A new Irish myth

By William A. Methven

Cover design by Design for Writers
Frontispiece by Philip Armstrong
Other illustrations and maps by Jenny Methven

Dedicated to my wife, Jenny and my son, Callum

the hare's vision

A new Irish myth

By William A. Methven

Published by Temair Publishing Ireland
Copyright © William A. Methven 2015.

ISBN: 978-0-9933950-0-0.

Ox Island, Ireland 575AD

© DOE - Historic Environment Division (HED)

Table of Contents

Prologue

"Fully have we made our chronicle.
Who will criticise it?
It has its middle, and its beginning,
And its end
Sufficiently have we followed their true history,
Much more do we know." ₁

Rain is falling on our land, renewing, refreshing and gently washing it clean of all blemish to begin anew. It seems like a holy baptism for all the world. The oak and the willow drink greedily to feed their growth and the river swells to occupy the full width of its banks. I see Muiream the otter, cousin of Feth Fio enjoying the fast flowing river as she travels at speed downstream to the bar mouth to feed. I wave to her. The world responds in its own way to heaven's gift of rain.

I sit by my desk in our scriptorium looking out over the unfolding scene, a view across the river to the pasture beyond and on to the king's rath, to a new beginning after the rain.

But the eye is fooled, dear reader. The stillness is deceptive. Great events passed through here: events that carried the fate of Christendom. At this close remove we cannot fully appreciate their outworking. That will be for you, the reader to assess in your day. I write for that reason. Your understanding of these events is important to us in this time and should be to you in yours. Without this record such history may be lost, washed away by the very water that constantly courses through and around this land and with it the loss of knowledge, wisdom and understanding.

I have penned this book with the help and support of others: many who witnessed part of the tale with their own eyes and others who have been guardians of the more ancient details. A small part of the tale and its participants I knew myself as a young novice. I can therefore bear some personal witness. However I had no part in the events and can claim no credit. I was but a bystander. I have no wish to inflate my role beyond that of the historian' although I can claim to have been there on that day in Druim Ceit to witness the miracles and the unfolding joy.

In all this I pray I have performed the historian's task adequately and fairly. At the turn of every page I have sought His guidance to be truthful and not to allow my own selfish ego to insert itself in the relating of these events. It has been my privilege to be the author and no more.

Nor was the writing of this tale done on my own initiative. As a humble monk I have no such power. It was the blessed Father Cormac himself who first inspired me to write this history before he left. As a young monk I was training in this very scriptorium and Father Cormac was admiring of my work.

He says to me, "Humanity can no longer live in ignorance of the true Word and its Light, brother. The story of these events must be told and I pray you to tell it. He will help you". He meant Lord Yeshua.

Then it was Abbot Colum Cille himself, close confidant of Father Cormac, who gave the final word before he returned to the community on Aio for the last time that I be given the time and the support to write this history; with the condition that it not be the subject of gossip and not be finished until after his passing. Colum Cille rests now and I pray that he looks down from heaven and finds my efforts to have been worthy of his confidence. Without his support this history would not have been written. Instead I would have been busy with the Gospels as they are written: a worthy task, but to an historian, they are an incomplete record. Such a comment may shock the reader coming as it does from a Christian monk, but you will understand as you read the history.

Now I must put down my pen. My cat and faithful companion, by name, Pelagius, tells me it is time for prayers. As I do not hear the bell any more, I rely on Pelagius. I rely on him for much more. He has been my ears onto the world in recent times and, being a cat, has eyes for the unseen. Without his kind intercession a deaf monk could not have completed a history that relies on hearing the spoken word and on seeing the unseen.

We pray in this place that in the years to come the role played by the heroes of this land in rescuing *the Word* from the dark and keeping its teachings alive in the light for the sake of all creation.

Brother Cuilenn
Monastery of Camus
Maigh Choscáin
Eriu

600A.D.

1 Mael Muru. Todd and Herbert, Historia Britonum, p. 271

BOOK ONE

1: The hare's vision

The monk watched the eagle gently soaring in the high, hot air in the midday desert sun. It was circling, watching something on the ground beyond the ridge of rock in the wadi. Some poor creature was being careless in the hot sun and being readied for the kill: perhaps a snake, a deer, a weasel, a hare or some such poor soul, the monk speculated.

God protect dear Zachariah, prayed the monk. Surely he was not out in this sun. The hare had met the monk in Italy many years before. The two had struck up a friendship and journeyed to the desert monastery together. Cormac mac Fliande was a wiry, muscular monk of some fifty years with greying, red hair cut in the Celtic tonsure. He worried that his friend the hare did not have much speed now to avoid capture from the eagle's death strike. While watching the eagle circling a memory was roused in Cormac, a vivid memory of when he and Zachariah had set out from Paestum in southern Italia several years before and when the hare had told him of his vision.

But suddenly the eagle dramatically altered its trajectory and swooped. As it did, there came a flash of memory and an intuition to the watching monk. He saw in his mind's eye that the hare's vision on that day in Italia was about to meet with the present time in the desert. All of a sudden Cormac knew in his heart that the summons he had received after matins that day to meet with his abbot was the beginning of the calling he had long been anticipating. The fact that the summons came from the abbot was significant. Cormac was ready. His years of study, prayer and fasting had prepared him for his destiny.

They had much in common, monk and hare. They had long conversations as Cormac sojourned in Paestum, a Christian settlement south of the River Sele in Lucania, eight days travel south of Rome. The young hare claimed to be the reincarnated soul of the ancient prophet Zachariah: a claim that the monk initially found disturbingly blasphemous and he chastised the hare accordingly. However that was not the only remarkable aspect to the young hare. His fleece was of a golden hue that shone in the sun and such hares were held to be sacred since ancient times.

This young golden hare stood his ground with the sceptical monk and Cormac for his part came to tolerate the animal's claims for himself. He found the hare's notions appealed to his Celtic humour. In fact in time Cormac came to be less sceptical as the hare debated theology and regaled him with tales of ancient Babylon. When the monk discovered that many of the hare's stories were based on visions, he became much less offended with the garrulous creature and his claim of ancient lineage. Visions were a vital part of the Celtic heritage. Cormac told the hare many tales of myth and legend from his youth, but unlike Zachariah, he made no claim about their veracity. That was for the listener to decide.

When Cormac left the hermitage in Paestum in the spring of the year 560A.D, he agreed that the hare would accompany him on his planned peregrinatio to the desert fathers in Egypt. Like Cormac, Zachariah had lost his family. The hare's tribe was lost to hunting wolves in the hills above Paestum the previous winter and he had come to regard Cormac as his only family.

Now in the desert many years hence, Cormac's mind wandered back to the day when he and Zachariah had set off from the province of Lucania. It was on that day that Zachariah that told him of his vision of the soaring eagle.

"Your need for company is a weakness of the flesh, hare, which you must address," said Cormac as they walked.

"And likewise your judgement of me, monk" retorted Zachariah.

"Ah I do admire your quickness of mind!" said Cormac. "I apologise my friend. You are welcome of course on my peregrinatio. The Divine is guiding me as I journey towards good faith and the company of a sacred hare is much valued. The divine walks with you also. So we are bound together you and I: two questing souls. So step lively, hare. We have many miles to cover before we meet the desert fathers."

"Thank you. Although my soul's journey is a different one from yours as you know."

"It is. All souls are unique: although we are all bound as one. You, friend, have a soul of quicksilver. My soul is likened to a meandering river. We have agreed upon this, have we not?" replied Cormac.

"That is exactly why I am a hare in this time. Its essence was suited to my own," said the hare and jumped high in the air to illustrate the point.

"I think you choose wisely, master hare", said Cormac. "Now can we journey in quiet contemplation? This talk is tiring and distracting. I wish to settle my mind while I walk."

"We can. But first, I must tell you of my vision,"

Zachariah had many visions which he shared with the monk. Some were enlightening, some were puzzling and some were nothing more than humorous tales. But Cormac had come to find them worthy of attention when, through one of his visions, Zachariah described Cormac's sad loss in his native Celtic land. Since this tale Cormac paid close heed to Zachariah's visions.

"Very well. We will be quiet when your tale is told." Cormac said to the skipping hare.

"It went like this" began Zachariah. "A man and his wife lived in some discordance in a small village not long after the time of Yeshua ben Pandira in Judea. The discordance was due to the man's ill treatment of his dutiful wife. He was arrogant, ill-tempered and sometimes even violent towards the poor woman. She for her part bore this abuse with a loving patience and looked for no more than that the man would give her shelter and food.

"The man's business as a tailor took him away for many days at a time, but sometimes he brought his wife to support him in these strange towns and on tiresome journeys."

"A loyal and godly wife is a blessing, but violence is an abhorrence," observed Cormac.

"Quite so. But listen, kind monk as my vision unfolds. The pair were walking with their donkey and cart to the next town to visit an important customer. The day was kind and the sky bright. It was a day in spring."

"Spring is a good time to set out," said Cormac as he looked delightedly at the spring weather and the growth unfolding all around them.

"Indeed." said the hare somewhat frustrated at the monk's interruptions. "An eagle was high in the sky above them. The man was vexed at the eagle's presence. An eagle had once stolen a bolt of cloth from his cart for which he had never forgiven the great bird and had sworn vengeance on it."

The monk sucked at his teeth and shook his head trailing his Celtic tonsured ginger hair about his shoulders at the word "vengeance".

The hare glanced sideways at the monk anticipating another interruption, but continued.

"The man and woman stopped to tie down the bolts of cloth in the cart as the eagle circled high above.

> *'It is he'* says the man to his wife. *'I recognise the white belly'*
>
> *'Shall we shelter under that tree, husband, until the creature goes away?'*
>
> *'No creature will hinder my work woman and he will not make a fool of me a second time!'* he said gesturing with his staff at the eagle. *'What does such a beast need with fine cloth?"* he shouts at the airless sky in torment. *"I have a customer to meet in the town before dusk and important business to see to. This bird will not cause me to tarry.'*

The hare was a great mimic and imitated the gruff voice of the tailor and the meek, bird like voice of the wife. He revelled in his performance.

> *'Perhaps it nests in the good cloth, husband dear'* says the wife.
>
> *'A bird nest in my fine cloth? Don't be a fool woman! He's a devil sent to ruin me. He's the soul of a long dead jealous tailor, I wouldn't wonder. He hates tailors for some reason and me in particular. His white belly reminds me of someone.'*
>
> *'Well you see many a white belly, husband, in the course of your work'*

"Can we get on with it, dear hare?" said Cormac. Zachariah was warming to his performance and Cormac feared this might mean a long story.

"Very well," said Zachariah. "Then the eagle changed course suddenly and swooped. The man raised his staff and roared defiance at the eagle. The woman shrieked. The eagle did not attack them but landed as nice as you like on a rocky cliff immediately above them. As it did, it dislodged some rocks which plummeted towards the pair on the road beneath. Soon a landslide ensued with the tailor and his wife in its path. The woman scurried beneath the cart, but the man was intent on protecting his property and clung to the donkey in case it would run off. He suspected the eagle's purpose.

"A large bouncing rock caught the man on the side of the head and he fell down heavily. Many other rocks fell on the cart dislodging some of the bolts of cloth. The eagle seizing his chance swooped down and deftly hooked a bolt of bright yellow cloth with its huge talons. He flew off into the sun with his booty.

"The woman watched the eagle fly off into the valley. As it did, the bolt of bright yellow cloth unravelled in its talons in a burst of colour and bright light: a gleaming banner against the blue sky trailed by the majestic bird. The woman gasped. Surely a sign, she thought. God help us, she whispered in prayer.

"The woman waited for the eagle to disappear into the wide sky with its shimmering banner. The rock fall slowly subsided. A heavy leather bag also rolled down the hillside and came to rest unseen by the cart. The woman crawled out from under the cart to see her husband lying in the dust with a wound on his head. What was she to do? It would soon be dusk and their destination was further down the valley. She cradled her husband, sang psalms to him and prayed for assistance as she pondered her predicament.

"Presently a traveller came running down the road. He himself looked in an agitated state. He was wearing a long white mantle and carrying a heavy staff.

>   *"Good woman, what has happened here?'* he calls to the weeping woman.

'We have been assaulted by a mythic beast from the air trailing a banner proclaiming I don't know what. It has killed my husband, sir' she wails. *'It is the end days as prophesised. God have mercy on us'*

"The traveller approached, examined the husband and from a bag produced a medicine which he waved in front of the injured husband's nose. Instantly he began to stir and revive. The woman, uneasy with the traveller and his magic potion, was nevertheless grateful to see her husband come to life. She kissed the hem of the stranger's mantle and thanked him.

"The husband for his part sat up and smiled a smile of loving openness that the wife had never seen from her quarrelsome husband in ten years of marriage.

'Good day to you both,' says he.

'Husband, how are you?' asks the wife expecting to be rebuked.

'Very well, I think' he feels his head.

'A rock hit you, husband dear. Sit quietly for a while. The eagle stole another bolt and has sent a sign to us,' she said expecting an explosion of rage. Instead he says;

'I know that eagle. It is the soul of old Abraham the tailor who taught me my trade. He is angry with me. I can't think why,' says the husband with a detached air.

'You cheated Abraham out of business husband, that's why. Don't you remember?' the woman replies.

'Surely not?' The husband looks perplexed and then regards the stranger benignly. The stranger smiles back.

'This man revived you, husband. I took you for dead.'

"Thank you, good traveller. My name is Leon. Master tailor and this is my wife....." he stops and stares at his wife. "Well, this is my wife." He turned away embarrassed and perturbed. He had forgotten his wife's name.

'God bless you both' smiles the stranger, not volunteering his own name.

"They began to clear the road of rocks to make a path for the cart. They reloaded the cart with the bolts of cloth strewn across the road. The stranger noticed the leather bag lying in the dust by the cart. He bent down and handed it to the tailor who disclaimed ownership of it, whereupon the stranger opened the bag. Inside were three scrolls tightly bound and bearing seals. The stranger examined the seals and muttered as he looked in the direction the eagle had flown.

"While he was examining the scroll, the wife was telling her husband about the celestial banner carried by the eagle. She sought confirmation from the traveller:

> *'Good traveller did you see the eagle carrying the banner on high?'* asks the wife.

"Looking into the sky the stranger answered gravely:

> *'I saw him, good woman. I think this is the message he was carrying.'*

"He held up a scroll. It was the same colour as the eagle's banner – golden yellow.

> *'What does it all mean?'* she asks. *'Are we in danger, sir?'*
> *'I must study this scroll,'* says the stranger. *'I must ask you both not to mention these events to anyone. These are indeed the end days of the old ways and great matters are afoot all round. Have no fear good people, this is God's work, not the devil's'* he says.
> *'We are simple people, good sir, and have no understanding of such things. We must travel on to the next town to sell cloth,'* says the wife. *'We have no concern with such matters. Come husband let us travel on.'*

"The husband appeared not to be engaged with the matters at hand, but was instead in conversation with the donkey.

'Will you journey with us, traveller?' asks the wife, concerned at the state of her husband's mind.

'No, good lady. I will tarry here awhile. Your journey will be without incident now. Be not afraid,' he says.

'Very well. We thank you for your help, traveller and wish you a safe journey also wherever you are going,' says the wife.

'I am already there,' says the traveller with a smile and sits down on a rock with the scroll. Then turns to the tailor and his wife, 'Remember never a word about these events.'

'Be assured of our silence, sir,' says the wife. The husband merely nodded benignly as he led the donkey down the road talking to it as he went and the donkey responding."

Zachariah stopped his narrative and looked expectantly at Cormac.

"Is that it, dear hare? Is that the conclusion of your vision? "asked Cormac.

"Not quite."

"Come; finish the tale so I can rest my mind."

"Well the traveller was you, good monk. You were the traveller in my vision," declared Zachariah with a proud smile.

Cormac stopped in his energetic walk, warm dust swirling about his sandaled feet. His pale Celtic skin flushed red at the hare's revelation, "The stranger was me!?"

"He was."

"Hmmmm. You wish to unsettle me hare, with your vision of eagles and banners and scrolls. What can this mean?"

"A scroll of great significance will come into your safe-keeping, Brother Cormac. It brings much light to the world. You will be charged with its safe delivery. This will be the crowning glory of your peregrinatio. More I cannot say for now."

"The world is in need of light. That much I can see. The eagle is a magical bird of great power and majesty. He is often used by the Divine," mused Cormac. "Very fitting, hare, very fitting. No doubt all this will be revealed to us in perfect timing," said the monk as he sought to regain his monkish composure. He fixed Zachariah with a stare in the hope of more prophesy on this matter, but the hare simply stared back. "Come, wise hare of the vision, we must set a good pace if we are to make the coast by night fall and be ready for this work. No more chatter if you please," said Cormac as he turned his face to the sun. He set out with a deliberate stab of his staff in the dust.

Zachariah was pleased with his prophetic vision and in his artful telling of it. He skipped along with great excitement and delight. He was looking forward to the imminent unfolding of this prophesy and the important role to be played by his friend the monk in the great events to come.

As Cormac rushed to a small wadi where he saw the eagle land, he spied the huge bird on the hot sand pacing around a rocky outcrop. She glared at the monk in defiance.

"What business have you here, dry monk?" demanded the eagle, annoyed that her hunt might be disrupted.

"I seek my friend, mother eagle" replied Cormac, not wishing to reveal too much to a hunting eagle.

"Well, be off! Your friend is not here unless it is this skinny hare under this rock that I seek for my meat," said the eagle. "Come out, hare. It will be quick and painless. Your destiny awaits and my children grow hungry. Do not cheat my family, hare. I warn you." The mother eagle flapped her great wings for emphasis.

"Zachariah, Zachariah are you there?" shouted Cormac as he stooped to see a cavity running through the rock by which could be seen daylight at the other end. In the middle, in the cool of the rock, was a frightened hare.

"Get the beast to go away!" pleaded Zachariah. "I am no one's meat."

"Get thee hence, eagle. Your meat is elsewhere," Cormac shouted through the cavity in the rock to the eagle glaring at Zachariah from the other side.

"How dare you! I will not be deterred by a dusty old monk! Perhaps you shall be my meat." The eagle quickly turned in a fury and began to come round the rock to confront the hare's protector.

Anticipating the attack Cormac picked up some large stones lying nearby and with lightning speed loosed them with practiced expertise at the approaching eagle. She flapped her great wings in a dance to avoid the stones.

"May the Great Sky curse you, monk and hare! The hare is pledged to me. He and I will be one day," said the eagle as she flapped her great wings again and took to the hot, thin air. "Keep your eyes on the sky as you travel, hare and monk," Within moments she was over the ridge and flying towards the mountains in the south.

"Come out. She has gone," said Cormac wearily.

A dust covered hare emerged from the cavity.

"Thank you, monk," muttered the hare as he dusted himself off. "These eagles come from nowhere."

"They come from the devil," said Cormac. "Be more careful, hare, if not for your own sake, then for mine. Your passing would grieve me, dear friend."

"Perhaps she wanted to carry me off to that beautiful land you often tell me of?" mused Zachariah ignoring the monk's pleading.

"Carry you off to Tir na n'Og?" asked Cormac. "Curb that imagination of yours, hare. I rather think your bones would be picked clean with great speed and left to be bleached by the desert sun. Mind, you may see Tir na n'Og in your afterlife."

"Mmmm it's good for one soul to feed another, I'm thinking."

"You seek a saint's martyrdom, hare? I'm not aware of any saint with ears like yours," said Cormac.

Zachariah preened his ears. "As a prophet in Babylon I was known for my distinctive ears. Are you forgetting St. Polycarp of Smyrna?"

"Ah St. Polycarp! There you are right, hare. St Polycarp had very big ears. It is true."

"Are we about to travel?" asked the hare recalling the eagle's parting remarks.

"I don't know. Aba James has just asked to see me with some urgency. I should be with him now if it wasn't for having to deal with that eagle," said Cormac shaking his head in bewilderment.

The hare's ears jerked upright at this news. "Events are afoot. Did you not hear the eagle? Eagles fly so high they can see the future coming," said Zachariah. "I am minded of my vision many years ago: the story of the eagle and the golden banner of cloth. I think the time is drawing near, monk. We must be ready."

"You have always had a liking for drama, hare. Could it be that we must watch the sky or one of us may be carried off into the future – to be skinned and eaten!" replied Cormac

"Mmmm. That may be so," mused Zachariah with a pensive look. The pair fell silent as they walked back towards the monastery reflecting on what could lie before them. Both could feel a stirring in the early spring air.

The monastery of St John the Short lay before them in an oasis nestling in a small valley. It was surrounded by tall palm trees, tamarisk plants and acacia bushes. The monastery was not a large one compared to some in Egypt at this time. It was founded by followers of John Colobos, a devout dwarf whose example of Christian obedience inspired many desert fathers.

John the Short had been tested by his aba. His old aba required the diminutive novice to plant a walking staff in the desert and to water it every day. John did this dutifully daily for three years, walking some twelve miles each day to do so. At the end of the third year the staff miraculously sprouted and produced green leaves. John the Short's example of obedience, forbearance and watchfulness grew to inspire many. The monastery he founded was built around the leafy staff, where it still stood as a great tree.

It was these qualities of John the Short and his tree that drew the Celt, Cormac mac Fliande to the monastery and although the small saint had ascended many years ago his great spirit lived on in the place. It was here that Cormac made his monastic cell, quiet and solitary in the still of the desert. Trees were important to all Celts. So St John's miraculous tree gave comfort to Cormac in his desert trials over the years.

This day Cormac was somewhat preoccupied. Aba James had never asked to see Cormac in the ten years the monk had been living amongst the Egyptian desert fathers. Aba James, *Hegumenos* of Scetis – the Father of Scetis – guided all the desert monasteries in the area. He was a close confidant of the Patriarch in Alexandria and such a man did not seek idle conversation.

Life with the desert fathers had taught Cormac much about monastic living and divine purpose. He had watched the journeys

of his fellow monks as they came and some went from the
monastery of St John the Short. All were on a journey, striving to
be closer to the divine. Cormac's life in the desert monastery had
been without event. It was a life focused on stillness and on God
through a strict discipline of study, solitary prayer, fasting and
manual work each day and long into the night. Nothing encroached
on their remoteness. Not for many years had Cormac dealt with
worldly matters and his monk's mind was having difficulty
contemplating his meeting with such a man as Aba James. To
reassure himself Cormac caressed the tree of St John the Short in
the courtyard on his way to the steps up to Aba James's quarters
beside the church. As he did so the warm morning air scented with
acacia blossom shook the ancient leaves and they gently brushed
the monk's upturned and stubbled face. Cormac smiled and winked
at the tree. This was a regular morning ritual for Cormac and the
tree never disappointed.

"Ah God bless you, John the Short. Grant me your strength for
what lies before me this day and in the days to come," he prayed to
the tree and set off reassured up the steps to await Aba James. The
tree continued to rustle its leaves as if waving at the departing
monk.

Cormac gingerly opened the stout door to Aba James chambers.
He tentatively entered the cool interior of a small whitewashed
room with a plain wooden bench and table on which was a ewer of
water and a simple cross on the wall above. Below the cross and
above the ewer was a note. It said in Latin: *"Crebrescunt faciem
amici, ut videat Dominus cutis"* *"Freshen your face, friend, so that
the Lord may see your skin."*

So Cormac cupped his hands and tenderly washed the precious
water over his face. The rose water was cool and fragrant. Ever
since his youth in Eriu he had loved the cool caress of water on his
skin. He dried himself quickly on his mantle: such bodily pleasure
was tempting. He wanted to bathe in the water. No doubt Aba
James was testing his visitors. Cormac sat down quickly on the
bench like a guilty pupil.

Inside the cool of the room with its pleasing rose water, an air
settled on the monk, easing his apprehension and his excitement
after his confrontation with the hungry creature in the wadi.

Through a small window he could see the air was becoming hot as the desert rose to her daily glory. He smiled to himself. His cool Celtic blood had at first fought and struggled with the desert. Its arid heat parched him cruelly. However he learnt in time that the desert understood the human condition. Her vast rolling sands and smooth rocks allowed the mind to quieten so that the soul may triumph. Her emptiness and scorching sand also offered numerous challenges to both the body and the mind. The desert was a perfect mistress with her stark contrasts of light and dark, heat and cold, water and dust. There was little nurture for the physical body or the self. Instead she nurtured the soul – if you let her. Cormac quickly came to understand why the divine had brought him to this place. There was no better place for a journey towards the heart of the divine than here in this desert of sand and rock.

The purples and greens and blues of the hills and loughs of his younger years in Eriu had been pleasing to the young Cormac, but they had tantalised and excited him offering numerous sensuous pleasures to distract and tease. The desert never tempted nor asked for anything. Cormac learnt that she challenged and subdued his self with her vastness. He was daily grateful for her discipline and in time he submitted willingly. It could be said that Cormac mac Fliande had fallen in love with the desert. He praised her daily. She for her part remained impassive and her harshness suited the Celt enormously.

Cormac's meditation on the desert was broken by the sudden presence in the room of Aba James staring at the seated monk with a benign smile.

"Will you join me in my room, Brother Cormac the Celt?" asked Aba James in a whisper.

"I will, father," said Cormac.

Aba James did not indulge in social conversation. It was not in the manner of a monk to indulge in chatter or gossip. Talking stirred the mind and with it, the ego. Cormac also was not given to many words, except when the garrulous hare provoked him, so it was not surprising to him when Aba James indulged in no social niceties on their meeting. He was a descendant of St John the Short, but he had none of the saint's diminutive stature being quite tall and angular with the look, Cormac thought, of a wise and gentle old dog. He even had the gait of an old dog. As he walked his monk's mantle swayed around Aba James like a dog's tail. The two remained standing as is the monks' practice.

After a moment of silence Aba James looked Cormac in the eye and said quietly: "Do you still seek martyrdom for the sake of your soul, our blessed Lord and our religion, brother?"

"I do, father" replied Cormac without batting an eyelid though his heart was pounding.

Aba James nodded in satisfaction. "You are greatly honoured. The Church is asking you to provide a vital service that may have some physical danger and distant travel attached to it. You will have to leave this place and travel across the ocean as a guardian of great importance."

Cormac swallowed hard. The eagle was right. He was to travel. And what of Zachariah's vision of the bright banner and the scrolls so many years ago? Was this about to become manifest?

Aba James continued to smile compassionately at the monk before him. He knew the Celt to be a devout and godly man who had shown great understanding of their ways as desert fathers. The Celt was a monk of some considerable spiritual and physical strength, that much was known. Both qualities Aba James sensed Cormac the Celt will need for the task ahead. Aba James knew that God had sought this monk out for important work: the detail of which he surmised. Such selection was a privilege for a monk seeking martyrdom. Nevertheless Aba James was concerned for the soul of this dutiful monk who had been under his care for some ten years and was, it seemed, to be thrown into a maelstrom of religious and political intrigue.

The Patriarch of Alexandria, Damianos the First had asked for this monk by name. Damianos had spent many years in the monastery of St John the Short as a young monk and then deacon. He knew of the red haired Celt who had arrived just as Damianos had departed in 567AD to become a secretary to Patriarch Petros IV in Alexandria.

"I can tell you that the Patriarch is vexed on a matter of the greatest importance to our religion. It was revealed to him in a dream that you are to help in a very delicate matter because of your connections with Eriu and her godly people," Aba James continued.

21

Then leaning close to Cormac he said, "I council you, Brother, not to involve yourself in Church politics of which there is a great deal in Alexandria as there are in all great cities of the world now. Are you a theologian, Brother?"

"No, Aba," answered Cormac, his mind racing to understand Aba James and surprised to be asked if he was a theologian. He would not have spent years in a remote monastery if he was a theologian. He had had long ago set aside these debates and affairs of the mind. However his studies in Alexandria before arriving at the monastery had taught him the arguments beloved of the theologians. His faith in the Word of Lord Yeshua was what guided the Celtic monk. He required no great philosophy. He had set himself a simple task in all his years as a monk: to follow the example of Yeshua in all things and to seek everlasting life in God's grace. He did this through the monastic life of purging the mind and body so that the soul can find its path to God.

However while Cormac mac Fliande strived to be a simple monk, he was an intelligent man and like many from his land, he was highly educated. He spoke and could read three languages: his own native tongue and also Latin and Greek. He understood philosophy, mathematics and astronomy which he had studied in the Catechetical school in Alexandria, so he likewise understood some of the great theological debates that had so riven the Church for many a long year. These debates were among men and women from the Latin and Hellene cultures who Cormac believed relished such controversy. His route to God was the Celtic way, through the senses tuned to the natural world and not through human intellect.

"As you know, we in Scetis do not concern ourselves with such affairs. We are monks engaged in our martyrdom. We do not seek these great debates of theology. The Patriarch is a good man, but I fear has concerned himself too much with such matters and has made enemies in Antioch and Rome," Aba James features assumed more the look of a sad old dog as he reflected on his friend, the Patriarch. "God has chosen you, brother. God is wise and has chosen well. Be not afraid. Though your faith will be tested as never before, be strong in the knowledge that you are God's chosen." At that Aba James placed a hand on Cormac's head.

"I pray I will be worthy, Aba. I am guided by God," said Cormac.

"You are, brother," said Aba James with some confidence. "And now I must ask you to prepare to travel this day to Alexandria where you will call upon the Patriarch and receive your mission. Go to the Church of St Dionysius in Alexandria directly where you will be met and instructed. I believe you know this church."

"Yes, I lived there before travelling to this place, Aba."

"That is good."

Looking at Cormac in silence for a moment, Aba James then said, "Brother, it is unlikely that you will return to this place. No one knows the mind of God, but it is unlikely. So we bid you farewell, beloved brother in Yeshua. Go now and prepare yourself for the journey. A caravan will depart on the next hour from the eastern gate. God go with you and give you strength and wisdom on your holy mission." Aba James smiled and reaching around his neck, removed a metal phial on a chain and placed it over Cormac's head. "I would have you take this for protection. It was St Mark's and was given to St Antony who gave it to the blessed St. John the Short. It contains the blood of Lord Yeshua and the tears of the Magdalene. Please give it to whoever needs Yeshua's protection the most."

Cormac looked up at Aba James quizzically.

"This will become clear to you, brother," said Aba James with a kind smile.

Aba James kissed the monk's bowed head. Cormac fell to his knees and prayed before his aba. Aba James replaced his hand on Cormac's head once more. "God and his many servants will protect you, Cormac the Celt. Go in peace and go with the word."

With that, Aba James was gone leaving Cormac kneeling in the darkened room, his hands clutching at the holy relic around his neck. He could hear St John the Short's tree rustling in the desert wind beneath the window. The holy relic that Aba James had just placed around his neck confirmed to the kneeling monk more than any words could do that this was no ordinary mission to bring the word to those without it. He clasped the metal phial even tighter and prayed to be worthy of Lord Yeshua and the Magdalene. Moments passed in the quiet sanctuary of the abbot's antechamber. Sounds of the monks fetching water from the courtyard reminded Cormac of the rhythm of the monastery. Cormac listened to its whispers. The world gently turned. As it did he rose and strode out into the midday desert sun to find his companion the hare. Cormac then began his odyssey beyond the desert fathers who had been his family for many years, following the path of his calling in quiet obedience.

Cormac knew his calling was to make new and very different demands. No less demanding of his soul and his body than those he had encountered in his days as a desert father. The long silences, the great heat and the light of the Egyptian desert had burnished him in body and soul like a polished metal. He was ready.

II: End of the beginning

Many great events start in small or inauspicious ways: they stir like small seeds blown on the wind or carried by a bird towards its ultimate destination and greater purpose. What fate there is for each seed only the divine or the fates can tell. Will it become a mighty oak that builds a king's ship to win a battle that founds an empire or will it be a small sapling that withers in the first winter of life? Nature shows us that no seed ever perishes completely. It gives birth to a life of some sort, an adult plant or food for another creature, a weevil or a bird. The seed carries an eternal imprint of its energy and its truth down through ages. It is at all times helped by witting and unwitting guardians.

It was in this way that the story I relate began and journeyed through the ages to the present time. This story begins with an ending: the ending of a human life, which like the plant that dies and sheds its seed to grow again, so too with the death of one human. In his death there was life resurrected. A seed of truth was planted out of which grew a bright light of hope that would journey far and wide through the generations.

Endings are beginnings as any student of metaphysics can attest. It was the death of the great martyr which begat so much history, joy and pain together. It is these great unfolding events that motivate my pen. They tell a tale for all humanity. They brought change: a change that is still resonating throughout the world. It is the eternal dance between good and evil, between light and dark, the call of the divine and the lust for power against the demand for truth.

It was Easter time in the year 36 A.D: the true Easter of Passover and not the Easter the Bishop of Rome later invented and sought to force on all good people many years later.

As dawn broke over the slumbering city of Jerusalem, two figures were busy near a tomb in the Bezatha burial grounds, just outside the city walls near Golgotha. Expectant pilgrims had arrived to fill the city for the great Jewish festival of Passover: pilgrims who rarely slept as they were in hourly anticipation of the arrival of their messiah. Some said he had arrived and some said he was dead. Passions ran high on all sides. The early morning air was charged with a heady mixture of apprehension and fear among the people. Beyond the people of Jerusalem stood the Romans, who shared no such passion and had one simple purpose that day: to maintain public order in this part of the empire just as in every other place.

In the dark of a tomb a body had been lying motionless on a stone slab wrapped in a white burial shroud which was stained with blood around the feet and hands from the execution two days ago. Even so, the blood was still fresh that morning.

The Roman guards removed themselves from the tomb to allow the two men space to work with the body. It was important to these two that the guards would not notice in the gloom that the body was not in fact lifeless. They worked quickly removing the burial shroud and folding it carefully.

The guards watched dispassionately as the two men carried a cruelly damaged and naked body out of a tomb and over the rocky ground on a litter. Briefly glancing back to check that they were not being pursued, the two litter bearers quickly left the burial grounds carrying the body. As they did so a cock crowed to welcome the new day.

When the body of a crucified Jew had been brought to the tombs in Bezatha at dusk two days previously on the evening of the Jewish Passover, these guards had been detailed to secure this tomb and let no one near it. At midnight on the second night came different orders to allow the removal of the body from the tomb in particular early the following morning. The guard sergeant was bemused by this change in orders, but a Roman soldier never questions orders, so they dutifully rolled away the stone blocking the entrance.

The same guards had officiated at many crucifixions. It was all a matter of routine and keeping order over an excitable people. There were anti-Roman zealots and revolutionaries mouthing blasphemies against the divine emperor under every stone: religious zealots talking about the messiah who would sweep away the empire.

26

There were also petty criminals to be dealt with. All miscreants had to be subject to the discipline of the cross.

The Master specified only two of his most trusted apostles for this delicate task. The Master had always been very cautious about who knew his mind and his plans. No one knew all of what he knew, not even the beloved disciple. The Sanhedrin and the Romans deployed spies everywhere: spies that would wreck the hopes and prayers of good people. He was a master tactician, of that there was no doubt. People followed him because they trusted him implicitly. They knew he was the one. John the Baptist had said so. And now the glorious triumph was in sight.

With the tomb empty the guards used the opportunity to get some much needed rest before they were stood down at the third hour. The Jewish festival of Passover had been a demanding period for the small Roman garrison in Judea. The Jews were in a highly excited mood this year with much talk about their God Jehovah and the imminent arrival of the messiah. All soldiers had been put on the highest level of alert for an uprising in Judaea led by this messiah claiming to be 'King of the Jews'. This claim mocked the divine Emperor in Rome. It was he who was King of the Jews and no other.

As the soldiers dozed among the tombs in the early light, a group of Sanhedrin guards led by a priest of the Great Sanhedrin of Jerusalem approached the tomb just recently vacated. Ignoring the sleeping Romans, they entered the tomb unseen, only to quickly re-emerge in an agitated and noisome state.

"Where is the zealot's body?" screamed one of them in Aramaic at the slumbering Romans. An officer of the Sanhedrin guard stepped in and repeated the question in Latin for the Roman soldiers. "Where is the body of the crucified Yeshua ben Pandira?" he demanded.

Gathering themselves to deal with yet more excited Jews, the sergeant of the Roman guard looked nonplussed and replied dully, "They took it as arranged."

"As arranged!? As arranged!? Who are 'they'!? We have come for the blasphemer 'as arranged'! Where is he?"

"Centurion Cassius gave us orders direct from the Prefect to allow the removal of this one from the tomb for reason of public order," said the sergeant. "We were told that two men would collect it. So when the two men came for the body of this Yeshua ben Pandira not an hour ago, they were allowed to remove him as arranged." The sergeant eyed the Sanhedrin guards suspiciously and challenged them in return. "You are not two. More like ten. Who are you!? What's your business here?" he demanded assuming the control that was his rightful place as a Roman soldier of rank. His men gathered about him.

"We are representatives of the High Priest of the Great Sanhedrin come to collect this zealot's body. If you doubt us your centurion should speak to Lord Caiaphas himself who awaits our return," said the Sanhedrin officer. "Who were these men who came?" he demanded in return.

The sergeant shrugged and made that dismissive two handed gesture typical of Romans which indicated that they were not at all interested in the matter that concerned these Jews. "Two men. They simply said they were here to remove the body of this Yeshua as arranged."

"They've got him," hissed the Sanhedrin officer in Aramaic. "They've outwitted Lord Caiaphas!"

The Sanhedrin priest held up his hands to quieten the agitated Sanhedrin guards. "High Priest Caiaphas will have to be told. They can't be far away. I will stay here in case any of his followers come to the tomb to dress the body."

"Surely they won't, not now. They have the body, sir," said the officer of the Sanhedrin guard.

The priest was highly placed. He was Caiaphas' nephew, Jonathan ben Ananus, his Segan in fact: his nominated heir and second in command. He drew the officer to the side and whispered, "Officer, I have made a study of this zealot. I know how he went about his business. Only a small number will know of this activity. Their plan is to falsely claim he has been "resurrected" according to their blasphemies," he spat. "The rest of his stupid followers will be ignorant of this deception and will be eager to wash the body and say Kaddish. If these followers arrive now they will believe we have taken ben Pandira's body. They will cause us great agitation. So I will reassure them and divert them, giving your men time to find where they have taken him," he said fixing the Sanhedrin officer with a steely look. "We must get an immediate message to the Lord Caiaphas of what has occurred here. You and some men stay here with me, but do not let the zealot's followers see you. Stay out of sight unless I call for you."

The Sanhedrin officer nodded and instructed his men.

Slowly taking off the regalia of a Sanhedrin priest, his turban and white sash, leaving only the long white tunic, Jonathan ben Ananaus shook free his tonsured hair to look more like a follower of Yeshua. He waited with the Roman guards for the blasphemer's followers to arrive at the empty tomb as he believed they would.

Indeed before the third hour two women arrived. He recognised one as the zealot's wife. The one called Mary who was always at his side. The priest feared she might recognise him. They had met when the arrogant zealot had threatened to destroy the Temple only some days previous. However she was greatly disturbed, her eyes dark and blood shot, her skin bleached white and taut with grief. She did not recognise the Sanhedrin priest without his gaudy ceremonial wear.

Jonathan held up his hand to stop them before they reached the tomb.

"We come to dress my dead husband," the Magdalene woman quietly asserted to the stranger in white. Her voice was strong in contrast to her physical demeanour.

"Why do you look for the living among the dead?" asked the smiling stranger. "See, he is risen as foretold," he gestured them towards the open tomb.

With a gasp the two women rushed into the tomb. Wailing was heard as the two distraught women saw only the shroud folded carefully and a small napkin. There was no body of the beloved husband and leader; just the pungent smell of myrrh and aloes. They held the shroud close to them and wept with a mixture of joy and grief. The second woman held the trembling body of Mary of Magdala as both examined the shroud.

As the two women re-emerged, blinking into the brightening light the stranger smiled reassuringly:

"He has risen and gone to Galilee and will see you there," the stranger said.

The two women stared at him for some moments, uttering not a word, struggling to understand what was happening, considering what was unfolding. Their faces stained with tears and eyes weakened from their long vigil. The priest hoped that the traumatised women would ask no probing questions, but accept what they were told. After all were not their beliefs and dreams being affirmed? Was this scenario not the fulfilment of their leader's blasphemous prophesies? The zealot was not dead, but resurrected and on the third day too. He waited in the still spring air facing the pair of mourners outside the tomb of the resurrected rebel. Awaiting their reaction to this momentous news, the stranger in white held his nerve and continued to smile beatifically. Many things would turn on this moment of deception.

The two women whispered in debate with each other. The one called Mary of Magdala stood in silence for a moment as if collecting her thoughts. Head bowed, her elegant hands clasped before her: a quiet dignity and strength descended upon her slight form. Then without another word she turned towards the city walls and left the burial ground, followed by her companion. Jonathan ben Ananaus watched them go with relief. It had worked, he thought, he had gained the Great Sanhedrin valuable time. The Nazorean would be resurrected after all; he smiled to himself at the great good fortune. Truly the great lord Jehovah's hand was in these deeds today.

"I suggest you follow them, officer." He said turning to the Sanhedrin guards hiding in the bushes nearby. "But follow discretely. They may unknowingly take you to the stolen body. Send for reinforcements. When you find the body bring it directly to Lord Caiaphas under close guard. Detain all those you find with the body. No one else must know we have the body. No one! Do not let anyone know the identity of the body. Hide its features. Otherwise you'll have this city in turmoil. Understood? I will meet you at the Temple where we will await your return with the body of the Nazorean. Lord Caiaphas intends to rid us of this dead messiah and his entire Galilean rabble this very day."

Events moved rapidly from this: events known to few men and women. My hand trembles as I write. These words carry with them the lives and hopes of many, then and now. Forgive me then if my pen stumbles for I too am human.

The two men moved at pace with the litter from Bezatha through the empty early morning streets of Jerusalem. All that could be heard was the bleating of the lambs that had survived the sacrifice of Passover. The city was resting momentarily after the excitement of the feast.

The battered body of Yeshua ben Pandira on the litter showed subtle signs of life, as he was jerked through the narrow streets. He breathed and he moaned occasionally. But the litter bearers did not react with any surprise; even though this man had been crucified two days before. Their concern was to get him to a destination safe from the Sadducees and the Romans who had plotted his demise. That was their task.

They slowed upon arrival in a narrow street in the Valley of Kidron in the poorest part of Jerusalem, just outside the city walls. A door flew open and the litter bearers were ushered quickly into a courtyard and up steps to a darkened room. The street was checked for pursuers and then the door was bolted and a guard posted.

Yeshua ben Pandira was lifted gently onto a table in the middle of a windowless room. The litter bearers waited in the shadows of the court yard. Upstairs in the darkened room three men stood around. Joseph of Arimithaea a rich merchant, a member of the Great Sanhedrin Council. He was also a secret apostle of Yeshua ben Pandira. Next to him stood another merchant, Nicodemus who while not an apostle was a close friend of Yeshua. The third man was Yeshua's brother James and one of the Twelve. The three moved closer to the outstretched body.

The room had been prepared for Yeshua's arrival. Lilies and poppies were arranged in large urns in each corner and the pungent aroma of spikenard hung in the room, but not even these pleasing appeals to the senses could diminish the sense of apprehension and nervousness that filled the air and the minds of the men gathered there. Their entire awareness was focused on the horribly disfigured and naked body of their Master laid out on the wooden trestle.

Bending over Yeshua, Joseph of Arimithaea looked at the battered and brutalised body of his beloved leader. Joseph's role in Yeshua ben Pandira's death defying strategy had been to persuade the Roman Prefect, Pontius Pilate that the bodies on the crosses on the day of Passover must not be allowed to remain there over the Sabbath. Joseph and Nicodemus, two respected merchants, the first a member of the Great Sanhedrin Council and the second a supplier of fine cloth to the Romans, had been successful in their pleas to the Prefect. Yeshua, along with two others had been taken down from the cross after six hours on the evening of Passover before the Sabbath. He was still alive while giving all the appearance of being dead to those people gathered round.

Examining the body with care Joseph said, "Thanks are to God for small mercies they didn't break our master's legs. But it's as we feared the spear thrust looks bad. It was not what he anticipated. We must pray that his healing powers will heal even this. I pray to God I did not fail our Lord in his mission."

The timing of his crucifixion had been critical. He needed to be placed on the cross the day before the Sabbath. The Judaic religion specified that dead bodies must not lie exposed on the Sabbath. So any bodies on the crosses on the eve of the Sabbath would have to be taken down. Yeshua knew that sometimes God needed human help to deliver his divine plan.

So unknown to the Romans Yeshua had been sedated while on the cross by the administration of a powerful dose of an opiate mixed with vinegar which helped him to withstand the enormous pain and also to appear dead. If this could be done he would be declared dead, taken to a private tomb and from there revived or 'resurrected' to claim his rightful place as the messiah, the bringer of Peace and God's Kingdom on Earth. With God's help he would sweep away the Sadducees and the Pharisees. The power of the Roman Empire would disappear and the Kingdom of God would rule in its place for all time.

This man had designed his own crucifixion; placing himself in the hands of the divine to protect and resurrect him so that he may return as the messiah to save and love the world. Was there any human design more incredible and more determined? Was there any greater sacrifice? Who would not follow such a one?

Nicodemus put his hand on Joseph's shoulder: "Do not reproach yourself, Joseph. Yeshua wouldn't. You did all you could. This is God's will. Let's keep our faith. He can heal wounds and raise the dead as we have seen."

"Come we must resurrect my brother with God's help" said James, anxious to see his brother restored to life.

"Have the opiate ready for the pain when he revives," said Joseph.

Joseph produced a phial and held it under Yeshua's nose. At first there was no response. The three looked to each other. Had he gone too far? Could even he come back? Then as the cock crowed once more Mary of Magdala appeared in the room and stood at the head of Yeshua ben Pandira. It was then he came back to life, slowly and painfully.

The three gasped. Yeshua also gasped, his gasp was one of pain. His mangled hand went clumsily to his deeply wounded left side and he groaned in pain and sorrow.

"Brother. It is us. The three and Mary. We are here. God has spared you from the cross. You are the Messiah," declared James joyfully.

Yeshua opened his eyes and grimaced.

Mary was the first to touch the wounded flesh. She stood silently cradling Yeshua's bloodied head in her loving hands. The three men did not touch their leader.

"Drink this water, Master," said Joseph holding a gourd to Yeshua's dried lips, "and take this opiate to soothe the pain."

They waited for Yeshua to speak. He regarded each of his most trusted followers in turn as he continued to grimace with pain. He waved away the opiate and took the water.

Finally he smiled lovingly at his wife above him and the three. They smiled back. They had their master back. The plan had worked. God's kingdom on earth suddenly lay before them all.

"My friends," he said. "The Messiah will not walk this earth in this time. The damage is too great for this body. My power is too weak to revive it. I am greatly diminished. The divine calls me. This wound is ...." He grimaced again. "I am being called. I will guide you from another place." He slumped back down.

The three men also visibly slumped and groaned quietly. James sank to his knees, ripping his shirt in despair, head bowed. Mary silently bowed her head with eyes closed.

Joseph was the first to recover: "What's to be done, Lord? We beseech you to stay among us."

"Some things are beyond even I, Joseph" said Yeshua with a weak smile. "But I will return, my beloved ones, when the time is right."

"What would you have us do, Master?" asked Nicodemus. Yeshua closed his eyes to the world for several moments. They awaited his consideration, something that could never be hurried.

Finally he opened his eyes once more and sipped the water.

Weakly he said, "In the tomb I had a vision of the world to come. A figure appeared from a far off land, in angelic form. She spoke to me tenderly:

> '*For now your work is done in the land of David, Yeshua ben Pandira*', she said. '*The Temple will fall and Jerusalem will be in darkness. Many of the House of Israel will die. A new faith will arise in the west under the Emperor and it will bear your name. The Emperor in turn will fall and in the end days men will come to this new faith seeking to maintain Rome's power. Their love for the divine and His creation will be corrupted by a love of empire. There will be a closing of minds and an intolerance of others. So the word must leave this land of David and go to a place of safety far beyond the temporal powers of Rome where it will become the light of the world, nurturing souls to grow to mighty oaks. It is written that a prophet has no honour in his own land.*'"

Turning his gaze upon Joseph of Arimithaea, Yeshua said, "Now you must carry the truth beyond this land, dear friend."

Holding Joseph's gaze he said, "Beware of those who come after me evangelising and claiming to speak my truth." His voice rose in strong emotion and Yeshua coughed painfully. He looked from Joseph to Nicodemus and to his brother, James for confirmation. "All of you will be pursued by the Sanhedrin and the Romans in the coming days. Joseph I trust the care of my beloved disciple, Mary, to you. You shall take her and *the Word* to a safe place beyond the

Romans until I return. James, you will safeguard the followers in the city and Nicodemus, you will assist Joseph in his escape, but stay in Jerusalem with James. *The Word* must not die with this body or with you. The light must be allowed to shine in another place for all to see."

"But Master, what of the lost sheep of the house of Israel?" asked Joseph mindful of Yeshua's mission to the Jews.

"You must lift up your eyes and make disciples of all nations, brother," said Yeshua. "If t*he Word* does not leave this land to be reborn, it will die with the Temple and this city. God wills it."

"I understand, Master," was all Joseph could manage in reply. The others nodded. In truth they did not have the strength to inquire further. Their minds were numb.

"Now bring the reed and parchment. Joseph you will write my testament as I speak. All four of you will sign as witnesses to my written words."

Mary supported Yeshua in her arms as he struggled to raise his head.

Few of Yeshua's followers fully understood his many instructions and demands of them. The Master's plan and how it unfolded was only known to him. Now it was clear he had anticipated that He may not survive and may wish to make His final testament. Yeshua coughed and as He did blood trickled down His chin which Mary wiped away. His body had little time left for this world. His struggle to keep the body alive was creating huge disturbances of energy around them.

As Yeshua spoke his last testament supported by Mary, Joseph wrote His words in the still of the dark and scented room. James and Nicodemus listened intently and prayed and wept. After speaking for some time, Yeshua sank back down. It was complete.

"Now all four of you witness these words by making your mark on the parchment," he said. "Joseph, you are the guardian of this document. Nurture it like a small flame that will light a great fire in the world. Take it beyond the reach of the Sanhedrin and even beyond the Romans and their allies, for they will douse the flame as they have destroyed my body and my Word in this land. With this light goes my true Word and wherever this light is revealed there the true church will flourish."

Turning to look into the eyes of Mary, Yeshua said, "You, my love, are of the light, the guardian of this broken body. Only my blood family must know of its final resting place. Bury it in the place I have stipulated."

Mary nodded, but still did not speak. It was a time beyond words.

At that, the one known as Yeshua ben Pandira, house builder, rabbi, husband, healer and prophet closed His eyes to the world. As He did so He gave up the human spirit and ascended to another place. Joseph of Arimithaea put down his reed. All four offered prayers and wept like children upon the naked body of their Master. They called out to God the father in their darkest hour of despair. The light of the world went out.

III: Caiaphas

Caiaphas could not tolerate the sedition that the Nazorean zealot was spreading. It disturbed the Romans. There could be no 'King of the Jews' under Roman rule. After criticism of his cruel handling of the Jews, it was Pontius Pilate's strategy to win favours in Rome. It was certain that if Pilate became embarrassed by an uprising led by a Jewish agitator he would exact a cruel punishment on Jerusalem and worst of all on Caiaphas himself for allowing such disorder among the Jews.

This Nazorean challenged the very basis of the Sadducees' beliefs and offended God himself. To them he blasphemed, he forgave sin, healed the sick, broke the Sabbath and even raised people from the dead. Only God could do such things. No human could claim nor do such things without offending God. This rural agitator had arrived in the holy city just days before Passover on an ass posturing as the messiah according to Holy Scripture. He then had the effrontery to throw the good merchants out of the Temple, calling the sacred place a den of thieves, threatening to destroy what God's anointed, the great King Herod, had built to the glory of God.

Much worse, this Yeshua ben Pandira made clear his contempt for the Pharisees and Sadducees, calling them hypocrites, false teachers, vipers, whitewashed graves full of dead men's bones and so on. This was no holy man, this was no Moses. This was a dangerous agitator who at a time like Passover was obviously planning an uprising. He was not the first that Caiaphas had dealt with in his ten years as High Priest. So Caiaphas knew he must act before God and the Romans did.

Caiaphas was incandescent with rage when he learnt of the removal of the Nazorean from the tomb before the Sanhedrin could itself remove the body. The plan was to parade the dead Yeshua ben Pandira through the streets of the city as a mere mortal and an imposter. Caiaphas was not accustomed to being thwarted.

Worse was to come for Caiaphas when he heard of the foolishness of his nephew, Jonathan, who postured at the tomb as an angel speaking of resurrection to confuse the Nazorean's demented followers. Now word of a resurrection was among the common people.

However Jonathan had some of his uncle's cunning. By sending these people out of Jerusalem to Galilee to find their risen messiah, Jonathan had bought the Sanhedrin valuable time in order to find the body. So all was not lost. They must find the body.

In the days that followed, the holy city was still swollen with pilgrims and in great ferment. High Priest Caiaphas and Prefect Pontius Pilate frantically sought to find the physical remains of Yeshua bin Pandira to disprove talk of a messiah.

As for Yeshua's followers their spirits moved from jubilation to despair as each twist in the street gossip was revealed and considered. Their Lord was gone from them physically and was not walking amongst them in physical resurrection as had been prophesised. They were like lost sheep under a Roman yoke. Who would speak for the sick, the poor and God's oppressed now? Where was truth and light? Were the people of Moses to remain slaves to the Romans forever, their leader vanquished as so many before?

Yet the miraculous disappearance of their Master's body and the presence of an angel at the empty tomb proved divinity was at work and gave hope. Yeshua was indeed the messiah. He was physically ascended to the divine and word was that he had promised to return. Then some said it was another Yeshua who died on the cross – Yeshua ben Barabbas leader of another Galilean rebellion, this one near the Tower of Siloam.

But Caiaphas was not to be confused by such street gossip. He dealt in the politics of men. The Sadducees cared nothing for the notion of resurrection.

Joseph of Arimithaea was arrested on the fifth day and questioned harshly by the Sanhedrin on the whereabouts of Yeshua's body in the heat of the Temple at midday. Fears grew that Joseph too would be crucified.

"Where is your rural rabbi? We know you betrayed the Sanhedrin and schemed with the merchant Nicodemus to have him released from the cross against God's will," demanded Caiaphas. "Why did you do so, Joseph of Arimithaea?"

"I merely sought to preserve the Sabbath according to the Law, Lord. No more. The spirit was gone from the body. We ministered to his memory and prepared the body in the tomb for his grieving family," answered Joseph calmly.

"He was dead. A Roman spear saw to that," sneered Caiaphas. "But we know he schemed to cheat the cross and you were his chief supporter!" screamed Caiaphas as he pointed his staff at Joseph in accusation.

"He did not survive the cross," affirmed Joseph in honesty and glared back at the High priest.

"So then you can tell us, Master Joseph of Arimithaea, where the body of this godless agitator rests now?" retorted Caiaphas.

"I cannot for I do not know where he was taken nor by whom."

In this Joseph spoke the truth. Only Yeshua's immediate family knew the whereabouts of his body now. Yeshua had stipulated this. He knew that the Sanhedrin would not question his grieving family. Joseph was deliberately kept ignorant of this final twist once Yeshua had dictated his last testament to him in the Valley of Kidron. This would save Joseph's life and allow Yeshua's body to lie undisturbed.

Caiaphas consulted with Jonathan ben Ananaus. Joseph of Arimithaea could not offer him the answer he so desperately sought, but to move against Joseph, a respected Council member and wealthy merchant without proof could inflame the people further. Frustrated he strode from the Temple and left the Sanhedrin Council sitting in awkwardness. Significantly his Segan, Jonathan ben Ananaus did not follow his uncle out of the temple.

In that hour power began to slip from Caiaphas' steely grip.

Caiaphas did indeed suffer the displeasure of the Romans. He had been unable to produce the dead body stolen from Roman custody by Jews. Less than a year after Yeshua's crucifixion Caiaphas' long reign as High Priest came to an end. He was removed from office by Pilate and replaced by his nephew, Jonathan. Within days Pilate in turn was removed from office by the Roman Legate in Syria for his incompetent handling of Jewish agitation and for bringing embarrassment upon the Emperor.

When Caiaphas and Pilate lost their powerful positions, Mary of Magdala and Joseph of Arimithaea, along with six apostles slipped out of Judaea helped by the merchant Nicodemus. They travelled to Egypt where they took ship to Gaul.

However Joseph did not bring with him Yeshua's Last Testament as Yeshua had instructed. Mary would not allow it. In this she disobeyed her husband. She had done so before. The risk she calculated was too great while the Romans pursued them. If they were caught the testament would be lost for all time. Arrangements were made for the testament to be smuggled out at a later date when Mary, Joseph and the apostles were safe.

There is one last twist to the tale before my pen moves on from this holy time to a later one.

Caiaphas was a stubborn and determined man as you would expect. In his exile Caiaphas' bitterness at his downfall did not diminish with ill health and old age. He was determined to be vindicated and Yeshua ben Pandira revealed as a common agitator lacking all divinity and by this measure to recover his own standing within the Sadducees and the Romans.

As he had done while High Priest, Caiaphas continued to use his wealth to maintain a network of spies throughout Judaea and beyond. These mercenaries – paid vagabonds of all kinds, searched unceasingly for clues to Yeshua's last resting place. And in the year 49 A.D, Caiaphas' doggedness was rewarded.

One of Caiaphas' spies, a Philistine called Achish, related a story to Caiaphas that had come to light from a family member who had nursed the merchant, Nicodemus. This old woman had told Achish that Nicodemus' mind was lost in his final days and that the old merchant rambled senselessly. However one thing he told her caught her attention because of his closeness to Yeshua ben Pandira.

Nicodemus related the events in the aftermath of Yeshua's crucifixion with clarity. He told his nurse of Yeshua's last testament given to Joseph of Arimithaea and even the nature of its content. Further, he revealed the identity of the guardians of the tomb – the two apostles who had carried Yeshua from the tomb and who knew Yeshua's final resting place. The last resting place held the manuscript, claimed Nicodemus.

Old and unwell and in a high state of agitation, Caiaphas excitedly called his secretary to him and dictated a letter advising the Sanhedrin of this important information and requiring them to arrest the two apostles immediately so that the Nazorean's mortal remains could be revealed and his myth exposed.

"Take this now, boy, to Matthias the High Priest. Ask him if he will call upon me this day to discuss this urgent matter," ordered Caiaphas to his secretary. "Go directly and swiftly. Speak to no one else on this matter, d'you hear?"

"Yes, Lord Caiaphas," said the secretary and left immediately with the letter for the High Priest.

However there was divine work afoot. The secretary was in fact a follower of Yeshua ben Pandira and worked in Caiaphas' house so that such events may be quickly ascertained.

Quickly Caiaphas' secretary made his way to James the Just, Yeshua's brother and leader of the followers in Jerusalem. The guardians of the tomb must be warned. They had only hours to act.

James called the two apostles to his small house in the Kidron Valley. One was the Cyrenian, John Mark; a young apostle who had hosted Yeshua's Last Supper in his family home at Cenacle and had accompanied Yeshua in his last hours of freedom in the Garden of Gethsemane. The second was another apostle, the Briton, Aristobulus. These two apostles had remained in Jerusalem while most others had left to spread *the Word*. They alone were the guardians of the final resting place and the last testament. They were well known in the city and would be speedily located once their identities were known by the Sanhedrin.

Huddled round a table in James' home, the three considered their plight. Caiaphas while elderly and unwell was still a dangerous foe. Together they prayed for guidance. It was given that same hour.

The secretary was sent back to his master to say he had delivered the letter as instructed and the High Priest would call upon him in the morning. This would give John Mark and Aristobulus time to move Yeshua's mortal remains along with the last testament and travel to a place beyond Caiaphas' reach. The continued presence of the two apostles in Jerusalem was now a threat to the word itself.

On returning to his master's home the secretary found the household in uproar. Caiaphas in his great excitement had been seized by many tongues and had fallen down frothing at the mouth like a rabid dog. Now he was lying comatose in his bed, unable to speak or move much more than his head. Caiaphas' crucial intelligence about Yeshua's last hours was now locked inside his being and would remain so until he passed some weeks later. The Sanhedrin would forever remain ignorant of these matters.

Praise be. This was indeed divine work.

Having moved Yeshua's remains for a third time to where it lies to this day, John Mark and Aristobulus left Jerusalem that night under protection of the dark with the last testament in their care and journeyed to Egypt, as Joseph of Arimithaea and Mary of Magdala had done some ten years earlier. Caiaphas's letter to the Sanhedrin went with them. Aristobulus travelled on to the islands of his birth in the far north where he spread the word.

The last testament remained in Egypt with John Mark as its guardian where it became known as '*The Word*' and passed into Christian legend. It brought light to the dark corners and out of this light grew the Church of Africa. In this way Mark became first Bishop of Alexandria.

It is Mark's guardianship of Yeshua's resting place and his role in protecting his Master's last testament that concerns us most here. John Mark, Yeshua's faithful litter bearer, remained bearer of his word not only in life, but beyond as we shall see.

IV: The Great Library: 575AD

The Berber horseman raised himself from the saddle to smell the flowers on the balcony as the caravan passed him by. He smelt the sweet, heavy aroma and smiled to himself as he picked one flower, kissed its petals gently and placed it in his headdress. Calmly he turned his attention to the street scene before him.

It was early spring in the great city of Alexandria. Star flowers were in bloom all along the Canopian Way. A procession was being led by a tall Christian monk who strode purposefully through the colourful street with a smaller man in a clerk's attire at his side. Behind them were many more monks leading a caravan of donkeys pulling several carts each stacked with wooden crates. They were making their way towards the Patriarch's palace on the other side of the city. So intent were they on their business and so aloof from the surrounding crowd in the late evening sun, that they did not notice the Berber on horseback watching them intently from the side of the market square. His dark eyes followed the monks and their transport keenly. As they passed him he quietly guided his horse in behind their caravan as it manoeuvred through the narrow streets around the market. His employer, the Bishop of Rome, would pay handsomely for information regarding the activities of the church in Alexandria, especially in regard to activities around the Great Library.

The small man – a library official, carrying a heavy leather bag, had to run to keep up with the tall, striding monk beside him. He was perspiring profusely.

"Father, father, I beg of you to slow down. In this heat such fast footwork is not good for one such as I." He was the Chief Librarian's Senior Editor. A man not accustomed to physical exertion, especially not in the hot sun.

"I understand your discomfort, good librarian, but we must not delay in the streets with our cargo, especially yours," responded the monk glancing around and nodding towards his leather bag. "His Holiness, the Patriarch will not rest until all this is under lock and key, in the Church's vaults."

This seemed to add to the Senior Editor's discomfort. "I wonder what can be so important" he said. "These scrolls …..No one will speak of them. On the one hand, the Chief Librarian laughs at them and on the other, Father Clement scowls at my inquiries and will not speak. They were kept by the abbot, not filed in our safe area. Can you enlighten me, brother?" said the official breathlessly.

The monk eyed him critically, but he too ignored the librarian's question.

The caravan had set out from the Great Library of Alexandria: one of the most outstanding libraries in the known world. It contained a huge volume of ancient scrolls collected from around the world from the time of the Ptolemy's when the city had been a centre of learning and enlightenment. It was claimed that the library held half a million scrolls. But the Senior Editor doubted they had ever been counted.

Now in this time the library was under threat, from both Christians and non-Christians alike. The rising power of the Christian Church and its pursuit of heresy caused it to take a critical view of any form of study that was not scriptural. The Great Library had hosted scholars from around the known world; men like the great Euclid and women like the philosopher, Hypatia, who was brutally slayed by Christians. These scholars studied the Great Library's scrolls and added many of their own as they sought new knowledge on subjects from astronomy to mathematics to geography and of course to religions of many kinds.

It was the latter that most disturbed the Christian Church. The library was suspected of holding many pagan tracts and worse: alternative translations of Christian scriptures suggesting different views of the Christ. In the Church's eyes these threatened the orthodoxy of Christianity, hard won after many years spent in bitter internal struggles since the time Emperor Constantine accepted Christianity. There had been many theological battles with the Arians, the Nestorians and the Pelagians, but more significantly, battles within the Church itself between the patriarchs in Alexandria, Rome, Antioch and Constantinople for supremacy and purity of interpretation of the Gospels. By the time of which we speak the unity of the early Christian Church had been fractured by strong views around the Holy Trinity and around Yeshua's true nature. The Romans and the Hellenes in their worldly ways had separated God into three – Father, Son and Holy Ghost – and talked of the Lord Yeshua in many obscure ways. The Church of St Mark the Evangelist in Alexandria took a strong opposing view, believing Yeshua to be the very godhead and not human. For this the Alexandrians were isolated and greatly abused by the Roman Church.

This difference in theology, coupled with the desire of the Romans to tolerate no dissension, fractured the Church for all time into East and West. And so now the Patriarchs of Alexandria and Rome were separated. They had locked horns over the true Word. Both were opposed to different forms of heresy and to each other's theology.

Indeed a previous Patriarch of Alexandria, Theophilus, had ordered that the Great Library be destroyed in order to have done with the pagan teachings of Plato and Aristotle and the like, but he was persuaded to delay until it was known exactly what the library contained within its many halls. It was known that there were writings of St Mark in the Great Library which must be preserved. Theophilus died before this enormous task could be begun and under continued Roman and Melkite persecution future patriarchs had little time to be concerned about the Great Library. It was not until the arrival from Scetis of the zealous Damianos the First, the thirty-fifth Patriarch of the Church of Alexandria and Bishop of Africa that attention focused on the Great Library once more.

Damianos worried about the growing power of the Sassanids to the east. These unbelievers had already sacked churches and libraries stealing priceless Christian texts in order to have their Arab scholars dissect and ridicule them. It was Damianos's view that if Alexandria was to fall into Sassanid hands the Great Library must be cleansed of valuable texts and taken to remote desert monasteries for safe-keeping.

It was this task of cleansing the Great Library that Damianos had set himself on his elevation to the Holy See in the Year of the Word

569. It had taken his clergy several years just to sift through and identify documents that might be sacred to the Church in Africa. It was the conclusion of this mammoth exercise that created the curious caravan through the streets of Alexandria that day in March in the year 575 A.D.

Over four thousand scrolls had been identified and stored ready for delivery to the Patriarch for further examination by the Church's theologians. But on that day, just as the exercise was terminating, three scrolls came to light in the final hall to be cleared that threatened, not just the Church in Africa, but the carefully constructed orthodoxies on all sides of the Christian Church.

These scrolls were bound together with a heavy seal and were hidden in a box in the corner of the hall.

The box had been opened by a monk and lay on a reading table for later examination. The significance of these scrolls might well have been overlooked in the rush that final day except for the fact that the Chief Librarian noticed a heavy seal on one of the scrolls.

"Fools!" he shouted to the busy monks as he brandished the scrolls. "Do you not recognise the seal of the Great Sanhedrin?"

The Chief Librarian, one named Rabanus, was a Jew of great learning and high status in Alexandria. He was an eminent geographer, who continuing in the tradition of the great Eratoshenes, had measured the earth and many lands within it. Such things appalled the Christian Church. God had made the earth and all things in it. What right had any man to put a measure God's creation? The Christian church clashed with Rabanus many times as he sought to preserve his guardianship of knowledge.

Men of learning were no longer set on high in the city of Alexandria. Rabanus was one of the last of a long line of Alexandrian scholars who had enlightened the world since the time of the Ptolemies. The Chief Librarian had daily to defend the library from Christian interference in its work. This latest assault by the Patriarch Damianos felt as though the Great Library was being raped of some of its greatest religious teachings in the cause of dogma.

The Chief Editor came scurrying at the sound of his master's raised voice. Together they carefully prised apart the heavy seal of the Great Sanhedrin.

"This seal dates from the time of the last temple in Jerusalem. I have seen them in the rabbinical college there," said the Rabanus.

When the seal was broken it revealed one short scroll written by the Apostle St. Mark, the first Bishop of Alexandria and all of Africa. It was part in Greek and part in Aramaic. Another slightly longer scroll was in ancient Hebrew. Most of the monks did not read or speak these ancient and obscure forms. Greek and Latin were their mother tongues. A further longer scroll was written entirely in Aramaic.

"So these could come from the time of the Christ?" asked Berossus, the Chief Editor excitedly.

"Haaa!" exclaimed the Chief Librarian. "Your Christ as you call him, Berossus, does not interest me as you very well know nor does this entire charade of theology you have become embroiled in through your cousin, the Patriarch. I rejoice that this is the final day of this nonsense and I can reclaim the Library for science and learning and be rid of these ignorant monks!" He snarled, looking over his shoulder to the monks busy examining the final shelves.

"But this is interesting," said Rabanus examining the scrolls. "Look we have two scrolls here: one written by your blessed St Mark. See his personal seal here." He pointed to a small seal in the shape of a cross. "Mmmmm. Mark writes in Greek as is his habit, but here he changes to Aramaic. Why did he do that? This other scroll has the seal of the Great Sanhedrin. Why would these be stored together?" he mused.

"The language of the Christ," observed the Berossus looking at the Aramaic text, and then bit his tongue for fear of angering his master again. "Ah yes," continued the Chief Editor in the more measured tones of academia, anxious to placate the learned Rabanus. "But the other is not, sir. It is in Hebrew. But I do not read these tongues," he confessed to the Chief Librarian whom he knew could read both and hoped he would volunteer an immediate translation.

Rabanus had remained aloof from the Church's interrogation of his library's Christian records. He was neither Christian nor theologian and he dismissed both as ignorant storytellers. Regrettably his Chief Editor, Berossus had become involved in the Church's affairs because of his own Christian beliefs and by the unfortunate coincidence that the zealous Patriarch of Alexandria, Damianos was Berossus' cousin. There had been a time when the Chief Librarian of Alexandria supported by five thousand students could have defied Ptolemy himself and locked the large bronze doors of the Great Library to any such interference, but those days were sadly gone. The African Church was on the rise and men of learning were scorned in the street.

However this time Rabanus' naturally inquiring mind was intrigued by his discovery. Although Aramaic was St Mark's native tongue, Mark was an educated Jew who had learnt to write fluently in Greek and had always done so, until now. What could Mark's use of Aramaic mean? He studied the text in silence watched eagerly by his Chief Editor.

Rabanus then turned to the second Hebrew scroll and read it too.

Eventually he smiled widely in satisfaction at his Chief Editor.

"My, my, Berossus, they have found something here. I swear by all the great scholars. This will give your cousin and his ilk a sore head." Rabanus' laugh echoed around the small marbled hall. "The truth is not a welcome bedfellow in your church, is it?"

"What is it, sir?" pleaded the excited Berossus looking at the two scrolls open on the table before them hopping from foot to foot.

Rabanus' only pleasure these past years had been to bait and tease the Christians scurrying about his library's great halls. He once secreted an old stick in an ancient Christian scroll. The earnest monks were convinced it was a piece from St. Anthony's holy staff; until a beggar was found in the courtyard complaining that his staff had been broken and one half stolen. The stick in the scroll matched the remaining part of the beggar's staff.

Now Rabanus would have his final amusement as he prepared to watch the departing Christians deal with the contents of these last three scrolls. He stayed his Chief Editor's pleadings with his large hands.

"Now Berossus you know I do not concern myself with religion and theocracy. These are matters for your church. You must take these scrolls to the Patriarch with haste. Believe me when I say that they will greatly interest him and his priests."

Rabanus guffawed and turned on his heels leaving his Chief Editor staring at the source of such amusement on the table. Berossus stood for a while considering how to tackle the Aramaic and

Hebrew texts. Then he remembered a young monk from Jerusalem among the one hundred strong cohort of scholar monks drafted into the library. This one translated several ancient tongues. He gathered up the scrolls excitedly and hurried off to find this young translator and release this hidden treasure to the world.

Arriving in the reception hall of the Great Library just before the office of None, Berossus sought out the young monk from Jerusalem: one Simon of Bezatha, insisting that he examine these latest scrolls without delay.

Some monks, who had noted Berossus' excitement, lingered curiously around the young Hebrew translator. Simon quietly ignored their excited chatter about the Apostle's scroll. The first scroll's large seal was broken when it was handed to Simon. His interest was stirred when he too recognised the distinctive seal of the Great Sanhedrin. He gently opened the first scroll written by St Mark. He noted the Greek, followed by the Aramaic: the language of Yeshua, now no longer spoken. Simon immediately reasoned that St Mark did not wish this scroll to be easily understood. Simon began to read silently. His eyebrows knitted and he looked up at the gathering crowd of monks.

St Mark began in common Greek:

"I, John Mark, the Apostle of Yeshua and Bishop of Alexandria leave to future generations this letter of Caiaphas, the High Priest of the Great Sanhedrin in Jerusalem and murderer of my Master. This was given to me upon Caiaphas' passing. I was charged with the safety of many things from the time of the Master. This document and its safe removal from the land of Judaea were among my many responsibilities. It bears true witness to great events and as such must be safeguarded by all who believe in Him and seek His true word.

Simon paused to assimilate the Aramaic text that followed:

"The events that Caiaphas relates in his letter to Matthias are of divine importance. I know his account of our Lord's passing to be a true one. For I, John Mark was Yeshua's stretcher bearer and am the guardian of his final resting place. My Master did not die upon the cross. He lived, was resurrected and was then taken up by God.

His mortal remains lie in Jerusalem city. He will return to walk among us as prophesised.

My Master's last teachings, referred to by Caiaphas – was written down by Joseph of Arimithaea as the Master lay dying of his wounds. The Lord Yeshua was greatly concerned for what would come after him. This Last Testament was brought by my hand to Alexandria where it inspired many to found the true church here in Africa. I leave the last teachings in your hands and trust in God's protection.

As our Master said: 'I am the light of the world. Whoever follows me will not walk in darkness, but will have the light of life.' The Last Testament is His Light, hide it and the truth will be hidden, darkness will be all around. Therefore for His truth to inspire others the last teachings must be for all men to see."

Then St Mark reverts to common Greek:

"Guard the Word. Heed The Word, not the lies. Others speak and claim to speak for Him. He suffered for our sins, was crucified, dead and buried and on the third day he lived. I saw all these things with mine own eyes. It was all that any man could give. It is for you now to take His Word forward to keep it in the light.

"God be with you in your hour of trial. He will give you the strength and the wisdom to await the revelation of His last teachings and His return. Let His light shine on The Word.

"In God

John Mark, Bishop of Africa, 1745600.5"

The young translator swallowed hard. His hands shook as he held the ancient scrolls. His young shoulders drooped as he felt a weight descend upon them.

"God", he prayed softly. "Give me the strength."

Simon prayed as he began to work through the Hebrew script of Caiaphas' scroll.

"Tell us, brother! What does the blessed saint tell us?" cried the monks assembled around Simon impatient for some news.

Simon reacted angrily in his nervous discomfort. He thumped the desk.

"I cannot concentrate with this crowd about me. Please Master Editor, send them about their business," he appealed to the Chief Editor.

"Of course, of course, brother monk. Be gone the lot of you to your work! Brother Simon must still his mind," the Chief Editor scolded. The monks departed gradually to the remaining tasks of cataloguing and loading the final scrolls, leaving Simon and the Chief Editor with the manuscripts.

This 'truth' from Caiaphas' scroll, when he found it, was overpowering. He poured over his translation for some minutes checking the syntax and looking for possible mistakes in his use of his Greek translation from the Hebrew. A word could subtly and radically change a meaning. His mind kept going blank as if it could not take in what he was reading. He kept bringing himself back to his task. He had made no mistakes in the translation, yet he sat and stared at the manuscript before him, turning it over again and again. He was aware that his hands were sweating and shaking ever more strongly. He looked around at his fellow monks in wonder.

He still doubted what he had read and translated into Latin instead of his native Greek. Still it was the same. The scroll was without doubt ancient and written in a style that he knew was current in the priesthood in Judaea at the time of the Christ. It did contain the seal of the Sanhedrin. The accompanying scroll was from the Apostle. Simon had seen others just yesterday and recognised the Apostle's own hand. The Apostle himself vouched for the second scroll's authenticity. He prayed to St Mark for guidance.

It was clear what the third scroll was. It was the Christ's last teaching written as he spoke before ascending.

Quickly, but carefully he put the ancient scrolls back in the leather bag. He noticed he was now alone in the great hall. The monks had left to say the hours. Simon set off to find Father Clement.

Clement, an elderly monk from Cyrenia, was still in prayers in the small chapel at the end of the courtyard. Simon had been so absorbed in these manuscripts he had forgotten the Offices: a serious misdemeanour. He waited in the cool shadows for the bell to sound at the end and approached Father Clement as he emerged into the afternoon light.

Startled by the young monk's sudden and urgent appearance, Clement remonstrated with him.

"What is it, boy that you linger in this way in the shadows like the devil? Were you not at prayer? We must still keep time for our calling, boy, in spite of the great demands," said the monk looking down at the scrolls Simon carried.

"No, I did not. At least, well…..I am sorry father, but my mind is distracted and disturbed. I must talk with you privately and urgently. It's some important scrolls. I need your assistance," said Simon hurriedly.

"'Privately'?! There is no 'privately' with us, brother. You know that. Have you something to hide from your brothers and from God? Besides, the abbot is waiting for me. Everything must be finished this day as you well know. I beg you do not distract me."

"In the name of our Lord I beg you, father, to give me a few precious moments. I have seen documents that have disturbed my very soul and I am in need of your guidance," pleaded Simon.

A gust of warm evening air fanned down the ancient courtyard and danced round the two monks, tugging at their habits. Simon clutched the scrolls closer. He could smell the desert mixed with sea air: a cocktail of great forces, energies in flow that the deserts of water and sand so often conjured up.

Clement saw the distress in the young monk's eyes and in the manner he was clutching the scrolls.

"Peace upon you, brother," said Father Clement. "I am sorry for speaking so roughly. It is not very Christian. Come into this room where we can speak. Mind it will still be in God's presence!"

"I know," Simon sighed with relief at the older priest's acquiescence. "These cannot be true! Please read them, father," Simon thrust the scrolls into Clément's hands. He had sought out Clement because the older monk had spent time as a scholar in Judaea and understood Aramaic and Hebrew.

"Now?" asked Clement.

"Father you will understand when you read." He spoke nervously and set out the three scrolls on a large reading desk by the high arched windows. "It won't take long. Please! Read this, the apostle's scroll first. Then the Hebrew text."

Clement could see that this normally very sanguine and studious young monk was indeed very agitated. Such excitement was very untypical. He had often chided Simon because of the volume of scrolls needing his expert examination. Much to his frustration Simon never took on the sense of urgency their task needed and maintained a quiet and methodical demeanour at all times. Now Simon was in a highly disturbed state before him.

"Very well, I will read them," agreed Clement sitting down at a desk in the corner of the study by the window to get the most of the evening light. He opened the two scrolls and at once noticed the Great Sanhedrin seal. The two monks exchanged looks. "Great Sanhedrin?" queried Clement. He had not seen one of these outside Jerusalem in all his thirty years as a scholar of ancient texts. The Great Sanhedrin had closely guarded its records. They were not a matter of public information to be passed around by gentiles nor found in far off places like Alexandria.

"Yes, it is," nodded the young monk. He was not able to say any more as he stood on the cool stone flags waiting for Clement's conclusions. He watched as Father Clement turned his attention to St Mark's Aramaic text Simon indicated by Simon.

After the first paragraph he looked up at Simon blankly. He again examined the seal and looked back at the Apostle's scroll. Then he resumed his translation as the wind picked up in the courtyard. Slowly he moved onto the second scroll with its ancient Hebrew.

> *"I, Joseph ben Caiaphas write to you in great haste Matthias the Most Holy, High Priest of the Great Sanhedrin of Jerusalem concerning a matter of great import to all Sadducees and right-thinking Jews.*
>
> *God has given me information on important matters relating to the impostor, Yeshua ben Pandira, the Nazorene zealot, which I must communicate with you in haste. This will enable us to finally expose the impostor to the people in the sight of God.*
>
> *A good man, although a Philistine, called Achish in my employ has learnt the truth of the Nazorene's death. Achish*

had befriended the merchant Nicodemus' nurse who related to him the old merchant's confession before his death. It reveals a truth that I have long suspected, Matthias. I am vindicated.

The Nazorene did not die on the cross. He conspired with Joseph of Arimithaea and Nicodemus to cheat the cross and be resurrected for all the people to see and to declare him "messiah" according to holy prophesy. It was his followers who stole his living body from the tomb under our very eyes and took it to another place for "resurrection". However his sinful healing magic deserted him and the Nazorene zealot died of his wounds sometime soon after. God be praised.

But before dying he dictated a testament setting out his so-called final teachings. This manuscript was to be taken by Joseph of Arimithaea to a far off place for safe-keeping, but the Magdalene forbade it. This manuscript remains hidden in Jerusalem. It is greatly valued by the Nazorene's followers. They believe it has divine qualities and that wherever this manuscript is revealed, they say, it will herald in the Kingdom of God on earth.

Mark you this, Matthias the Most Holy, the Nazorean's secret resting place contains this manuscript and it is known to only two of his apostles – the Cyrenian John Mark and the Briton, Aristobulus. It was they who stole his living body from the tomb and carried it to Nicodemus for care. They can lead us to the tomb and to the manuscript.

My Lord, High Priest, if we move quickly we can arrest these two thieves and expose the Nazoreans for all to see. Yeshua ben Pandira's mortal remains will reveal that he was just a man – a troublesome peasant, not God and not a messiah. We will be vindicated in our defence of God.

Through these steps we will find this liar's manuscript and destroy it too before his followers find it and another 'messiah' to lead the people against our divine authority once more.

I am old now and unwell, Matthias. Before I die God has now called me once more to provide this service. I humbly ask you to call on my house without delay to discuss these

*matters and so to lay our plans. I ask you to send a message
in return with my secretary when I can expect you.
  God's servant,
  Joseph ben Caiaphas"*

The sun was low in the sky as Clement finished reading the scrolls.
The air in the room had cooled and the shadows were lengthening.
Both monks, the young and the old, shivered as they stared at the
third remaining scroll bound by a rich white fabric.

"I haven't examined the third scroll, Father," said Simon. "I, I
haven't the courage, I don't…"

Clement in a whisper and swallowing hard said, "Pray with me,
my brother."

The two knelt by the large desk and prayed for some time.

"Now come with me to the abbot" said Clement as he carefully
rolled up the scrolls. He grimaced as he did so. Simon noticed the
old monk's changed demeanour and his own anxiety increased.

The two left the study quietly and made for the abbot's quarters on
the west wall of the Serapeum.

V: The City of Derry, Ireland. 2015

A featureless government office gave no hint of its exotic contents. The walls were battleship grey with furniture to match. In a corner of the room were heavy glass display cases. The feature that interrupted the greyness was a display of colourful pictures and maps of an archaeological excavation on one wall along with a data projector. From an open window could be heard the sound of a busy street below and a busker playing a flute. The music added interest to the drab room.

A meeting was about to begin chaired by Sir Francis Hedding, whose role as a senior government mandarin was unclear to those attending, but he had called the meeting and it was known that he acted on behalf of the British Prime Minister.

Sitting at the bottom of the large table was Bryony MacDirmaid: a young field archaeologist who had recently taken on the management of her first dig in Dunseverick, a rural settlement on the north coast of Northern Ireland. She was thrilled to be appointed by Heritage Ulster, not only her first dig as Supervising Archaeologist, but also in her favourite part of the country, her beloved north coast. Yet on a warm sunny summer's day here she was sat in a dreary government office in the city of Derry surrounded by a strange collection of eminent people. She felt uncomfortably out of place.

Sir Francis at the head of the table opened the meeting without saying much about himself, beyond something self-deprecating about being the Prime Minister's "concierge" which gave everyone the intended impression that he was some kind of high level emissary. He downplayed his position in a style reminiscent of old British spy stories. Sir Francis went round the table and asked each person to introduce themselves. It became obvious to Bryony that it was indeed a bizarre gathering reflecting the central issue they had to discuss. Their names went by in a blur. There were senior clergy, one representing the Roman Catholic Cardinal of Ireland and one the Anglican Archbishop of Ireland; there was a theologian from Oxford; the Chief Executive of Heritage Ulster Sheila Donald who Bryony knew; Bryony's line manager in Heritage Ulster, Sean White; an Israeli specialist in bible history and Hebrew from the British Museum; someone from the National Trust whose land she had been digging on; a senior civil servant from government communications; an eminent historian also from the British museum, Professor Margery Dugdish, whose work on early British and Irish Christianity Bryony had read; a senior civil servant from the Northern Ireland Executive; a forensic archaeologist from the Ulster Museum who had worked with Bryony on the find, Benedict McTavish, and finally a grey, balding secretary sitting next to Sir Francis taking notes. No minutes would be issued, Sir Francis added and no one was to take any notes, apart from the official secretary.

"So like your old school master I'm going to ask you to put all your pens and jotters away, please" said Sir Francis. They had already been asked to leave their mobiles and laptops outside the office.

"Well" said Sir Francis "This is a strange and delicate matter which I have been asked to look into with you all and I thank you for coming along today. Our deliberations will be reported back to the Prime Minister who has taken a particular interest along with, the Archbishop and the Cardinal of course," Sir Francis nodded to both clerics, "with a view to mapping a way forward" Then his avuncular manner changed abruptly, "I would remind you all that you have each signed the Official Secrets Act and that all these discussions are held under the Act. Nothing discussed here must be repeated to anyone not here today and must not be written about – email, text, report, especially to the media. Nor must you speak about it on the phone, mobile or landline, even to each other and especially not to friends and family, no matter how trusted they are to you. No conversations in public places between you about this matter. The consequences of breaking these rules will be most severe. You are all in positions of great trust. Please do not betray that trust. Do I make myself clear?" he glared around the table. There were nods and mutterings of assent.

"Good!" and the avuncular manner returned. "First we must be sure of what we have got before us" he gesticulated towards a large portfolio in the middle of the table. Bryony's heart missed a beat. That was her find he was referring to. She enjoyed telling a good story and this was one, but she knew she must remain professional, none of the embellishment she usually gave her reports. If asked to speak she would remain calm and objective. This Sir Francis looked the type that would cut you in two if you winged it, never mind the rest of them now staring at her around the table.

"Let's start at the beginning. Miss..... MacDirmaid" Sir Francis began, consulting his notes for her name. "Your archaeological dig found these manuscripts, did it not? So we must start with you." It was said almost as an accusation.

"Yes. I did."

"Please talk us through how this happened, where you were working and why you were there in the first place. You may use the map and photographs of the area on the wall: if you would be so kind."

He waved to the map of Northern Ireland with his bifocals and photographs on the wall at the top of the room behind him and swivelled his chair around to get a good view.

Bryony swallowed hard and got up. She had rehearsed her presentation. A voice in her head said: "Go on! Tell the story."

"Heritage Ulster had been excavating in Dunseverick on the north coast with the permission of the National Trust following a substantial landslide on an outcrop near the harbour. The landslide has revealed some interesting features. The dig first of all revealed the chalice." She pointed to a projected photograph on the wall.

"The purpose was to identify if any other artefacts existed from this time which is the 6th century AD," began Bryony slipping into presentational mode. She could see how nervous Sean and Sheila Donald were; hoping no doubt that she didn't let the side down in such a forum or slip into her notorious storytelling mode. Everyone seemed tense. She spied a pointing stick and gladly armed herself with it, brandishing it like a weapon in case anyone considered attacking her. Feeling stronger she continued. "We had excavated to a depth of two meters on various locations around the landslip. The landslip had revealed what transpired to be the stone wall of a later church built in Norman times and probably on the site of an older Patrician or Columban church. It was here below the north wall that we had been focusing on. We were finding a variety of interesting artefacts in these locations here and here, Roman and Greek coins and some interesting pottery and of course the silver chalice just here." She smiled proudly. The silver chalice of Greek origin was as great a find as the Ardagh Chalice. Sean gave her an encouraging smile, but no one else seemed bothered that such a priceless artefact had been unearthed. Even the clerics were stony faced.

"The Dunseverick Chalice as it has become known has been dated to around the mid-6th century AD. It is in fact very similar in design to the Ardagh Chalice found in Ireland from around a century later. But this chalice is not Irish in origin because of the Greek lettering on its base..." Bryony went on. She realised she had to move on from her favourite topic to the focus of the meeting. "This encouraged us that this location here, was of particular importance. The chalice was found at the same level as a wooden floor believed to be the original church. At a depth of 1.3 meters below this level, we discovered the heavy oak box which on examination contained the manuscripts wrapped in linen inside a heavy leather bag. The soil type around the box indicated that it was infill. In other words the area around the box was excavated for the box to be buried. Although it appeared to be done in a hurry as the box was upside down as if thrown......."

"What does the writing on the chalice say, Ms MacDirmaid?" asked the cardinal's representative.

"*'The people of Hibernia and their bishop are dear to God and His church'*" replied Bryony. "We believe the bishop referred to be Columba, because of the images of the dove and the oak leaf used on the chalice."

"Thank you, Miss MacDirmaid" cut in Sir Francis eager to move things along. "Questions at this stage?"

The Israeli from the British Museum asked "Were there any distinguishing marks on the box?"

"Yes. A carving in old Irish said: "'*Solas do ghlóir mo praises'* *'Light for the glory of my praises'*. It also had an ornate carving of a square Celtic cross." said Bryony and pointed to a picture on the wall of the chest.

"And has the chest been dated" he asked.

"Yes. It's much older than the chalice: around the first century AD and made of French oak from the Pyrenees. It has created a puzzle for us. It is the earliest carving of a Christian cross found in these islands – Ireland or Britain."

Both clerics' brows furrowed at this.

"So a puzzle for you archaeologists and historians, but we need to move on to the meat of the issue – the manuscripts. Can you tell us something of them as you found them and then we'll pass onto.........Mr McTavish for his scientific analysis?" said Sir Francis.

"Yes. There are four documents in scroll form written on papyrus: three short and one somewhat longer. They were found in excellent condition inside the leather bag which itself was badly scarred. Inside the scrolls were some seeds, pressed wild flowers, some sand we think of Egyptian origin and a pebble" explained Bryony.

"Wild flowers, sand and a pebble?" asked the British Museum representative again.

"Yes the sand is Egyptian, the seeds are barley, the flowers are bog iris and dog violet and a small basalt pebble lying lose in the chest from a riverbed" answered Bryony.

"Anything else, Miss MacDirmaid?" asked Sir Francis.

"It is probable that the chest was dumped in a hurry because of a Viking raid." Bryony hurriedly stated before her session was ended. This was the closest she came to storytelling. She had no time to elaborate on some of her other theories and sat down quickly. Sean smiled and winked at her, pleased that she had curbed her need to develop the story.

"Good! Mr McTavish, enlighten us with your science please about these manuscripts before we move on to what they actually contain" said Sir Francis.

Benedict coughed loudly as he always did when asked a question. He stood up.

"No need for you out here I think, Mr McTavish. Just tell us from there" said Sir Francis, 'Unless you have photographs to point to?"

Benedict McTavish confirmed he had no need to do any pointing.

Bryony blushed at the suspicion that her field expertise was not all Sir Francis was interested in and felt an anger rise in her as she alone had been asked to standout front.

"Tell us first of all how certain we can be of the date of the manuscripts" said Sir Francis.

Benedict coughed again and Sir Francis winced at such repeated annoyance.

"Carbon dating of the papyrus and the ink puts the manuscripts firmly in the 1st century AD, sir. But the leather bag is much later, around the 6th century AD and made from Egyptian cowhide. The box chest as Ms MacDirmaid has said is also from the 1st century. The barley seeds are from the late 6th century," Benedict said confidently.

"And is there any room for doubt on the date of the manuscripts?" one of the clergy queried.

"Very little. We use the latest methods to cross reference both parchments and the inks used." said Benedict. "They've also been checked by the British Museum, the Israel Museum in Jerusalem and the National Museum in Alexandria all of whom have expertise in this field. We used much more advanced dating methods than were used to examine for example, the Turin shroud. There's little doubt of their age"

Bryony smiled to herself, flattered that this should be in the same league as the Turin Shroud controversy.

"The geographical origin of the scrolls is more difficult to pin down precisely without a translation of the text, but the papyrus and the ink are of a type used in what was the Levant and the Euphrates valley around the 1st century AD," continued Benedict eager to show his expertise.

Bryony day dreamed of that magical time on the north coast in the summer just past when she and Sean shared the joy of the discovery. Her hobby was storytelling so the events of the summer gave her plenty of material. It was as if the ancient worlds were being unlocked under their feet. There had been great light on the north coast that summer with big, bright skies overhead and a shimmering sea below. She felt tremendous energy and a freedom to do whatever she wanted. Then in bed one morning Sean had an idea that they should go deeper in the location where they had found the chalice, beneath the floor of the church to see what lay beneath. Bryony joked that her chalice was not enough for him. She teased him that it was some sort of Freudian or Celtic urge to do with the dark of mother earth stirred up by the chalice, she said. Sean accused her of being weird. Joking aside Bryony argued that more excavation could damage the floor, but Sean persisted and he outranked her.

He was the boss so they went deeper, coming in from the side to save the floor and there it was within two days of digging: that they found the upside down chest with its carvings, revealing its ancient manuscripts. They were promptly rushed off to Belfast for the forensics and an embargo was put on talking to the press.

It was different after that. Sean became very intense, rarely made love to her and certainly never like before. He told her that he still loved her, but that he felt under a lot of stress and couldn't settle until they knew what was in the translations. When they got the dating results from Benedict in Belfast that provided a lift and Sean's mood lightened for a short time.

Then came the uncertainty around the translation that went on all autumn. They packed up the dig for another season at the end of September without knowing what was on these amazing scrolls. Sean was getting annoyed with the translator in the British Museum. Back in Belfast after the summer it was weeks before they got any feedback from the museum where the scrolls had gone for specialist translation after Benedict had dated them. Two of the scrolls were written in ancient Aramaic and needed a specialist who was enormously difficult to get hold of. He was quite often abroad and when they did get an email from him he was downright evasive. They couldn't understand the problem. Surely they saw this as important. Bryony suspected he couldn't do the translation and was bluffing. Sean said no, he was a leading worldwide expert. A serious player who knew something but wasn't saying, said Sean. They lobbied within Heritage Ulster, but that did no good. They knew nothing either.

Meanwhile the restoration and dating of the chalice gave Bryony huge pleasure and a welcome distraction from the scrolls. Then one day she was called to a meeting with Sheila Donald and Sean in Heritage Ulster's head office in Belfast. She thought it was just a progress meeting to review things and manage any future media attention, but a government official was present. Something was odd about Sean's behaviour. He wouldn't give her eye contact and stared at the table uneasily.

"There's been a development on the scrolls" Sheila Donald announced matter of factly, but she also appeared nervous and looked from Sean to Bryony. "We have a final translation."

"Hallelullah!" exclaimed Bryony. "What do they say?"

"Well, we have some formalities before we tell you" Sheila went on uncomfortably, smiling weakly.

"Formalities!?" asked Bryony.

"Yes. I'll cut to the chase. These are immensely important historical documents. You must have gained that impression when you found them and we got the dating and origin. It's unlikely we will ever deal with any discovery as important in the rest of our professional careers," Sheila said and, as Bryony nodded. Sean just kept his head down, looking at the table. The government official sat there impassively. "The scrolls are also immensely sensitive in what they tell us" she said as she placed her small chubby hands flat on the desk for emphasis.

"What is that, Sheila?" asked Bryony.

"Before I tell you that I, we must ask you to sign the Official Secrets Act," Sheila said glancing across at the official who took the cue to open a file.

"What!?" giggled Bryony. "This is archaeology in Northern Ireland. What have we found? The Celtic Ark of the Covenant? The Irish Dead Sea Scrolls?"

"Exactly," responded Sheila with a weak smile.

"Shit. This isn't happening," whispered Bryony glancing at Sean who this time returned her bemused look. She could see her chalice being relegated. Just her luck!

"But before I share this with you both I must ask you to sign these papers" said Sheila as she passed the forms from the official "Then we can get on. It is simply a device to make you aware you are being given privileged access to very sensitive information and you must respect our need," glancing at the official, "for you not to reveal the contents of these scrolls to anyone beyond the people in this room. Not colleagues, family, loved ones, not your very best and trusted friends and certainly not the media. OK?"

They both nodded silently. Stunned at the situation they suddenly found themselves in.

The official spoke: "Please also do not commit anything to writing on this either. No email, no texts or tweets to each other. No phone calls, mobile or landline, where anything about the content of these scrolls could be listened in to. Speak only about this matter when you are alone in a room where you cannot be overheard. No conversations in public places where you could be overheard. You are now being asked to sign the Official Secrets Act. Is that clear?" he looked from Bryony to Sean for their assent.

They signed the forms and the official put them back in his folder.

"Ms Donald will brief you now. I will leave. Even I don't know the content" he smiled and left.

As the door clicked shut after the official. They sat in stunned silence for a moment. Then Sheila Donald spoke.

"I can't give you a full translation away with you for obvious reasons, but I can let you read this one copy which is held in my safe. It must not be copied. I will say something first of the contents. The provenance of these scrolls has been carefully established hence the delays that have frustrated all of us. They have been examined by experts in the British Museum, Israel and Egypt," she took a deep breath. "The second document, the shorter scroll, was written by the Apostle Mark while he was Bishop of Alexandria in Egypt in 67 A.D..." She hesitated and looked up at the stunned faces. Sean and Bryony looked at each other. All at once Sean had that old look on his face he had when they found the chalice: a mixture of boyish thrill and an expectation of real adventure.

"The shortest scroll was a note from a Christian monk working in the Great Library in Alexandria in 575AD where Mark's scroll was found, but it is written on Irish vellum, not papyrus. The Library contained several writings of Mark at that time apparently. So it was easy for them to establish provenance. This is the only record of Mark's writing that has survived as far as we know bearing in mind that the Gospel of Mark was not as far as modern biblical scholars can determine actually written by Mark the Apostle. The Great Library was destroyed around 610 A.D. by the Saracens apparently," she looked up to see two faces intently regarding her, "Mark introduces and vouches for the authenticity of the third, longer scroll in Aramaic. The longer scroll is the..." Sheila Donald hesitated, swallowed hard and laughed nervously. Then spoke in a rush, "is the final teachings of Jesus Christ dictated on his ......his deathbed and written by Joseph of Arimithaea. The final scroll is one written by the High Priest present at the time of the crucifixion, Caiaphas who was apparently aware of the last teachings and was desperate to get his hands on them, but failed. I don't know how well you both know your bibles" she smiled wanly. "The significance of these authors should not be lost on both of you. These scrolls you found in Dunseverick are the only known surviving witness statements to the final moments of Jesus Christ. These people were his contemporaries: Caiaphas, Mark and Joseph of Arimithaea." She paused and looked down to compose herself.

Sheila Donald was a regular church goer, a daughter of the kirk having been brought up in the Free Church of Scotland on the Isle of Lewis. Her father had been a lay preacher. The bible was the cornerstone of her childhood. Now the Christian faith was about to be redefined by the contents of these scrolls and the bible reedited after hundreds of years and she Sheila Donald of Lewis was a part of it. It was much more than an archaeological find or a history story to her. It would change her Christian faith gained at her father's knee.

She looked up from the papers in front of her with tears in her eyes, "You'll have to forgive me Bryony and Sean. This is very trying for me. You probably know that I'm a committed Christian: always have been. My parents saw to that," she laughed self-consciously. "I know neither of you are church people and I don't judge you, but for me these scrolls challenge all Christians. As a professional historian I must respect their provenance. This is no fake or heretical writing. I cannot dismiss this."

She shook her head and took out a hanky. Bryony put out a hand to hold Sheila's arm as she talked. She was struggling to understand why stuffy old Sheila Donald was getting so upset. Wasn't this good news for Sheila? Witness statements to the crucifixion!

Personally as an archaeologist with some little Christian faith, Bryony had sometimes wondered about the historical Jesus. Was he a myth or a real historical figure? Where was the evidence of his existence? Now there seemed to be some. Yet here was Sheila, a devout Christian, very upset at the prospect. Why did these scrolls upset her so?

She pushed the A4 sheets of plain text across the desk to both of them. "Please read the rest," and remained in the room while they read the translations of the Latin, Greek, Aramaic and Hebrew contained on the four manuscripts they had found that previous summer in Dunseverick.

"Now for the scrolls that are central to this," Sir Francis announced jolting Bryony back from her day dreaming in to the grey room, "Dr Shamir, would you take us through the four scrolls in some detail?"

The secretary went round the room closing the blinds and semi-darkness descended on them. Bryony felt it set the scene.

The British Museum's expert on ancient Semitic languages Dr Jacob Shamir rose and went to a blank screen on the wall; there was a flash of white light as the projector kicked into life. The screen displayed ancient writing on faded parchment.

"We have four scrolls in the find. Two short scrolls. The most recent is in Latin written by a sixth century monk who carried out translations into Latin in the late sixth century, then another partly in Greek and partly in Aramaic authored by St Mark dated 67 A.D. vouching for the authenticity of the two earlier scrolls which are one in ancient Hebrew written by the High Priest Caiaphas around ten years after the death of Jesus, but we can't be exact, and then a much longer scroll in a form of Aramaic used only in Galilee around the time of Jesus, written we believe by Joseph of Arimithaea claiming to be the last teachings of Jesus dictated by Jesus on his 'death-bed', so to speak, around 36 A.D. This scroll is apparently co-signed by Joseph of Arimithaea, Mary Magdalene, James - brother of Jesus - and Nicodemus. But we cannot be certain of these signatures as there is no corroboration, that is no other signatures to compare them to.

"All this in effect helps us with the dating. Three of the four scrolls effectively introduce the fourth larger scroll: the one in Aramaic, the one we will refer to as '*The Word*' in accordance with Christian legend.

"This is the most recent scroll," he said moving to the next slide. "A note, if you like, in classical Latin from a scribe, a monk who claims to have translated the other scrolls. It is on Irish vellum." He glanced across the room at the two clerical representatives who had stirred from their sulky reticence to lean forward to the screen. "He is in effect testifying the authenticity of the other scrolls."

Dr Shamir read:

> *"I, Brother Simon formerly of the Great Library of Alexandria in 575AD do attest that these manuscripts previously held by St Mark are authentic. One is written by the High Priest Caiaphas and the other by Joseph of Arimithaea in the presence of Our Lord.*
>
> *The Patriarch of Africa, Damianos the First banished these to the farthest reaches of Christendom and us with them. God grant us peace and His strength."*

He went to the next slide.

"This is the scroll written by Mark."

Those in the room were fixated on the slide showing the rhythmic script on the brown papyrus scroll: written by a hand that had undoubtedly been touched by Jesus.

"St Mark begins in common Greek:

> *"I, John Mark, the Apostle of Yeshua and Bishop of Alexandria leave to future generations this letter of Caiaphas, the High Priest of the Great Sanhedrin in Jerusalem and murderer of my Master. This was given to me upon Caiaphas' passing. I was charged with the safety of many things from the time of the Master. This document and its safe removal from the land of Judaea were among my many responsibilities. It bears true witness to great events and as such must be safeguarded by all who believe in Him and seek His true word.*

"Then there is this by Mark in Aramaic:

> *"The events that Caiaphas relates in his letter to Matthias are of divine importance. I know his account of our Lord's*

passing to be a true one. For I, John Mark was Yeshua's stretcher bearer and am the guardian of his final resting place. My Master did not die upon the cross. He lived, was resurrected and was then taken up by God. His mortal remains lie in Jerusalem city. He will return to walk among us as prophesised.

My Master's last teachings, referred to by Caiaphas, were written down by Joseph of Arimithaea as the Master lay dying of his wounds. Lord Yeshua was greatly concerned for what would come after him as a result of an angelic vision he experienced in the tomb. This Last Testament was brought by my hand to Alexandria where it inspired many to found the true church here in Africa. I leave the last teachings in your hands and trust in God's protection.

As our Master said: 'I am the light of the world. Whoever follows me will not walk in darkness, but will have the light of life.' The Last Testament is His Light, hide it and the truth will be hidden, darkness will be all around. Therefore for His truth to inspire others the last teachings must be for all men to see."

"Now St Mark reverts to common Greek:

"Guard the Word. Heed The Word, not the lies. Others speak and claim to speak for Him. He suffered for our sins, was crucified, dead and buried and on the third day he lived. I saw all these things with mine own eyes. It was all that any man could give. It is for you now to take His Word forward to keep it in the light.

"God be with you in your hour of trial. He will give you the strength and the wisdom to await the revelation of His last teachings and His return. Let His light shine on The Word.

"In God

John Mark, Bishop of Africa, 1745600.5"

A clergyman quickly crossed himself "Those numbers, what are they?" he asked.

"It's the Julian calendar. It's 11 March 67 A.D. in the Gregorian calendar that we use today," answered Dr Shamir. "It is believed St Mark was martyred around 68 A.D. in Alexandria, but we can't be certain. He was believed to be some fifteen years younger than Jesus. So he would have been in his fifties when he wrote this."

Dr Shamir paused for other questions and looked round the room. He knew people needed time to absorb what they were being shown before he moved on to the main scroll. The one labelled as Caiaphas's letter. No one asked a question.

He clicked onto the main scroll.

Professor Margery Dugdish of the British Museum cut in.

"Jacob, I was going to ask how we can be sure that this third scroll is authentic. Sparing the blushes of the clergy present, but could the Apostle Mark or someone else have faked this scroll to promote their own views? This was a common practice among the followers of Jesus at the time as you know to promote their cause." she smiled deprecatingly across at the clergy who did not smile in return. Historical research and religious belief were awkward bedfellows.

"I'm glad you asked that Margery, provenance is everything here. There are a number of reference points.

"At its most basic we know from our dating techniques that these documents were of the time they claim to be. The papyrus, the vellum, the ink and the languages used. We also have the evidence from the monk Simon that places the St. Mark scroll in Alexandria in the 6th century and we know Mark became the first Bishop of Alexandria and died there in the 1st century.

"Most convincingly there are the seals on the St Mark scroll and on the Caiaphas scroll which have been tested and are of the 1st century.

"Finally, the story of the crucifixion written by Joseph of Arimithaea claiming to be the last teachings of Jesus differs significantly from the later stories in the New Testament and does quite frankly cut across what later became Christian orthodoxy about what happened after the crucifixion.

"Mark was an apostle and loyal follower of Jesus. The Christian bible places him in the Garden of Gethsemane. The Last Supper was held in Mark's family home. In modern police parlance Mark has no motive, other than to tell the truth. There is no known political or religious motive for him to fake such a document which has the potential to alter later views of Jesus and possibly to undermine Christianity before it became a separate religion from Judaism.

"My own view is that Mark wanted to get the truth out in the first century, but at some point *The Word* is buried in the Great Library with this covering note from him.

"Let's be clear on one central point here. These documents have stronger provenance than many that make up the story of Jesus' life and crucifixion. I say that as a historian without any religious axe to grind here" he said looking at Sir Francis and then to the clergy.

"We must appreciate that at this time – 67 A.D. – Christianity did not exist as a separate religion from Judaism. It was at this time still a Jewish sect and many of the apostles were still practicing orthodox Jews. It was Paul who began the process around this time of disconnecting the 'Christ followers' from Judaism. We must also be clear that the books of the New Testament, Matthew, Mark, Luke and John, which document Jesus' life and crucifixion and further developed that disconnection from mainstream Judaism begun by Paul, were not written until towards the end of the 1st century with several further revisions and were not written by anyone who had met and known Jesus. There are many misconceptions. The Apostle Mark is not the Mark who wrote the Book of Mark," he smiled at his audience as he revealed this common misconception. The clerics remained stony faced, unwilling to enter into any controversy. "The Apostle Mark moved to Alexandria to found a church in Africa in 49AD when he would have been in his mid, thirties. As I have said, it is believed he was younger than Jesus by around fifteen years. He was a teenager at the time of the crucifixion.

"I hope I am making myself clear?" Dr Shamir asked the room.

"Thank you, doctor. That's been most helpful. I never did get to grips with the good book" interjected Sir Francis shaking his head. "Before moving onto what this document written by Joseph of Arimithaea actually tells us, which is the meat of the thing, have you more history that you feel we need? I'm sure many of you here," he gestured to the clergy and around the table. "know a lot of this background. But thank you for reminding us, doctor."

People nodded in the way people do at meetings whether they know something or not. Sir Francis' finely tuned antennae picked up that the clergy were becoming increasingly annoyed with the lecture on biblical history from a non-Christian. He needed to lower the tension that was building in the room. He wanted no sectarian strife at this meeting. There were more than enough religious sensitivities to manage.

"No, Sir Francis, that covers the key elements."

"Who can tell us anything about what may have happened to these scrolls between ancient Alexandria and a remote Irish shore in the 21st century?" asked Sir Francis.

Benedict McTavish raised his hand tentatively.

"Our tests revealed a number of traces on the leather bag which help us know where the scrolls went after Egypt. The leather at that time was quite absorbent so it has retained a number of clues" he paused to look at his notes, "There were traces of mud only found around the Irish midlands and pollen of plants very typical in Ireland at this time – the dog violet flower, bog iris, barley seed and distinctive flint found only along the north coast of Ireland and heavy deposits of sea salt indicating a long sea journey. There are no traces of anything to suggest a journey through mainland Europe or England. So we think the scrolls journeyed from Egypt all the way by sea to somewhere in southern Ireland and from there to its final resting place in Dunseverick, which at the time was the location of a major fort on the north coast. Students of early Irish Christianity will be well aware of the strong links in the 5th and 6th century between Egypt and Ireland through the desert fathers. Given the carvings on the chalice it is possible that St Columba or Colum Cille, as he was known at the time, became the custodian of the scrolls. Quite what he made of them and why they came to be buried in this location remains a mystery. They may have been hidden from invaders such as the Vikings as Bryony suggests. But we can't be sure."

"May we see the original scrolls?" asked Sir Francis gesturing to the display cases. The secretary wheeled the heavy display cases into the centre of the room where everyone gathered round.

There was a hushed silence as they took in the ancient documents.

Bryony moved closer and was looking intently at the documents on display.

"Where's St Mark's seal?" she asked looking at Doctor Shamir.

Dr Shamir moved closer.

He opened the locked case containing St Mark's scroll and with gloved hands lifted the ancient scroll to examine it.

He then looked at the other scrolls while the others watched. He physically paled.

"These, these are not the scrolls I examined. The text is quite different. St Mark's seal is gone. It was here earlier this morning. The originals have been replaced with these, these poor copies with changed text. It's gibberish! Who has done this?" he exclaimed accusingly at those gathered round. Sir Francis in turn regarded him coldly. The room fell silent. All that could be heard was the flute player busking in the street below.

VI: Alexandria, Egypt. 575A.D.

Zachariah settled himself on the sacks that he was resting on. He stroked his long ears thoughtfully and closed his eyes. He always did this before falling into his dreamtime from which he would awake with fresh insights and new visions.

Zachariah's sleep was not disturbed by the cart's motion as it trundled over the desert tracks towards the city of Alexandria. They travelled in the dusk and early morning to avoid the heat, but also to avoid the *Mazices*, the nomadic tribesmen of the western desert who raided the monasteries and plundered their caravans.

Cormac had watched his beloved monastery of St John the Short slowly disappear from view the previous day. Now they were travelling out of the region of Scetis with its settlements of desert fathers and through Al Asqeet. The journey to the city of Alexandria would take four days. On the way pilgrims had asked to accompany Cormac's caravan back to Alexandria for protection, but the guard of Berber horsemen assigned to the little caravan had warned them off. It seemed that Cormac was to remain separate from any other desert travellers. This disconcerted Cormac as there was an ancient tradition in the desert to give assistance to pilgrims on their way. Cormac remonstrated with the guards, but they were implacable.

They shook their heads and declared loudly in Coptic, "No strangers are allowed, Father. *Mazices* are all around!"

They indicated the hills and made a motion with their hands to their groins and spat in the sand which left Cormac in no doubt of the consequences both to the guards, if they allowed anyone to accompany this monk on his journey and to any *Mazices* who would dare confront the Berber guards. Simultaneous to the guards' declarations, the horses kicked up clouds of sand to lay their own emphasis upon their riders' opinions. As Cormac had no wish to upset such fine beasts, he accepted their case and that of their riders without further debate. Placing his hood over his face he said vespers inwardly and was rocked to sleep by the motion of the caravan.

 When Cormac awoke they had stopped for the day at the edge of Al Asqeet as it widens out to the broad plain taking Egypt down to the sea and Alexandria. It was in Al Asqeet that Yeshua had first lived with his family as a babe in arms after their flight from Herod in Judaea. It was why St Anthony, leader of the early desert fathers had chosen this place. To the desert fathers Al Asqeet had a more powerful association with Yeshua than Jerusalem. Cormac had sensed the energy of the child Yeshua throughout his time in the desert. He had felt the presence of the Christ a number of times. Always by the monastery well and always he felt tremendous joy from the encounters and a clear sense that one day he would be called to provide a service.

 Cormac watched the desert night close in. The colours changed from the reds of sunset to a dark inky warmth, then a refreshing coolness settled upon him. The calmness of the desert dusk allowed the mind to be still. The membrane between worlds became thinner.

 It was as if the desert was taking an outbreath after the heat of the day. This outbreath allowed Cormac's consciousness to take flight, to seek insight and guidance in the holy stillness of the enfolding dark.

 Visions of his time many years before in the holy city of Alexandria came to Cormac as he sat in the dark of the desert. The city was the seat of St Mark the Apostle and was where Cormac and Zachariah had landed on their arrival in Africa from Europe many years ago. The pungent smells and the hot air of the desert came to Cormac's nostrils: the bougainvillea and jasmine that flowered on every street in the spring, the incense from the temples and the churches, the smell of the spice carts as they made their way from the harbour. Most of all he remembered the agora with its merchants, beggars and its rich mixture of itinerant philosophers. Many of the philosophers were Greek in origin: Sophists, Cynics, Platonists, Epicureans and Pythagoreans, most were also followers of Egyptian gods such as Serapis and Isis. Their practice in the agora was to challenge Christian monks on their beliefs while they were on their frequent walks from the Catechetical School to the Church of St Dionysius. One such philosopher was the elderly Ausonius accompanied by his young and very able daughter, Melania.

Like all philosophers Ausonius and Melania debated and lectured to earn their living. Melania was already showing a sharpness of mind in excess of her years. People talked about her as the new Hypatia. Cormac prayed the girl did not meet an end like poor Hypatia. The great pagan philosopher and daughter of Theonas was skinned alive and torn limb from limb by a Christian mob in the year 415 A.D. In a city once praised for its philosophers, such pursuits had become decidedly risky. By the sixth century the hierarchy of the increasingly powerful Christian church in Alexandria, together with the Patriarchates in Rome, Constantinople and Antioch, was strongly opposed to all thought that challenged the growing Christian orthodoxy and all that was not firmly embedded in their interpretation of agreed Christian scriptures. Alexandria was now the seat of the powerful Coptic Patriarch and his followers, the miaphysites.

Nevertheless Ausonius and Melania continued to ply their age-old trade in the busy agora along with a dwindling band of other scientists, preachers and politicians pursuing their need to speak freely. Philosophers used this public platform to sell pamphlets and promote their classes in the nearby lecture halls.

Cormac became something of a willing foil in Ausonius' debates. He was drawn to the old man for his courage, clear mind and integrity. He enjoyed Ausonius' lightness of touch and his sharp mind and even sometimes got the best of Ausonius, provided his daughter did not intervene on her father's behalf. Her mind was sharp and she was well schooled in Greek sophistry.

On the occasion that came to Cormac's memory as he sat in the desert gloom, Melania had not intervened. In fact she intervened less and less as her father became bitterly opposed to the growing power of the Christian Church in Alexandria. Cormac sensed that Melania was growing in discomfort and in concern for her father's well-being and her own. History was not on their side.

75

"So our good friend the monk here believes that the Christian god is not one entity but three like the great Isis, Horus and Osiris. They have the father, Son and Holy Ghost. So this Christianity is nothing new. It is a copy. Is that not so, good monk?" Ausonius began to a curious crowd.

"So Saul of Tarsus teaches, Master Ausonius. But Yeshua never said so. You must read the Gospels if you are to lecture the good people of Alexandria on such matters." Cormac retorted.

"I don't lecture, my Celtic friend. I merely ask."

"Reading educates the mind, good Ausonius. In all humility I encourage you to read the Gospels. Then you will find no reason to ask," said Cormac to cheers from the crowd. To suggest that the great Ausonius was not well read was a humorous, if disrespectful allegation.

Ausonius countered: "But you Christians like to preach, do you not? The floor is yours, good monk. Preach to us about your three gods and I will tell you about ours, then we will see which the copy is."

"We monks do not preach, "replied Cormac. Cormac then spoke to the crowd reluctantly. As he did so, he saw Melania watching him with concern. He sensed she did not wish her father to gain the advantage in this debate. "But I will say this: there is one God on high. The same God as Yeshua worshipped. No other. The trinity is an expression of the different natures of God: divine, human and spiritual, nothing more."

"Ah! So you are a follower of the Christian heretics and philosophers of our own great city, Origen and Arius and the like, brother monk?" Ausonius quizzed provocatively.

"I am a follower of Lord Yeshua and no other, sir."

"And what of this Yeshua? Is he the Son of God, born of a virgin just like Dionysius and Mithras and therefore God himself, as many in this city believe or is he human like you and I, as your Bishop Nestorius has declared in Constantinople?"

Cormac knew he was being drawn into an area of theology that was dangerous in Alexandria. Alexandria was home to the miaphysites: a strand of Christian theology that declared Yeshua or Jesus as the Greeks called Him, to be of the same nature as God and therefore not human. A bitter dispute had arisen within the

Christian church since the Council of Nicaea in 325 A.D. and culminating in a great schism after the Council of Chalcedon in 451 A.D. Rome compromised and declared that Jesus was both human and divine; Constantinople inspired by Nestorius, declared that Jesus was human, not divine. Alexandria, under the influence of the Patriarch, Cyril and his successors, forcefully asserted that Yeshua was divine, not human and of one divine nature only.

These fine theological arguments had created great passion, division and bitterness within the early Christian church. In this time the Coptic or Miaphysite Church was becoming ever more powerful in Alexandria. Non-Christians such as the Jews and the pagans, once equal partners in the great city of knowledge, were being forcibly marginalised by the Patriarchate of the Coptic Church. Cormac did not wish to be tempted into this debate by Ausonius' polemics, especially in the Agora surrounded by *bouleutai* keen to report his words to the *parabalini*, the Patriarch's militia. He had to be cautious to avoid the sinking sands of heresy. In the city Cormac had learnt from the greatest teachers how to defend himself from the clever words used to entrap through the use of parable and such devices. Such showmanship by the great Ausonius was to be the old man's downfall. Cormac admired his search for truth, but shared his daughter's caution.

"Master Ausonius we all know you to be a great philosopher," the crowd mumbled their ascent. "So answer this: as many of you know I have a hare for a companion. He is a good fellow, but eccentric. He claims to be the soul of the great prophet Zachariah and can converse on any subject. His visions are certainly as prophetic as the great Zachariah. So I ask myself and now you: is he hare or human or divine or indeed all three at once, good Ausonius?"

The crowd laughed at the monk's proposition and demanded Ausonius to answer. The hare was a sacred creature to all Alexandrians and his wisdom was not challenged. Moreover Zachariah was well known to the crowd in the agora. The hare was not reluctant to take advantage of such a position and regularly deflated skilled philosophers with his clever questioning.

Ausonius paused to consider as Melania whispered to him. But he waved her away. Cormac sitting in the dark of the desert night could remember Melania's twinkling eyes from beneath her curling golden hair as she looked him up and down from the steps of the temple beside her father: perhaps wondering if this monk was friend or foe.

"Er hem....The hare is a sacred animal much valued by the great Horus. I will not insult him. Your hare is a great, yet perplexing fellow, monk. That much is true. I cannot say with any certainty about his true nature. I am no scientist," Ausonius admitted.

"Just so, Ausonius. You see a simple hare perplexes even a great philosopher," Cormac said to the crowd. "How difficult then is it to know the true nature of Yeshua?" Cormac smiled to Ausonius and Melania. He noticed her smile of relief that a lengthy and highly controversial debate had been avoided. He walked on to the applause and the cries of the crowd. Others, priests from Patriarchate, watched in silence.

Cormac was nevertheless pleased with his victory that day in the agora: none was more pleased than Zachariah himself when Cormac related the tale. Later Cormac was to wince at the memory of this puffed up monk, full of books and learning and clever words. However he was to soothe himself with the knowledge that his clever argument had saved the day for both he and the dogged Ausonius. Cormac had come to believe that this principled old philosopher was risking his own life and that of his daughter in his brave questioning of the rising power of the Christian Church.

Hearing of his latest debate with Ausonius, the principal of the Catechetical School advised Cormac to avoid the agora.

"It has become a battle ground I fear, and many good men like Ausonius may suffer. Please, take care brother, that you are not one of them," the principal cautioned.

Cormac took the caution. Reluctantly he avoided Ausonius and Melania from that day forth. Their battle with the Christian Church was not his. Although as a true follower of Yeshua he held concern for their welfare.

It was not long after this event that the Patriarch's militia, the *parabalini* brutally expelled all the pagan philosophers from the agora as the Christian church consolidated its hegemony in the city of Alexandria. Pagan temples were either torn down or converted to churches. Pagans were persecuted and, under threat of death or exile, converted to Christianity. Scientists and geographers were forced out of the city. Even the Great Library near the Serapeum came under threat.

Some months later, concerned for Ausonius and his daughter, Cormac was guided to seek them out. He found them living in the Boukolia where they were now among the *anexodos,* the poorest in Alexandria. Unable to work as a pagan philosopher Ausonius' and Melania's income was much reduced. Their pamphlets no longer sold in the same quantities as the Christian church frustrated distribution and the lecture halls were now closed to pagans. Ausonius was repeatedly attacked by Christians both in verbal and physical assaults. His health deteriorated and his spirit was broken. Melania was spat at in the street. Both took the bread charity from the Patriarch along with all the other marginalised and urban poor. Melania sold spices in the agora and the surrounding streets to buy necessities and to pay for their meagre rooms. The twinkle had gone from her beautiful young eyes and no philosophy passed her lips.

It vexed the monk to contemplate how his church had done such things. It was true that the early Christians had been sorely persecuted at times by the Roman Empire and by the Jews, especially in Alexandria. But this cruel vengeance was not what Lord Yeshua had taught. This was a time, Cormac believed, to show Yeshua's love and forgiveness and to change the manner in which power is exercised. Ausonius and Melania were Greek in origin and had never preached religious intolerance themselves nor advocated the mastery of one people over another. Pagans they might be, but no harm was ever done by their philosophy to any Christian. As a Celt, Cormac well understood the pagan ways as they were still taught by the ancient ones in his land. To him there was little to argue about between the ancients and Yeshua's teachings. Indeed there had been no such antagonism in his native land. He could not understand the fear of paganism that arose in the breasts of Christians and the violence that followed on the heels of this fear. Daily he prayed to Yeshua for the protection of the pagans and their beliefs.

When Ausonius passed away a few months later, Melania was forced to work as a hand maiden for one of her father's creditors: a rich Christian merchant living on the Canopian Way. This merchant took advantage of her status and shamed her with many menial tasks.

Cormac discovered the lady on the Canopian way near her master's house. She was walking in an entourage behind her master's caravan.

"Good lady, how are your spirits," Cormac enquired in a whisper. Melania's face was etched with fatigue.

"Good monk. How well it is to see you," she smiled grimly through her shame. She hesitated and then said, "I am pledged to this man to repay my father's debts. He uses me sorely, if truth be told. But Isis has been my protector. I have a clean bed and a full belly. And you good monk, how fares your studies?"

"I am well, lady. I continue my studies at the Catechetical School. They are almost complete or will have to be soon, I believe."

"This is not a good time for those who seek the spirit in all things. Where will your life take you after your studies?" Melania enquired.

"God is guiding me to join the desert fathers. But my faith is being tested. My church in Alexandria is a vexing thing. Their treatment of those such as you and your father has disturbed me. It is not the faith of Yeshua that does this," said Cormac all in a rush of strong emotion.

"Have a care, brother monk, in what you say," Melania's eyes locked on Cormac's. "They seek power, sir. They are Greeks and Romans. Power is their currency. I know it is not the way of your Lord Yeshua."

"The Celts in my home land do not seek power over others in this way. It is foreign to me. My people never had an empire or a government, but neither have we been conquered," said Cormac with a rueful smile.

Melania smiled. "I remember. I remember you telling my father in the agora in one of your debates. He took a keen interest in your people."

They both smiled at the memory.

"There is little written down to study about us," said Cormac. "Pythagoras taught my people much, lady. Your father was a very great Platonist. I much admired his work."

"Take care who you confess this to, brother," Melania advised. "My father was lucky to die in his bed. The great Hypatia was skinned alive and torn limb from limb by Christians," she shivered at the thought as she spoke.

"Just so." Cormac paused and considered. "Will you allow me to help you, good lady?"

"In what way can you help me, sir and why?" Their eyes met and an understanding passed in the moment between them.

"There is a monk I know by the name of Vitalios with a mission based in St Metras' church near the Sun gate. He helps prostitutes end their immorality and begin life anew. He is well supported by a rich benefactor and is looking for help with his mission."

"I doubt if he would look favourably on one such as I. They call me a pagan witch. I know nothing of such things as prostitution, sir. I am a virgin. Though my master has boasted to many that he will enter me at the next full moon," Melania's voice broke as she confessed this.

Cormac risked touching Melania's arm to comfort her. Again the same energy passed between them.

"We must move quickly then. Vitalios is a good man. He needs good women such as you to help him in his work. Will you allow me to approach him on your behalf?"

"I could not give up my religion to follow him, sir."

"Vitalios is not a dogmatist, lady," Cormac reassured. "His work involves him with citizens of every kind. He does not judge or even preach. He needs the help of one such as you. Nothing more," said Cormac.

"Very well, but he must know I follow the Goddess."

That evening Cormac spoke to Vitalios. The arrangement was made shortly thereafter for Melania to escape her serfdom on the Canopian Way and to live and work with the monk Vitalios among the women of the shadows.

On the day Cormac left Melania in the care of the good Vitalios something happened which was to change the nature of the monk's life. As he turned to leave Melania with her guardian in the courtyard of the mission, Melania knelt before Cormac and kissed his garment while pledging her affection for him and her gratitude for the great service he had done her.

"Please lady, there is no need. I have done my Christian duty, no more," said the monk.

"You always treated my father and I with respect, sir, more so than any other Christian. My father looked forward to your visits to the agora and your debates, as did I. We both grew to love you and your Celtic playfulness. We were saddened at your absence. Now with this act of great love we are bound to each other in spirit across the divide of our beliefs. Although we serve our different gods, I am now bound to you as your loving sister." said Melania with her tear filled eyes fixed on his.

Cormac was uneasy with her directness. He had had no intimacy with a woman since living with his wife in Eriu. His vows as a monk placed strict rules upon his relations with women. Although marriage was possible, no physical contact was allowed. Now this woman was touching his garment and speaking of a love that was not possible.

"I am bound to Yeshua, lady," he reminded her.

"And I to Isis. It is not a physical connection I speak of," said Melania. "I am a virgin and wish to remain so."

"I too have a pledge of celibacy."

"It is a pledge I hold in the utmost respect, sir. Does your pledge prevent friendship with women? Did your Lord not associate with many women?" asked Melania.

"He did. We are talking of spiritual relations. The conditions are strict and you are not a follower of Yeshua, lady," Cormac added pointing to a great difficulty in this city between pagan and Christian.

"I understand your Lord Yeshua consorted with all manner of persons and helped them. Are you a dogmatist in matters of love like so many others in this city?" she asked.

Cormac watched a smile flicker across Melania's face. A smile he had seen many times in the Agora. She had always liked teasing him. He knew he was drawn to the lady and was unsure of his true feelings for this young woman: feelings that would be tested by any pledge on her part.

"I love and serve Yeshua, lady" Cormac insisted while she still held his garment.

"As I serve Isis. I have pledged a love to you, Cormac the Celt and wish you to know this before you leave. I ask nothing of you in return except that you know of my loving gratitude for your friendship."

"My love is for all beings and for God. My calling as a monk ...."

"You are permitted to love your brothers and sisters, sir" she interrupted.

Cormac stood silently in the courtyard. He hesitated only because he knew this frank encounter with Melania challenged him to define his relations with women. It was discomforting to experience such declarations from a woman and from a pagan. It was true that he had long held the lady in some affection, but had persuaded himself that these were selfish, base emotions that he had foresworn as a monk. Now that the lady had been so forceful in declaring her own wishes and setting them in a spiritual context, he was conflicted. There were also dangers in this city to be associated with a pagan whether man or woman. However his Celtic heart overruled him.

"Very well, lady. I am honoured and affected by your sisterly love and pledge my own brotherly love and respect," Cormac said.

Melania remained kneeling.

"It is good. We are bound together as two journeying souls. We both knew this from the beginning. I knew you in another life, brother. But that is for another time." Melania stood and smiled at the perplexed monk. She turned and walked away, leaving Cormac alone in the courtyard with his heightened emotions.

Cormac did not see Melania before he left the city. He did not leave because of the lady's declarations. He was tormented in many other ways and felt the tug of the divine upon him.

The great city which had once charmed Cormac, no longer did so. A man of strong faith, he was saddened by the steady decline in Alexandria. Alexandria's glory was much faded in many ways, as if an actual light had been extinguished. The knowledge and richness of spirit that had drawn the monk like so many from across the world was fading. Even the beacon on the great lighthouse of Pharos appeared to dim. The Hellenes and their learning no longer held sway. The Ptolemies were no more. Even the mighty Roman Empire was gone. The city had new ways and new masters.

Yet Alexandria was Christian. It was a rising Christian power that now governed the city: a power that had become rich and mean in its manner and showed intolerance to others. While Rome no longer persecuted Christians, these Christians now in turn persecuted any who did not believe their strict orthodoxy, such as Jews, pagans and even other Christians. This new Church resisted free thought, art and science, demanding adherence to the scripture in all things. It was a narrowness that did not bring the promised enlightenment of salvation.

Cormac grieved in his soul that this was the creation of those who claimed to follow Yeshua. For his own part he sought a freer path of service closer to his Lord Yeshua and not tormented by the ego and its need for the learning found in books.

It was at this dark hour of despair that God guided this conflicted monk to seek solace in the clean air of the desert like many before him.

"Scrolls you say, monk?" asked Zachariah. "So my vision all those years ago is coming to pass?"

Cormac's companion had woken from his deep slumber and startled the sleeping monk.

"Good hare, you startled me" said Cormac.

"Scrolls?" repeated Zachariah

"Yes and back to Eriu" said Cormac.

The hare nodded. "That is interesting. It is even more interesting to know that these scrolls carry the fate of Christendom in their words and you are to be their guardian."

"I am?" said Cormac in close attention.

"Wait and I will explain my vision further," said the hare with great authority. "I saw you riding on an eagle's back through high winds and seas and black nights into the far north. Finally the eagle landed on a great sunlit hill on a verdant island. There waiting for the eagle was a wolf with four white swans and a hare, me. All were gathered there to help you journey onwards with these scrolls."

"I see" said Cormac waiting to see what more the hare had to say.

"High in the sky was a second eagle, a dark eagle with feathers as black as night. He seeks the scrolls for another and swooped in that instant to carry them away. Moving quickly the wolf brought you with the scrolls to shelter while the swans fought off the dark eagle. With urgency the wolf guided you along a passageway under the great hill where an ancient people lived. He understood these scrolls and knew of their great importance. He promised to help you and some others secure the scrolls for all time."

Cormac waited. Zachariah hesitated.

"Well, hare?"

"There was a great white light in the north that you had to journey towards with the scrolls. A white dove was there. It was there that you had to bring the scrolls. You were pursued by the dark eagle. He was dogged in his pursuit of the scrolls and sought to kill the light."

"What of the scrolls? What is written on these scrolls?" asked Cormac.

"Ah now that's the really interesting aspect, monk. Normally I could see such a thing, but a fine veil surrounds these scrolls. I am not permitted to read them. I pressed the eagle and he told me they carry great truths brought to the earth by Yeshua himself. 'Liberty for all from emperors and bishops' was all he would say. 'You must see that the monk must not falter', he added at the end and fixed me with his eyes as only eagles can and flew off across the ocean."

Hare and monk sat for a while; taking in the vision. Finally Zachariah spoke in hushed tones:

"Your task is great, good monk. Of that there is little doubt. This is your calling, your mission in this life. God has called you like no other; even I was not called in such a way while I dwelt in Babylon. Your time has come to be resurrected. Are you ready?"

With his eyes closed Cormac whispered, "I am ready."

"I will remain at your side in the usual manner, fear not,"

"You bring the wisdom of the ages, good hare." The two companions smiled at each other.

"Let us sleep, brother. Tomorrow we will reach the great city of Alexandria and begin our odyssey," said Cormac.

VII: The Consistory

In the early spring of 575 A.D. the Pope of Alexandria, the Patriarch of the Holy See of Saint Mark and Bishop of Africa, Damianos the First sat in his Consistory in a state of some agitation. He held delicately in his hands the three ancient scrolls from the Great Library. Though he was a man much renowned for his kindness and his dedication to God and his holy church in Africa, he was also a man of his time and place; his mind fixed on the religious orthodoxy of his patriarchal lineage. His dark Syrian eyes now showed torment mixed with sadness. His face no longer held the repose of one who is possessed by certainty. There was within him an angry sentiment that none who knew him had seen before. Damianos had the demeanour of a tortured soul, no longer that of a holy man who talked to God.

"What trial is this that has been visited upon us, *Oikonomos*?" he asked in anguish. "As a young monk in the desert I heard of the legend of *The Word* that came to Egypt with the blessed St. Mark and then on his martyrdom was taken out of Alexandria to the desert with St Anthony. They say that with this holy manuscript St Mark founded the church in Africa and St Antony led the way of the desert fathers who have inspired so many. No one living has ever seen *The Word*. It was excluded from the Holy Scriptures. Some even doubted its existence. Now it is here in my hands, hidden in the Great Library all this time, hidden perhaps because Christians could no longer understand what was written. Yet you tell me *Oikonomos,* that we cannot show *The Word* today. How sure can you be? " asked the Patriarch.

"As you know, Holy Father, there are *Arians* and *Chalcedonians* who would use these scrolls against the Church of St Mark. Peter of Callinicum for one, *Nestorians* in Constantinople for another. They gnaw at our African faith, Holy Father. They would use these scrolls to destroy all we have built here," said the *Oikonomos*, the one known as Acacius.

"Then our history has trapped us, Acacius. Are we defying God's will!?" shouted Damianos in torment.

"There is theology here that is beyond one such as I, Holy Father. But perhaps *the Word* is destined to benefit others now."

The *Oikonomos* was the Patriarch's chief administrator and advisor in all temporal matters. He managed the powerful Presbytery in Alexandria and beyond. He knew well never to mix his temporal concerns with those of the Patriarchy. The two men were alone in the Consistory. Damianos sat in a large, beautifully carved ebony chair draped in fine Egyptian cloth.

"These scrolls have been attested to be true, Holiness," said Acacius. "Father Clement has had them re-examined. The apostle's own hand has verified both the scrolls of Our Lord and of the High Priest, Caiaphas. The apostle's scroll bears St. Mark's holy seal. We know the writing to be his from other documents in the library. It would appear that there is little doubt of their nature, Holy Father."

"It was surely not for this that I have been called to high office by God himself?" Damianos asked wearily. "To see *the Word* revealed and then to be hidden again, to leave this land. But if we keep it here it will surely destroy St Mark's Church in Africa!" he said holding the scrolls aloft.

"I believe that to be so, Holy Father. They must leave us. But they will no longer be hidden. It will inspire others in far off lands. That is our satisfaction."

Damianos' voice reduced to a hoarse whisper choked with emotion.

"It tells us that Yeshua ho Xristos was …. was human, He was resurrected, yet died a short time later of His wounds. God, I ask forgiveness for these words as a poor sinner before you in this place." Damianos bowed his head and continued. "It is written here that before our Lord ascended He wrote this last testament that was to be carried to some far off place. If this is true….." his voice lowered for he was about to blaspheme and kissed a cross around his neck, "how can one such as this be the Son of God, a divine being?"

87

"I am not a theologian, Holy Father," said Acacius again, not wishing to be drawn on the delicate issue of Yeshua's divinity. His concern was with the temporal survival of the church in Africa.

"I am sorry, my dear Acacius, I should not involve you in such matters and you should not hear such blasphemy from your Patriarch's lips" said Damianos. "But I cannot confide in my bishops. Their faith is a precious thing. I cannot shatter it. Their faith is built on the miaphysite faith that the Xristos is God, no other. He is not a man, like us! He did not die!"

The Patriarch slammed the arm of His chair. He was not a physical man, but the force of this action caused a heavy jewelled ring to fall from his thin index finger onto the ornate carpet of the Consistory. The Patriarch gasped in horror. The *Oikonomos* quickly retrieved the ring for his Patriarch. The ring of the apostle must never leave the hand of the Patriarch. Damianos quickly replaced the ring on his finger. Trembling, he handed the scrolls to his *Oikonomos*. He no longer trusted himself with them. He sought to regain his composure.

"Must I remind even you, Acacius, of the plague caused by the Emperor Justinian's blasphemy against God and His church here in Africa? The discovery of *the Word* brings that risk to us again, Acacius. If others discover this truth we risk both His wrath and the ridicule of non-believers. Does God wish *the Word* to be revealed here? For people to know that the Son of God was not divine? I am guided that he does not. This is why I have come to you on this highly delicate matter. I do not exaggerate, dear Acacius, when I say that on this matter rests the future of the church in Africa."

"Indeed, Holy Father. I will serve the Church in this matter diligently," said Acacius remembering the pain that the plague visited upon his young family all those years ago. "You will know, Holiness, that the Bishop of Rome is taking a close interest. His spies are among us. Already he has heard of our work in the Great Library and rumours of the discovery of some important scrolls there concerning the nature of the Xristos. The fact that we will not reveal their exact contents to him has heightened his curiosity."

"I know. May God curse him! Now we have the pleasure of his infamous emissary, the black priest, Augustine of Nubea, in our cloisters this very day," said Damianos. "We cannot and must not let the Roman Church know of *the Word*, Acacius. They would bring another plague upon us if only to achieve the hegemony they desire over the Christian Church. Yet we are conflicted. To go against the apostle's wishes would be unthinkable."

At the mention of St Mark, Diamanos kissed the ring that had just been retrieved from the floor.

"Brother Augustine asks to see you, Holy Father," said Acacius.

Damianos dismissed the suggestion with a wave.

"You deal with the fellow. Send him back to the Bishop of Rome with a story to satisfy him. Make it a good story though. This Augustine is not one to be easily discouraged. He is like a hunting dog on a scent, they tell me. He has already secured many relics and sacred scrolls for the Romans. They wish to hold all knowledge and power in the Christian world, the devils."

Turning to the scrolls he said, "Although it is clear what we must do, I am tormented further, Acacius. *The Word* was brought here by St. Mark and through it he built the Church in Africa. By sending it away, do we risk everything?"

"The Church in Africa has survived many things, Holy Father; Roman persecution, plague and heretics. Its roots are deep and much stronger. Perhaps it is God's will that others are helped now as we have been."

"Ah my wise *Oikonomos*! You see so clearly what I have seen," said Damianos with some relief. "I have been seeking guidance from the divine and from the blessed apostle on this challenge he has sent us, Acacius. To destroy *the Word* would be a sacrilege against the wishes of our blessed saint and bring the wrath of God upon us, but my vision is that *the Word* must leave our Church in Africa in this time. We are right to send it far from us and beyond the reach of Rome, but it must also be to a Christian country where *the Word* will flourish. Pagans too must learn, Acacius, so they can mend their wicked ways. If the Bishop of Rome possessed *The Word,* he would use it to destroy us.

"I am guided to send *The Word* far to the west, to a place that would suit our purposes. Come and see, Acacius." Damianos walked over to a large table in the middle of the Consistory where a map of the world was displayed. He pointed to the very edge of the known world. "The island of Eriu in the great western ocean has known the Xristos since the first century. As you know, we trade with this place and our desert fathers know the people of Eriu. Legend says that Joseph of Arimithaea with some apostles journeyed there when they left Judaea and would have brought *the Word* with him to these islands had not God intervened to bring it to Africa to build this church here instead. It is fitting that *the Word* should travel to this island now."

"The destination is a good one, Holy Father, but who will carry *the Word* safely there and who will be its guardian in Eriu?" asked Acacius.

"There is a powerful Prince of the Celtic Church in Eriu, Prince Colum Cille who will be a worthy guardian. He is also an ordained monk and an abbot in those lands. The desert fathers speak highly of him. Most importantly he is no friend to Rome and her machinations. Rome never conquered this land. He will know what is best. Let him deal with this. If God favours him, Colum Cille will be enabled to build a true church in Eriu which will last the ages, as St Mark has done here in Africa."

Damianos took a date from a silver bowl and continued to set out his strategy while he ate.

"Colum Cille is a holy man by all accounts. He will be guided to do what is right. I am told that he has a strong desire for redemption from his past sins as a royal prince and also the plague ravaged this island. So Colum Cille will be mindful not to further offend God." He paused to examine the dates. "Now I know of one of his followers, Father Cormac the Celt. He is a seniores in my old monastery of St John the Short in Scetis. He was ordained by Colum Cille. I have today sent for this Celt. He will be with us within the week. I am guided that this monk can be entrusted with *the Word* and will carry it to the prince."

"It is a heavy burden for a simple monk, Holy Father. Can this Celt be relied on?" said Acacius.

"He is a good and a brave monk, honed by the desert. He is not so simple. Aba James speaks well of him. I would trust him. Yet he's whimsical like many Celts. He is known to converse with a hare who claims to be the soul of the prophet Zachariah. Ha! The hare guides him in many things I am told, but let not that concern us.

My guidance is clear on this matter. This Celt will take *the Word* to Prince Colum Cille."

"Very well, Holiness," said Acacius raising his eyebrows. He knew the Celts to be a mystical, yet pious people. Many of their priests were followers of Pythagoras as well the Xristos. In the areas of astronomy, mathematics and philosophy they were highly civilised. They spoke to the trees and to the beasts claiming that all God's creation was equal in His eyes.

"Have two of our best ships been made ready to sail, with soldiers in the second vessel for protection," Damianos demanded. "Get me Master Igider. None can sail faster and more surely than he. The ships must be provisioned for a long journey. The monk must leave as soon as he is instructed. He must not be allowed to linger in the city. That could be fatal with this emissary on our heels."

"Such ships would be ready to sail in five days at the earliest, Holy Father. I will escort the monk to the ships myself and see him on his way. The *parabalini* will give protection in Alexandria and on the journey. I will have a letter of introduction for you to sign," said Acacius. "Though once the monk is on the island, we cannot ensure the safety of *The Word*."

"Find a merchant, one trusted by us in Eriu. Send him a message to guide our monk to Colum Cille. He will be richly rewarded," said Damianos. "God will protect *The Word*, of that I am sure, Acacius, provided there is no foolishness. But mark this; the sea captains must not know their vessels' destination until they have departed. I do not want anyone in Alexandria to know their destination beyond you and I. Secrecy and divine protection is the only surety. If knowledge of these scrolls comes to light we will need an army to protect them."

"I will give the captains a letter of instruction to be opened only when they are clear of the great lighthouse. The *parabalini* will guard the ships while they are in dock and at sea. Master Igider knows the sea roads to the western ocean well," said Acacius.

"Good. The Bishop of Rome has spies everywhere and now his emissary is among us. We must take great care in all that we do to maintain total secrecy. What of the monks in the Great Library, the ones who read *The Word*?" asked Damianos. "There were two of them. What has become of them?"

"As agreed, Holy Father, I offered them the choices we discussed," said the *Oikonomos*. "Neither of them wished to be martyred as saints and to reach heaven."

"Such selfishness in a monk is sinful. City life and learning has made them soft in their faith and too attached to this world. This is the harm places such as the Great Library can do, Acacius. They forget God and study the words of men instead."

Damianos considered the dates further.

"Have the young scholar go with Father Cormac to Eriu. They will need his services as the translator of the scrolls. Send the older monk to Aba James in the desert. Both must swear a vow of silence and travel under different names. If they fail in this, they will become martyrs."

"Indeed, Holy Father, I will see they understand the penalty for speaking.. What should the monk be told, Father?"

"At the moment no more than he is to travel to a far off place in my service on a mission of the utmost secrecy and importance," said Damianos. "See to it that *the Word* is sealed with my personal seal. He must not read it. Only Prince Colum Cille will do so."

"Yes, Holy Father. There will need to be a letter advising Prince Colum Cille, explaining matters, also sealed."

"Just so. Draft it and we will together sign it. We will tell the monk a little more of his mission when he meets with us, but how much more I am not sure yet," said Damianos. "Now I must pray, Acacius. This business weakens my spirit. Bring the Celt to me after matins on the day he sails. We will instruct him and send him on his way. Then we can put this matter behind us, God willing. Lock the scrolls away and mount a guard before you do anything else."

With his composure now somewhat recovered, Damianos the First concluded, "We are being greatly tested, *Oikonomos*. That much is clear. We cannot know His reason. We must be strong and wise. We hold Christendom in our hands," he gestured with his opened hands. "God bless you, my dear *Oikonomos*, for your steadfast support in our hour of need."

VIII: The message

The horsemen did not wish to linger in the city. They had been ill at ease ever since arriving at the Moon Gate early that morning. The desert was the Berbers' sea and they were its fish. In the city they were out of water. As soon as they had deposited their monk with his meagre baggage and the strange hare at the Church of St Dionysius as ordered, they took flight and left loudly cursing the city of Alexandria and its nonsense.

Standing in the courtyard of the church in the early morning air Cormac looked around at the buildings he knew from many years before. He had had a room at the rear of the church and studied in the Patriarchate's library as well as in the Catechetical School and occasionally in the Great Library near the Serapeum. As time went on, however the Great Library was frowned upon by the Church because of the many pagan texts it contained and his attendance there was discouraged.

Cormac had studied and mastered the craft of the scriptor during his time in the Church of St Dionysius. He had copied the psalms and the Book of Mark several times in uncial text, becoming quite expert in the mixing of colours. He had become known for his frequent use of verdigris, a vivid green that Cormac confessed reminded him of his native land. He sometimes drew green scenes in the margins of fields and trees which displeased the abbot, but intrigued many others and drew them to read the text.

Now, above the courtyard he could see the Consistory where the Patriarchate held council. Beyond the Consistory were the Patriarch's living quarters. Cormac had never been in these rooms, only the bishop and senior members of the Presbytery entered there. In the centre of the courtyard was a large wooden cross marking the burial place of St Dionysius, a previous patriarch and behind this cross were the broken remains of a statue to the god

Dionysius. The church like many in Alexandria was a former pagan temple.

Cormac knelt to give thanks to the saint for his safe delivery to Alexandria. While kneeling he sensed a presence beside him, but, not one to be disturbed at prayer, he continued with his eulogy to the saint.

Someone coughed. Still Cormac continued to eulogise. Then the person knelt beside him and prayed likewise.

Cormac finished his prayer and stood erect to see that the one kneeling beside him was known to him. It was Brother Finian who had been a novice when Cormac had lived in the church. He was a Pict from the northern kingdom of Dalriada which bordered Cormac's homeland of Eriu. Like Cormac he had travelled through Europe to arrive in Alexandria. Brother Finian stood and greeted Cormac. His face had a shadow on it that Cormac sought to read.

"You are very welcome back among us, Father Cormac the Celt," Finian said. Then turning to Zachariah he said, "And of course Master Hare you too are welcome."

Zachariah nodded in return. He noted the monk's air of concern.

"I am so glad to see you, Brother Finian the Pict" said Cormac smiling broadly and asked, "How goes the scriptorium?" in an effort to hear the tone of the monk.

"It is well, brother. We use a little less verdigris than when you were with us," Finian remarked without a smile.

"I fear I will have no time to change that, brother."

"Your stay is not for long?" asked Finian anxiously.

"I believe my stay may be short lived, brother,"

"I see. It is God's will. I have instructions to take you to your room and to ask you to attend the Consistory promptly after matins tomorrow," said Finian.

He looked quizzically at Cormac. Ordinary monks rarely entered the Consistory. This was where the Presbytery managed the affairs of the church in Africa and met with the Patriarch on lay matters. Cormac gave no sign that would indicate to Finian the nature of his meeting. He knew so little himself, but also knew to be discrete on the nature of his presence. Moreover, gossip and idle conversation was not encouraged among monks on any matter.

In spite of this rule, Finian spoke again: "Your visit comes at a strange time for us, brother."

"Strange, brother?" asked Cormac.

"There is a nervousness in the air that was not here before. Meetings go on in the consistory long into the night. Huge volumes of scrolls have been removed from the Great Library and brought to the Consistory. The Patriarch does not move among the people as before. Yesterday an emissary of the Bishop of Rome arrived. Now you return to us without explanation. Where is the Holy Spirit, father? The peace is disturbed. It has gone from this place of God," said Finian his face turned to Cormac in an agony of questioning. "I pray you are here from the desert fathers to return the divine peace to us."

Cormac placed a hand on the monk's shoulder. "Brother, I cannot say for certain why I am here and I am bound by an oath of secrecy. I await my mission."

"I should not have pressed you, brother. Please forgive me," said Finian.

"You are forgiven. Have faith, brother. These are temporal matters and will change with the winds. God is with us through all time and will guide us," Cormac said.

"Perhaps I should seek the desert fathers like you, brother. The city has become sick and is clawing at my faith,"

"God is within you, brother, wherever you are," said Cormac.

"Have a care who you say that to, brother. Many in this place would call that heresy. God is in heaven not in the breast of man, they say" said Finian

"You and I from the Poetic Isles know differently, brother," said Cormac. "But we will keep our counsel."

The two monks walked in silence through the cloisters to the cells at the rear of the church where Cormac had lived before. Zachariah skipped behind them, but still did not speak.

Finally Cormac broke the silence between them.

"Go to the desert fathers if that is your true guidance, Brother Finian. Aba James in Scetis will welcome you. You should know that the desert is a harsh mistress, but a sure way to the heart of the divine if you honestly seek to know that truth."

Finian nodded silently, believing he had said enough on the matter.

"It is the same room as before, father. We wanted you to be at your ease on your return to us," said Finian smiling weakly.

"You are as always kind to me, bless you brother," replied Cormac looking round the small room. It was unchanged except perhaps for a new wooden bed and a chair.

"You are welcome to eat, father," Finian gestured to a small table with a jug of water and a plate of bread and cheese on it, "and to join us for the offices in the church. May the Lord Yeshua hold you in his loving embrace, Father Cormac."

"And you, Brother Finian," replied Cormac. The two monks smiled and held each other's gaze. They bowed in unison to the cross and with that Finian departed.

Cormac set down his sack containing his bible and his cloak and placed his staff in the corner. He straightened the small wooden cross hanging at an angle on the wall and prayed briefly before beginning to eat the food. The bread was good. Alexandria was renowned for her bread. All of Egypt's grain came through her streets on its way from the fertile fields along the Nile to the huge warehouses on the Eunostos, Alexandria's harbour. In return for the shipments of grain to the four corners of the known world, all kinds of merchandise flowed into Alexandria: silks and spices from India, precious stones and tapestries from Byzantium, perfumes from Carthage, medicines from Greece and tin and salt from the Britannic Isles. Since the demise of the Roman Empire and the expulsion of the Jews from Alexandria, the grain trade was controlled by the Church making the Patriarch of Alexandria one of the richest and most powerful men in all Christendom. Many felt such riches did not sit well with sacred office; although it is true that the church dispensed free bread in Alexandria to the poor and to pilgrims. Each morning the city was filled with the smell of baking bread and the noise of the carts that delivered the loaves to the citizens. This morning was no different than it had been when Cormac last occupied the little cell. The rattle of the bread carts could be heard in the street beneath the high window.

As Cormac sat quietly eating he noticed that underneath the cheese was a small piece of folded parchment. He leant over and unfolded it. On it were written two words in Greek:

"Save Melania".

The name did not surprise the monk. She had been in his dreams of late and therefore knew that she would in some way feature in his return to Alexandria. Cormac nodded knowingly to himself and sat savouring memories as he likewise savoured the bread and cheese.

"What is written, monk?" asked Zachariah looking at the monk.

"It's this." Cormac said, showing the scrap of parchment to the hare.

"Ah of course!" exclaimed the hare. "She's one of the swans: in my vision with the wolf on the hill." Zachariah handed the note back to Cormac.

"You mean she is to travel with us?"

"Exactly"

"But why? This lady has no business with the Church and it would appear that we have to undertake a long and hard journey on Church business. That would be difficult for such a woman," Cormac said. "How would we care for her? No you go too far, hare. My bond to Melania is not yet broken it is true, for I dream of her. But travelling with us? How do you know one of the swans in your vision was the lady Melania?"

"I knew when I saw her name written on that note. I saw a swan."

"Ex tempore dico, my friend," said Cormac.

"Certainly not! The great Zachariah of Babylon does not pretend like some cheap actor or dream poet. I deal in divine visions, nothing less. As well you know, monk." Zachariah spoke sharply and was rather insulted at Cormac's suggestion.

"Forgive me, Zachariah. It seems I am guilty of my own accusation. But, tell me, why this lady? She is an educated lady although a pagan."

The hare had begun to sulk and would not respond to Cormac. Instead he stared out the high window, his ears thrown back in annoyance.

"Good hare, I have apologised. Forgiveness is a virtue." Cormac touched the hare's back.

"Very well. I forgive you, monk," conceded the hare. "The lady Melania is in trouble of some sort and we must go to her. If she stays in this city she will die."

"This city contains many intrigues, hare. We are here but a few brief moments. How can this be? Melania was living in Vitalios' community near the Sun Gate engaged in work with the women of the shadows."

"That was some years ago, monk. I believe her circumstances may have changed, but I cannot say in what way. We will have to seek her out," said Zachariah.

Cormac sat in silence to consider the implications. He sensed a movement of the fates. The journey had tired him and his mind was in a fog. His years in the desert had taught him how to play the fates like a skilled musician or an actor in a drama. He had watched the energies move across the sands, but that was in the desert where many things were clear. Now in the crowded city he sensed that matters would move very quickly in the coming hours. His faith would have to guide him moment to moment.

He knew he was pledged to look after this lady, but also bound to make this journey for the church. He wondered how he would be permitted by the Alexandrian church to bring a pagan woman on this journey. Only in special circumstances were monks allowed to be in the company of women and then they must be women of the faith.

"Good monk, you hesitate when the energies demand your action. I think I know why," said Zachariah.

"You claim a lot, hare,"

"I do. Allow me to say. The lady is dear to you and that leaves you uncomfortable with your vows, especially on a long voyage. Look how you blush!" said Zachariah bluntly.

Cormac nodded quietly.

"This is of the flesh, monk. You must put this to one side and go forth with this business," said the hare. "The lady needs you and you may need her. You are both actors in this great drama; nothing more. Do not confuse this with other matters of the flesh. Do you wish to become like your friend, the Pict befuddled and confused by this city's fraught affairs?"

Cormac turned to look at the hare who continued to speak.

"If the lady is to accompany us then God has a hand in it, as well you know. Let the divine guide you, monk. Now you are returned to the city you are fast taking on the ways of thinking and worrying and postulating. Soon you will be philosophising like Plato or worse, agonising like the Pict" said Zachariah nibbling some bread casually while speaking profoundly.

"You are right as ever, my friend, and I thank you for your wise words at this time," said Cormac as he finished the bread and cheese and drank a little water. "Very well. We will seek out Vitalios' this day and through him the lady, Melania, and all before our meeting in the Consistory in the morning. Come, we have little time!"

Cormac was on his feet, grabbing his staff and moving out of the cell with a contented hare in his wake. A desert wind moved through the cloisters behind them. Monk and hare felt the warm, sandy wind on their backs as they left the precinct of the church to find the lady Melania.

Watching them depart was a dark, silent figure in the shadows of the cloister: the Nubean monk, Augustine, the Bishop of Rome's emissary.

IX: The Lady Melania

The *bouleutai*, the merchants of Alexandria, still sold their many wares in shops and stalls along the Canopian Way: spices, pottery, fine jewellery, glassware and cloth dazzled Cormac's eyes with bright colours of blue and green and yellow. Trade appeared to be brisk with many wealthy *honestiores* moving from shop to shop accompanied by their servants and slaves haggling for the fine goods on their masters' behalf. Scents of perfume billowed from workshops around the Caesarion. These mixed with incense from nearby churches, the smell of fresh bread, sea air from the Mediterranean and the hot wind carrying desert odours to make a heady mixture of the sensuous, the natural and the divine. In this way Alexandria had not changed for centuries. It was a mixture of all these.

The sight of the wealthy, the *honestiores*, in their fine robes alongside the beggars, the *anexodos*, in their desert rags, was still a disturbing sight for many. The Church forbade begging. Strangely the church of Yeshua ho Xristos now found poverty distasteful and wealth a sign of divine beneficence. However the Alexandrian Church at least understood its duty to its poor and fed them in workhouses; perhaps motivated as much by a desire to remove the sight of begging as by Christian charity. For their part the *bouleutai* seemed to have grown in number since Cormac's years in Alexandria and now dominated the Canopian Way. It was a city in great flux. The change that had driven Cormac to the desert had continued apace. The glory of ancient Alexandria as a seat of learning, perhaps the greatest the world has ever known, was in this time much faded. In the place of the men and women of learning in the grand buildings, streets and squares created by Alexander and his generals were now busy merchants and the Coptic Church.

The Christian church dominated the city's public places and public affairs in both sacred and temporal matters. Trade was encouraged because the merchants paid taxes to the church. After centuries of persecution under the Romans, the Christians of Alexandria had emerged as the one supreme authority following the empire's demise. The Church was now creating its own empire founded on the power of its carefully constructed religious orthodoxy and its hierarchy of patriarchs, bishops and priests. The other inhabitants of the city – the pagans and the Jews, were no longer tolerated by the city's new rulers. All the pagan temples had been turned into Christian churches and the pagans made to convert or be exiled, even the great temple of Poseidon on Pharos was now a church. The temple of Isis Pharia survived because Isis was a powerful patroness of sailors and sailors were important to the city's life blood: maritime trade brought the church and the *honestiores* their riches and power. So these remaining pagan superstitions were grudgingly accommodated.

The Jews, once so vital a part of Alexandria's life and learning, were now confined to the Delta quarter in the poor northeast of the city having been expelled from the rest of the city by St Cyril in the fifth century. It was to this quarter that Cormac and Zachariah made their way to seek out the monk, Vitalios and his assistant, their friend, the lady, Melania.

In his years in the desert Cormac's senses had grown accustomed to singularity and simplicity. Now as he walked with Zachariah along the tidy streets and grand colonnades there was so much for the senses to absorb. Yet Cormac was eager to make his re-acquaintance with this old city and, if truth be told, to meet with the lady Melania. The feminine energy of both the city and the lady had come to exercise a sensuous fascination over the desert father in his years of exclusion; an influence that sat uncomfortably with his vows as a monk. The energy that drew him back could not be denied and Cormac knew in his heart that he had to surrender to its demands. He acknowledged that such a force came from the divine. It was for him to determine how he should react. So it was on that early spring morning with a yellow saffron light bathing the city, monk and hare strode purposefully through the streets on a mission to find the lady Melania.

Cormac recalled the street housing Vitalios' mission in the Delta Quarter. It was a narrow, shadowy street that allowed Vitalios to run his mission without attracting undue attention. It was housed in a series of buildings grouped around a courtyard. There was only one entrance where access was by a heavy door made from the thickest cedar with stout hinges and bolts. This was a measure to safeguard the women sheltering inside from their masters' greedy attentions. Vitalios fed and housed these poor women and gave much needed protection, as much he could without force of arms. Inside he taught the value of faith to fallen women and in time many were enabled to become true followers of Yeshua, ministering in turn to other fallen women in the city. Some even became desert mothers and many bore children that were brought up in the church.

Cormac and Zachariah arrived at Vitalios' mission by the seventh hour with the sun at its highest. Zachariah pulled on the bell rope by the great door. Inside could be heard the bell ringing and voices singing. A peephole opened.

"Who calls?" said a woman's voice from inside.

"Tell Father Vitalios it is Cormac the Celt and Zachariah the Hare. He will know," said Cormac.

The trap door closed and the two were left on the street.

The great door was then swung open and Vitalios stood beaming. He was a large bearded Greek with irrepressible energy and a voice to match.

"My Brothers in Yeshua!" he declared throwing his arms open wide.

"It is us," said Cormac grinning.

"Too long have I waited for your return, brothers."

"And I" said Cormac as the two monks embraced.

"And Master Zachariah, I see. The city finds you well?" said Vitalios to Zachariah.

"It does, monk," said Zachariah. "How goes your mission?"

"Ah! My mission," said Vitalios. "I will tell you inside. Come quickly"

"We have not much time, Vitalios. We must return to the Church of St Dionysius before the day's end."

The door closed behind them and they were led to Vitalios' private quarters off the courtyard. It was a simple room with a bed in one corner and a table and chairs and leading off this was a small church.

"We must pray, brothers," said Vitalios and led Cormac into the small church.

The two monks knelt before a cross. As they did Cormac noticed a picture of Mary of Magdala alongside a statue of the Goddess, Isis, on an altar under the cross.

They knelt in quiet prayer for a few moments and then returned to the living room where they sat drinking cool water and eating some bread and dates.

Without wasting precious time Cormac began, "It is the Lady Melania, Brother. I have a message to see her."

"I know. I sent you that message, Cormac," said Vitalios sadly. "Brother Finian told me of your imminent return to the city. The lady is in great danger and I am hoping you can help her. She will listen to you. I have done all I can."

"What danger is she in?" asked Cormac as he felt his heart beat quicken.

"In her time here with us in the mission the lady held to her beliefs as she declared to us she would and I did not interfere," said Vitalios his large brown hands moving as he talked. "She was a compassionate and diligent assistant in every way. Many of the women who come to us are pagan and the lady was well placed to support them."

"You speak of the past, brother. What of the lady today?"

"Some months ago the lady established a temple close by, dedicated to the Goddess Isis. She said the goddess guided her to do so. The lady believed that she owed a debt of gratitude to the goddess for protecting her. I tried to dissuade her, telling her that it was Yeshua that protected her, but she was not persuaded. As you may know, brother, the Church in Alexandria has outlawed pagan temples and threatens harsh penalties for those who defy them."

"I know this," said Cormac.

"For a while the temple thrived. Many of the women seemed to find some reassurance there. Although they would always return to Yeshua here," Vitalios smiled in satisfaction. "This month has brought a change with the Lychnapsia Philocaliana, the Festival of Light. It is a pagan festival honouring the goddess, Isis. On the night of the festival the *parabalini* attacked the temple. They tried to hold the lady Melania but she escaped. Instead they took another poor woman and burnt her in the street, brother."

"May God rest her poor soul," said Cormac shaking his head in horror.

"Amen. But Brother, the lady will not be deterred. If she continues with the temple she will die I fear, and die horribly. I have prayed for her. But she will defy our God and the Church."

"Where is the lady now?" asked Cormac urgently.

"Why, in the temple. It is close by."

"We will go there now, Vitalios. We have no time to spare for the lady or for ourselves. If we are to help her it must be on this day," said Cormac.

"Are you in some danger too, brother?" inquired Vitalios.

"No danger, but we must return to the church before the day's end." Cormac felt he must tell his old friend something. "We are leaving this land, brother and will not return. We believe we are bound for my homeland, the island of Eriu on a mission for His Holiness the Patriarch. No more can I say nor do I know. So we must part and not meet again in this world, dear Vitalios," said Cormac embracing Vitalios with some force of emotion.

"Take care, my brothers in Yeshua. It has been an honour to know you both. Many challenges await you. But we will pray for your safety and the success of your peregrinatio," said a sad Vitalios.

They left an anxious Vitalios to find Melania and secure her safety and that of the other women if they could. As Cormac and Zachariah made their way along the narrow backstreet to the temple of Isis they did not notice the same shadowy figure that had watched them in the church cloisters. It was Augustine, the Bishop of Rome's emissary lingering in an alleyway as they passed.

The temple was housed at the very end of the same long and narrow street. It was a former temple to Apollo, Roman God of the Sun. A side door was open and inside they could hear women singing praises. As they entered and walked through an archway towards the sound of the singing they saw the statue of Isis in the centre of the temple. As soon as Cormac and Zachariah approached they were startled by the sight of naked women dancing round the statue of the goddess. The women stopped their ceremony and examined the visitors nervously. Cormac immediately turned his back on them in embarrassment. He had not seen the naked female form for many years. In fact the only naked female he had ever seen was his wife and that only on feast days. In that moment in his mind's eye he saw her again, his wife Moninna, standing before him naked on the night of Beltaine. Her flesh was drawn taut by the famine, but in spite of her hunger she sought to please him. On her head she wore a crown of hazel and primrose and in her dark belly hair she had marsh marigolds. Days later she was struck down with the plague and died soon after.

Zachariah could see the vision in Cormac's mind.

"Let her go, monk. These women are not Moninna." whispered the hare.

Monk and hare heard a sharp collective intake of breath. All the women had bowed to the floor. It was in honour of the golden hare, a sacred animal in the religion of Isis. Zachariah's presence was a good omen and calm descended on the nervous women.

Cormac recovered his composure but still kept his gaze averted and said, "We seek the lady Melania. Is she among you?"

Then a voice from across the temple chamber responded in sweet but firm tones. It was the lady Melania, "You must know men are not permitted in the temple. You must leave now, monk. The hare is an honoured guest."

"It is I, lady, Cormac the Celt, returned from the desert. We need to speak with you on a matter of importance."

"My brother is come back with his sacred companion!" Melania cried. She began to approach Cormac and Zachariah while the rest of the women remained bowing.

"Steady, monk. She wears no clothes," warned Zachariah who did not avert his eyes the whole time enjoying the adulation. "Have a care, lady. This monk cannot look upon your nakedness."

"My brother should know his sister is still a virgin and a priestess of Isis. He should therefore not be offended by my nakedness," said Melania approaching through the crowd of naked pagan women who watched perplexed as their priestess walked towards this monk and sacred hare.

"Still you will offend me. Have pity, sister," said Cormac shielding his eyes.

"Very well," said Melania who stopped to collect a gown of fine fabric offered by another woman. The gown did little to cover her flesh, but it was enough. She bowed once more to the hare.

"You must leave the temple or it is I who will be offended, brother. Come to my room. Master hare can stay if he so wishes" said Melania in a reverential tone to Zachariah and led the red faced monk off to the side.

"Zachariah I need you with me!" said Cormac. Zachariah did not argue in spite of the attention he was enjoying.

"Excuse me, but my friend needs me," said Zachariah to the bowing followers of Isis unwilling to upset or disappoint them. He understood that naked women could suddenly become emotional.

In the quiet of the room Cormac and Melania were able to regard each other without further hindrance. Melania looked tired. Her face had aged somewhat as lines appeared around her gentle eyes. Gentle eyes that showed strength and delight tinged with anxiety. She had lost the puppy fat of youth and was now a woman fully matured and wise.

"It is good to see you back in our city, my brother. You look well. A little older and thinner I see. Your god has been good to you in the desert?" Melania smiled.

Cormac's skills in social conversation were much diminished from his years in the desert. There was urgent business to be done. Yet his sharp eyes took in the lady and showed his concern.

"My God is with me at all times, sister. Seeing you does please me. Often I have remembered our friendship and prayed for your welfare. It is about your welfare that brings us here. We are all concerned about your fate if you remain here doing this work."

"My fate?" said Melania beginning to frown a little at the monk's interference in her religious devotions so soon after his return to the city.

"Yes. Vitalios has told me just now of the attack on your temple and the burning of one of your number," said Cormac.

"The goddess always protects me as your god protects you. Do not be concerned for me."

"Forgive me, sister, but your goddess did not protect the poor creature that was burnt to death in the street outside."

Melania was suddenly quiet. "She had not become a follower and was not under the goddess' wing. It is like your baptism, brother. Once you are a follower you are protected from such things."

"I will not debate with you, lady. I am guided by the divine to bring you with me on a journey where you will be cared for. This is not your city any longer. You must know it is a dangerous place for pagans. Many temples have been closed and many pagans have been killed by the *parabalini*. The land I am bound for will allow your form of worship. In my homeland the pagans still practice. You will be safe there, my sister. You have said that we are bound to one another," said Cormac.

Melania regarded Cormac quietly and nodded gently. She felt his concern and recognised the significance of his proposal. Monks were not allowed to travel with women, least of all a pagan woman. That could cause his excommunication. Such a step would be a grave one for this monk. She glanced over her shoulder.

"So you are returning to your homeland. Has your god dispensed with your services here?" she teased. She needed to hear more from him.

"He has not, sister. He has guided the Patriarch himself to send me on a journey to my island on some important business in the coming days, perhaps on the next day."

"I thank you for your concern, my brother. I know of its significance for you. But your Patriarch would have me dead if I came with you and I have a duty here to these women and Vitalios. Therefore I cannot leave."

"It is Vitalios who has sent me to offer you protection to leave this city! He fears for your life here, as I do. The Patriarch will not harm you if you are travelling with me. I swear it. Lady, I am pledged to bring you to safety as God is my witness," said Cormac desperately.

"I too am pledged to my sisters here in Alexandria. You and Vitalios have never understood the power of Isis. Isis will protect us," said Melania with resignation.

Then Zachariah began to speak, "Lady Melania," he began. "Hear me. I have seen a vision where you journey with us to an island in the north. It is your destiny. Do you question the hare's vision?" His piercing brown eyes challenged her.

Melania could not meet the hare's eyes. She shook her head in confusion. She knew of the hare's powers and as a follower of Isis respected his divinity. But she had committed herself to the women of the temple. The two paths could not be reconciled.

"I do not doubt you. Tell me more of your vision, Master Zachariah" asked Melania.

Zachariah told her of his visions of the scrolls and of Cormac's journey on the back of an eagle to a far off island in the north where he was protected by four white swans, one of them being Melania.

Now without speaking Melania lifted a charm from around her neck and held it for Cormac and Zachariah to see. It was made of the purest white ivory hanging on a fine silver chain. It was of four white swans.

"My mother gave it to me on my first cycle and told me I was born on an island on the Nile guarded by four swans" said Melania. "It was prophesised at my birth that I would end my days on another island surrounded by swans. Swans are my protectors. They are the hand maidens of Isis. It is why I am eternally pledged to the goddess."

Zachariah smiled and Cormac nodded with some relief.

"Swans are mythical beings in my land too, lady," said Cormac. "It is decided then. You will come to Eriu, my sister?"

Melania did not answer. She closed her eyes and was silent for many moments, and then she spoke softly.

"Destiny, destiny. How often I hear that word." She examined her ivory swans thoughtfully. "It is made manifest I cannot deny it, brother. Yes I will go with you." She sighed as she looked sadly over her shoulder towards the temple and the daughters of Isis that she would leave behind.

X: Departure

That morning at matins the Patriarch appeared ill at ease and so too was his deacon who performed the service. The service was a hurried affair. There was no oblation, no Sanctus and no homily to the gathered crowd. To the consternation of those present the Patriarch did not give his daily blessings to the poor. Instead he fidgeted with his worry stones throughout, glancing repeatedly at Acacius. At the second epiclesis he hurried off without waiting for the communion, followed by Acacius. They walked towards the Consistory leaving the deacon to complete Matins with the communion and to comfort those who had hoped for the Patriarch's blessing.

The matter of the holy scrolls weighed heavily on the Patriarch's mind; heavier since a complication had arisen in the night regarding the well laid plans for the despatch of the ancient scrolls.

Acacius had met with the Bishop of Rome's emissary after vespers the previous evening in order to discourage any further interest of his in the scrolls. Before Acacius could relay a well-rehearsed story to explain the secrecy, Brother Augustine was able to confirm that he knew of the planned dispatch of Cormac the Celt to the island of Eriu with the scrolls. However the emissary appeared not to know their content. In response Acacius insisted that this was untrue and enquired about the emissary's sources.

"A monk in the city confessed it to me," said Augustine with relish, enjoying the *Oikonomos'* discomfort.

"Who? Which monk is spreading this idle gossip, brother?" probed Acacius.

Augustine calmly ate some grapes from his mantle and smiled. "I don't know his name, but he was eager to help the Bishop of Rome in his quest for the truth, as you should be, *Oikonomos*. This charade of a separate church in Africa will not last for much longer. The Sassanids are moving their armies ever westwards from Persia.

Soon you will be vassals of the heathen Arabs and your church will be destroyed. The Bishop of Rome seeks to help you resist them and to protect our holy relics in Africa. Arabs are a threat to all Christians and to these sacred scrolls, are they not, *Oikonomos*?"

Acacius was too skilled a diplomat to be ensnared by the emissary's crude manoeuvrings.

"You must forgive me, brother, but such politics are beyond me. I serve God and my church, no other. Is it not enough that our grain ships feed the church in Rome?" said Acacius keen to remind the emissary of Rome's dependent relationship with the Church of Africa. "I can advise you, emissary, that Alexandria is a city full of gossip and idle tongues. Our monks can be simple folk from the desert whose tongues can often wag senselessly on matters that they do not understand."

"This monk was no simple fellow from the desert, *Oikonomos*. He was an educated Greek. He was no simple desert father," said Augustine. "So there are no vessels bound for this island in the morning?" asked the emissary.

"None carrying these scrolls that you talk of, I assure you. It is a busy harbour and vessels leave all the time carrying grain and other goods to the four corners of the globe. There may be vessels bound for the island you speak of. I cannot say for certain," said Acacius masking his shock that the emissary also knew the very day of departure.

"I know the harbour well, *Oikonomos*," said Augustine. "I stroll there most days taking in the air and all the excitement of trade. No doubt I shall be there tomorrow. It is a matter of some sorrow that you will not join with the Bishop of Rome in this matter."

As the emissary turned to leave, Acacius' tone changed abruptly.

"I am minded to share with you the Patriarch's sentiments, emissary. How we manage our affairs in this place is a matter for the Holy Church of St Mark and for God. Should the Bishop of Rome or his servants cause us any disquiet, the matter of Rome's grain supply will come under close scrutiny."

"Ah! The Church of Africa's true nature is revealed. These must be very important scrolls, *Oikonomos*, for such a threat to be issued by a Christian to other Christians," said Augustine.

"As a Nubean you will know the loving nature of the Church of Africa, brother. It gave you sanctuary and educated you while you were an orphan, did it not?"

"It gave me to a leper who abused me! It was the Church of Rome that rescued me!" snapped Augustine.

"Then protect yourself from abuse the second time, brother and return to your guardian, the Bishop of Rome forthwith."

"That I cannot do!" Augustine turned, leaving Acacius pondering what to do about this determined emissary.

In the Consistory after matins the Patriarch glared at Acacius.

"How does the emissary know so much of our plans, *Oikonomos*? Only you and I know of this," the Patriarch said accusingly.

"The Celtic monk knows he is departing today. He must have gossiped in the city."

"But he does not know where he is going. Even the ships' masters do not know this!" said the Patriarch. "How does this emissary know this? Our plans are in ruins! The Bishop of Rome will get these scrolls and ruin us!"

"Not if we move quickly, holiness. The emissary is a lazy dog and does not rise until the third hour. Besides his breakfast this morning will return him to sleep for some hours. This will give us time to have our monk well on the way. The emissary has no ship capable of sailing the distance or of catching our vessels. He will be lucky to get back to Rome without drowning in the vessel he has at his disposal."

The Patriarch forced a smile. The two men smiled at each other.

"Once again God comes to our rescue with your wisdom and guile. You do well to listen to Him, *Oikonomos*. Very well let us send our Celt on his way within the hour. Bring him to us."

Cormac had been waiting outside the Consistory since matins, as he had been instructed. At matins he had offered himself up to God and was now eager to be on his way with Zachariah and of course the lady Melania. All that remained was to inform the Patriarch of his travelling companions. Yeshua would guide him.

As Cormac was ushered into the Consistory by the *Oikonomos* he prostrated himself before the Patriarch seated on the dais. There were no other members of the Presbytery present.

"Arise, brother and come forward. We have urgent business to transact before we send you on your way," said the Patriarch.

Cormac arose and still bowing he kissed the extended hand with the ring of St Mark.

Holding the sacred scrolls before him, Acacius got to the business in hand without delay: "These scrolls are to be transported to the island of Eriu, brother. They are the most important and sacred of scrolls in all of Christendom. The Church of St Mark trusts them to your care."

Cormac bowed solemnly, but showed no outward emotion.

"We cannot tell you their content. It is better that you do not know, but you will know that their contents must not be revealed to any living soul. You must not allow these seals to be broken and the documents read." Acacius showed the sealed scrolls to Cormac and then placed them in a heavy leather bag.

"Whoever reveals the contents, brother," said the Patriarch quietly from his vantage point on the dias, fixing the monk with his dark eyes, "will be damned in the eyes of God to suffer for all eternity. None of your Celtic penance will suffice for such a sin as viewing these scrolls or publicising their contents. The one who views them without authority will be damned for all time. You must never allow these scrolls out of your sight, not for a moment. Is that clear, Father Cormac?"

"It is, Holy father."

Acacius continued: "This much you may know. You will be landed in a place in Eriu and met by a merchant known to us. He will take you to a monastery nearby. From there you will journey to meet with the Prince Colum Cille. I believe you know the prince."

"I do. He ordained me many years ago. Does he know of these scrolls and expect my arrival, Holiness?"

"He does not," said the Patriarch. "But we know him to be a holy man of great wisdom and power in the land. We know of this man and admire his work for God. You will give the scrolls into his safe keeping with these words from me."

Acacius placed another sealed scroll in the leather bag. "It is for Prince Colum Cille to decide the matter of these scrolls and their continued security. At that point your work for the Church of St Mark is done and you will keep our blessings for ever for the great service you will have done us."

"This letter of introduction from the Patriarch will ensure your safe passage through Eriu," said Acacius handing another scroll directly to Cormac. "Here also is some gold that will help you along your way." Acacius handed over some gold coins to Cormac in a small cloth bag. "Only spend what you have to, brother and give the rest to Prince Colum Cille to help build his monasteries."

"I – I have never handled such a thing as gold nor any kind of money, Holiness. It is not used in Eriu."

The Patriarch raised his eyebrows.

"Nevertheless take it, brother. If men need persuading use it. Whatever is left at the end of the mission Prince Colum Cille may use to build a monastery or church in our name. We will send you desert fathers to help," said the Patriarch smiling at Acacius. He had not thought of such an outcome until now. He began to see an outpost of the Church of St Mark on this island in the western ocean. That would displease the Bishop of Rome and no mistake.

"You will be accompanied by a young monk from Jerusalem," continued the Patriarch. "He has taken a vow of silence which must not be broken. So do not question him. His name is Bartholomew. Once he is in Eriu you will see that he joins a suitable house of God and maintains his vow of silence. You are better travelling alone, brother. You will be less conspicuous."

Cormac made a motion to speak.

"Yes we know about your hare, brother. If you are foolish enough to bring him on such a journey as this, so be it. We will not interfere, but he is to mind his tongue. I hear he is a garrulous creature," said the Patriarch.

There was a silence and Acacius motioned Cormac to speak.

"Holy Father, thank you," said Cormac. "It is not just the hare. I am pledged to bring another with me, my sister."

"Sister! You don't have a sister here, surely?" said the Patriarch in surprise.

"She is my spiritual sister. I knew her father, Holy Father."

"Who is this woman? Is she a sister of the Church? Do I know her father?"

Cormac swallowed hard, but he had already determined that he would not leave without the lady Melania.

"No Holy father. She is not of our faith. She is a pagan, but a good and righteous woman. Her father was the philosopher, Ausonius."

"What! Is this the woman who spoke in public in the agora and now sets herself up as a pagan priestess in a temple defying God? No pagan woman will sail on our ships. I forbid it."

"Forgive me Holy Father, but our sailors are mostly pagan and worship Isis," said Cormac.

"Do you argue with me monk? This pagan woman will not accompany you. Now go!" demanded the Patriarch and pointed to the door.

"I cannot go without this woman, Holy Father. If she remains here the *parabalini* will slay her like Hypatia. You must find another to take these scrolls. I will remain in Alexandria." Cormac reached out the letter of introduction to return it to Acacius.

"Do you defy your church and your God, monk!? Are you obsessed with this pagan?" cried the Patriarch and turning to Acacius said, "This is not the monk we need, *Oikonomos*. Aba James was mistaken. Find another. Send this fellow back to the desert to cure his urges and see that he is flogged for consorting with pagans."

"Find another at this hour, Holy Father? The ships are ready. The Roman emissary cannot be delayed beyond this day. He will be upon us and discover the truth," said Acacius.

"I humbly beg your attention, Holy father," said Cormac with his head bowed.

"You may speak, brother," said Acacius reassuringly.

"The hare has the gift of prophesy, Holiness. It is known. He has seen a vision where the lady is a white swan and protects us in Eriu from a black eagle that would steal the scrolls. He saw this before we knew the nature of our mission. I believe it is a sign from God, Holiness," said Cormac quietly.

"By all that is sacred!" bellowed the Patriarch. "Swans, eagles? What drivel you Celts busy yourselves with? I have heard this hare

114

was loose tongued. It was he who told the emissary of the destination!" He looked at Acacius for confirmation.

"I assure you he did not, Holiness," said Cormac appealing to Acacius. "Zachariah has the wisdom of the ages and would not do such a thing. Talkative he may be, but not about important matters. But there is more to say with your permission, Holiness."

Acacius held up his hand before the Patriarch could respond. "I believe we should hear the brother out, Holiness," said Acacius.

"Talk, monk!" ordered the Patriarch.

"Many of the sailors place great store in the pagan goddess, Isis, Holiness," began Cormac. "This lady is a priestess of Isis. She will bring reassurance to these sailors on such a long voyage."

"This is becoming a Greek comedy, *Oikonomos*, and a blasphemy to add to blasphemy. We are fools to allow it. God will punish us for mocking Him," said the Patriarch flatly.

"We have little choice, Holiness," said Acacius. "These are unusual circumstances in all regards. Perhaps we need to match unusual with unusual. If we trust this monk to deliver the scrolls, then we must accept these strange terms and let him go this day with the pagan woman. It will be one less problem in the city, Holiness."

The Patriarch hesitated. He looked at Cormac and stroked his beard for several moments.

Finally he said: "Do you pledge to the Church and to God to deliver those scrolls intact to Prince Colum Cille, monk?"

"Before God I do, Holiness," answered Cormac.

The Patriarch and the *Oikonomos* looked at one another while Cormac remained still between them. He awaited his fate and that of Melania and Zachariah.

"Very well, monk. Be gone from us with your strange band, but on one condition," said the Patriarch wagging a long thin finger at Cormac. "This pagan priestess is not to speak in public and is to be taken into the care of Prince Colum Cille along with the scrolls. He will decide her fate, not you nor any other. I hope and pray he slays her or if he is so minded, places her into a monastery for correction and salvation. In this way we may pacify God for giving her succour."

"I accept this before God, Holiness," said Cormac. He knew Colum Cille would never accept an unwilling member into the church.

"Then go with God, brother, and with our blessing on your divine task," said the Patriarch and signalled that the interview was concluded.

As Cormac bowed and left the Consistory, Acacius followed him, carrying the heavy leather bag containing the scrolls.

"You are full of surprises, brother. Please, no more. I will accompany you and your companions to the harbour and see you safely on the vessel to take you to Eriu," said Acacius. "Where are your companions, brother?"

"They await me in my room,"

"Fetch them now. Hurry, brother."

As the strange band of *Oikonomos*, monk, hare and priestess left the Church of St Dionysius for the harbour of Eunostos they were surrounded by an armed phalanx of *parabalini*, the Church's militia. They had instructions to protect the party at all costs and to see the monk and his companions safely aboard the vessel in the harbour without interference. In addition they were instructed that no other vessel was to depart the harbour that day. Moreover if a black skinned monk were to intervene he was to be slain instantly.

The *Oikonomos* eyed Cormac quizzically as they stood on the wharf of the Eunostos – the great western harbour of Alexandria. All round them was noise and activity as the *fellahin* loaded the patriarch's grain ships moored alongside. Up to thirty ships left every day taking grain to all corners of the known world – Rome, Constantinople, Carthage, Antioch and even as far as the Britannic Isles. They returned with spices, tin, gold and many other precious goods for the patriarch's treasury to be managed by his *Oikonomos*, Acacius. Acacius waved a brightly coloured silk scarf before his face in an effort to keep the dust and the flies at bay. The stour rising from the bags of grain as they were transported from the warehouses filled the air and choked the throats of those unaccustomed to such conditions.

They stood by the two large vessels that were to transport them to Eriu. One was to carry Cormac and his group and the other carried soldiers and archers in case of attack. The vessels were equipped for fast passage through the sea with thirty oarsmen on each side. The oars were fixed upright in the vessels and beside them on benches sat the crew of over sixty men lined up either side awaiting departure. In addition to the oarsmen were two masts for sails: one large central mast and a secondary smaller mast at the bow. In the stern was a covered area for the storage of provisions and the comfort of the ship's master and his guests.

These were not vessels of trade, but vessels of war; made for the fast transport of an army and for the engagement of the enemy at sea. The crew were free born *Maghreb*s and Berbers, heavily muscled and skilled sailors from Cyrenia on the North African coast who had been specially selected for such a long sea journey at speed. These men had sailed to Eriu and beyond many times. Some claimed to have sailed far in the western ocean beyond the sea roads to unknown lands to trade with a red skinned people. The sea was home to these men much more than the land.

That morning the ships' crews were eyeing the sky and the wind critically as all sailors do. Conditions were not favourable for departure as a strong northerly wind fixed the vessels tight to the harbour side. It would be a struggle to depart and make weigh against such a wind, but their orders from the Patriarchy were to depart without delay whatever the conditions.

Their anxiety and that of the vessels' masters was heightened by the fact that no one knew their destination port. This was an unusual circumstance. Rumours abounded. Some said the Patriarch had declared a holy war on Rome; others that Rome had sent vessels to attack Alexandria and these vessels were part of a fleet sailing out to repel the invaders. Nervous speculation grew as the strange party from the Patriarchy surrounded by militia men arrived on the harbour and stood beside their vessels. The Patriarch's *Oikonomos* and a phalanx of *parabalini* escorted a tall red haired monk with a sacred hare and a fair haired Greek woman. The anxious crew made pleadings to the goddess of sailors, Isis, to protect them from evil.

Acacius motioned Cormac to a quieter corner of the wharf away from his companions and the prying eyes. Cormac was reluctant to leave the lady Melania and Zachariah in the company of the *parabalini* and the nervous sailors. Melania had been in a state of great disquiet since she had arrived at the Church of St Dionysius on the third hour. Her disquiet had increased tenfold as she found herself in the company of the murderous *parabalini* and now all these agitated sailors and soldiers. It was not a place for women of sensitivity and good breeding. Both Cormac and Zachariah sought to reassure the lady, but their words were of little comfort. So Cormac instructed Zachariah to watch over the lady closely as he moved away to speak with Acacius.

"You will miss the desert, father. You spent many years with the desert fathers. Did you not?" Acacius asked softly.

Cormac had sensed since their first meeting that the *Oikonomos* was closely assessing his character and his ability to successfully carry out the great task assigned to him by the Patriarch. Now he was in a corner of the wharf for one final examination from the Patriarch's diligent adviser before Cormac boarded the ship with his precious cargo of scrolls. After that, all was in God's hands.

"The sea is a desert too, sir. I will be at home with God in that place." Cormac replied in an attempt to reassure.

"You are a sailor then as well?" continued the *Oikonomos.*

"In my youth I helped my father fish."

"You were not pledged to the monastery as a child, father?"

"No. I became a *manaig* – a lay monk, on marrying the abbot's daughter and only later did I become a full brother in Yeshua."

"Ah yes, you Celts deny the celibate life. Intriguing." Acacius mused, eying Cormac curiously for a moment and then probed further. "Why later did you become a brother in Christ and leave your family?"

Cormac grimaced and looked up at the open sky beyond the Caesarion. He hesitated and then spoke with a voice from a deep wound. "My wife and children were taken up in the great plague, sir. God called me then, as he also called them, but to a different place."

Acacius nodded silently in full knowing. He himself knew the pain of such a calling. The plague had ravaged Alexandria and his own family. In this revelation he had the reassurance he needed. A man who could survive such loss and live in the desert with God and the devil could shoulder the burden given him by the Patriarch.

"God has spared you for a reason, father. Perhaps the reason is here with us now," Acacius said as he gestured towards the leather bag before them.

"I believe it is so, sir" Cormac nodded as he took a deep breath to soothe the pain of memory. "I have been prepared for the trial."

Cormac had not mentioned his wife and children for twenty years. They had been locked inside him since their dreadful passing. The two men stood in silent partnership acknowledging their understanding. On an impulse Cormac whispered the names of his dear ones to the sky, "Moninna, Ternoc and Etgal". The sound was like a solemn song. All at once they were out upon the hot air of Alexandria, far away from their native home; his wife and their twin sons. Their souls had been set free by his simple words of confession.

Cormac sighed in blessed relief and with his out breath, three small birds landed on the leather bag at his feet. They were swifts. The warehouses along the waterfront abounded with such birds; birds he had known well as a boy in Eriu and also as a desert father in Egypt. These creatures united his worlds as messengers between two ancient places: Eriu and Egypt. Now they were here to see him over the seas and back to Eriu. He smiled lovingly at the birds. They cocked their heads and smiled back just like Moninna, Ternoc and Etgal had often done across the corn and over the wall of the lower meadow.

"Nothing ever ends, everything lives on, dear soul," the birds said to him.

"Something further you must know, father," said Acacius unaware of the birds' communication with Cormac.

He moved close to Cormac and, as he did so, the three swifts flew off and in a broad sweep of the great harbour perched on the top mast of one of the vessels. Some sailors noticed them.

Speaking softly Acacius said, "The Bishop of Rome is keen to obtain these scrolls, father. He does not know their contents, but if he did he would surely use them to destroy us here in Africa. He has sent an important emissary, Brother Augustine of Nubea to obtain them. He is in the city now, but we have waylaid him so that you can make good your departure. He will follow you, father. We cannot stop him forever. Somehow he knows you are bound for Eriu."

"I understand," said Cormac meeting Acacius' worried eyes.

"When you told us of the hare's vision concerning the black eagle pursuing you, I knew it to be true. You see Brother Augustine is a black skinned African. He is known to be ruthless in his pursuit of the Bishop of Rome's desires. They call him "the bishop's eagle". So have a care, father. Augustine will pursue you. Of that I have no doubt. You will be safe at sea with our protection, but once on land you will need to travel quickly and in great secrecy. You must not let the pagan woman or the hare slow you down or reveal your mission, I beg you."

"They will not, sir," said Cormac as he looked across the harbour to the great lighthouse and their point of departure from Africa. He doubted that a black skinned monk would travel unnoticed in Eriu and that gave him some reassurance.

Just then the *parabalini* brought a young monk into their presence.

"This is Brother Bartholomew, father," said Acacius holding the young monk's arm. "He has taken a vow of silence which must not be broken. He will accompany you and will be placed in a monastery on your arrival as I have said."

Brother Bartholomew kept his eyes cast down. Cormac regarded him. He was young, there was no doubt, but there was an air about him that spoke of a keen intelligence and an artist's sensitivity. His Hebrew tonsure was similar to Cormac's own celtic style of hair: shaved at the forehead and long at the back and sides. Bartholomew stood clasping and wringing his white, ink stained and bony hands before him. It was obvious to Cormac that this young Judean monk was not there of his own freewill. Cormac guessed he was a scribe and wondered at his vow of silence. A scribe needed to talk to his fellows to organise the much needed collaboration his complex work often demanded.

"Come father, your party is complete. We must not delay any longer," Cormac heard the *Oikonomos* say. "You must take ship and be gone from us. Look," Acacius shouted gesturing to the sky, "the wind has changed in our favour! God is with us!"

It was true. As they had talked on the waterfront, the wind which had been pinning the vessels to the harbour wall now veered to a steady westerly breeze: ideal for departure and their onward journey. The spirits of the Cyrenian crew visibly lifted. The *Oikonomos* motioned to the master of the first vessel and the crew leapt as one to embark followed by the crew on the second vessel carrying the soldiers and archers.

And so it was that Cormac mac Fliande and his companions left Africa in a grand manner, on board a large vessel of war flying the holy standard of the Patriarch of Alexandria and Bishop of Africa, bound for Eriu, the land of his birth and bound for high drama by all accounts.

God had called him. But the devil was on his heels.

XI: The Great Green

The leaving of Alexandria was a holy moment for both Cormac and the lady, Melania, for different reasons. It was in Egypt that God had healed Cormac's broken heart and had given the monk new life. Cormac, the broken and childless farmer from the island of Eriu had come to know his God and his place in the world through the desert fathers. He had been reborn in the sand where the prophet, Yeshua had spoken to him in his solitude.

Now a new vision was born on the sea of the wide sky and the broad wind. It was a holy trinity that Cormac recognised, holding and bathing the life of the humans, the birds and the fish alike. As the vessel cleared the great harbour Cormac knelt on the swaying deck of the vessel and gave thanks to this elemental trinity. He recited the prayer of St Brendan the Voyager:

> *Help me to journey beyond the familiar*
> *And into the unknown.*
> *Give me the faith to leave old ways*
> *And break fresh ground with You.*
>
> *Christ of the mysteries, I trust You*
> *To be stronger than each storm within me.*
> *I will trust in the darkness and know*
> *That my times, even now, are in Your hand.*
> *Tune my spirit to the music of heaven,*
> *And somehow, make my obedience count for You.*

He prayed that this divine contract would carry them all to safety in Eriu and from there to the completion of their mission with Colum Cille, known to Cormac by the name Crimthainn, the fox. It was not for nothing that Colum Cille was known as the fox to his early followers.

The lady Melania wept as the vessel sailed gently past the Temple of Isis on the island of Pharos leaving the city of Alexandria behind on the port beam. She knew Isis was guiding her far away from the land of her birth. Such a departure to a distant land had been prophesied by the High Priestess of this temple on Melania's seventh birthday. She had patiently awaited its manifestation, but for now Melania wept in memory of her family and particularly for the guidance of her father: the golden days in the lecture halls of Alexandria and of debate in the agora alongside her beloved father.

Her world had been governed by the magic of Isis and the philosophy of Socrates as taught by the great Plato. The philosophers and the goddess had guided Melania for most of her life. They taught that what the eye cannot see is no less real. Now she was following that belief in the unseen worlds by trusting in divine guidance. She trusted that this monk and the visionary hare were indeed part of this unseen force calling her beyond Alexandria and away from all she knew.

As the strong westerly wind from the Levant took the vessels swiftly out of the Eunostos and past the Great Lighthouse with little need of rowing, the master of their vessel turned his attention to the papyrus scroll and maps he had been given by Acacius with instructions only to break the seal and read once past the Great Lighthouse. Like his crew, Master Igider was of the Berber people, an ancient seafaring tribe from the North African coast. As he studied the scroll and maps closely on his small after deck he mumbled to himself and nodded, glancing across at the Christian monk and his followers as he gave one map to his navigator.

The small group of travellers huddled together on the stern deck of the patriarch's fastest vessel closely watching the sailor read the scroll. All of them were apprehensive now they were on the open sea and at the mercy of these Berber sailors. All of them that is, except the young silent monk, Bartholomew. Since boarding the vessel he had crouched by the stern looking fixedly at the vessel's wake, showing no concern or interest in his companions or the crew. He played mournful tunes on a small flute. Cormac was uncertain where this flute fitted within Bartholomew's vow of silence. However he was minded to let the matter rest as the music might soothe them all on their journey.

The master folded the scroll and the other maps into his shirt for safekeeping. He walked over the swaying deck to where Cormac and his companions were gathered with Alexandria slowly receding from sight in the morning light. He looked at them curiously: his gaze resting on the lady Melania for some moments. He looked her up and then down until she was made quite uncomfortable.

He turned and bellowed to the crew in *Maghreb*, the language of the Berber people. All that Cormac and his companions could distinguish was the word "Eriu" in the master's guttural tongue. There was a murmur throughout the vessel and many turned to look at the passengers and at the lady Melania in particular. The look was not menacing, but it was intense. They appeared to be discussing her. Melania moved behind Cormac pulling her cloak close about her.

"Why do they stare at me? What was in that scroll the master has?" she pleaded.

Cormac shook his head as perplexed and concerned as Melania.

"Instructions for the passage, no more. Be calm, lady. You are safe," He tried to reassure her, but the interest was disturbing. Cormac wondered what the *Oikonomos* had written in the letter that would cause the sailors to react to the lady in this manner. Zachariah's high trembling laughter broke the mounting tension.

"No, monk, it is not a threatening interest," Zachariah said, for the hare could understand most tongues. "They wonder if they have an Egyptian princess on board."

"Why do they think that?" asked Melania incredulously.

"Their fathers' fathers carried Princess Meritaten, eldest daughter of the Pharaoh Akhenaten to Eriu many generations past. It is an old tale passed down. They suspect you follow in Meritaten's path. It is good. They will be wary of you. Just behave like a princess and we will all be treated royally," Zachariah chuckled.

"Meritaten?" mused Cormac. "Ah! The one called Princess Scotti who gave her name to the people of Eriu."

"Just so, monk."

"It is a legend of my people. You are in good company, lady." Cormac smiled at Melania in relief.

Melania suddenly stiffened with anger, turned and moved from behind Cormac to stand in full view of the crew: the wind tugging at her robes. She declared loudly and hotly.

"Do not mock me, sailors! I am Melania, priestess of the goddess Isis and follower of the great philosopher, Plato," she asserted proudly. "I am no Egyptian princess. I am Greek from Alexandria."

At the sound of the word "Isis" there was a sharp intake of breath and greater murmuring.

The vessel's master gestured at his men to be quiet. As he strode across the deck towards Melania, Cormac moved closer to her. The master spoke Greek haltingly.

"You are priestess of Isis?" he asked gently.

"I am, sir" Melania said hotly.

"Ah! Then you are welcome, lady. It is good for us to have priestess of the goddess so close on voyage. She will protect us with you here. I am called Igider: the Eagle in your tongue." He bowed and smiled.

Turning to his crew he bellowed in *Maghreb* once more. The crew cheered, stood and as one they also bowed to Melania, who for her part raised her arms intuitively to accept the adulation.

"Well played, lady," whispered Zachariah.

"I do not play, master hare. I am a priestess of the goddess Isis, the goddess of sailors. These men are right to worship her and not the Christian god. Through me Isis will protect us on this voyage. All is well."

"And you were right to follow my vision, lady," Zachariah reminded her. "The eagle is with us and will indeed see us safely to the island," he said indicating to the vessel's master, Igider the Eagle.

Cormac saw Melania's fear disappear in a moment and a new strength come to her form: so all was well. Once again Zachariah's visions carried much truth. An eagle was indeed carrying them to Eriu.

All at once Melania appeared at ease with her new surroundings, no longer a nervous and fearful woman, but a priestess of the waves where strong men, even eagles looked to her for help. As a child and a young woman in Alexandria she had been forbidden to go near the great harbour for fear of abduction. She had never known sailors and indeed feared their coarse ways. Now among these men she was no longer fearful, but was reborn, her status as a priestess and a woman at last respected by men.

For his part Cormac simply saw the hand of God moving across the waves to protect them. He and Zachariah had prayed to God all through the night for the lady's well-being. Now they smiled knowingly at one another. The first hurdle had been surmounted, their faith rewarded once more.

At that very moment the vessel leapt in the waves like a wild beast straining to be let loose of its chains as the wind sprang at the huge sails. The crew ran to adjust the ropes and shackles.

Melania beamed at her companions and holding her brightening face upturned to the wind said, "Isis is with us! See, brother the wind comes directly from the temple on Pharos. Now your eagle can fly, master hare!" she shouted in joy and held her arms out as if to fly herself.

She pointed back across the ocean towards Alexandria where the island of Pharos was now barely visible. On this island were the only pagan temples allowed to remain by the church in North Africa: huge temples to Poseidon and Isis had been built by the Ptolemies to watch over sailors. Without these temples not a vessel would move from the harbour. Where trade was concerned the church could be very pragmatic.

"Indeed, lady," replied Zachariah returning her smile. Although he believed the wind came several more degrees to the east, from the direction of the holy city of Jerusalem. To Zachariah's mind it was God's wind that spurred them on. If it filled the lady's heart with pleasure and strength to believe the wind came from the pagan island, it would be churlish to argue with her. It was good to see her come into her own. God's purpose in bringing the lady out of Alexandria was fully revealed, even if it meant a pagan goddess was to be adulated. The sight of the lady in bloom filled the hearts of both monk and hare with a bright joy and love. It was written that God was magnanimous towards nonbelievers. Yeshua had said so: "*In my father's house there are many mansions.* "Here and in this moment it was so.

The sea roads from North Africa to Eriu and the Britannic Isles were ancient well-travelled paths since the time of the pharaohs. These Berber sailors knew the roads well and had many folk memories from their ancestors of epic voyages to the northern isles. Igider did not use the astrolabos given to him by His Holiness, the Patriarch and beloved of master sailors throughout the Mediterranean. It was used to navigate a path plotting the sun, moon and stars. Igider knew the roads well and steered by the stars and the sea birds. Since he was a boy the birds had spoken to him as they flew beside his vessel. It was they who gave him the name "Eagle". The great gull, the little tern, the even smaller swift, the cormorant, the goose, the great heron, even the sea eagle spoke with Igider and gave him the wisdom of the sea. He fed them scraps of freshly caught fish as they perched on his deck and talked. They told him of the weather to come from the west and he took their counsel. They also told him of unseen vessels, their business and settings.

Now with Isis guarding his vessel little could go wrong, Igider reasoned. But for amusement and to reassure his superstitious crew, he frequently asked the lady to sit with him as he steered the vessel and talked with the sea birds. It seemed that more than the birds, Melania's presence at the master's side encouraged the crew and gave them energy when fatigue was upon them. No sailor wished to disappoint the goddess. Melania for her part welcomed the friendship of this Berber and was fascinated by what he told her of the sea and its ways.

Igider was proud of his vessel; the fastest in the Patriarch's fleet, proud of his mastery of it and proud of his appointment as her master by the Patriarch.

The vessel he sailed was a newly built Byzantine dromon, of the type famously used by the Emperor Constantine in the Battle of Hellespont and for that reason much loved by the Patriarch. She was a monoreme by design, that is to say she had one row of oarsmen, not three like the large Greek trireme, favoured by Alexander and Pericles. However the big trireme was unstable beyond Mediterranean waters. Like the triremes, the smaller monoremes were war ships not traders. They were low in the water for stability and had a shallow draft with strong hulls suited to ramming or beaching if the need arose. Monoremes with a strong crew of thirty oarsmen on each side could move at speed using oar or sail according to the conditions. For this reason these vessels were suited to the fickle western ocean where the sea and wind would play cruelly with a vessel: at times threatening to overwhelm and at others becalming sailors for days without wind to sail by.

Their vessel still smelt of the new canvas, pine, cedar and fresh pitch above the aroma of stale sailors' sweat. Igider loved the smell of the wood in particular and caressed the broad cedar timbers of her thwarts and decking as he guided her through the warm Mediterranean, the *Great Green* as Berbers knew it. His love of wood came from his youth in Cyrenia working in the forests with his father. He was to have been a woodsman or possibly a house builder but for the birds calling him to sea and far off lands. As a sailor during the winter it was Igider's pleasure to build fine fishing boats for the Berber villagers. Come the spring the Eagle always left with birds on board a grand vessel with an important commission in his tunic.

Igider the Eagle became renowned throughout the *Great Green* as a true master of the sea and the wind. Even though he was not a Christian, he was favoured by the Christian Patriarch in Alexandria who held Igider's seamanship and trustworthiness in high esteem. His Holiness commanded the biggest fleet in the *Great Green* and had given him many senior commands in recent years. Now he gave him the pride of his fleet and trusted him to deliver this emissary monk with precious scrolls to the Britannic Isles and under great secrecy.

The rhythm of the sea took over their lives as they journeyed west along the North African coast towards the Pillars of Hercules and from there out into the western ocean and north to Eriu. On days when the wind dropped, Igider ordered the sails lashed and the oarsmen bent their backs over their benches. A new rhythm took over as the vessel responded to human energy: a deep drum beat kept the oarsmen in time. The oars of all sixty men sliced through the sea as one.

Cormac found the powerful rhythm deeply soothing as it vibrated through the vessel. He prayed and sung the psalms he had first learnt as a boy in Killabuonia, but he departed from strict practice and sung these in rhythm with the vessel much as he had done with his father and his uncle when they fished in the bay and took supplies to the holy brothers on the Skellig. He even broke off at times to sing some fishermen's songs that his father had taught him. The songs told of a fisherman's love for the fish and the sea that held them, for the sky and the rocks and of course for the wife who awaited his return. He sang the words of his favourite poet, Amairgin:

> I am the wind that breathes upon the sea
> I am the wave of the ocean
> I am the murmur of the billows
> I am the ox of the seven combats
> I am the vulture upon the rocks
> I am a beam of the sun
> I am the fairest plants
> I am a wild boar in valour
> I am a salmon in the water
> I am a lake in the plain
> I am a word of science
> I am the point of the lance in battle
> I am the God who created in the head the fire
> Who is it who throws light into the meeting on the mountain?
> Who announces the ages of the moon?
> Who teaches the place where couches the sun, if not I?

Often when Cormac sang, the three swifts would land on the stern guardrail at his back and listen with their heads cocked to one side. The meditative rhythm transported Cormac back in his mind's eye to that time of careless youth in Eriu. There was food aplenty in those days and fun too in the fields and on the beaches and in the sea. He recalled his child's curiosity at his first encounter with Coptic monks. It was on the Skellig. He remembered their gaunt brown faces and bony hands as they reached down from a crag to snatch the supplies that his father and his uncle had brought them. They said little in their strange tongue except for:

"Bless yez both, Aduar and Lorchan, and the child. We pray for yer safe return. Go with God."

Cormac's father waved at them, but he said nothing in return. The Copts had little of the language of Eriu. He and his brother were concerned with saving themselves and their small boat from being dashed on the rocks of the skellig by the swell of the deep sea. They took such risks in their service to the gods, Christian and Celt. Manannan, the Celtic sea god was very powerful. They believed a grateful Manannan mac Lir would bring them good catches of fish and through his gratitude Manannan's daughter Aine, the goddess of Love, Summer, Wealth and Sovereignty, would keep their soil fertile. For many years this had proved to be so.

But Manannan was a trickster and his daughter was cruelly abused. So one year the summer never came, the crops failed and there was famine. Then in the second year of sunless skies the vengeful Balor brought the yellow plague to the Celts. Many were taken.

Cormac's family were every one plucked from the earth by the plague and the famine. Out of a family of eight brothers and sisters only Cormac now walked the earth and he the eldest too. Cormac's beautiful wife Moninna was taken in the flower of her womanhood with her belly full of child along with their two bright sons, Ternoc and Etgal.

It was the Christian God and men like Crimthainn in the monasteries that had saved the country from complete destruction. Some said it was the old ways that had cursed the land, that the old gods had lost their way. Some believed that Lugh would once again defeat Balor and order would be restored. Others that it was a judgement on the fighting and killing between the tuatha, the clans. Few knew for sure. It was in these dark times that abbots, Crimthainn among them, told the people of Yeshua and gave others belief in His salvation. It was the abbots who were clear that Yeshua would save the land and its people. Their belief was infectious. They called the people to the monasteries. People sought sanctuary for practical reasons too, for food and safety as well as the reassuring word of Yeshua. In time the people were saved and the land was restored and so the monasteries swelled with monks and sisters.

Cormac had no sense of what it would be like on his return. He had heard from other pilgrims that Crimthainn was still walking the land, saving many souls along with his uncle Earnan and cousin Fiachrach. So too were many other great men and women too: Brendan of Birr, Íte of Killeedy, Brendan of Clonfert, Comgall of Bangor and Senan of Scattery. They said that the sun had returned, the crops grew and the sickness healed.

But back in those days of dark and sorrow it was not a land Cormac believed he could any longer find peace with. Soon after he was ordained by Aba Crimthainn in Durrow, Cormac left for Gaul to find martyrdom. If not a martyr's death followed by everlasting life, then redemption and resurrection in this life. In truth it was guilt that had driven Cormac to leave his home and his land: guilt and shame that he had lived and failed in his sacred duty to protect his loved ones.

But Aba Crimthainn and Lord Yeshua spoke reassuringly to Cormac in Durrow and Yeshua again in Gaul calling him to the desert to be healed, to be made whole and to find God. In those days Cormac had thirty years on this earth. Now he was returning with fifty-five years on his life but with a lightness of being and a spiritual strength given to those touched by Yeshua, chosen to bring sacred scrolls to the land of his birth. He prayed daily to Yeshua to give him the strength needed for this task in Eriu, a land of many shadows for one grown accustomed to the light of the desert.

They passed the coast of Sicilia with Carthage to the west and sailed on without event under cloudless skies into the Berber Sea. On the thirtieth day both vessels anchored in a small sandy bay on the North African coast of Mauretania, then on a signal from Igider's vessel small skiffs set out from the shore towards them. Anxiously Melania asked Igider for an explanation.

"These are my tribesmen, lady" he said proudly. "They bring food and water for our journey through Western Ocean."

None were allowed to leave the vessels and travel ashore. The second guard vessel put soldiers on board to ensure no one left or talked to those provisioning the vessels. Igider quietly threatened that any man revealing their destination to outsiders would have his tongue cut out. He then apologised to the lady Melania for his rough talk and reassured her that her tongue was safe.

The provisioning was necessary before they passed through the Pillars of Hercules and into the western ocean. The land of Mauretania was judged to be safe by the Church of Alexandria and beyond the reach of the Bishop of Rome. The ports on the coast of Hispania would have been a natural choice on such a journey, but foolhardy in the extreme under the circumstances. Hispania under the Visigoths was now loyal to the Roman church and the Visigoths would be pleased to plunder the Patriarch's vessels.

After thirty days of continuous motion on the open sea it was refreshing to feel the vessel at rest in calm waters. The group sat below the stern deck in the shade to eat some dried fruit and biscuit and to enjoy the restfulness of not having to be braced against the motion of the vessel. Cormac viewed his companions to check on their well-being after a month at sea.

The lady Melania's fair skin was now ruddy and weather beaten, her hair stiff with sea salt and bleached by the sun, but she seemed well and at ease with her challenging surroundings.

Zachariah's coat was like the lady's hair, bleached and thick with salt. His ears had been troubled with heat blisters, but a regular application of oil gave him relief. The hare was not at ease on the open water and spent much of his time dozing in a basket under cover in the stern cabin.

Buckets of fresh water were brought on board for them to wash off the salt. Igider was mindful of their comfort; especially Melania's whom he had allowed to make use of his cabin for her ablutions.

The young monk with the vow of silence, Bartholomew, continued to be detached. He rarely communicated with the others, except at times to indicate his thirst or hunger. Cormac had no desire to tempt the young monk into speech. He knew the importance of silence to the soul.

"How are you, my friends?" asked Cormac as they ate. "I must know how each of you is after one month at sea."

They remained silent, intent on eating their food.

Cormac continued, "The Eagle tells me that with a fair wind we will reach Eriu after another month. That will be at the time of the festival of Beltaine. The land will be in full bloom."

Still there was silence. Then the lady spoke with a smile: "I hear this is a Celtic fertility festival, brother where people jump naked through fire to be cleansed and fairies walk the land."

"It is true that changelings are abroad and the earth is most fertile" admitted Cormac, not wishing to be drawn into all the pagan practices of Beltaine.

"Women too are fertile at Beltaine. I hear there is much coupling at this time," smirked Melania keeping her eyes cast downward on the bowl of food. She could sense Cormac's discomfort.

"It is said that any child conceived at Beltaine is most blessed. I was myself conceived at this time" said Cormac maintaining an air of detachment, pretending not to notice Melania's teasing. He had encountered her provocations before.

"So you believe in the power of the old gods, brother," teased Melania.

"It is not a question of belief, sister. It is the cycle of nature over which God rules supreme," said Cormac not rising to her bait.

"I thought your St Paul and Augustine of Hippo taught that the act of procreation is sinful and that children are born into the world full of sin," continued Melania.

"Ah! You wish to engage me in theology lady just like the old days," laughed Cormac unable to maintain his sober demeanour.

Melania too laughed as she recalled the scenes of such debate in the agora with Cormac and her father.

"Paul and Augustine were fools!" Zachariah declared abruptly.

"Why so, Master Hare?" asked Melania in all seriousness for she would not tease the hare.

Before Zachariah could respond Cormac interrupted, holding up a sun burnt hand he said, "Friends this is not a time for debate on such matters. We must measure our situation. How is each of you in soul and body?"

"Well," said Melania simply. "Once I have washed the sea off."

Cormac looked to Zachariah, "Tolerable, monk," the hare responded. "I am not a sailor, as you know,"

"Indeed, but your soul and body, hare?"

"They are in harmony, monk," answered Zachariah.

"Brother Bartholomew, we do not wish to interfere with your vow of silence. Nod if your soul and body are well; shake your head if they are not."

Bartholomew shook his head and pointed to his head and then his tongue.

"Are you troubled in your vow of silence, bother?" asked Cormac with concern.

Bartholomew nodded.

"It's not *his* vow of silence, monk," interjected Zachariah.

"How is this so?"

"It is imposed by the Patriarch" answered Zachariah.

"He has taken a vow of silence, nevertheless."

"It's simple. He translated the scrolls we are carrying. He knows what is written on them. He carries the secret, does this one," said Zachariah by way of explanation for the lady Melania.

Bartholomew glared nervously at Zachariah and looked about him to see if many others had heard. He was obviously still very afraid for his safety since being brought on board the vessel. He was very aware that there were those who would break his vow of silence with torture.

"Be quiet, hare" hissed Cormac. "You will endanger Brother Bartholomew and all of us."

"Ignorance will endanger us, monk, not the truth. If this one could speak he could tell us what it is we are carrying to Prince Colum Cille and we would not be travelling blind."

"Master Zachariah, can you not see what is on these scrolls?" asked Melania.

"No, lady. There is a very powerful veil cast about them. Even I cannot see through it," answered Zachariah.

"Who has put such a veil there?" asked Melania.

"Why, the Lord Yeshua himself, lady," said Zachariah simply.

The group remained silent for a while. They did not question Zachariah's views. But Bartholomew looked intently at the hare and from him to the lady and the monk, eating quietly while this news was digested. Only Bartholomew did not eat.

Presently Cormac smiled kindly at the nervous young monk, "I will ask the Eagle for some scroll and quill. I found writing a great comfort while on silent retreat."

"Surely writing would be difficult on a seagoing vessel, brother," enquired Melania.

Cormac considered. "I have never attempted it. It would be troublesome. It is true. I will ask the Eagle for slate & chalk. He may be able to get some from shore before we leave. We will also use the opportunity to learn the language of Eriu. It is important that you can communicate in some fashion. The language is very different from Greek and Latin, but I will give you enough words." He quickly left the group to speak with Igider.

Zachariah shook his head in disbelief. "He takes a very simple view of matters, our brother. He may expect you to write out the Psalms on slate in his native tongue before we disembark," he said looking at Bartholomew who closed his eyes to avoid further engagement.

The lady Melania smiled. "Brother Bartholomew, you can use the slate to pass messages to us," she said to encourage the young monk. Zachariah began to think the lady shared the same simple approach to matters.

"It is arranged," said Cormac returning from Igider and smiling at Bartholomew. "Be not concerned brother. You are under Yeshua's protection as are all of us along with these holy scrolls. God hear our prayer." Cormac looked skyward and held his hands open to heaven.

"Amen," said Zachariah earnestly.

"The peace of Isis is upon us," said Melania quietly.

"Soon we will sail through the Pillars of Hercules and out into the western ocean," said Cormac reflectively as he ate a final biscuit.

"Have you sailed this western ocean, brother?" asked Melania.

"I have not, sister. The Eagle tells me it can be a rough passage, very different from the *Great Green*," said Cormac pointing to Igider. "He has been told by the great sea birds – the albatross and the great gull, that the weather in the west is storm driven at the moment, but that it will ease as we travel north. So we must be prepared for some challenges. The Eagle is an experienced master in the western ocean. As are his crew. We are in good hands and of course the Lord Yeshua will guide us safely to our destination."

It was dusk as the provisioning was completed including the slate tablets and chalk as promised for Brother Bartholomew. The vessels immediately weighed anchor and left the sanctuary of the small bay for the open sea in the gathering gloom. They could not risk spending even one night in the bay. Igider's instructions were not to overnight anywhere until they had reached Eriu. Vessels at anchor in the dark were an easy prey for stealthy brigands.

It was indeed true that the Western Ocean was of a different character to the *Great Green*. The waves were the size of sand dunes and moved slowly like great beasts causing the crew to work twice as hard to maintain the vessel's forward motion. For some days they made slow progress along the western coast of Hispania with a strong north-westerly wind threatening to drive them on to the shore and into the hands of the Visigoths.

Even Cormac became ill at ease with the conditions. The huge sky and sea disturbed him much more than the empty desert. In the desert you could stop and rest. The sea was relentless giving no time for peace of mind. To Cormac so used to quiet contemplation this was vexing. He played continuously with several small pebbles he had collected during his peregrinatio. He clasped the relic tightly around his neck and recited quietly the Yeshua Prayer, "*Lord Yeshua the Christos, Son of God, have mercy on us*," over and over again. Brother Bartholomew watched him intently from within his silence and appeared to be silently joining Cormac in the meditation.

On the fortieth day Cormac's meditation was disturbed by shouting from the crew. Igider came over to them pointing at the eastern horizon. There on a promontory of land was a huge lighthouse similar to the Great Lighthouse of Alexandria.

"It is the Tower of Hercules, my friends. Due north of this is our destination, Eriu," Igider said as he gesticulated to the north. "The ancients used it to find your island. It is good. But first we must escape these devils." He pointed at the huge dark cloud

approaching from the north, darkening the whole sky. "And him."
He pointed at a vessel coming from the coast towards them.

Igider swore in *Maghreb*. "We cannot run in this wind. Our guard
vessel will deal with this fellow," he said pointing to their support
vessel which had already turned into the approaching storm to
confront the stranger from the shore. Soon it was lost in the
growing swell and neither vessel could be seen.

Igider ordered the sails lowered and made fast. He cast a sea
anchor off the stern of the vessel. The sea anchor was a heavy
canvas bag which when filled with water dragged behind the
vessel, slowed it down and provided much needed stability in the
heavy seas. He told Cormac and the others to go to the lower deck
and strap themselves in securely or they would be swept overboard.

"The Bishop of Rome, he sends this devil to us. Soon the sea will
boil. Get ready all of you." Turning to Cormac, Igider shouted,
"Father, take care of the lady."

In his desperation Cormac reached out and grabbed Melania as the
vessel heeled wildly straining on the sea anchor. It was the first
time Cormac had touched a woman since he buried his wife in Eriu
many years before. Such contact was forbidden for monks. He felt
the tenderness of her, so different from the roughness of men.
Monk and priestess noticed the sharp pulse that shot between them,
but neither reacted to it. The needs of the moment were driving
them, for that there would be no apology.

"Brother, I thank you but I must be where Poseidon and Isis can
see me to save our vessel," she broke free and ran half stumbling to
the main mast where she asked Igider to bind her to it with heavy
rope. Igider did so and checked the binding carefully. Cormac
blessed the lady and went below praying for her. He tied
Bartholomew and himself to a wooden stanchion. Zachariah leapt
into a barrel that was tied to the stern mast holding heavy ropes.

"Hold fast all of you and pray to God for us all," shouted Cormac.

Melania proclaimed at the top of her voice to the gathering storm
from the base of the mast:

> "*Isis, who was and is and shall ever be daughter of the earth
> and sky,*

I honour you and sing your praises. Glorious goddess of magic and light, I open my heart to your mysteries. Protect us all,"

This was heard on the wind by a passing seabird that altered course and landed on the vessel before the lady like a tame house bird. This reassured Igider and his crew greatly. They recognised the sign at once, grabbed the bird and swiftly sacrificed it to the gods, smearing its blood on the vessel.

None of this was seen or heard by Cormac on the lower deck who would have protested such slaughter. He still clasped the holy relic tightly and prayed that the approaching vessel was not from the Bishop of Rome carrying the Nubean emissary, Augustine. All day and all the night Cormac recited psalms and Melania made her pleas to Poseidon and Isis. The vessel rolled wildly but was held. By whom it was hard to tell: God, Poseidon, Isis or by the sea anchor.

As dawn broke with a weak sun all were exhausted. Igider was first to speak:

"The vessel, where is she?" he said quietly.

The support vessel carrying the protective cohort of soldiers and archers was not to be seen. All day Igider scanned the surrounding sea mumbling to himself. They waited with their sea anchor still in place, but no ship appeared. Cormac prayed for the souls of the soldiers and crew.

By mid-afternoon with a freshening southerly breeze Igider gave the order to ship the sea anchor and make way. Such a breeze would carry them all the way to Eriu if fortune smiled on them.

So it did. It blew for a week. As each day passed they could see why Igider was known as the eagle. Their vessel flew through the waves on the southerly breeze guided by Igider as if he was riding the back of a giant eagle, joyous in his element. This joy was felt by all on board and the fears of what had happened to their support vessel and the pursuing craft subsided in their bubbling wake.

On the fiftieth day a shout was heard from the top of the mast:

"Eriu! Eriu!"

Cormac fell to his knees and gave thanks. As he did so, three little swifts landed on the railing beside him. He smiled at them and as they had done in Alexandria, they smiled back.

BOOK TWO

XII: Arrival

With his eyes closed Cormac could smell the land beyond the wide estuary as Igider eased the vessel onwards. He could smell his birth home. The scents reached inside him, stirred his guts and made his heart quicken and his chest fill. They were scents of moist green grasses, the pungent odours of the damp soil freshly dug, the warm dryness of the beach and the bitter saltiness of the glistening kelp mixed with the fragrance of the heather from the hills. Even the sea smelt as it did when as a boy he fished with his brothers, his father and his uncles. Now his mouth watered as his stomach looked forward to the cooked fish on the evening fire. Yet his nostrils instinctively searched the airs for another smell: one that had pursued his leaving of Eriu as a young monk. He was like a nervous stag testing the air for the source of an old threat. It was a smell that had masked all others, sickly and heavy. It travelled from hillside to shore from field to home where it hung like a stain drenching the people in the foulness of plague and then famine. The smells that had nurtured him as a boy and defined him as a man, giving meaning and continuity to the tuatha were bleached from the land by death. When the old smells left the land taking all he knew, Cormac set off to find what he had lost.

The plague they call the Justinian plague had come out of Constantinople leaving devastation in its wake. At the end of the plague's reach in Eriu it was accompanied by crop failure over three summers and a consequent famine. The people turned to the Christian God in their desperation. Leaders like Crimthainn or Colum Cille, as the world came to know him, heard the cry of the people.

It is true that Crimthainn brought the Christian God to heal the land and to save its people. Like many, Cormac had sought his guidance and reassurance. But the newly ordained Brother Cormac could not find it in himself to remain at Crimthainn's side. He felt impelled to live as an itinerant monk and to find a wholesome land in which to be at peace with the Christian God. Crimthainn did not reproach Cormac for leaving his people.

"Ye are being called, brother. I can hear the call even if ye cannot. One day soon ye will hear its voice it and understand why you left," Crimthainn told Cormac as he prayed with him in the monastery of Durrow. The great Crimthainn had the second sight and God spoke to him. "Soon I too will be called to leave this land. But we will meet again, brother. Our work together is not done. Now go! We both have much to do in the years ahead"

Those words of Crimthainn still rang in Cormac's ears.

First Cormac travelled to Gaul where the plague was all around and the people in dreadful torment. To his horror he discovered that he had journeyed towards the awfulness, not away from it. He learnt that the plague had travelled through Gaul from the east and on to Eriu in the west. One day in great despair and surrounded by death, Cormac heard the confession of a dying Frankish monk in a monastery by a great fast flowing river.

"Confront the pain and with that the illusion of death, my brother," said the old monk. "Understand its lessons and become its partner in life, just as Yeshua had done. Let go of all attachment to your own comfort and safety. Only in this way can you transcend the pain of mortal existence, understand the mind of the divine and then serve Him and all his creation."

So Cormac abandoned fear and surrendered to the needs of the people. He journeyed south into the land of the Ostrogoth ministering to the sick and the dying as he went. In time he understood the plague and with that came an understanding of the mind of the divine. It was at this time he met Zachariah. It was not until he took ship with Zachariah in Brundisium for Africa that the odour of death left his nostrils and Cormac at last felt his soul break free on the waves, cleansed and free. Later in the desert he learnt in a vision by the well that it was Lord Yeshua who had spoken to him in Gaul in the form of the old monk.

Now he had come full circle back to the land of his birth and with a mission that would bring him back to his old teacher, Crimthainn, just as he had foretold a lifetime ago.

As he smelt the freshening airs from the approaching shore Cormac detected none of the old foulness. The land had indeed been cleansed. Opening his eyes he gave loud thanks to the broad sky, to God and also to Crimthainn. Looking around he could see the closeness of the land on either side. Ahead of them was the island in middle of the estuary. It was as Igider had told him. They were in the mouth of the great river Sionann and the island ahead was Inish Cathaig. Its high tower was an unmistakable landmark for Igider to find.

Cormac's companions saw his joy and felt it too. The sun was high in a blue sky, the cool wind was fresh from the land and the land seemed to beckon to them.

It was Zachariah who spoke first: "Is this what your birth land does to you, monk? Where is the desert father of quiet contemplation?" he teased.

"He is before you, hare, as always. Desert fathers rejoice in a land reborn," said Cormac.

Zachariah leapt onto the cabin roof the get a better view.

"That is Inish Cathaig with the high tower of the monastery of Senan" advised Cormac pointing to the land. "We are to land there. Senan is a great monk like Crimthainn. He is sure to help us."

"It will be good to feel the land beneath my feet again, in the company of a great monk or no," replied Zachariah.

Melania beamed at Cormac, delighting in his pleasure.

"The land feeds you, my brother. We are at our journey's end. I am happy that you are come home," said the lady Melania. She pulled her cloak about her in the cool northern air. "By Neptune, it is cold. Will it stay like this?"

"It is early spring, lady. Soon the air will warm. The monastery will have a fire for us. It is a tradition of hospitality in my land," said Cormac reassuringly.

The young monk Bartholomew remained silent. His vow of silence weighed heavily upon him. The sea voyage had also taken its toll and his health was failing. His companions worried for his welfare.

"Come Brother Bartholomew and see the land," said Cormac to encourage the boy.

Bartholomew shuffled over to the side railings of the vessel beside Cormac to see what lay ahead.

"Here is our destiny, brother. Here we will do God's work. All of us,"

The young monk smiled weakly to Cormac, not wishing to be churlish to the joyous monk.

"Look a boat comes to greet us!" shouted Zachariah from his vantage point. A small craft rowed by three men had set out from the island. It was long and low in the water, moving swiftly towards them.

Igider shouted: "You are home, Father Cormac, you are home! Look they come to greet you. Are they your brothers?"

"They are not my blood brothers. All my blood brothers passed on many years ago," replied Cormac quietly. "But these will be my brothers in Yeshua now."

"That is good. Come let us be ready to disembark you all," said Igider as the sails were dropped and the oarsmen braked the vessel to a standstill.

As the craft came along side Cormac spoke his native tongue to the rowers. He spoke it like a foreigner being many years unpractised. But it was enough to explain they had travelled far and were to meet with Father Senan. The rowers threw a cross of St Brigit onto the vessel as a greeting. Brother Bartholomew picked it up and examined it.

"My friends, it is a sad day that we must leave you," said Igider. "I was told to tell you that this man will meet you here and take you onwards. I cannot say his name," he pointed to a name on a piece of parchment.

"Tocca mac Aedo," read Cormac.

"Do you know him?"

"No, but I understand he is a merchant who trades with the Patriarchy and will help us," said Cormac.

Igider drew Cormac to one side.

"Be careful, father. The Bishop of Rome wants what you carry," he said pointing to the leather bag now around Cormac's shoulders. "I believe he has taken our support vessel." Igider glanced back at

145

the horizon. Their support vessel had never reappeared after turning back to challenge the approaching vessel off the Tower of Hercules, but neither had any vessel followed them since.

"We will be careful, Master Igider," said Cormac. He prayed silently that they would find Crimthainn quickly before Rome's emissary caught up with them. "You too must have a care on the return journey."

"We are accustomed to danger, father, but you?" Then with a big smile he pointed to the lady Melania. "Well, you have also the Goddess Isis," he said "She is an angel, father. Take care of her. She has protected us all during this voyage. She will protect you now. I love this woman like a......like a sister. She would be the only reason I would not go to sea again, but stay close to her."

Cormac realised Igider was tearful as he regarded Melania.

"We all love the lady, Igider. We love you too for bringing us safely to Eriu. You are, as I was told, a great sailor. The Holy Father chooses wisely. Thank you, my brother. You have served God and his Church well," said Cormac as he embraced the big man.

Igider kissed Cormac's cheeks repeatedly much to Cormac's embarrassment. Igider laughed at the monk's discomfort.

"Why you get red in the face, Father? I hear men in your country suck each other's breasts," he laughed.

"That is true. It is an old tradition of the tuatha," admitted Cormac.

"We have made good time on the voyage. No one has followed us by sea. So you are ahead of Rome, father. May you move swiftly over this land to your destination," said Igider.

Cormac agreed but wondered where he would find Crimthainn. He hoped most of Eriu would know the whereabouts of the great abbot. Yet he was not one known to stay still for long. Where Crimthainn was last week may not be where he is today. It was Cormac's fervent prayer that with maturity the abbot would have slowed down and could be easily located.

As the time came to leave the vessel all the crew had gathered on the upper deck to see them off. Igider was not alone in crying freely as they saw the lady lowered to the boat. She stood in the small craft and raised her arms to them:

"Isis is with you on your journey home, my sailors!" she shouted and the sailors cheered in joy.

With that the small boat set off for the island. Melania tried to remain standing with her arms outstretched to the sailors, but it was impossible as the boat rocked in the swell. Cormac had to catch her as she almost fell overboard. Instead the lady sat at the stern with her arms reaching towards the watching sailors. They returned her gesture of affection until Melania safely reached the island. She had never known the love and respect of such men and it had touched her deeply. Her tears flowed freely and fell on the land of Eriu as they stepped ashore.

XIII: Inish Cathaig

The land around was low, providing clear views on all sides of the island and the estuary beyond to the mainland. The monastery was built close to the shore and near the landing site where the newly arrived strangers had just disembarked. As the group walked towards the monastery they found their legs unsteady beneath them, accustomed as they had been to the perpetual swaying of their vessel these past weeks. Cormac had to lean on his staff to steady himself and Zachariah fell over more than once, much to his annoyance.

"If there are hares on this island they must be laughing at me!" he exclaimed.

"They will conclude that golden hares are strange fellows who find the act of walking a straight line somewhat difficult," laughed Cormac. The levity while it vexed Zachariah helped release the tension they all felt in the moment of finally arriving in Eriu to begin their mission on land.

To gather their senses they stood still for a while and watched Igider sail away from them back to Alexandria with the huge red sails aloft. Three swifts flying overhead swooped down close to them almost touching Cormac's red head and flew off over the estuary towards land. Cormac watched them go and then each said a quiet prayer for Igider the Eagle and his good sailors who had become their family and friends these weeks at sea.

The monastery was made up of a number of small roundhouses of wattle and thatch grouped around a rectangular wooden church. Behind this was a tall stone-built tower. This structure was familiar to Cormac as such towers were built in Egypt to anchor divine energy to the earth close to monasteries and also to act as a food store and a refuge when under attack. They were guided to the church by their boatmen to give thanks for their safe arrival, all except for the lady Melania who was taken by boat to a crannog supporting another roundhouse in a sheltered harbour close to the shore. The founding father of the monastery, the ancient Aba Senan, forbade women on the island. With the crannog below low tide it could be argued that the women were not on the island. The seclusion suited Melania who gladly set about washing two months of the sea from her and resting her tired bones.

As he knelt in the dark of the church, Cormac could feel the profound change in his surroundings seep into his being. All was quiet and still now, unlike the bright light and constant motion and sound of the vessel on the western ocean. Through this quiet he could feel the nearness of the Holy Spirit. He sighed deeply in a profound relief and gave thanks for this moment and for his safe return to his homeland.

"Ye are welcome among the land of the free people, Brother Cormac. We are honoured with yer presence among us here on Inish Cathaig," whispered the elderly Aba Senan in the broad tongue of the people of *Iarmummu* while he lay on a wooden bench holding onto Cormac's hand. He was the comarba or founder of the community of monks on the island. In his other hand Aba Senan held the letter of introduction from the Patriarch.

"It is an honour to be here with you, Aba Senan," responded Cormac bowing his head and smiling to the revered old monk.

As he had asked, Cormac was alone with Aba Senan in his small hut. The abbot's living quarters were set beside the church in the middle of the enclosure on a small rise of land near the shore. It was a roundhouse made of hazel wattle and thatch. There was no fireplace. The only furniture was a wooden table and two stools and the only concession to comfort was a woollen blanket for the elderly monk.

"The desert fathers have been our inspiration in this place. Some have passed through here on pilgrimage north. Ye are privileged to be one of their number, brother" Senan said.

"I am, father."

"Yez have come far and in great haste. I am honoured to have this letter from the Holy Father in Alexandria. But I cannot read any more, my eyes see only God's beauty and not the work of men. The letter has been read to me. We are bound by God to help ye on your holy mission, brother and are humbled to be chosen by the Holy Father."

A blackbird sang outside the door and Senan stopped to listen, before returning his attention to Cormac.

"Yez need to find Colum Cille? That's a task and no mistake. We hear he is exiled to the far north beyond Eriu where he has a large community on an island," said Aba Senan.

"Exiled?!"

"Yes. It was his choice I hear. We involve ourselves in no gossip here. So ye will not have it from me. But he is beyond Eriu. That much I can say. He copies my island practice, does the noble prince," he chuckled to himself and then wheezed, lying back down on his bench.

Cormac studied the old abbot's lined face. It was weathered from many winters on Inish Cathaig. The eyes still sparkled with a flame and a humour, while his body was old and weak after years of denial.

"I must ask, father, about the plague and the famine. When I left Eriu many years ago the land and the people were ravaged by it. Is it still with us?" asked Cormac.

"No, brother, its ravagings left us many years ago. The land and the people are restored, thanks be to God and our work here and throughout the land. That's one challenge yez will not have to face on your mission," said Aba Senan. Turning to the letter from the Patriarch he continued, "This Tocca mac Aedo that was to meet yez is not here. He is a merchant that often passes through here and supports us, but we have not seen him since Eastertime," said Aba Senan.

"Where is he, father? I must find him," asked Cormac.

"That I cannot say. Merchants' business is not my affair, brother."

The old man saw the concern on Cormac's face.

"I know ye have this burden, brother and we must help ye," Aba Senan said relenting. "Ask Brother Mael to come in. He stands outside and knows the affairs of men in *Iarmummu* and even beyond."

Brother Mael was the Aba's close confidante. He was a much younger man and dealt with the more worldly aspects of the community.

"Brother," said Aba Senan to Brother Mael. "Tell us. Where is that merchant, mac Aedo?"

"Tocca mac Aedo has fallen foul of King Tigernaig and is in hiding, aba" replied Brother Mael.

"Hiding? Hiding where?" asked the aba.

"We learn that he has been given sanctuary by his tuath, the *Maic Brocc* near the mouth of the great river, aba"

"Tigernaig is a ruthless young scalpeen, brother. I have had a few quarrels with him myself, but he leaves us alone. Just as well or I'd bring the wrath of the heavens down upon is head!" exclaimed the old man.

"We will go to this merchant in his hiding place, then," said Cormac.

Brother Mael looked from his aba to Cormac. Senan shook his shaggy grey head.

"We would not advise travelling there on your own, father. Not with the party ye have. The *Maic Brocc* are at war with the king" said Brother Mael to Cormac and turning to Aba Senan, "With your permission, aba, I would suggest we send someone to guide Father Cormac to Tocca," said Brother Mael.

"Yes that is wise, brother. We must assist the brother with his holy mission as the Patriarch has asked us," said Aba Senan.

Emboldened with his aba's permission Brother Mael continued speaking directly to Cormac.

"Brother Eochu is a *Maic Brocc*, knows the land and seeks martyrdom. He could guide yez."

"Ye forget Brother Eochu is doing penance for eating too much. He sleeps on a bed of nettles every night for forty nights. I doubt if he could make the journey in his present condition, brother. Ye must find a more able bodied soul," said Aba Senan.

"Ah yes, aba. I forgot, forgive me" said Brother Mael. He thought for a moment. "There is another here who is close kin to the *Maic Brocc* and knows the land better than most."

"Who is that, brother?" asked Aba Senan.

Brother Mael swallowed hard and appeared nervous.

"Why the boy, Fiacc, aba," he said.

"Is he still with us!? I thought he had left to cause trouble elsewhere. Yez know my views on boys who are not bound to us, Brother Mael. He caused great confusion with the sheep. He has not the makings of a monk or a shepherd either," said Aba Senan.

"Forgive me, Aba. I believed ye knew he was still here" said Brother Mael. Turning to Cormac he said, "This boy was rescued from the estuary by the brothers. He was very weak from nearly drowning and we have restored him to health now."

"Can we burden our brother with this boy?" asked Aba Senan.

"I think we can, father. The boy knows *Iarmummu* better than many his age and he has travelled widely. He knows the paths and the *Maic Brocc*."

"You find yourself, a desert father, in strange company on this holy mission, brother?" mused Aba Senan regarding Cormac quizzically aware of his strange band. "Now we are adding to it with this half drowned wayward boy."

"God has chosen to challenge us, Aba. I cannot deny it. But neither can we refuse His test," said Cormac growing accustomed to the attention his strange band attracted from churchmen.

Aba Senan nodded in agreement. Brother Mael used the moment to press home his proposal.

"The boy is now strong and fit and wants to leave here. He can guide ye to his kin folk and the merchant Tocca" he said to Cormac looking nervously sideways at his aba.

"Rest here for tomorrow is the Sabbath. Then take this boy with yez away from here with our blessing. God go with yez on your mission, Brother Cormac. Brother Mael will make the arrangements. Now it is Espartu. We must go to the church."

Aba Senan spoke again as Brother Mael helped him from his bench.

"When ye meet Prince Colum Cille tell him Senan sends his blessings and tell him Senan has completed the riddle. If he were to visit me I will confide in him. He will know what it is I speak of," the old monk chuckled to himself.

"I will, father" agreed Cormac.

That night Aba Senan died quietly in his sleep.

For Cormac the next day was taken up helping to comfort the monks who had only known the one abbot. The death of their long serving comarba was a heavy blow, but Senan's nephew inherited the role as was the custom. So the mantle of Senan was passed on to his kindred that day.

Brother Mael though was greatly disturbed and sought out Cormac for counsel. They walked together to the west of the island.

"Father I have committed a grave sin," he confessed when they were well away from the community.

"Speak brother and unburden yourself," replied Cormac calmly.

"This boy that we spoke of is not a boy. He is a girl called Bretha" said Brother Mael and saw Cormac's surprise. "Aba Senan would not allow women on the island, yet the girl was close to death. So we cut her hair and dressed her as a boy to deceive our aba. Now he is no more. I cannot confess to him this dreadful sin," said Brother Mael in tears.

"Deceiving your abbot is a serious thing to do, Brother Mael. It must have weighed heavily upon you."

"It has," said brother Mael through sobs. "We sought to save the girl. Aba Senan was a good comarba, but he had strong views and may have forced us to cast the sickly girl adrift and let God decide her fate."

"Was there knowledge of the girl among you, brother?"

"No. There was not. Sinners we may be, but we are not beasts of the field" said Mael emphatically.

Cormac could understand the monks' deceit in order to protect the girl, but such deceit never prospers. It would have been better if they had faced their aba with the truth and trusted the divine. Some abbots, like Senan, believed the presence of women distracted men from worship. They took their guidance on such matters from St Paul and St Augustine, but not all did so. Many also took their guidance from Lord Yeshua who consorted freely with women. In this time there were many nuns living alongside monks in monasteries. Some became abbots like Deirdre of Killeedy and Senan's own sister Imy of Killimer whom Senan helped found a nunnery.

"You would have done well to be honest with your aba, brother. God would have protected the girl" said Cormac. Placing his hand on Mael's chest, "You have a good heart and we all err from the path of truth, brother. We are flesh and we can learn. I hope the girl is grateful to you and to God."

"That's the thing, father, she is a strange child," Mael took in great gulps of air such was his relief at Cormac's words. The deceit had been an awful burden to him. "She is the daughter of Failge Berraide, the *file* and has much of the old magic about her. That's also why we did not wish to cause offense by casting her adrift," whispered Brother Mael for fear of being overheard. The old ways still had a strong hold, even on monks. "I must ask ye now to give me my penance for my deception, father. So my sin can be cleansed from me."

Penance was a tradition developed by the celtic church in Eriu as a means of expunging sin so it was not a burden carried throughout this life and into the next. As a desert father Cormac carried high status with his fellow monks and was in a position to levy penance.

Cormac prayed for a while and then said to Brother Mael: "You will erect a cross here and each day at this hour you and all the monks who carried out this deception of your aba must come to this place and say a prayer for Senan's soul and the successful conclusion of our mission in Eriu for the sake of Lord Yeshua. You will do this for one whole year. In this way will you sin be lifted from your souls."

"Your mission must be very important, father, for such a penance"

"I believe Christendom may depend on it, brother" said Cormac repeating the words of the Patriarch and fixing Brother Mael with a steely look to emphasis the point. "Your penance will perform a great service, not to me, but to the Holy Patriarch in Africa and above all else to Lord Yeshua himself."

"The penance will be done, father," Brother Mael bowed and kissed Cormac's hand.

XIV: Iarmummu

It was early morning when they left Inish Cathaig with a cool mist calming the waters of the estuary. Dolphins played with the boat as the oarsmen made good headway on the incoming tide. Cormac sat at the stern and trailed his hand in the water as he had done in his boyhood. He was glad to be moving towards his goal – finding Crimthainn. Although the location of his old mentor had given him some concern, morning prayers had brought him assurance that the matter was in the hands of God. For now he was content to play with the water and to share in the dolphins' obvious delight in God's creation.

From the boat the 'boy' Fiacc guided the boatmen and soon pointed to a large copse of willow on the southern shore.

"We should land there to find Tocca," he said.

Once on shore and with the boatmen departed for Inish Cathaig, Fiacc let out a squeal of delight.

"Blessed Aine! I am well pleased to be off that monkish place!" he looked around at the group awaiting his instructions as to which way to go. He smiled at this strange band looking to him for help. "Firstly, my friends, I'm a girl, not a boy! If ye have any doubts ye can see!" she held open her tunic for anyone wishing to examine her breasts. No one did. "My name is not Fiacc. It is Bretha, daughter of Failge Berraide," she looked around for a reaction to her father's name and her exposed breasts. There was none. "Well he's a great *file* and I will be one day too."

"We knew you were a girl," said Cormac smiling calmly. "Brother Mael told me. Please cover yourself, child."

This only served to deflate Bretha who adjusted her clothing with a scowl, deflated that neither her announcements nor her breasts had sufficiently impressed or shocked her companions. She noticed the young silent monk, Bartholomew staring at her furtively and stuck her tongue out at him. He immediately looked skyward to avoid the attention of this strange, uninhibited girl. He had never met a girl like her before, but then he had not met many girls since he left his sisters in Jerusalem as a ten year old to take holy orders with the monks in Alexandria.

Bretha was slightly built with tousled red hair, green eyes and quick, confident movements. She wore the clothing of a boy, brown linen tunic, baggy pants and leather boots. In truth she behaved much like a boy. Around her shoulders was a red cloth bag.

With composure restored Cormac in an effort to find common cause with the young woman said, "My cousin was the great *file*, Flann mac Cuilleanain."

Having a close family member as a *file* confirmed a certain social status on the whole family. In a land with little written down the spoken word carried great power. This is why the *filid*, the poet class held such status. They held kindred histories, legends, rituals and even laws in their verse.

At that Bretha's smile returned and she retorted:

> *"You frightened pale sheep,*
> *that ploughmen will dine with*
> *ye famine, grey as grease*
> *from a cracked,legged*
> *brass candlestick"[2]*

"Just so. My cousin also had a fondness for the satirising. But It is an ungodly form," said Cormac.

"Shouldn't we be introduced?" said Zachariah bouncing up to regard the girl more closely. He was intrigued by her.

"Oh my! One of the sacred ones! Which family are ye, master hare?" Bretha asked Zachariah.

"Family, child?" he asked.

"Aye, of the Tuath Dé."

"Oh I am not of them, child. I am Zachariah the prophet from Babylon recently arrived with my friends here from Egypt," said Zachariah.

[2] Translation: Christian Druids, Minahane, p. 59.

"No matter. A talking golden hare is most sacred. Your riddles will do well in *Iarmummu*, Zachariah the Hare from Babylon,"

"What is *Iarmummu*?" asked Zachariah.

"It's where yez are!' said Bretha. "From the great lake in the north to the ocean in the south and in the east as far as the border with the *Laigen* is the Kingdom of *Iarmummu* and Tigernaig is its king." She spat after saying the king's name.

"And what of Eriu?"

"They say Eriu is an idea in men's minds," Bretha shrugged. "I've not been there. I might go one day, when I'm a *file*, and I'll satirise their kings, should they offend me." Bretha giggled.

Melania too was fascinated by the young girl: her language, her appearance and the energy around her. Speaking haltingly in the language of Eriu taught by Cormac, she asked, "What is a *file*, Bretha?"

"A *file* is a *file*. They weave magic with words. They keep the history and ways of our people. Their words have much power to heal or to wound," said Bretha proudly. "My father satirised Tigernaig. That is why Tigernaig is at war with the *Maic Brocc* and the Hen is in hiding. The Hen is what we call Tocca. The Hen did a lot of trade with the king on behalf of the *Maic Brocc*."

"The *file* is a poet in Eriu, lady" said Cormac in further explanation. "Their words carry much force in this land. As Bretha says their words carry great power."

"What did your father write to cause a war?" asked Melania.

"He doesn't write. His words are spoken, memorised and repeated by others. Only the monks write. He said: ' *Ye expulsion of the foot, ye cuckoo's recompense, ye blackbird's disappearance....*"[3]

Cormac held up a hand to stop Bretha in full flow. As a follower of Yeshua he had no liking for the ungodly nature of satirising.

"Why did he do this to your king?"

"Tigernaig stole a great shield belonging to the *Maic Brocc*. It was a shield given them by the Tuath Dé in the old days" said Bretha. "Since my father satirised him Tigernaig has walked with a limp." She giggled.

---

[3] Translation: The Christian Druids, Minahane. P.53.

Cormac pursed his lips. He had hoped for a more auspicious start to their arrival in Eriu. The famine and plague may well have gone, but local wars it seemed had not. He recalled that Eriu had many tuatha or clans who frequently fought over land or a perceived insult of one clan upon another. It is true that the *filid* composed some beautiful verse. Cormac's cousin had been a fine *file*, but many others misused their powers and caused distress. It was said by some that the satirising of the old gods by some *filid* had caused the plague and the famine. He had no wish to be embroiled in the affairs of the *filid*, especially when they had fallen foul of a king.

"Can you take us to meet Tocca mac Aedo?" asked Cormac anxious to be about his business.

"I can. He stays with my father at Mungair, half a day's walk from here" said Bretha. "Why do yez want to meet Tocca?"

"He is contracted to perform a service for us," said Cormac briefly.

"Yez are a strange band," mused Bretha looking round at the four standing on the shore awaiting her direction. "A monk, a sacred hare, a foreign lady and this dumb boy. There is mystery here."

"There is no mystery. We are pilgrims journeying north to meet with followers of the Lord Yeshua there," said Cormac abruptly anxious to allay any suspicions and gossip. He knew the people of *Iarmummu* loved gossip as much as they loved music and fighting.

Bretha looked at them each closely. She sniffed the air like an animal and looked all around at the sky above. She tossed a flat pebble in the air, caught it, examined it, looked at the sky again and said: "Then pilgrims I shall take ye to the Hen. Come."

She set off at a brisk pace with the others following behind on a narrow path between green meadows along the shore. A lightness of spirit came to Cormac as he felt the caress of the cool grasses and smelt the scent the dog roses and elder in the spring air. It was true, Cormac reflected, the famine had left the land. God had cleansed Eriu. Many fields were under cultivation, some with barley and some with flax, others with carrot and cabbage. There were prosperous farming settlements nearby and people working the fields, but Bretha took them past these without stopping to introduce her strange band.

As they went Bretha gathered plants and herbs, placing them in the red linen bag around her neck. She nibbled almost constantly on a variety of plants and berries. She passed some to Zachariah. There were many flavours the hare had not tasted, some bitter, some sweet, some hot on the tongue.

After crossing a small river they turned inland where the morning mist had gathered more thickly. They moved through marshland where Bretha advised them to stick close to the path.

By mid-day they were approaching a high mound of earth with men carrying swords and clubs watching from its wooden ramparts. It was a fort or a *rath* as it is known in Eriu. Bretha shouted a greeting to the men and they waved to her. She took the group through an opening in the *rath* into an enclosure with several roundhouses of different sizes made of wattle and thatch. Smoke curled through the top of each dwelling. Many children ran about as did chickens and geese.

Cormac recoiled at the sight of such young healthy children. They stirred the buried horrors of his boys, healthy and strong one moment, then before the day's end sick and dying in his arms. Children held the potential for such wretched unpredictability. Now he saw that his belief in the healing qualities of the desert had been a sad illusion. The desert had merely shielded him these many years. In that place the only demons were his own and he had mastered them. Yet no child had ever disturbed his quiet contemplation. There were no reminders of his tragic parenthood. Now as he was confronted with so many youthful spirits dancing and shouting all around him, he realised he had merely come full circle in his spiritual journey. He could see that Eriu would continue to test him, plague or no plague. In his mind's eye he saw and even heard his golden haired and rosy cheeked boys calling his name lovingly in the fields; a cry of joy that turned to one of terror as they saw that their father could not save them from doom. Cormac closed his eyes to shut out the awfulness of his failure. It was then that he felt the tug on his mantle.

"Please God, not this," he pleaded quietly.

Opening his eyes he looked down at a child standing at his side. It was a boy slightly older than his own had been, but not yet ten. The boy's face was turned up to Cormac revealing large eyes of dark pools with a gentle focus.

"I am Connor of the Dreams. You are welcome, Father Cormac," the boy began.

"Thank you, Connor of the Dreams. You are kind," replied Cormac with a smile, wondering to himself how the boy knew his name.

"Ye have travelled far in your heart and yer head, father. In my dreams I have seen ye. I know of the pain this land holds for ye."

"How do you know these things, boy?"

With a sudden movement Connor of the Dreams held out his right arm to reveal a stump without a hand.

"Eochu, the great wolf took my hand in the forest and in return gave me the gift of second sight. It was a good trade....."

"I am glad it was, boy."

"....because now I can help ye, Father Cormac."

"How so, child?"

"Yer kindred who passed in the great plague now watch over ye; yer wife, Moninna and yer sons, Ternoc and Etgal as well as yer many brothers and sisters. Ye are dearly loved and well protected. Ye must know this and have faith, Cormac mac Fliande."

The boy's dark eyes held Cormac in a soft, knowing gaze as tears began to form in the monk's eyes.

"God bless you child," whispered Cormac smiling down at the strange boy as he considered what Connor of the Dreams had said. It was clear the boy had the gift.

As if knowing what was on Cormac's tongue to ask, Connor continued, "Firstly, I cannot tell ye how this affair will end. That is forbidden. Know only this, the protection of yer kindred cannot interfere with yer destiny. When it is yer time ye will join them. Secondly yer kindred do not blame ye for their fate. The nature and timing of their passing was written on their souls from birth, as it is on yers. Simply know that ye are loved by them, well protected and that yer kindred live on in Tir Na n'Og."

Before Cormac could respond Connor of the Dreams turned and walked away. He was ignored by the other children as he went. He turned to smile reassuringly and wave with his one good hand at Cormac, before disappearing behind a nearby barn, leaving Cormac to reflect on the strange encounter. As he did so tears of relief fell down his cheeks.

With a smile Zachariah who alone had seen the encounter said to Cormac, "Rejoice, monk, rejoice," and turning, ran off into the nearby woods before the children encircled him. Children were always intent on chasing him or pulling at his ears. So he had learned to avoid their company.

Now instead of chasing Zachariah the children were milling around Bretha. It was clear she was popular with them. She for her part was tender with them.

"Where have you been, cousin Bretha? Where have you been?" they shouted as they gathered around her eager for news of her adventures.

"I was swimming with Uasal the swan and living on an island with some old men until these friends came and brought me home to yez," she said by way of introducing the strange band standing behind her.

"Were the old men the wise ones?" a child asked her.

"Uasal is very wise, the old men less so and quieter."

"So now ye are wise. Will ye make us wise Bretha?"

"Yez are already wise, beautiful ones. What plant is this?" she held up a plant from her bag.

"Devils Claw," they shouted.

"It stops girls bleeding," shouted a boy with a smirk.

"See! Yez are wise too," Bretha said. "Now go! I must speak with my father."

The children scattered.

A man small in stature appeared in the doorway of a large roundhouse. He was gaunt with long grey hair falling down over a purple tunic and a bronze torc around his neck caught the morning light. His face lit up as he saw Bretha.

Bretha waved to him and met his smile.

He took her in his arms and they kissed one another.

"Bretha, my little calf where have ye been? They told me ye were drowned swimming with the swans. I thought the swans had taken ye, like your mother" he said in sorrow.

"No, father. I wasn't drowned. I was swimming with Uasal the swan and her family until the monks pulled me out of the water. Like ye, they thought I was drowning. Have ye been well, father?" Bretha asked gazing with concern at her father's gaunt features.

"I have been worried on many scores, daughter" said Failge Berraide sadly. "First we have this dispute with the king and then I lose my daughter to the swans. It has not been easy. But now ye are back. That is a good sign." He embraced her again and reaching down held her buttocks. "You still have the buttocks of a boy, Bretha. Those will not get you a husband. Did the monks starve you?" he said disapprovingly.

Bretha laughed off her father's concern.

"Their food is meagre. It is better to have a boy's buttocks around the monks, father. They do not take kindly to the presence of women." Bretha turned to the others standing behind her. "These are my friends, father, from the far off land of Egypt, Father Cormac, the lady Melania and Brother Bartholomew and…." She looked around. "Where is Master Zachariah?"

"Ah! He is visiting the woods," said Cormac quickly. "He will be with us presently."

"You are all welcome to Mungair and to the *rath* of the *Maic Brocc*, friends. Thank you for bringing my daughter to me. My name is Failge Berraide," he said as he bowed and whispered to Bretha, "Monks travelling with a woman and a foreign one too! What is this, daughter?"

"She is a high born priestess of a powerful goddess and they are pilgrims travelling north, father," muttered Bretha. "Father Cormac is their leader. He is from Eriu. I sense they are good people who mean no harm. They wish to meet the Hen who they have business with."

"I see" nodded her father reassured. He respected his daughter's judgement in many things since her mother had died when she was but a small child. Failge turned to the group with a smile, "Tocca will be here this evening. He is travelling back from the great lake after some trading. Please come in. My home is yours. There is beer, bread and some barley stew. Please sit." He motioned to chairs covered in deer hide inside his roundhouse. "You can rest here tonight. Bretha will show you to our guest house where you will be comfortable."

Tocca did not arrive that evening, but in the morning as the sun was climbing over the estuary the merchant appeared wearing fine garments which were mud splattered from his journey. He was younger than they expected, heavily built but with a small pointed head and a nose that resembled a hen's beak. In his hair he wore colourful feathers. He had a nervous twitch which made his head bob like a hen's and the nervous energy of one accustomed to trade and to searching for opportunities much like a hen would seek out grubs. Far and wide Tocca mac Aedo was known as Tocca the Hen.

While he discussed affairs with Failge Berraide and the need to recover relations with the king if trade was to improve, Tocca picked at morsels while his head continued to bob. The king had closed the coast to the west and the great road to the east. The *Maic Brocc* were in need of salt for preserving meat and of iron for smelting. Tocca suggested bargaining with the king to recover the shield. Failge was not persuaded. The king had broken the law by taking the shield without the tuath's agreement. The judge had set the honour price of twenty cumals and pronounced that Tigernaid must also return the shield to the tuath. It was known that no king was above the law in Eriu.

Cormac and the others waited patiently for the merchant to finish eating. He noticed that Tocca repeatedly glanced at his leather bag containing the scrolls which never left Cormac's side.

Tocca belched, passed wind, pushed his plate away and turned to Cormac.

"My friends I am honoured to be of service to His Holiness the Patriarch. The *Maic Brocc* have traded successfully with the church in Egypt since my father's days. We trade fine tunics and jewellery for salt from Africa." Tocca the hen showed off his fine red tunic and silver rings. "But this affair with the king has stopped all that. It is a sorry time, my friends. Our trade is much reduced." He stared at the floor, his head bobbing all the while as he spoke.

Looking up he continued, "The Holy Father has honoured this poor merchant. I am to help yez travel onwards from here. Is that so?"

"That is correct, sir" Cormac answered. "We are on important business on behalf of the Patriarch and need to find the Prince Colum Cille as soon as possible."

"Colum Cille?" exclaimed Tocca the Hen and sucked in his cheeks to make a loud clucking noise that made Bretha giggle. "Colum Cille left this land many summers ago. He is on the Island of Aio far to the north of Eriu near Alba. Yez have a long journey ahead, friends." He glanced again at Cormac's bag.

The news of Crimthainn's exile and now his location on this distant island was worrying. Cormac had hoped they could meet in the monastery of Durrow where they had parted many years ago after Cormac's ordination. The monastery was but a few days journey away. A journey to the north of Eriu and then on to another shore was a worrying prospect. The longer they travelled the greater chance had the Bishop of Rome's agents to find them and seize the scrolls.

"Do you know where this island is?" Cormac asked Tocca the Hen.

"I know those who do. It is many days' sail from the coast in the north and there are no vessels like the one ye arrived in, father. These are small open craft."

It was evident the Hen knew much more about them than Cormac would wish.

"Ye will have to journey from here to the fortress of *Dun Sobhairce* on the northern coast. Yez will not be in *Dun Sobhairce* before Samhain. There is a cruel sea on the north in winter. Yez may have to wait the winter out. It may be Beltaine before you reach Aoi," said Tocca the Hen. "There are some on the way who would be curious about such a group as yers and what merchandise ye carry. The land to the north is full of the *fianna* and worse, the *Dibergga*," he said glancing at the bag again and then at the lady Melania. "Yez will need men to protect yez, father. Good men. This will be costly. Can ye pay such men for all those days and nights?"

"God is our true protector, sir" replied Cormac. "But yes we can pay for practical assistance."

"That is good. There are many on yer path north that cannot be trusted. The *Breifne* for one. Only yesterday they tried to cheat me." He spat. "The *Calraige* are at war with the *Argialla*. Who knows about the *Ulaid* and the *Ui Tuirtre*? The alliances keep shifting." Again the Hen made his clucking noise. "Trade is a complex business, father. News of what's what with the tuatha is a valuable commodity."

Tocca the Hen stared at the group, his head all the while bobbing. He looked to Failge Berraide for confirmation.

"What Tocca says is true, friends. A group such as yers will have difficulty over such a distance. Our people are good but there are those like the *fianna* who are brigands" said Failge.

Tocca the Hen then assumed a quiet, more confidential tone, his neck craned towards Cormac so only he would hear.

"Father, I know ye carry a package of great importance for the Patriarch. He has asked me to help ye reach Colum Cille safely. That is all. But Tocca is a wily merchant. That is a scroll bag at your feet and I also know ye are pursued by the Bishop of Rome" he nodded at Cormac to allow the impact of that news to be felt. "I do not wish to know more. This is not in the interest of Tocca. But I would caution ye to consider yer way of proceeding. Such a group as yez is not the way."

"What are you suggesting, master merchant?" asked Cormac directly.

"That ye entrust yer package to my most loyal couriers who for a fee will deliver yer package to Prince Colum Cille in half the time yez will take – if yez ever get there."

"That is impossible. I must go myself. I am responsible for the safety of my companions," said Cormac looking to his worried friends. Even Bretha seemed concerned at what was unfolding for her new companions but being a girl she knew not engage in the discussion.

"Father, Tocca is right" said Failge Berraide. "He is skilled in these matters. His couriers are good men and they travel fast. They know these lands. Let them take yer package to Colum Cille."

"I cannot. I am pledged before God to deliver this by my own hand."

The discussion was brought to a swift conclusion by guards shouting outside in the enclosure.

"The king approaches, the king approaches!"

Tocca the Hen flapped his arms in frustration.

"What direction?" Tocca asked a guard.

"He rides with the sun."

That at least signified that the king came with friendly intent.

Failge Berraide and Tocca the Hen left the roundhouse advising their visitors to stay inside.

Outside warriors from the tuath ran with weapons to the entrance of the *rath* to challenge the king. Tigernaig had arrived with over one hundred warriors in chariots and on horseback. Barely sixty people of the *Maic Brocc* defended the *rath*, some were women and some even young boys. The tuath's own king, Bruidge, was in the north of their lands selling cattle, leaving Failge Berraide as the most senior tuath member to deal with King Tigernaig.

After initial exchanges of threats and insults, Tigernaig asked to meet with Failge Berraide and Tocca mac Aedo. The king held aloft the bronze shield he had stolen from the *Maic Brocc* and declared he wished to trade it. Curiously the Bishop of Emly was also present. Such things were not normally a concern of the Christian church.

Failge and Tocca the Hen agreed to let Tigernaig along with the bishop to enter the *rath* with four stalwarts.

The king strode confidently into the enclosure with his stalwarts and the bishop following behind. He looked far from friendly. The king was short, powerfully built with a long black beard. On one arm he carried the magnificent bronze shield. It was true, he walked with a slight limp as Bretha had said as a result of Faille's satirising. It was not good for a king to show such infirmity.

Tigernaid snorted as he saw his tormentor, Failge the *file*. His dark eyes flashed with anger. In contrast the Bishop of Emly's kept his eyes fixed on the ground before him as he stood beside the king.

Fidelmid Tigernaig was the King of *Iarmummu*, one of the five kingdoms of Eriu. He had been a strong military leader who had conquered the weak *Eoganachta* to gain power. However he was not a good king. A good king must be just and fair in his lawgiving. Tigernaig was not such and many tuatha disliked him for his lack of judgement. His theft of the shield was a case in point. No good king would carry out such a crime upon his own people, particularly on the *Maic Brocc* who were skilled merchants in trade. The theft had caused war and a disruption to essential trade.

Tigernaid threw back his cloak to expose his left breast. It was a custom in Eriu for powerful lords to offer their left breast to be sucked by those seeking protection, provided the lord wished to offer protection. Once done this creates a bond between the two – the protector and the protected. It was seen in many situations as a peace offering and one not to be lightly rejected. No one present took up the king's offer of his exposed breast. None of the *Maic Brocc* sought his protection.

Insulted the king fixed his angry gaze on Failge and Tocca the Hen who stood in the centre of the enclosure with the tuath watching on in interest from a discrete distance.

Finally Tigernaid spoke in a booming voice addressing the entire enclosure: "I am here among yez, *Maic Brocc* because yez are a valued tuath in *Iarmummu*. The tuatha of *Iarmummu* beseeched me to talk with yez to end this bitterness between us." A disbelieving murmur went through the tuath. "I am a humble king who hoped that the *Maic Brocc* would gift this wonderful shield to their king, their protector from the *Eoganachta* and in so doing their king would be protected in battle by the shield's magic. It grieves me that the *Maic Brocc* begrudges their king this shield and would have their *filid* satirise me." Tigernaid fixed his gaze on Failge who returned the gaze in full measure with a gimlet eye.

"In the interests of all the tuatha of Iarmummu I am here today with the good bishop to propose an end to this ungodly behaviour and this begrudgery." Tigernaid fell quiet and looked to the bishop who took the signal and stepped forward.

"I wish to speak with Father Cormac, the desert father. I believe he is amongst you" said the Bishop. "I am Finian, Bishop of Emly. I wish to speak with you father regarding your holy mission to Prince Colum Cille. I wish to help you on your mission and in so doing restore peace to these troubled people. Will you speak with me in the presence of Christ, father?"

Failge shot an inquiring glance at Tocca the Hen. Only through Tocca could the bishop have known of the monk's presence in the tuath. The Hen kept his beady eyes fixed on the king. Slowly a door opened in the roundhouse behind Failge, Cormac emerged alone into the early morning light clutching his leather bag. He came to stand next to Failge facing the king and the bishop.

"I am Cormac of the desert fathers, speak what you wish, father and I will listen."

"Greetings to you father. We are privileged indeed to have a desert father among us. God bless your mission," began the bishop. "Your mission to deliver holy scrolls to Prince Colum Cille is known to us, father. I am told that these scrolls are important to the church and to all of Christendom. We are anxious that they are safely delivered. Allow us to help you complete your sacred mission, father, in a spirit of Christian brotherhood."

Cormac held his composure at the revelation that the detail of his mission was known to these people. He had looked to a cloak of secrecy.

"Thank you, father bishop. How will you help us?"

"King Tigernaig will use his enormous power and influence throughout Eriu and with the four kings and the high king to see that the scrolls are delivered safely and that you and your companions come to no harm."

"I see" said Cormac simply.

The bishop went on in spite of the monk's reticence.

"King Tigernaid wishes to return the shield of the *Tuatha De* to the *Maic Brocc* as a sign of his goodwill and he also offers to take charge of the scrolls and to see them safely to their destination."

At this news of the return of their precious shield the tuath cheered. But Failge raised his hands to silence them.

"From this moment on, all relations and trade routes will be returned to the *Maic Brocc*" said the king pressing his advantage and hoping to isolate Failge. "I pledge this shield as a sign of my goodwill." With that he placed the shield on the ground between them. "I ask in return is that you, Failge, *File* of this Tuath, cease your satirising of me and remove the injury you have inflicted upon your king." Tigernaig pointed to his foot. An injured king would not remain king for long. Kings in Eriu must be unblemished.

Failge's demeanour had blackened as he stared at Tigernaig and the Bishop of Emly. Even his magnificent torc had lost its brightness. The bishop would not return his gaze. While Tigernaig's eyes betrayed an inner smirk. Tigernaig obviously believed his bargain was a good one that the tuath could not refuse. He relaxed his posture and stood with his hands on his hips confident of a positive outcome, even allowing that he had ignored the honour price of twenty cumals.

"Tell me Fidelmid, how ye knew of Father Cormac's presence among us this day?" asked Failge, noticeably not using the king's title.

Tigernaig looked to Tocca the Hen. It was Tocca who replied pleadingly: "This is a good trade, Failge. We regain our sacred shield and our trade routes. The war will be over. These are just some Christian scrolls"

"Ye have betrayed yer tuath, Tocca," snapped Failge. "Why are these scrolls so important that a king and a bishop would journey here and make this offer? What is it ye are not telling yer tuath? Speak now or I will satirise ye throughout the land!"

Tocca the Hen flapped his big arms in supplication.

"The Bishop of Rome has offered riches to those that secure the scrolls for him. All of Eriu is looking for this monk and these scrolls. Only I knew that he was coming here with the scrolls. That was priceless knowledge that I used to benefit my tuath in this time of war. I did nothing wrong. I should be praised!" said Tocca defiantly.

"In my house on this day ye tried to cheat these scrolls from this good monk! How much did Tigernaig pay ye for this information, Tocca?" asked Failge quietly.

Tocca the Hen shrugged and toed the earth.

"Ye have betrayed yer tuath because this trade was never discussed in council. Ye have negotiated behind our backs. Ye have also betrayed our guests. The *Maic Brocc* are famed for our hospitality since the time of our first born. We do not betray our guests. That's why the *Tuatha De* gave us this shield. Have ye any idea what would happen to the *Maic Brocc* if we betray the *Tuatha De*?" Failge's voice was raised so that the tuath would hear his words.

An answer came to Failge from behind.

"The *Maic Brocc* will be cast to the four winds. A famine will be visited on your lands. I, Iucharba of the *Tuatha De* promise this, if the shield is lost to the *rath* of Mungair." A tall figure came forward slowly from the shadows near the barn. He was black haired and dressed in a black tunic and hunting cloak. His skin was the purest white that reflected the bright sun like the shimmer on water. His eyes flashed like those of a wolf. As he passed the Hen

169

he touched him on his shoulder and Tocca fell to the ground paralysed, gaping and blinking up at the sky. The tuath gasped.

Iucharba stood without fear between Tigernaig and Failge. "For four hundred of your summers the *Maic Brocc* has been helped by the *Tuatha De* as have many others in *Iarmummu*. We have taught you much and in return you have given us a portal to the land that was once ours. All that will be shattered if this shield of Eogabal is traded. You, Tocca mac Aedo betrayed us." He pointed to the blinking Tocca lying on the earth who squealed in fear. The Bishop of Emly sank to his knees in prayer.

"There will be no trade. The shield will remain in Mungair. The scrolls will remain with the monk," said Iucharba staring at King Tigernaig.

Tigernaig was not one to be denied. With a roar he went to draw his sword. As he did so Iucharba raised his hands skywards. With a rush of air four large swans swooped low over the *rath* and landed in a circle around the shield and Iucharba. Tigernaig and his bodyguards charged them. Before Tigernaig could bring his sword down on the first swan a golden hawk fell from the sky upon the bodyguards wounding two with its talons. Distracted Tigernaig hesitated for an instant and in that instant the largest swan sprang at him: with two swift thrusts of its beak to his eyes it blinded the king. Tigernaig fell back holding his bloodied eyes and screaming. His bodyguards drew back towards the entrance where the king's warriors were now fighting to get to their fallen king.

Iucharba calmly picked up the shield and gave it to Failge.

"The *Maic Brocc* did no dishonour, Failge. Your people are safe."

Turning to an alarmed Cormac he said: "Quickly monk, get your companions and follow me. You must leave here at once. Follow me."

XV: Rome, 575A.D.

"I will accept your punishment, Holy Father. I have failed you" whispered Augustine as he lay prostrate on the cool flagged floor of the Lateran Palace at the feet of the Bishop of Rome.

Immediately he had learned of the Celtic monk's escape to sea with the scrolls, Augustine had sailed back to Rome from Alexandria. It was clear that no ship's master in Alexandria would agree to take him in pursuit of the Patriarch's own vessels and his own vessel was too small to make the voyage. So, Augustine had little alternative but to return to Rome to confess his failure to the Holy Father. Never before had Augustine been outwitted to return empty handed to Rome. Always he had brought good news, even victory to the Holy See. This time he had miscalculated the resourcefulness of the Alexandrian heretics and they had bettered him. The scrolls were lost to the edge of Christendom. Now his standing as the Holy Father's feared emissary was open to question. Augustine had cursed the Patriarch and his smirking *Oikonomos*. If spared, he promised to return to exact vengeance on the smug heretics.

The coolness of the floor and the proximity of the Holy Father brought discomfort to Augustine. Painful memories flooded in of when he last lay on such a floor with a dominant male figure standing above him.

In his mind's eye Augustine could see himself as a young boy growing up happily on the shores of the Nile in lower Nubia. His birth name was Ouggamaet. He could see the morning he was sold into slavery by his father to pay family debts. The boy had then been taken by his new owner, a rich Greek merchant by the name Libanius, to the city of Alexandria on the Nile delta. Libanius was a devout member of the Christian church or so it seemed, attending church regularly in the Caesarion where he would rub shoulders with important clergy, even the Patriarch himself. Such happy coincidences were good for business. Libanius would often return from the Caesarion to his household greatly pleased with orders for his high class linens and silks. In celebration of this he would either beat the young Nubian for pleasure or take him to his bed, depending on his taste for lustful gratification that day.

Ouggamaet prayed to the gods to free him and to smite his sinful master. An answer to his prayers appeared to come when Libanius became afflicted with leprosy. Mercifully he was less able to beat Ouggamaet, but still he took him to bed and taunted the terrified boy with the prospect of becoming a leper.

Libanius travelled far and wide seeking a cure to his leprosy and his absences gave Ouggamaet respite. But on his return he would take his bitter disappointment out on the boy.

Lying on the hard, cold floor of the Lateran Palace, Augustine could feel a rage building in him towards the man above him. It seemed to flow from the floor and into his body. How dare this man seek authority over him! What right had this old fool to stand in judgement over him? His submissiveness to an older man filled Augustine with a mixture of self-loathing and rage. He knew he had to get up from the floor before the anger exploded, but he dared not move until the Holy Father gave him permission.

The Holy Father could see Augustine's distress and knelt beside the stricken monk.

"Get up, my son. There is no need for this. You did not fail. If you but knew it, you have succeeded. As you always do," said Catelinus smiling down on Augustine. "I have long thought that God works through you more than most, Augustine. I wish you would understand this."

A bemused Augustine quickly released himself from the floor's cold grip and brought himself to his full impressive height

"How can this be, Holy Father?" he whispered half in demand and half in plea. The Bishop of Rome looked into Augustine's dark eyes and stepped back. He knew well what lay within.

"You report that the scrolls have gone to Eriu in the Britannic Isles. That is invaluable information for us, my son. You have done well to learn this."

"Why? It is at the end of the earth, father. They sent them there because it is far beyond our reach" said Augustine fighting to regain his composure before the Holy Father.

"There is the hand of God in this, Augustine. Do you not see it? The Church in Eriu is heretical, still pagan, and seeks to resist and challenge our authority. They are also close to the heretics in Africa. It is not surprising they have sent these scrolls to Eriu. They must be very important to them, important that they keep them from us."

Augustine looked blankly at his master. He knew him to be a wily politician as well as a godly churchman. During his pontificate this Bishop of Rome had, with Augustine's considerable support, protected the independence of the church in Rome from a succession of armies. First came the Germanic tribes of the Goths and Ostrogoths, then the Emperor Justinian from the East followed by the Lombards from the north: each sought hegemony over all the land from Lombardia in the north to Calabria in the south. Only Rome in the middle lands had remained largely independent of all these forces due to the efforts in recent times of the Bishop of Rome, Ioannes III and his considerable emissary, Augustine the Nubian. From this position of independence the church continued by stealth to extend its influence over the Frankish kingdom and the Germanic peoples in the north and much of Iberia to the west. It was the Britannic Isles that yet remained beyond the Church of Rome.

"In my prayers I received guidance that these scrolls will lead us to control over the Britannic Isles. God has placed the scrolls in these islands for a very good reason, Augustine. They are the keys to these pagan souls for us."

"We have no allies in these lands, Holy Father," said Augustine.

"That is no longer true" smiled the Bishop of Rome. "Our friend in the Frankish Kingdom, the good bishop, Gregory of Tours knows the Britons well and tells me of a young ambitious prince who seeks our baptism and our support."

The two men smiled at one another.

"We have brought several young princes to kingship, have we not Augustine? Now you see the hand of God and your honoured role within His desires."

"I do, father. Please forgive me for my lack of faith and ungodly behaviour. I struggle like a poor sinner at times. Your faith in me and His faith in me give me the strength to do His work," said Augustine recovering his composure.

"I know of your struggles, my son. It is your cross and you bear it with fortitude. It has been my privilege to guide you these many years."

Augustine knelt and kissed the Bishop of Rome's ring finger, but the touch of another man was not comfortable. In his tortured mind, Augustine always saw his tormentor, Libianus, horribly disfigured with leprosy and pitifully calling his name in his lodgings in Rome. Libanius had come to the city of Rome to attend an eminent doctor. This time he brought Ouggamaet with him as a guide because of his failing eyesight. The boy saw his opportunity in the strange city when his master sent him to fetch water. Ouggamaet ran off for the water and never returned. He left Libanius wailing, half blind and alone in his lodgings.

Ouggamaet became a beggar to survive. But begging in the City of Rome in these times was not a good trade especially for a black skinned boy. The city was almost deserted; the rich were in flight; their houses in disrepair from many years of neglect. In desperation one day Ouggamaet approached a well-dressed gentleman for some food. The gentleman told the boy to follow him to his house and he would give him food. Fearing a repeat experience of what he had just escaped from, Ouggamaet refused. The gentleman could see the boy's mistrust.

"Very well, if you will not come with me I will have you arrested for begging and sold into slavery. Which is it to be, boy?" asked the gentleman.

Ouggamaet felt he had little choice but to follow, at a safe distance.

The gentleman was a high ranking member of the Senate and a bishop in the Christian church by the name of Catelinus. He did not harm or misuse Ouggamaet. Instead he won the boy's confidence and took him into his household. Catelinus treated him well in every respect. In fact he came to love the boy as a son and under his tutelage Ouggamaet flourished, becoming educated in science, geography, Latin and the faith of the Christian Church. At sixteen the boy was baptised into the Church of Rome taking the name of Augustine, inspired as he was by the life of St Augustine of Hippo. At eighteen Augustine became a priest ministering to the many poor in that sad city and he was given a beautiful bronze cross by Catelinus. The cross became a symbol of Augustine's ministry which he carried with him at all times. He frequently held it aloft as he progressed through the devastated streets of Rome and beyond.

It was a time of many trials and uncertainty for the once great city of Rome. The Emperor had long ago left for Constantinople and the imperial city had become abject. The Ostrogoths had sacked Rome in the year of 550 A.D. leaving the small number of people that remained in a state of poverty and devastation. Only the Church of Rome now stood between the people, their city and oblivion. Many believed that the city would become like Troy, lost to legend. It appeared that all the peoples conquered by Rome were now arriving at her walls to seek retribution for past cruelties. So it was that Augustine grew to manhood in this precarious city with Catelinus as his mentor and holdfast.

However the colour of his skin told against the boy. Even in the church of God it seemed he was not fully accepted. Repeated slights further embittered Augustine's ever fragile nature. Although he strove to follow the Christ's example in all ways, Augustine still lived under a cloud from his earlier life as a slave and a concubine. He prayed to St Peter many times daily to be released from the burden of his painful youth, but the burden would not leave Augustine. Nightmares weakened his spirit over the years and when vexed he was hot tempered and prone to a vengeful nature which left him further racked with guilt. The influence of his adoptive father, Catelinus could not resolve Augustine's worsening plight. Until, that is, an act of God elevated Catelinus to high office, the highest office in the Church of Rome: Bishop of Rome in the year 561 A.D. He took the title Ioannes the Third.

In this way Augustine from Nubia found himself called to the side of his adoptive father, now the Holy Father, and thrust into the high politics of the Church as the Bishop of Rome's trusted emissary. This powerful role soothed Augustine's troubled soul and he grew to a man of standing. Trusted by the Bishop of Rome and feared by those in high places, Augustine would travel widely dealing with

175

the many and murky challenges facing the hard pressed Church of Rome. He faced down princes and kings in the pursuit of the Rome's revived ambition to become powerful in faith, instead of in arms and to make itself anew as the "City of God".

So in this Year of our Lord 575 A.D. and on this day of April, Augustine found himself again called by his Divine Father and his Holy Father to perform another service.

"I am growing old, Augustine. Soon you may have a new master in Rome. This may be your last act of service to this bishop," said Catelinus to the kneeling Augustine.

"No, father. You will live long. It is God's will."

Augustine's hand tightened on Catelinus, not out of love for his adoptive father, but out of anger that he would never be considered a candidate for such high office. Always the servant, always overlooked as others of higher birth and fairer skin became bishops and it was he who was left to risk his life in the dark arts of church ambition.

"I am growing weak, my son. I have seen seventy years, most in the service of the Church of Rome."

"Then do not send me away. I am needed here. The Lombards threaten us and the Emperor is a fool! You need me here!"

"God has made His wishes known, Augustine. We are His instruments. You must go and go quickly while I am still on this earth to guide your mission."

"God will not take you with such important work to do"

"There will be others to follow in the work" said Catelinius. "Now listen to me Augustine, you will travel north to Gregory of Tours in the Frankish kingdom of Neustria. Here is a letter of introduction. He will effect a meeting with this prince. Work your divine alchemy on this prince and convince him of our friendship and support. See how he can become our servant and we his master? In this chest are one thousand gold solidi as a token of our good faith. One for each year that this prince's family will reign should he pledge himself to us. Give this to the prince with the offer of much more if it is needed to secure these scrolls and our church in those islands. He himself will be beatified in the eyes of St Peter. Here is our written pledge to him." Catelinus handed Augustine a papal scroll with a heavy seal.

"These sacred scrolls of Alexandria will be difficult to find in a strange land. Their tongues will be strange to me" mused Augustine.

"God will bring them to you, Augustine. Has he not always shown you the way? We have arranged a sister who was born in those islands to accompany you. She speaks the language of both Eriu and of Britain. Treat her well and with respect, Augustine. She recently nursed Governor Narses of his injuries. You would make a powerful enemy if she came to any harm" said Catelinius fixing Augustine with a glare. "She will be your valuable servant in dealing with these people. Travel to Eriu and make their king the same offer with this second chest of one thousand solidi. Alternatively, I hear their land is full of monks with powerful abbots. One of them will have the scrolls. Find out who this monk's abbot is. He will have the scrolls or know where they can be found. Offer our patronage. If he will accept Rome as his authority we will help build a truly Christian church that will be like a shining beacon to all the peoples of the Britannic Isles. The abbot's name will ring through the ages. He will be much favoured by God. If he hesitates set the young prince at his throat." Catelinus sat down and breathed heavily. "So Augustine this is God's will and remember what we have learnt together over these years: if you support both sides to a conflict you will always triumph. The scrolls are the bait for both factions. Don't you see? But make no mistake, we must have them. Without these scrolls I sense all this could be at stake" said Catelinius looking around the high vaulted ceilings of the Lateran Palace.

"What are these scrolls that they would exercise the Alexandrians so?" asked Augustine.

"When I was a young priest, an old desert monk told me of a legend that the last testament of the Christ was held in Alexandria. It had been brought there by St Mark. The legend said that wherever this testament is revealed the true church of the Christ will be built. However the testament also revealed truth about our faith that, as the church in Alexandria became rich and powerful, it wished to suppress. So it was hidden in the Great Library. I am guided that this is what they have in their heretics' hands in Alexandria. That is why we must possess this testament. The last testament of the Christ must be in Rome to guide the one true church."

"Why would they dispatch the scrolls to such a distant land, yet not destroy them in Africa?"

"They cannot destroy them. These are sacred scrolls and to destroy them would risk God's fury. That is why we must find them. They must be held here and not in some muddy hovel on a distant godless island to be discovered by pagans and used against us. Bring them back to St Peter, Augustine. Then you will have rest, I promise you."

"To have rest in God's eyes and to serve you that has been my only goal, father. I pray that such a goal will keep you on this earth. Live long enough, father to see me return with the scrolls and the Church of Rome praised in the Britannic Isles. "That is also my prayer, my son, and to see your salvation before I die."

XVI: Gaul

The Roman roads through the land were still passable even though the empire had retreated far to the east. The armies of the invading Visigoths, Ostrogoths and the Lombards valued the Roman road system for rapid troop movements across Europe and continued to maintain them.

Augustine with his interpreter, Sister Dorothea, as well as a wagon master and a single guard made good progress in the clement spring weather. In these turbulent times members of the church still travelled unmolested. Brigands and purse thieves avoided the clergy for fear of inviting the wrath of the Almighty. The intimidating presence of a tall black monk gave additional surety.

Augustine watched his female companion closely. She was a woman in her prime of some eighteen years with marble white skin and long brown hair. She spoke Greek to him with a Celtic accent that irritated him. He disliked and distrusted women for their weakness and their corrupting influence. He had bitter memories of his own mother who while loving her only son, abandoned him to slavery. Since then he had come to see all women as hypocrites. These virgin sisters of the church were no different, in some ways worse, to Augustine's mind. Some had seduced him over the years in moments of weakness and he hated them for exposing his foibles before God. He had in return punished the fallen sisters severely for their sins to show God his heart felt repentance. Augustine wondered when this Sister Dorothea would spring upon him with her carnal lust and was therefore ever watchful.

Sister Dorothea was initially unsuspecting of Father Augustine's thoughts. She was enraptured by the natural world, her face always cast outwards and upwards smiling at the sky and at the birds dancing in the spring air. And yet she observed all the offices. So when not smiling at the world she was engaged in prayer; seated across from Father Augustine she was blissfully unaware of how he regarded her. He sneered as her large breasts shook before him beneath her gown with the motion of the wagon. This was how the female worked her sin, he reflected quietly. Praying to our Lord while she displayed her breasts in such a manner was the mortal sin of the arch hypocrite. He wanted to throw the hypocrite out of the wagon and make her walk to Tours as punishment for her display and to show her that Augustine could not be tempted, but he was mindful of the Holy Father's warning to treat this one with respect. He vowed he would disappoint the seductress with her dancing breasts. His Godly discipline would triumph supreme.

To begin with Dorothea talked little to Augustine, whose manner she found unsettling. He took no pleasure in the passing scene as she did. Her excited remarks about the pleasant birdsong or the signs of green shoots all around, met with a grunt or a frustrated sigh from the emissary. As the Holy Father's representative Augustine was a man of some standing and austere reputation who appeared weighed down with important matters which Dorothea considered should be distracted with the beauty of God's creation. However she began to appreciate something of his inner torment when she realised the focus of his attention was not the passing scene or prayer to the divine, but her breasts. She had dealt with troubled men like Augustine before who, having been denied their mother's love, were fixated on the breast for evermore. This uncomfortable realisation only encouraged Dorothea to distract the emissary even more with talk of celandine and pine bunting and her fascination with a raven that she believed had attached itself to them. She named him Isaiah after the biblical prophet. However this manner of flippancy which bordered on blasphemy only did further harm to Dorothea's cause with the emissary.

Within a week of leaving Rome by road they were in the port of Massalia and two days later arrived at the Abbey of St Andrew in Avennïo Cavarum where they were to rest for two days in the nunnery before a ferry would take them up the great river Rodonos to Lugdunum. Augustine could be free of the woman as she stayed with the sisters. He breathed more freely and was glad to be released from the torment of Sister Dorothea. His first task on arrival was to demand angrily that the abbess bind up Sister Dorothea's large breasts in the traditional manner. In this way she would provide no further distraction to him or offence to God. The frightened abbess apologised profusely for the sinfulness of her sex and hurried off to find the wayward sister. Dorothea would be bound up and given the penance as set out by Augustine. She would read aloud St Augustine of Hippo's Confessions each day until it was complete. Augustine of Nubea never tired of his saint's inspirational writings. He found them always a perfect sinecure for the affliction of hypocrisy. Besides, it would prevent the sister's compulsion to engage in idle chatter about the sky or the trees or this raven she appeared to be unnaturally attached to. When she finished she could start at the beginning again. Content with these arrangements Augustine retired to his rooms to meditate on the strategies that lay ahead.

Augustine's chief point of contact on his way to the Britannic Isles was Bishop Gregory of Tours in the kingdom Neustria. This high born cleric was a recent appointment to the bishopric having been consecrated the previous year following the death of old Eufronius. Gregory had been a deacon in the city for many years and was well regarded by Rome, being a well-known campaigner against the heresy of the Arians and the Pelagians who numbered many in Gaul and in the Britannic Isles. He had rebuilt the cathedral of Tours destroyed by fire and shown himself to be skilled in his dealings with the ruthless Frankish kings who valued his wise counsel.

Augustine was most interested in determining how Gregory could help further the church's ambitions in the Britannic Isles, especially in the most westerly island of Eriu. The young prince referred to by the Holy Father could be key. He would make it his business to speedily discover the prince's true worth to the church, his weaknesses and his desires in order to support them in whatever way he could to achieve the recovery of the scrolls and the domination of the Church of Rome in both Britain and Eriu. Something the mighty armies of the Roman Senate and the Emperors had failed to do. But the army of God would now accomplish this feat with Augustine at its head, Saint Augustine of Nubia: God's general.

The next day Augustine ordered that their sailboat be readied to depart by the sixth hour in order to avoid incurring penance for travelling on the Sabbath. It was four days' journey to Lugdunum by ferry, the Sabbath being five days hence. Augustine was pleased to see that the breasts were well bound and would provide no further distraction. The sister herself seemed somewhat subdued and her eyes were red. Augustine wondered if Dorothea had been chastised by the abbess, beaten perhaps for bringing shame to her sex. These virgin sisters applied harsh measures to their own sex at times. Content that order and his authority had been established, he allowed himself a benign smile at Dorothea as they settled themselves on board the river boat. She returned the smile meekly and looked down at her hands clasped on her lap. Tears flooded her eyes and she bit her lip nervously.

"Have the sisters chastised you?" asked Augustine in a matter of fact tone. He had no wish to show concern, mainly because he felt none. It was merely his lurid fascination with suffering.

"No Father. They did not chastise me, but they bound me very tightly." She could not tell this monk the real reason for her display of strong emotion. If she confessed her condition of womanhood to this man he would likely throw her in the river to cleanse her. So she lied to avoid the risk, "It is the river, father. The deep water disturbs me."

"Your faith must be stronger, sister. You have many long miles of river ahead of you. First we travel the Rodonos to Lugdunum and then we will travel the river Liger to Tours. We do God's work on behalf of the Holy Father. What greater protection could you seek? Do you doubt that we are divinely protected?"

"No, father. I do not. It is a weakness of my sex. He will give a poor sister such as I the strength to do His work. Please forgive me"

"Ask His forgiveness, sister. Not mine."

She closed her eyes to avoid his glare and prayed to the saints and to the angels to give her strength for the journey with this man. As she finished her prayers she heard the cry of a raven high above the river. Looking up Dorothea saw the same raven that had followed them from Massalia, the one she had named after Isaiah. It was like seeing an old and trusted friend come to give succour in times of difficulty. She felt reassured and drawing her strength from the great bird's power, Dorothea settled contently back in her seat.

Augustine eyed her suspiciously wondering where this one was drawing her comfort from: God or from the beast in the sky?

To unsettle her, Augustine barked, "Begin the reading, sister".

This jolted Dorothea out of her contemplation. She would spend the next eight days in penance reading from St Augustine's Confessions, a book she did not enjoy. Unhappily she saw little of the passing scene of springtime in Gaul along the river. Purple herons standing sentinel all along the river banks beneath the leafy willow and the oak, eyed the stately passing of their sailboat. Beavers and otters splashed in alarm at the encroachment of their river that was last disturbed by Caesar as he slaughtered the Celtic tribes in tens of thousands. In that time the rivers ran red with the blood of heroes and the screams of their children defiled the air.

Dorothea could understand why Father Augustine so admired his saintly namesake. The saint disparaged women. During his ministry he had done much to influence Christian orthodoxy on the role of women. It was indeed a sore punishment for a woman to read. However as Dorothea read, Father Augustine was soothed and remained in quiet satisfaction as the days passed on the gentle rivers of Gaul.

They arrived in the city of Tours as dusk was falling. The great river of Liger had been kind to them and had ferried them smoothly to the city. It was the evening before Easter and the city's walls glowed red with the setting sun. The city displayed a mood of expectation for the celebrations of Easter day: the high point of the Christian calendar. Augustine and his assistant, Dorothea were taken straightway to the residence of Gregory of Tours in the monastery of St Martin of Tours. In spite of their long journey, they were given no food only water as the people were fasting in the approach to Easter. On Easter Day there would be feasting to celebrate the risen Jesus.

Vespers in the cathedral led by the bishop himself gave Augustine an opportunity to appraise Gregory of Tours before their meeting on the day after Easter. Gregory was a diminutive figure made all the smaller by his garments and the grandeur of the cathedral. He was no taller than a half grown boy. Yet his voice was surprisingly strong and carried throughout the cathedral as he led in the praying of the psalms. Quietly Augustine chuckled to himself as Gregory stood on an ornate crate in order to be seen giving the blessing of St Martin. He could not doubt that the Holy Father was mistaken in placing confidence in the little bishop, but still he wondered.

It was set that Augustine would meet with Gregory and Prince Artur after Terce on the day following Easter in the bishop's chambers. Augustine had elected to bring Sister Dorothea with him, although Gregory spoke both Latin and Greek fluently, so no translation would be necessary, he assumed that this young Celtic prince would have no other tongue except his native one. Besides, he liked to have a witness present when conducting meetings of this nature. He found that kings and bishops always had witnesses present and often used them to concoct false versions of their agreements.

Gregory greeted Augustine warmly and ignored Sister Dorothea. Augustine had long ago ceased the habit of kissing a bishop's ringed finger. He believed that as the Holy Father's emissary he was the equal of any bishop and dared any to challenge his assumption. Gregory had his deacon in attendance; a young man of a pale disposition who said nothing throughout their meeting.

Gregory's eyes were on a level with Augustine's chest. They were bright blue and twinkled with a keen intelligence in a large head.

"It is an honour to have the Holy Father's representative among us at Easter, father" began Gregory.

"It is an honour to be before you in Tours, Your Grace. Word of your ministry here travels far and the Holy Father is much in admiration" replied Augustine. He handed over the letter of introduction. Silence descended on the group as Bishop Gregory read the letter and then placed it inside his robe.

"The Holy Father is well I trust?" said Gregory.

"He is very well, thank you," said Augustine. The true state of the health of the Bishop of Rome could not be admitted for fear of rousing his enemies. "The church is well in Tours and around, Your Grace?"

"We are blessed with the support of the Franks. King Caribert is most assiduous of our welfare: though there is much rivalry with his three brothers in Austrasia, Burgogne and Acquitaine. But that is where the church provides the glue that holds these kingdoms together and away from each other's throats."

"Quite so, Your Grace" Augustine agreed. "How may I find this Prince Artur and what do you know of him?" Augustine was not one for small talk and gossip. He had pressing business to expedite.

At the mention of the name Sister Dorothea twitched in her chair. The two men paid her no heed.

"The hand of the Almighty has brought the prince to us, father. He is in Armorica, not two day's journey from here. The angels walk with you, which I can see with my own eyes. To have the prince so close when you need him is God's work indeed. But why would this not be so? You are the Holy Father's emissary," said Gregory. "Many of the British live in Armorica now, having been forced out of Britain by the heathen Angles. The prince is in the Forest of Brocéliande acquiring horses for his army."

"What do you know of this prince, Your Grace?"

"I hear of him, but never met him. He is Christian, young, but already a power among the hard-pressed British people. He is a formidable general in battle, a skilled horseman and a slayer of many heathens in his holy crusade to drive them out from a country yearning for the church. He leads a cavalry troop of one thousand horse of his fierce Celtic tribe called the Gododdin."

At that Sister Dorothea exclaimed and dropped a cross she was carrying.

For the first time both men noticed her only to return to their conversation.

"He is an ideal ally for the mission you have been set. His army drove many of the Scotii out of western Britain and back to the island of Eriu in recent times. The Scotii are a nation of heretic rascals following the teachings of that fat old hound, Pelagius. They plunder the land of Britain; steal their women and young men bringing them into slavery and debauchery. This prince will be eager to engage in further battle, I am sure. I hear the Gododdin have broken with the Celtic Church and seek the protection of the Church of Rome" said Gregory with satisfaction.

Augustine smiled at this news. Once again he was God's anointed; in the right place at a fortuitous moment But he was distracted by the woman fidgeting. He stared at her to silence her.

185

"I have some men who know the prince and will guide you to him in the morning, father. But there is more important news. A merchant from Eriu who trades in fine jewellery and cloth and is known to us arrived here not three days ago. He says he knows of the location of these scrolls and he even knew that the Holy Father had dispatched an emissary to find these scrolls for the church. He had hoped to meet you here."

"How could he know such things?" asked Augustine suddenly on the edge of his chair.

"It is merchants' business to acquire information in the course of their trade. They often amaze me. As we did not know you would visit us, father, the merchant would not delay and travelled on to Prince Artur's encampment in Armorica. He hopes to meet you there."

"This is very good news. I am minded to leave at once, Your Grace. I need your men to be ready within the hour" said Augustine standing up abruptly.

"Will you not rest another day father? I am told the prince will be in Armorica for another week."

"I cannot. God has brought us together in this place. We must seize the divine moment he has provided. Your news is good and I thank you for your intelligence. The Holy Father will be most pleased, as I am. May you walk with God."

As the diminutive Gregory wrestled himself off his great chair to bid farewell to the Holy Father's emissary, Augustine was already leaving the room followed by a nervous looking Sister Dorothea.

As Augustine walked quickly back to his quarters he turned on Sister Dorothea.

"What is this behaviour before a bishop, woman?" he snarled. "You fidget and fidget, and then you exclaim and throw the holy cross on the floor! Do I need to have you whipped to settle your twitching? Do you seek to embarrass me? I need you to be quiet, to observe, to listen and when necessary to translate. Not twitch like a devil on a spit!"

"I – I"

"Well what is it? Are you possessed woman? For I will have your demons cast out this very day."

"No Father!"

Dorothea hesitated and gathered her strength even as she trembled with fear and foreboding. She would have to confess her past to this man otherwise he would surely have her flogged and exorcised for possession.

"This Artur you refer to is my brother, father. It was a shock to hear his name."

"Your brother?!" Augustine's mind began the rapid calculations surrounding to such information. This familial bond would tie the young British prince more closely to the Church. This was good, he calculated.

"Yes. But there is more to my history that I must tell you, Father. I cannot hide it any longer. As a girl I was taken by the Scotii from my family's lands in *Rheged* and used as a bondswoman for some months until my brother rescued me."

"Then you have a brother to be proud of, sister. Many had no one to rescue them from such a plight," said Augustine thinking of his own history.

"Yes, Father."

They walked further along the cloisters as Augustine considered the information. He stopped.

"Sister, are you a virgin?"

Tears welled up in Dorothea and she began to weep. This was the awful truth she feared some day she would have to face. She clutched her cross tightly to her bosom.

"I will ask you again, sister. Are you a virgin? Bondswomen do not remain virgins do they?"

She shook her head.

"No father they do not. I was used by men of high rank and some merchants too."

Augustine felt a divine rage building within him. Sisters of the Christ found not to be intact were flogged, cast out of the Church and often disowned by their families. This one had lied to the Church and to God.

"You harlot!" roared Augustine in outrage. He tore at her gown. Dorothea screamed in terror. He was about strike her when a still small voice inside him advised Augustine to proceed no further.

He realised that if this one were cast out and punished, as she deserved to be, her brother the prince would become an enemy. He could not afford such an upset at an early stage in his mission. Political calculations had to be made for the greater good. Dorothea had fallen to her knees, weeping and clutching the torn gown to her. Some monks came running at the sound of the commotion.

"The sister was attacked by a rabid hound, brothers. Quick! He went that way. The beast must be stopped," said Augustine. His mind was as ever fast moving and cunning. The monks ran off to find the beast.

Augustine helped the weeping Dorothea to her feet.

"Forgive the emotions of an old monk, sister. I too was enslaved as a boy. Such evil raises strong emotions in me. Come, we will soothe your pain."

Augustine brought Dorothea to his room. He needed to restore her and to know more of this one's history and that of her brother. He sent for another gown for Dorothea. Sitting down he offered her some water. He sat across the room and watched her regain composure and drink the water. He could understand how men had been tempted and had made use of her to gain some physical satisfaction. She had a prettiness about her and a shapeliness to match. This one could torment the weak, as Augustine knew only too well. However he must be careful. This woman was now key to the Church's plans.

A sister returned with a new gown for Dorothea. Augustine ordered that she undress Dorothea and fit her with the new gown. He did not leave the room, but watched as Dorothea was undressed by the sister. No one would dare question a high ranking cleric such as Augustine or suspect that his motives were base, certainly not a lowly sister. Under her gown Dorothea's flesh was smooth and white. Augustine noticed she had strong shoulders, thighs and buttocks. He reasoned she must come from a good bloodline where the women could carry many children. Her tribe were warriors of the highest order. Perhaps the women fought too. However this one had forsaken all that to serve God. Except that she had deceived the Church. What other deceits was she capable of?

He noticed the bindings around her breasts that the sisters in Lugundum had applied on his orders. They dug into her skin.

"Do those bindings trouble, you sister" he asked, making an effort to display compassion.

Dorothea raised her arms to cover her chest.

"T-they do, Father, But I can endure it."

"Sister, loosen the bindings until they are comfortable for Sister Dorothea."

The sister dutifully helped Dorothea remove the bindings until her breasts were exposed. Augustine closed his eyes and prayed for strength to endure the test of his vocation. Quickly the two sisters worked to rebind the breasts less tightly to save further distress to Father Augustine. Once Dorothea was fully dressed the sister was ordered to bring food. As the other sister departed Augustine shared the food with Dorothea in an act of generosity designed to assuage her fears and loosen her tongue.

"I mean you no harm, sister. Of that you must be sure. You, like I, have suffered at the hands of sinners" he said while smiling and holding up his hands in earnest placation of the frightened Sister Dorothea. "But if we are to work closely together, I must know the full facts about you."

Dorothea looked at the emissary and swallowed hard.

"I understand, Father."

"Please tell me why you deceived the Church to become a Virgin of Christ."

"Please believe me, Father when I say I did not set out to deceive the Church. During my time in Eriu angels watched over me, they spoke to me and promised that I would be returned to my people and to the Church. This kept my faith strong. After my brother rescued me and brought me back to the Kingdom of *Rheged* in Alba they spoke to me again and said I had a duty to God who had saved me to become a sister in the Church. In the Church in *Rheged* there is no rule that a woman must be whole to become a sister of the Christ. Then our king sent me to Rome to study because we want the Church of Rome to be our Church in *Rheged*, in fact in all of Britain to save us from the Scotii and the pagan Picts and Angles."

"And have you continued to lie with men since becoming a sister of Christ?"

"No Father I have not."

"Do you enjoy being with men? Do you have cravings of the flesh now?"

"No I do not, Father"

"How many times did you sin in Eriu?"

Dorothea closed her eyes in anguish to recall the memories.

"Many times."

"Why did you lust after them so frequently, sister?"

"I didn't lust after them at any time, father".

Dorothea wept.

"My master made me drink wine and tied me down while he pleasured himself. I could not stop him. I tried to run away, but he brought me back. Sometimes he shared me with his friends."

"Did you become with child?"

"Thank the Lord, no. They gave me medicine that they said prevented this. If I had had a child they would have killed it or enslaved it. God be praised that I had no child" Dorothea continued to weep.

"Indeed. Now tell me about your brother, Prince Artur" said Augustine.

Dorothea quietly recovered her composure, ate some cheese and fruit. She smiled at the thought of her brother.

"His name is Arthnou in our language, but others call him Artur. He is not a prince. He is Guledig of the *Goddodin*. He is a general: a great one, known throughout the land. He leads one thousand horsemen into battle against the pagan Picts, Angles and Scotii who would seek to take our land and enslave the Christian British. His horsemen drive the pagans into the sea. But he is a good Christian, father. The Gododdin broke with the Celtic Church after I was taken by the Scotii and now they carry Rome's standard. My brother has sworn to avenge me against the Scotii."

"The Holy Father has heard of your brother's great bravery for Christ and wishes to help him defeat the heresies of the Scotii and to bring the holy Roman Church to these islands. The Holy Father would make your brother king of the British."

"My brother has no desire to be king. He is a soldier. Urien is our king. He rules the British."

"All men have desires, as you know sister. What is your brother's?"

"To serve the Christ, to serve his people and to avenge me," Dorothea said with pride.

"That is good and noble. We can help him in that noble cause. Will you help the Holy Father help your brother and your people?"

"Of course. I am the Holy Father's handmaiden, Father."

"Then in one hour we shall leave to find your brother. There will be no more said about your sinful past, sister, now that you have confessed to me. God has brought you here to face the past and the nature of your sin. Be grateful for this opportunity to wash away the sin in service to the Holy Father. Our Christ said, 'Pick up your cross and follow me'. We two must do this."

"Thank you, Father. I will serve you and the Church loyally."

XVII: Armorica and beyond

Artur had been sent by King Urien of *Rheged* in northern Britain to Armorica in western Gaul to meet with the British expelled by the Angles from eastern and southern Britain. An army was being raised and plans laid to finally rid Britain of the Angles in the east, the Scotii in the west and the Picts in the north. Artur could move freely in Armorica, an area of Gaul that, like Eriu had not been penetrated by the Roman Empire and still continued to enjoy its independence in spite of the ambitions of the Franks in Greater Gaul.

Artur was a young man, not yet twenty-five, who had risen to command the Gosgordd of the Gododdin: an elite army of three hundred fearsome horse soldiers within the one thousand strong Guletic cavalry. Under Artur's command the Gosgordd had carried all before them in their fight to rid Britain of the invaders.

In the dark days after the departure of the Roman legions Artur's ancestor, Ambrosius Aurelianus, a Romano-British general, created the Gosgorrd modelled on Roman cavalry regiments. With the Gosgordd, Ambrosius Aurelianus fought and defeated the Saxons under the Vortigern. Now his descendant carried his torch for the British. Artur rode into battle carrying the torch aloft as tradition demanded, but now also carried the standard of Christ the Saviour.

In the great forest of Brocéliande near the port of Alet in Armorica preparations were nearing completion. Fifty head of large cavalry horses had been newly trained for battle by Artur's men over the winter. They were to be taken back to Britain to increase the size of the Gosgordd for the coming campaign. These were horse specially bred for their size and strength to break through the enemy's lines and withstand the fury of battle and the chase.

As Augustine and Sister Dorothea drew near to the British encampment on a flat area of land, the pungent odour of horse dung and sweat hung in the air. The earth shook with the hooves of many heavy laden battle horses. There were men's shouts and horses' snorts beyond a thick bank of hornbeam to their left.

Dorothea's heart beat fast. These were the sounds and smells of home that she had not heard for some time. She knew her beloved brother must be close at hand. However she worried how he would react to Father Augustine. Artur held the Church of Rome in high regard and believed the salvation of the British people lay with the church, as did she, but she was not so sure of the emissary's opinion. Artur was still young and dealt plainly and honourably. Leading men in battle required these qualities. Father Augustine dealt in a world of intrigue and politics that Dorothea's time in Rome had taught her had little to do with plain speaking and honour. In addition, she was sure her brother had never seen a black skinned man and did not know how he would respond to one. It was well that she was present. God's hand was upon them all, she reasoned.

There was a gap in the hornbeam thicket that took them through to a large clearing bounded by oak and beech on two sides and a lake on the other. The clearing was full of activity and noise. Men and horses were everywhere. To one side there were three large thatched roundhouses, several barns and a fenced area for horses. The wagon master took them straight towards the middle of the three roundhouses and at once Dorothea saw her brother leaning on a sword watching their approach with curiosity. Artur's guards on the edge of the forest had stopped their wagon to interrogate them and had ridden with them to the encampment. Artur was of fearsome expression in spite of his youth with a dark thick beard and piercing eyes. He was clothed in a leather smock with heavy cloth leggings tucked inside riding boots.

As they drew near, Artur recognised his sister. At once his fearsome appearance fell away as he thrust his sword in the ground and ran forward to greet Dorothea. In one swift movement he was standing on the wagon and lifted her out. Her decorum as a sister of Christ was lost in delighted squeals as she smelt her brother and felt his strength. Many soldiers turned to watch their Guledig greet the arrival of strangers to the training ground. Artur was not usually so playful and certainly not with women.

"Sister! It is you, my little sister of Christ!"

"It is brother. My, you have filled out since I last saw you. You look and smell like a full grown wild boar. What happened to your poor nose, Arthnou?"

"It turns itself up at the smell of Angles and Scotii and now will stay like this until they are driven from our land. So it is written," he joked. In truth it had been broken in battle. The one who broke Artur's nose lost his head the very next second.

They laughed and he held her by the shoulders ignoring decorum for a sister of Christ. Their language was unknown to Augustine who remained patiently seated in the wagon observing the welcome spectacle and assessing the young warrior.

"You look well, sister. The Church of Rome has been good to you."

"It has, brother. Such things I have seen and learnt! I speak both Latin and Greek now as King Urien wanted."

"That is good. You must teach me the Greek. I can read the Latin and speak it if I have to. Sister, who is this with you? Has he the plague? You have not brought the plague back from Rome to us?"

Dorothea laughed at the horror on her brother's face.

"No brother, I have not brought the plague. He is a dark skinned man from Africa, far beyond Rome. There the people are all that colour. It is the hot sun that does it, I am told."

"I have heard of such people, but never saw one until today. I could not suffer to be burnt so by the sun. I will approach him and see him more closely."

"No, brother. You must know he is a high-ranking emissary of the Holy Father come to meet you, my brother. He has affairs of state to discuss with you about the Church of Rome. It is good news, brother. He brings the Church of Rome to our land!"

"He is the one!? We have been expecting him since a merchant arrived with news of his coming."

Artur and Augustine silently regarded each other. Turning to Dorothea he said: "Sister these are matters that should not concern you. What is afoot here? First a Scotii merchant arrives talking in riddles about sacred scrolls in Eriu that the Holy Father desires most strongly and then my sister arrives with this dark man from the Holy Father? I have an army to make ready, I have no time for mysteries. "

"Be quiet, Arthnou! Your fame has travelled to Rome. The Holy Father has said your name! The Church of Rome is coming to our land. Isn't that wonderful? These scrolls are very important too. I hear they are the very words of the Christ. The emissary's name is Father Augustine. He is very powerful and clever, Arthnou. He is the Holy Father's foster son. I believe he can bring great good to the Kingdom of *Rheged*. But tread warily when dealing with him. Always remember you too are powerful. You are Guledig of the Gosgordd and an ally of King Urien."

"I never forget it, sister. What language does he speak?"

"Not our language. That's why I am here, to speak for him when needed. He speaks Latin and Greek. The miracle is that they did not know you were my brother nor of my past until today. I had to tell Father Augustine. He was understanding, I think. So you see God's hand in this, guiding the Church of Rome to us, to save us from the pagans!"

Artur considered: "I do, sister. You have been chosen by God, sister, as God's instrument. That is clear. The angels were right. They did not punish you in Rome? I worried about you in Rome. They insist on virgins. Did any man touch you?"

"No I was not touched by any other than the Christ. Please say no more, brother. It pains me. I was not punished as they did not know. Father Augustine was enslaved as a child also."

"I must speak with him. What does he want from us? How can we help the Church of Rome become a force in the land against the pagans?"

"I will let Father Augustine speak. I must not speak for him. It is forbidden."

Artur may have presented as a simple soldier, but he was no one's fool. He spoke to Augustine in his native tongue, although he was quite able to converse in Latin. Artur calculated that this would give him time to think of his responses while Dorothea translated.

While the two men exchanged pleasantries they began the process of assessing each other. It was clear that Augustine wished to win Artur over and gain his trust and that Artur was anxious to gain the active support of the Church to secure Britain against the pagans. However while both men had an understanding of the great matters at hand and were naturally cautious with each other, time was not on their side. For Artur, Britain was being harried from all quarters by pagans and heretics and his army was being readied for a major campaign. Augustine for his part must secure the scrolls before they fell into the wrong hands – pagan hands – and were misused against the true church. So matters could not be delayed out of natural caution between strangers.

As was the custom, Artur welcomed Augustine into his roundhouse and offered food and drink. Augustine ordered that a chest be brought with him from the wagon.

"May I be permitted, Guledig, to address matters at hand?"

Artur noted the emissary used his correct title. This one knew his business, he mused.

"The Church of Rome has admired the British people for many years, Guledig. Britain was a vital and proud part of the empire and its people loyal Romans. It saddens us that such a proud people are afflicted with pagans and heretics in recent times." Augustine paused to allow Dorothea to translate.

Artur nodded and smiled, but remained quiet.

Augustine continued: "The Church too has been a victim of the empire's demise and has had many pressing matters to attend to in Rome. We have had similar incursions of invaders and an empire in some disarray. But now God has vanquished many of our enemies and allowed His church to grow as scripture prophesised it surely would."

Augustine paused to drink some wine and continued,

"So in regard to Britain, the Franks in Gaul have, through God's guidance, helped the Church to thrive in this land, sadly not in Armorica. And now the Holy Father offers Britain the active support of the Church of Rome, Guledig."

Once again Augustine paused for Dorothea's translation and watched Artur's reaction.

Artur smiled, but again remained silent. He sensed the emissary had more to say. These sacred scrolls had not yet been mentioned.

"The Holy Father is mindful of your needs to raise an army equipped to subdue and expel the Scotii, the Picts and the Angles. The church can call on many resources, spiritual and temporal, to help with this and also to build fine churches in a land finally at peace with itself and with the one true God."

As Dorothea translated, Augustine threw open the chest revealing the gold solidi he had carried from Rome. Artur leaned forward.

"This is one thousand gold solidii given into my hand by the Holy Father himself who asked that this be given to you, Guledig, to use as you see fit in subduing the pagans and establishing the church in Britain. If more is needed it will be provided."

Augustine fell silent, sat back and waited for Artur's response.

Artur took his cue and weighing his words mindfully said;

"This is a happy day for us Britons, emissary. It is four generations since the legions left our shores and now word reaches us that they have even left Rome itself, but the Church has held a steadfast torch for God against the pagans all this time and now she comes to us. It fills my heart with joy to hear your words of comfort, emissary. Britons have waited in faith for the Church to reach our shores and prayed that the day of holy celebration would come before the pagans engulf us. That day has come and the gift of gold is gratefully received." Artur smiled at Augustine and fell silent again.

Augustine sat forward once more.

"I thank you for your words, Guledig. There is a pressing matter that pains the Holy Father and challenges us all. He asks that we together attend to it without delay, for it threatens the foundations of the church in Britain."

Augustine paused and Artur waited.

"Sacred scrolls, vital to Christendom itself, have been stolen from the Church by the Scotii and brought to Eriu. These scrolls contain the very words of our Christ and must be returned to us before they fall into pagan hands. Should you help the Holy Father retrieve these scrolls, Guledig, you will be exalted in heaven itself and a large cathedral will be built in your honour in Britain."

Artur responded,

"This would be an honour, a holy quest no less to secure the Church in Britain. The Scotii are rascals who have long afflicted these islands. They still worship the old gods, while claiming to worship the Christ. They are hypocrites. They steal our women and our cattle and treat both the same." Artur spat into the fire and continued,

"I would say this in return, emissary. While the Scotii are rascals, no one knows this more than I, it is the Angles in the east who press us most hard. We are in Armorica to bring war horses and soldiers back to Britain to help drive the barbarians from our shores this summer. A diversion in the west would not be wise at this time. The quest for the scrolls in Eriu could begin in late summer."

Artur watched closely the emissary's response to the difficulty he raised. Augustine did not immediately reply. He let a silence settle on their discussions, for he knew a merchant had travelled to meet with Artur with important information about the scrolls. It concerned Augustine that this young general had not revealed this. Did Artur already know the location of the scrolls? Was he toying with Augustine?

Artur broke the silence,

"But God's hand is on this holy quest as we good Christian men know. He sent a messenger from Eriu to us, not a day previous. He is a merchant who claims he has seen these scrolls in Eriu and knows who holds them. He has been searching for you, emissary and hoped to meet with you here to give you his news. He will speak to no other on the matter. I will have him brought to us immediately."

Augustine visibly relaxed and drank some more wine. He said nothing of his prior knowledge of the merchant.

"But I counsel caution, emissary. We have long experience of the Scotii. Their merchants are tricksters of the highest order. This fellow could be sent to confuse us with false information."

The merchant was brought into the roundhouse by Artur's men. He looked ill at ease and unkempt as he walked cautiously forward to the centre of the roundhouse where Artur and Augustine sat in conference. A nervous smile fell from his face as Dorothea screamed.

Artur and Augustine turned to Dorothea in alarm.

"What is it, sister?" asked Artur. Dorothea was on her feet like a startled deer looking for escape. Artur held her, but she would not be held and broke his grip.

She pointed at the Scotii merchant standing perplexed in centre of the gathering with fire smoke swirling around his head. It was none other than Tocca mac Aedo, Tocca the Hen of the *Maic Brocc* in *Iarmummu* who had been struck down by Iucharba of the *Tuatha De* in Mungair. Tocca had recovered from the magic spell and at once set out to find the Bishop of Rome's emissary who was seeking the sacred scrolls. There was a valuable trade to be done, Tocca reasoned and Tocca mac Aedo was never one to miss good trade.

In her native tongue Dorothea half screamed, half sobbed an oath, pointing at Tocca.

"He was one of them. He defiled me in Eriu while I was a bondswoman. He treated me cruelly."

Tocca looked around bewildered.

"The sister is wrong. I would never touch a sister of Christ," he said looking at an equally bewildered Augustine who, not understanding the language, stared from one to the other.

"Are you sure, sister?" asked Artur of his sobbing sister.

"How could I forget such a creature!? It's him. They call him Tocca the Hen." Dorothea embraced herself in distress.

Tocca still had feathers in his hair and the unmistakable appearance of a hen. He made for the doorway, but Artur's men blocked his escape.

With lightning speed Artur drew a long bladed knife and held Tocca by his hair.

"This is a lie! I swear it!" Tocca crowed.

Artur held one of Tocca's ears and sliced it off with expert precision and threw it in the fire. Tocca screamed in pain.

At this Augustine was on his feet ready to intervene to save the precious merchant with valuable information, but his path to Artur and Tocca was blocked by Artur's men.

"Stop this! He knows where the scrolls are!" shouted Augustine, but no one was listening. A dark mist had descended on Artur that his men knew well from the battlefield. No man could withstand it, emissary or no.

Still holding Tocca by his hair Artur snarled into Tocca's good ear: "How would she know your name, you chicken of the dung heap!?"

Tocca whimpered. He knew protest was useless. He had had many young British girls on his travels. It was usually part of a settlement in trade. He could not remember this one.

Without further hesitation, Artur held up Tocca's smock exposing his protruding belly and sliced him open spilling his steaming intestines onto the ground at his feet. Screaming Tocca made a pitiful attempt to hold onto his falling intestines. Dorothea was brought forward to face her abuser. She held her eyes closed and was praying for Tocca's soul.

Lifting the disembowelled Tocca to his knees Artur commanded in a voice from another world: "Open your eyes, sister".

As Dorothea opened her eyes, Artur slit Tocca's throat from ear to ear. She continued to pray aloud with tear-filled eyes fixed on the dying Tocca. Artur held him upright until he breathed his last and then threw him down at Dorothea's feet. Stepping over the body, Artur dipped two fingers in the warm blood and made the sign of the cross on Dorothea's forehead. She fell to her knees still praying while crying and was carried gently by Artur's men out of the roundhouse.

Tocca's body was dragged out and straw thrown down to soak up the blood. Artur wiped his blade, placed more wood on the fire and resumed his seat opposite the emissary who had also resumed his, there being little else to do.

"What right had you!?" demanded Augustine.

Artur responded calmly in Latin to Augustine who glared at him. "It was necessary, emissary. The spirit of the Holy Ghost came upon me. I could do no other. My sister was defiled by this man while a bondswoman of the Scotii. Now she is avenged and a cloud has been lifted from her spirit. He has answered for his sin as God wanted. Now he too is cleansed."

"I am referring to making the sign of the cross on her forehead and in blood! What sacrilege is this?"

"My sister had to be avenged. Her soul was in torment," said Artur.

"Only God and His earthly servant, the Church, have that power, Guledig. The Church has much to teach you."

The two sat in silence reflecting further on the developing circumstances. The slaughter appeared to have satisfied Artur who sat quietly before the fire, while anger continues to stir Augustine.

"That man knew the whereabouts of the sacred scrolls. You could have kept him alive until we had this information! He was sent by God to me!" said Augustine slamming the arm of his chair in angry frustration.

"Emissary, I assure you anything that chicken of the dung heap had said after my sister identified his sin would have been suspect. He would have told us any story to save his saggy skin."

"Now we have the whole island of Eriu to search! Where will we begin?" Augustine's eyes blazed and his nostrils flared accusingly at Artur.

"Not so, emissary" Artur's tone was calm and reassuring before the emissary's rage. "We know where this creature came from before he travelled here. That is where the scrolls will be."

"Where was that?"

"The kingdom of *Iarmummu* in the south, in the village of Mungair. One of my captains was born there and knew this man. He will guide you."

This placated Augustine somewhat.

"He will guide me, Guledig?" asked Augustine. "No, you will accompany me and supply me with men. Your sister is pledged to me as a translator. She serves the Church, not you. These are the wishes of the Holy Father. Will you defy him in your arrogant ways?"

"I am pledged to obey the Holy Father. But if I go with many men to Eriu, Britain may fall. In addition my presence will attract attention that will impede your mission. This will not serve the Church's cause."

Rolling up the sleeve of his cloak Augustine said,

"Look at my skin, Guledig. Do you not think a black skinned man from the Church of Rome travelling in Eriu will not attract attention? I will need men to ensure these scrolls accompany me back to Rome. If the Holy Father should lose his emissary and the sacred scrolls, he will not look favourably on you or on any of these islands, I assure you. Besides if you do not wish to see your sister enslaved and abused in Eriu once more, you will provide proper protection."

Artur stared at Augustine silently. He would not accompany the emissary to Eriu. He could not leave Britain while the preparations for war were under way, scrolls or no. Such actions would risk everything. He did not wish to have much needed men diverted from his planned campaign in the east against the Angles, but what the emissary said was right. He risked his sister and much else if he did not protect the emissary and the scrolls. He was also intent on these scrolls remaining in Britain. Artur understood that the very words of the Christ would secure the church in Britain like no buildings or armies ever could. He could see that these scrolls were now as important to Britain as any army. On this Artur would not compromise.

"Very well, Emissary. I will provide sufficient men and one of my captains, Ros Failge, to protect your mission and my sister In Eriu. But my presence will not be helpful to you in Eriu or to the future of the Church in Britain. I will remain in Britain to protect our lands from the pagan Angles and to prepare the way for your return with the scrolls to Britain to found the holy Church. This is the outcome desired by God."

XVIII The sidhe

(The underworld)

"I will not stay silent! My vow is a falsehood designed to hide the truth."

Startled, they turned to look at Bartholomew who had uttered these words in the soft light of the room where they ate.

"My silence risks all our lives, but worse than this, it puts *the Word* of the Christ at risk," continued Bartholomew.

"Brother, your vow is…." began Cormac.

"I would be condemned for all time!" Bartholomew shouted at Cormac. "My true name is Simon of Bethaza in Judaea, not Bartholomew. That's another deceit. I am a scholar and a monk. It is I who translated the scrolls and was forced to take a vow of silence by the Patriarch to hide the truth for the Church. My teacher, good Father Clement, who helped me, has been banished to the desert in silence."

Pointing to the leather bag held by Cormac, Simon with trembling hand and voice said: "What you have been given by the Patriarch to carry, Father Cormac, are the last words of the Christ as written down by Joseph of Arimithaea from His words as He lay dying. It is witnessed by Mary of Magdala, Nicodemus and James the Just. It was brought out of Judaea by St. Mark to Egypt.

"It has been hidden for many years in the Great Library. Now they have sent it away to this land to be hidden once more. The Church fears the truth as spoken by the Christ. But I will remain silent no longer."

The one now called Simon glared at Cormac. His tortured young eyes burnt with anger and pain. He expected to be reproved by the older monk. Instead Cormac simply stared at the leather bag in his arms, cradling it like a delicate flower.

Simon's outburst had been in his native tongue of Greek. So Bretha understood nothing of what he had said, being fluent in her own native tongue only. However she had sensed the young monk's distress since their first meeting and wished to understand his torment and help him, if she could. Instinctively she held Simon's arm and sought to catch his eye to offer comfort in whatever language she could. Simon in his agitation remained focused on Cormac, unaware of Bretha's attention.

Cormac, Melania, Bretha and Simon were sitting at a large table in a room next to one of the great halls of the *Tuatha De*. Iucharba had led them to this place of safety in the underworld immediately after the violent confrontation with King Tigernaig in the overworld of Mungair. None dared to follow them into the world of the *Tuatha De*.

These were Eriu's 'old people', sometimes known as the 'fairy people' who had ruled over the land before the invasion of the Gaels had forced them to flee. They had built a kingdom under the hills and mountains known as the sidhe, where they lived separately and in contentment separate from the overworld of the Gaels whom they no longer sought to challenge. To the *Tuatha De* the overworld of their ancient memory had vanished and had been replaced in their view by the harsh world of the Gael with their brute physicality, rivalries and rude manners. Then during the Justinian plague the old gods had asked the old people with their power of magic and healing to help the overworlders find a new way of being as the plague had created despair and destitution.

In their wisdom the *Tuatha De* knew that a balance between the two worlds would bring benefits to both. Now in this time there began to be alliances formed between the Gael and those in their underworld chambers of the sidhe. Those Gaels with a mind to see could understand the benefits that arose from such an alliance during the plague. Others among the Gael were resentful and suspicious of the motives of the 'old people'. It was for good cause, some Gaels said, that their ancestors had driven the *Tuatha De* to the sidhe.

Since they had been victims of great injustices in the past, the *Tuatha De* detested unjust and brutal rulers, such as Tigernaig of *Iarmummu*. More than this, King Tigernaig had made an enemy of the people of the sidhe by stealing the Shield of Eogabal which they had given to the *Maicc Broc* as a token of friendship.

Neither overworlder nor *Tuatha De* could interfere in the affairs of one another unless help was asked for and was to the higher benefit of both. For example they would not intervene to settle petty rivalries and neither could they be won over by clever words or persuaded by promises of riches or land. For this reason it was difficult for those of low minds and poor morals to engage productively with the *Tuatha De*. In fact many brigands would receive a singed beard for even daring to make an approach.

The people of the sidhe knew of Cormac's arrival as soon as he and his party had set foot on Inish Cathaig. The ambition of Tigernaig to obtain these sacred scrolls and sell them to the Bishop of Rome convinced the *Tuatha De* that this matter needed their attention.

Iucharba had left Cormac and his friends to rest while he made some arrangements for their onward journey. As they sat in silence around the table taking in Simon's revelations, a degree of calm descended on the four after the violent confrontation with the king in Mungair. The air in the underworld had soft warmth that bathed them gently in both body and mind. There were fragrances too in the still air that tantalised. In one moment the aroma of herbs like mint and thyme and sage teased the nostrils. This would then change to scents of incense or freshly cut wood or grasses. As they breathed the air in the sidhe, the situation in the overworld that had just been left so hurriedly behind by the four, became clearer and less charged with emotion for them. Even Brother Simon's state of high anxiety was moderating as the moments passed. In a quietened mood, they began to play a game naming all the fragrances that wafted around them. Cormac and Bretha excelled at those connected with nature while the lady Melania and Simon were skilled at naming the incenses and some spices; until a point was reached when the lady Melania smelt the presence of her dead father and in tears realised that these fragrances were being generated by their thoughts. Perhaps, she suggested, a device to compensate in the sidhe for the absence of real stimulation. Were fragrances in the sidhe a means of communicating thoughts and emotions?

Their discussion of this phenomenon was interrupted by the return of Iucharba. His appearance had altered much since he had emerged from the underworld to take command of the confrontation with King Tigernaig. Now in the world of the *Tuatha De* his dark features had changed. His hair assumed a golden colour and his eyes were bright blue, yet still wolf-like, his face was softer featured in the light of the sidhe. Yet there was no doubting it was Iucharba; the voice retained the commanding depth and tone that was instantly recognisable.

"I have made arrangements for you to travel northwards along the River Sionann towards Colum Cille. There are monasteries by the river and lakes that will give you shelter," said Iucharba smiling at the four. "The boatman, Feth Fio, knows the land and can be trusted by you. He will bring you to your destination."

"Will he bring us to Colum Cille on the island of Island of Aio?" asked Cormac.

"Colum Cille will now meet you on the north coast of Eriu. He will leave his community on Aio shortly" said Iucharba.

"How do you know this of Colum Cille?"

"Colum Cille knows of your arrival and has made arrangements to reach the north coast soon," said Iucharba.

"But how does Colum Cille know about us?" asked Cormac alarmed that news would have spread to Colum Cille so quickly.

"We told him" said Iucharba plainly. "Colum Cille has worked with the *Tuatha De* since the time of the plague. We help the prince in many ways because he understands our ways and works to bring light to the world."

Iucharba looked at each of the faces staring at him in wonder. Both Cormac and Bretha knew of the legend of these people, but neither of them had conversed with them or been in the sidhe. There had been no such contact between Gael and *Tuatha De* during Cormac's young years in Eriu and he had never heard Colum Cille talk of them.

Iucharba saw Cormac's doubt.

"Do you doubt what I say, monk?" said Iucharba coldly.

"Forgive me, but how can you have told Colum Cille of my presence in Eriu. He is on the island of Aio many days journey to the north?" asked Cormac.

"Look about you, monk" said Iucharba simply. "Do you think the *Tuatha De* live in a world like yours? This is the sidhe, not the overworld. Know this, the prince remembers you from Durrow and hoped that you had found God's comfort in the desert after the sad passing of your wife Moninna and your sons, Ternoc and Etgal. Does that satisfy you or will I tell everyone how you met the lovely Moninna during the festival of Beltaine?"

Cormac smiled. Not many beyond Colum Cille knew these things about his earlier life in Eriu.

"Forgive me for doubting you, Iucharba. We are grateful for your help. It has been a long journey and the burden has been heavy."

"The *Tuatha De* will help lift that burden where we can, but do not assume we will always be able to help as we have done here. The old gods have bound us to certain limits," Iucharba said while his piercing eyes took them all in.

He continued: "There is more that you should know. The Roman emissary has now landed on the south coast with a party of twenty horse soldiers from Britain. He aims to trade with the kings of Eriu and the abbots to obtain these scrolls for his master in Rome. The emissary will offer much in return. If they refuse, the emissary believes he has powerful support in Britain and Gaul to conquer Eriu and seize the scrolls for the Church of Rome. The merchant Tocca mac Aedo travelled to meet with the emissary, as we thought he would. Tocca was killed before he could reveal to the emissary that your true destination is Prince Colum Cille. The emissary believes the scrolls are in Mungair, where the merchant met you. So he journeys there."

"But the merchant is lying on the ground above us. We left him there but a short time ago. Put there by you," said Cormac.

"No. In your measurement of time that was some time ago. Time in the sidhe is flexible and can be bent to our will. You have been here longer than you think, in your time. The merchant recovered, journeyed to Gaul to find the emissary and was slain."

"Then we must leave at once" said Cormac getting up from the table only to find himself thrust back down by some invisible force that seemed to come from Iucharba's raised hand.

"The emissary will take some time to get to Mungair. You will also travel faster by water than the emissary will by horse," smiled

Iucharba calmly. "Feth Fio will not be here until morning in the overworld. So you are invited to spend the night in the sidhe and then journey onwards."

Iucharba held up a long finger and continued talking. "However before he died, the merchant revealed all that he knew to a British military chief: that you will deliver the Christ scrolls to Colum Cille in Aio and not in Mungair. This information was cleverly kept from the emissary by this chief before he slew the merchant for the rape of his sister. This general detests the Scotii for their raids on his people, in particular for the enslavement and rape of his beloved sister. He has ambitions to build a strong *Chresten* church in his own land of Britain that will be a buttress against the pagan Angles and Saxons and believes these Christ scrolls will strengthen this church. His motives are not base like the emissary's. He seeks the true word of your Christ for good reasons, as do you and Colum Cille. He commands a powerful army in north Britain and plans to invade Eriu to capture the scrolls if he can. This general's motives are not base and for that reason the *Tuatha De* will not be able to help you as we can with this emissary. Colum Cille will need all his skills as a diplomat and strategist to deal with this general. In many ways these two are very alike, both Chresten with ambitions for their people and their faith. We find this a fascinating struggle for the Christ scrolls that you carry and are pleased to be able to help good spirit in this drama, where we can."

"Who is this general?" asked Cormac.

"If I say his name it will feed his power. He is, like Colum Cille, the descendant of high druids and is guided by the old powers while he seeks the new. He, like Colum Cille, understands the true power of the Christ scrolls."

A twinkle came to Iucharba's eyes.

"This man's sister is now a sister of Christ in the service of the Bishop of Rome, even though she was raped by her owner while a bondswoman. She now travels with the emissary as his translator. The British general will want his sister safely returned to him, will he not? We will see which is stronger: the ties of blood or faith. Your God does indeed work in wondrous ways, my friends." He laughed quietly and looked round at the group who were listening intently to his words. "But knowledge is power, is it not? You know your enemies now. So proceed in confidence."

Turning to face Simon, Iucharba continued, "As a scholar you know the facts, but there is more to these scrolls than a scholar's facts. For now you have revealed their origins to your friends and that is enough. Reveal no more. I counsel you all to speak no further on this matter to any other before you meet with Colum Cille. We will guide you where we can, as will your own God," Iucharba said reassuringly and smiled his lupine smile while looking around at all four. "Now I will take you to your room to sleep. Your minds need rest and in the morning I will bring you to your boat on the river."

XIX: Immram

(Boat journey)

Rain was falling as they emerged into the bright light of the overworld accompanied by Iucharba. The fresh air of the early morning laden with rain felt heavier than the air of the sidhe. The entrance to the sidhe was concealed by a copse of ash and beech on the side of a large mound looking westwards towards the River Sionann. Early morning song of the blackbird greeted their arrival into the overworld and bluebells carpeted the ground in the shade, their scent hanging in the still air. After cautiously seeking permission from the spirit of the place, Bretha and the lady Melania began to pick bright blue bunches. As the rain became heavier they gathered under a large sheltering ash tree. Iucharba began speaking in grave tones.

"It seems we have under estimated this emissary, friends. Since we spoke he has changed his route and now heads directly towards the High King in Temair. It seems he will not seek out the scrolls in Mungair as was hoped, but will look to secure the early support of the High King himself to obtain the scrolls. He has many inducements to offer."

All at once the rain stopped and the birds fell silent. It was as if all creation was listening. Everyone looked to Cormac for guidance.

"This is not the news we hoped for in our prayers," said Cormac. "If the emissary can win over the High King, then the scrolls are in great danger."

"Father Cormac, you are correct," said Iucbarba. "While you remain outside Colum Cille's protection you are very vulnerable and more so now that the High King may pursue you for the scrolls rather than the Bishop of Rome's emissary on his own."

"We must make haste to Colum Cille before the High King and his agents can reach us," said Cormac. "Your boatman must take us up river with all speed, Iucharba."

"Feth Fio has the swiftest boat on the river. But the emissary is now on the Great Road to Temair and with fast horses will arrive with the High King in a day, maybe two."

"We cannot wait here. We must find the boatman and be on our way," said Cormac and set off towards the river without looking back for further discussion or agreement. The others followed his lead.

As they arrived on the jetty, a small figure emerged from behind a clump of thorn on the river bank.

Without turning to look Cormac said, "Welcome, Master Hare. We are pleased to have your company once more. You are well in yourself?"

"I am well, good monk, though tired from my exertions of late."

Cormac regarded the hare curiously, but asked no questions.

"You look well, monk, as do all our friends. But a little burdened perhaps," said Zachariah examining the group gathered on the jetty with a steely eye. All were delighted to see the hare, though a nervous energy hung round them as they contemplated developments.

"We are hard pressed, hare. Much has happened in your absence. But our good friend Iucharba of the *Tuatha De* has been our stout defender and adviser" said Cormac.

Iucbarba had not followed them onto the jetty, but stayed close on the river bank. He bowed to Zachariah who returned the gesture and then pointed to a boat approaching the jetty.

"Feth Fio will now take you onwards towards the source of the river. In the land of the Ui Maine, at the great monastery of the Meadow of the Sons of Nós, a trusted servant of Colum Cille, by name Luigbe, will meet you and take you onwards. The *Tuatha De* wishes you well in your sacred mission. We will help where we can, but the sidhe in the northern lands of the Ulaidh is not strong. Farewell."

With that he waved and walked up the hillside, from where he stood like a sentinel observing their departure from the shelter of a tree.

211

The group watched Feth Fio bring the boat alongside the jetty. He was a small man who with great agility leapt up onto the jetty to tie the boat on. As he did so he took in the group standing expectantly. His small head bobbed and his whiskered face twitched busily as he secured the boat and examined his passengers. He wore a brown cloak against the rain, but his head was unprotected revealing thick short brown hair.

"Which one of ye is Father Cormac mac Fliande?" he asked.

"I am" said Cormac.

"I am Feth Fio, master boatman of the River Sionann" he said proudly. Then shaking a bony hand with long nails at Cormac, "A traveller told me yez do this in Egypt. So Feth Fio wants to show willing."

Cormac stood perplexed, eager to be on the water and not sure what the boatman had in mind with his hand gestures.

The lady Melania whispered to Cormac: "I think he wants to shake hands."

"Of course," said Cormac who shook Feth Fio's hand.

Feth Fio then went round each of the group in turn to shake hands, even though shaking hands with women was not a custom practised in Egypt. He stopped at Zachariah licking his lips either in nervousness or in the expectation of a meal.

"Is this one coming too?" he asked Cormac.

Zachariah looked appalled.

"Yes, this is Zachariah our companion" said Cormac.

"I don't normally take hares, except to eat. They didn't say anything about pet hares. This one's a strange colour too," said Feth Fio stroking his whiskers thoughtfully.

"I am Zachariah, the Prophet of Babylonia who happens to be a hare at this time. Do not disrespect me, sir. I am no one's 'pet' or their dinner. I am a golden hare!" said Zachariah glaring defiantly at the boatman and rising to his full height.

"Ah! A changeling. Why didn't you say? I get a few on the river, more up north where we're going. Always get on well with changelings. The reason may be obvious. You're welcome on Feth Fio's boat, Master Zachariah."

"Thank you," said Zachariah smiling with satisfaction.

"We are anxious to be upriver, Master Feth Fio" said Cormac eager to communicate their need for urgency to the boatman.

"This I know, Father Cormac. Master Iucharba has made me aware of your need for haste," said Feth Fio. Then holding up a bony hand he continued, "I have no need to know any more, Father. All my years on this great river have taught me that if I am told no tales, I can carry no tales and no one seeks me out for what I know. That's how I have kept my skin all these years."

Feth Fio attentively helped each into the boat. His boat was a curragh fashioned with rods of alder, covered with ox hide stretched on the frame and sealed with sheep fat to keep it watertight. It was light in order to move fast through the water, but was extremely strong to withstand the wind and waves. Feth Fio's craft was large enough for a party of twelve and could be sailed or rowed. It was to become very familiar to them in the coming days on the long journey up the great river.

To balance the craft Feth Fio divided the party, with Cormac and the lady Melania in the stern and Bretha and Simon in the bow. Zachariah being lighter took up a position in the middle, alongside Feth Fio who manned the oars.

Before they departed and much to Cormac's consternation, Bretha asked Feth Fio to stay his oars. She made a votive offering of her gathered bluebells to the goddess of the river, throwing the flowers onto the surface of the swirling water. The lady Melania then cast some bluebells to the four winds asking Isis once again to support their journey. Cormac and Simon watched the bluebells float gracefully away on the river current. With the pagan gods placated, both monks began singing the Credo as Feth Fio bent his oars at the beginning of their race northwards to meet with Colum Cille's emissary.

That night they stayed at Cill Dalua, in the monastery of Molua, still in the land of *Iarmummu*, where word had spread that sacred scrolls were in Eriu brought from Egypt and sought by the Bishop of Rome. The monks were agog at the arrival of this strange band carrying sacred scrolls. So much so that Cormac and his companions began to doubt that staying in monasteries was the wisest strategy. Anyone, High King or no, could find them simply by asking at the monasteries along the way.

For this reason Simon refused Molua's offer to join his monastery. Simon's refusal was a relief to Cormac, even though it was the patriarch's wish that the young monk should be secreted in a monastery on arrival in Eriu and it was clear that Simon was greatly in need of spiritual support: support that Cormac could not easily provide while travelling. Cormac suspected that the young monk's crisis went much deeper and he was experiencing something of a crisis of faith. Simon alone knew the contents of the scrolls. So only he grappled with the message of Yeshua's Last Testament. Cormac prayed that this experience would draw Simon closer to the divine.

They left Molua shortly after matins as the sun rose. Cormac took the oars alongside Feth Fio and the two oarsmen greatly increased the speed of the boat as they headed against the strong flowing river and out into the great lake. Once in the great lake they hoisted the sail to take advantage of a southerly breeze and freed from the task of rowing, both Feth Fio and Cormac showed themselves to be expert fishermen. By evening they had many good-sized trout to eat.

They resolved not to spend the night in the nearby monastery of the 'Land of the Two Streams'. The evening was a gentle one with a soft breeze coming off the land and a clear sky after much rain. So they slept as best they could in the boat with the sail for protection. At sunrise the next morning Cormac took Simon with him to the shore to say matins. As they looked east to pray they saw the sky streaked with the red of sunrise. It was a holy time that needed no church to see the divine.

Matins was brought to a sudden close when the sound of a woman's screams was heard coming from the lake behind them. Running to the shore that fell steeply to the water they could see Bretha swimming and shrieking, not in terror but in delight as an otter swam with her. The two were tumbling together in the water, each trying to catch the other. It was clear that Bretha was naked. Seeing that she was in no danger Simon walked off towards the boat in no humour to understand the unbridled joy. Cormac sat down a discrete distance away to watch the sunrise before they would have to set sail once more on their race northwards. In truth he enjoyed the sounds of Bretha's pleasure as she swam. Her squeals were matched by those of the otter.

Presently she called to him breathlessly.

"Father Cormac, can ye help me out? This bank is very steep," she said. "Mind, I'm naked so ye may want to close yer eyes to save yer monk's blushes."

Reaching down with his eyes duly closed Cormac said, "Take my hand, child."

With one heave Bretha landed on the grassy bank beside Cormac who steadfastly kept his eyes closed.

"Fetch your clothes, child. We will need to be gone as soon as the sun is up."

Cormac resumed his position watching the sunrise while Bretha dressed behind him.

"That Feth Fio is a divil. He nipped my behind," she said as she dressed. "But I pulled his tail hard for good measure."

Cormac took the confirmation of Feth Fio's nature quietly. Feth Fio was a changeling. He had suspected as much from Feth Fio's demeanour and movements. There was a lot of the otter in him.

"There's a dragonfly on yer shoulder, Father," said Bretha as she came over to Cormac and sat beside him.

"I know. He was there all through matins. He may be a dead monk come to watch over us," he laughed at his joke.

"No. That's Colum Cille keeping an eye on us," said Bretha. "He's whispering in your ear, 'Get me the scrolls, Cormac, before that gobshite from Rome' he says."

Cormac regarded Bretha solemnly.

"My joshing annoys ye, Father, doesn't it?" said Bretha blushing under his stern gaze.

"You're an imp. But there's no harm in you, child, only good."

They sat quietly.

"Tell me, child, why did you wish to travel with us on this dangerous journey?" asked Cormac.

"A poet needs to experience the world, father. Otherwise what would I have to say in my words? I'm composing a great epic poem about this adventure. It'll be the talk of all the *filid* down through

215

the ages and ye'll all be immortalised like the great Cú Chulainn or
Ulysses. This will be a greater legend than Táin Bó Cúailnge once
my poem is finished."

"That's quite an ambition," said Cormac.

"How long were you in the desert, Father?"

"I lost count of the years. Perhaps ten."

"Is it very different from Eriu?"

"Imagine a beach but no sea and sand dunes stretching away as far
as you can see and a sun as hot as the fires on Beltaine night," said
Cormac.

"Why would you go to such a place?"

"God is there."

"Is he not here in Eriu?"

"He is now, child."

"What of your family in Eriu?"

"All taken up by God."

"In the famine and plague?"

Cormac nodded.

"Did you have a wife and children?"

Cormac nodded again. "Two boys," he whispered.

At that two small birds flew close overhead. Cormac and Bretha
both watched them fly off to the north. Tears came to Bretha's eyes
as she saw the deep longing in Cormac's heart to join the two birds.
Instinctively she reached out and held Cormac's hand. Cormac did
not resist.

"And you, sweet child? You carry a loss too."

"My mother died giving birth to my brother. They both died."

"They all watch over us from heaven where we will re-join them,"
said Cormac.

"When we were in the sidhe my mother came to me during the
night"

"So did Moninna, Ternoc and Etgal come to me," said Cormac
smiling.

"There is magic in this land, Father."

"I know, child. There is magic everywhere. We are magic. We will
need all the magic there is to get these scrolls safely to Colum Cille
and live to tell the tale."

He paused and turned to Bretha, looking into her big green eyes and beyond. Bretha held his gaze.

"I need you to keep a watch over Brother Simon, child. Will you do that?"

"Simon doesn't need I" she said.

"He needs friendship" said Cormac. "His mind is troubling him. These events have disturbed him greatly. Only he knows the contents of the scrolls. That's a burden even for the most strong. He is young and still soft. When the mind is troubled it puts the soul to flight and the body becomes a wandering thing."

Still holding each other's gaze, Cormac continued, "Teach him your language, child. He is a scholar. The learning will distract the mind and allow the soul to fill him again. Let him discover another's language. Use the wisdom of the old people that is deep within you, Bretha."

It was as if Cormac could see inside to the very heart of her. Bretha smiled and nodded, "I will, father. If he will let me."

"He has his choices to make, as do we all. With God's grace and our support he will make the right ones. God has honoured each of us with great challenges." He broke his gaze and looked down at Bretha's bosom, "Keep your vestments buttoned up," said Cormac reaching out and buttoning Bretha's smock. "He is chaste. Temptation of the flesh will only feed the body. It's his soul that needs fed, child. Do you understand?"

"I do, father. I'll keep meself buttoned up and me legs closed around the young man, but only him, mind."

Cormac grimaced. Bretha could not resist teasing the gentle monk. She was an imp as he said, but it was her way of showing love.

Getting to his feet, Cormac said, "Now the sun is up we must be on our way."

As they walked to the boat Cormac said a silent prayer seeking God's forgiveness for speaking of such things as magic and asked for a blessing for Bretha.

XX: Arrival in the Laigin

Cathair Mar knew in his gut when the large three-masted vessel appeared on the horizon off the coast of the Laigin in the southeast of Eriu that it was the arrival of the Roman emissary. The *Ard Ri* had sent a message throughout the land that wherever the emissary put ashore he was to be brought to the great *rath* in Temair without delay. So now it would fall to Cathair Mar as chieftain of his kindred, the Uí Bairrche, to meet with this emissary and conduct him to the *Ard Ri*, the High King of Eriu.

The gentle shores of the lands of the Ui Bairrche were much favoured by traders from west Britain, Gaul, and Hispania because the great road brought their goods inland to the rest of Eriu. Traders came in single-masted vessels with shallow draft that were much smaller than the grand vessel now off the headland. So Cathair Mar was persuaded that this three-master was no trader, but perhaps carried the emissary from Rome. Besides, whispers among the many merchants had said that the emissary was journeying through Gaul and would most likely come ashore in the land of the Uí Bairrche and travel northwards to the *Ard Ri* in Temair along the king's road, the Slighe Chualann.

The industrious Uí Bairrche had built a stout harbour where vessels could moor and be sheltered as the wind blew across the channel and the waves crashed. As a result trade had greatly increased and with it their standing and prosperity. Such standing would surely grow should the kindred conduct the emissary to the *Ard Ri* safely. Cathair Mar prayed to the gods, the god of the *Chrestens* and the gods of the Celts that he, as the Tuatha Ri – the clan chief , would deliver the emissary to the *Ard Ri* without the evil eye, given the bad blood between the *Laigen* and the *Ui Neill* whose chief, Ard mac Ainmuirech, was now *Ard Ri* in Temair.

No such emissary had ever set foot in Eriu; although some said one came in the time of Lóegaire mac Néill, son of Niall. In the monasteries there was much talk of these sacred scrolls that had arrived in Eriu brought from Egypt by a monk from Eriu, a saintly and wise desert father. They said these scrolls came from the Holy Land itself and contained secret prophesies for all mankind. For this reason the Bishop of Rome sought them. But who is the Bishop of Rome to make such a claim, asked some. These scrolls belonged to God. So let God decide.

Cathair Mar was not a judge or a bishop to assess these matters. He was elected to lead his tuath, the Uí Bairrche. This had not so far involved him in the affairs of kings and bishops. He would deliver this emissary to the *Ard Ri* and return to his farm and his people and have done with sacred scrolls.

He collected the council of the tuath and together they waited for the arrival of the vessel as it made its way ever closer to the shore and with its steady progress came a sense of unease to Cathair Mar. A warm southerly breeze blew across the wide green sea that morning, but only the one vessel was in view where normally there would be several. It was as if this vessel was a large fish that had frightened off all the smaller ones. In spring there were always vessels in sight carrying wine, cloth, salt and more besides. The council were unsettled by such an empty ocean. What could this mean? they asked.

They appealed to Manannán mac Lir, the god of the sea. Manannán had been a good friend to the *Ui Bairrche* in recent times by allowing them to build their stout harbour. But Manannán could be a trickster when the mood was upon him and he was friend to the *Tuatha De* who were mixed up in this whole business of sacred scrolls. No one knew what games he and the *Tuatha De* would play. You had to have your wits about you when dealing with Manannán.

The answer came from Grundmael the Farsighted as he arrived, running from the headland.

"The vessel carries soldiers and horses!" he said breathlessly.

"How many, Grundmael?" asked Cathair Mar.

Grundmael could not count, but threw down pebbles on the ground to represent the number.

"Twenty," said Cathair Mar.

"Why does an emissary need these horse soldiers?" asked another of Cathair Mar.

Cathair Mar thought and said: "The Church of Rome does not know this land. Perhaps their bishop fears we will attack his emissary."

"We should gather the war band, Cathair Mar. In case they slaughter us where we stand" said Cathair Mar's brother, Daire.

"Daire is right, Cathair Mar. We cannot be sure this is the emissary. He may be a brigand come to plunder."

"Very well, but keep them out of sight lest they provoke these soldiers needlessly" said Cathair Mar.

Dorothea regarded the tall, gaunt figure of Augustine standing precariously at the bow of the vessel as it leapt and dived towards the sandy shore where they could see men gathering to meet their arrival. Augustine's large hands clasped the rigging tightly for support: it was the first time Augustine had stood upright for several days. Over his back was slung his bronze crucifix.

Sea sickness had laid the emissary low during their passage from Armorica. He was not a natural sailor. However his present anxiety for dry land was driven not by a selfish concern for his own well-being, it was his all-consuming commitment to the task before him that drove Augustine to be ashore in search of the scrolls. His personal welfare was not a matter he considered, nor in truth should it be for any servant of God. His holy mission was all. His body and mind was as always bent to the service of his master.

Dorothea did allow herself to ponder which master the emissary served: God or merely the physical incarnation of the Holy Father who was also Augustine's foster father, Pope John III. She had never seen the emissary pray. He observed none of the offices and read none of the gospels. His only display of his religion was the large bronze cross he carried with him at all times and his fondness for the writings of his namesake, St. Augustine of Hippo.

She had nursed Augustine throughout the voyage as he wretched and writhed on an empty stomach, unable to eat or drink for long periods. He was not an easy patient. He cursed the sea, the wind, the vessel and its sailors as agents of the devil. He complained of her nursing and threw the food she brought him overboard believing in his delirious state that she was trying to poison him; at one point mistaking Dorothea for his mother, accusing her of abandoning him as a child and now returning to kill him. He wept, convinced he was dying. Instead of calling out for God's salvation, he called for his mother. Dorothea thought he might indeed die and prayed for him fervently. Augustine recovered: principally because God had given him the constitution of an ox and so now he stood at the bow of the boat ready to confront this strange land with all his might. He was fully recovered but with no gratitude shown to his kindly nurse.

Returning to Eriu stirred mixed emotions in Dorothea. She had seen no visions urging her to return to the land of her enslavement. Nevertheless here she was about to set foot on this island once again: this time in service of the church and no longer as a bondswoman and concubine.

It was fitting, Dorothea believed. There had been many kindnesses shown her during her captivity by the people of the land that she should return in kind. But it was God's infinite kindness which had given her salvation. During captivity Dorothea had pledged her life to God without thought of return, yet in return God had caused Artur to free her. She had no doubt that she was freed in order to serve Him.

Her brother had been greatly helped by a powerful Scotii chieftain of the *Dal Fiatach* kindred in the north of Eriu, outraged that some of his people enslaved women and children. Dorothea's master was a cruel beast who gave his hunting dog's greater consideration. He was a pirate who made his living raiding the shores of Britain from his land on the northeast coast of Eriu to plunder and enslave the weakest. The pirate escaped certain death by being absent on his foul business when Artur accompanied by the chief arrived to save Dorothea. Before leaving they burnt his house and barns to the ground including the foul hovel that had been Dorothea's prison.

Artur, like his sister, pledged himself to God from that day. He also repaid the chieftain by helping him prosecute a war against rival kindred and from this a strong bond was formed between the two men and between their kindred. Dorothea was pleased that her torment had united the *Dal Fiatach* and the Gododdin in mutual interest and had enabled her kindred to see that not all the Scotii were 'rascals'. Dorothea could see that God's hand was upon the whole affair and gave herself into His care completely.

As they drew close to the shore the sails were dropped lest they drive the vessel too hard into the sand and break the masts. Many oars were deployed to expertly guide the vessel bow first onto the shore. Riding the waves, it slid with a crunch onto the beach. Dorothea said a prayer seeking God's guidance for what must now lie ahead.

The council of the Uí Bairrche were gathered on the beach headed by Cathair Mar with their warriors out of sight in nearby woods. They regarded the beached vessel with its many soldiers and horses with concern.

Without a backward glance Augustine leapt ashore clasping his bronze crucifix. He had never been outside the boundaries of the Roman Empire. He understood Rome's customs and practices and knew no other. Yet he boldly set foot on a land with very different ways, largely unknown to the Romans and never subdued by their legions. This was not a consideration for Augustine. He would subdue this place where the legions had failed and for the Bishop of Rome not the Emperor; with himself, Augustine of Nubea, as God's representative. This was his moment. He believed he was come into his own divine destiny. With this conviction he strode towards the Uí Bairrche and holding the cross upright in the bright sun, rammed it into the soft sand in front of them. Confronted with this sight of a large black skinned monk carrying a bronze cross before him, the council stepped back a pace. Then Augustine called for Dorothea to be brought ashore so he could talk with those gathered.

Ros Failge, the captain of the troop sent to Eriu by Artur, would not allow Dorothea to leave the boat until four of his men accompanied her. Artur had commanded Ros Failge that he was to protect Dorothea beyond all other considerations. Even the sacred scrolls were secondary to his sister's safety and as a member of the Gosgordd, Ros Failge was bound by their strict code of chivalry and loyalty. So it was that Dorothea was carried ashore on a litter like a princess, much to her embarrassment and to the annoyance of Augustine. Yet her presence greatly reassured the Uí Bairrche.

They saw that she was a Sister of Christ with some standing and such a one would not be brought onto a battlefield.

Cathair Mar with his broad sword in his belt and flowing red hair stepped out from the throng of the council and in the tongue of Eriu he said: "I am Cathair Mar, Chief of the kindred, the Uí Bairrche and this is our Council. We are people of the Laigin. This is our land. What is yer business here with British soldiers and horses?"

Speaking through Dorothea Augustine said: "We are here on God's business, Chief Cathair Mar. I am Augustine of Nubea, an emissary of the Holy Father, the Bishop of Rome and these are his men. I am here on important church business to meet with the abbots of Eriu on sacred matters. The soldiers are here to protect me and the goods I carry." Unknown to Augustine Dorothea added, "We mean no harm. We are honoured to be in the land of the Uí Bairrche and seek your permission to travel onwards on our church business, Chief Cathair Mar."

Cathair Mar consulted with the council as they cautiously eyed the horse soldiers. No one present had ever seen a black skinned man. They had heard of such and believed that because they lived close to the sun they were favoured by the gods.

"No druids are harmed in this land. Even the brigands, the fiann and the *dibergga* leave druids unharmed and will give one such as ye a special wide birth, Lord Emissary. These soldiers will grow fat in yer service," said Cathair Mar. "Who do ye seek in Eriu, lord?"

"I seek the Abbot of Mungair in the kingdom of *Iarmummu.*"

"That is far to the west. Perhaps three days travel from here," said Cathair Mar struggling to hide his surprise at the emissary's desire to see only a lowly abbot.

"We know this, Cathair Mar. All the Bishop of Rome seeks is that the good people of the *Ui Bairrche* allow us to be on our way peacefully. Do this and I will see that you are mentioned in prayers in Rome, Chief Cathair Mar," said Augustine.

Cathair Mar consulted again with the Council while Augustine waited impatiently glancing to Dorothea who smiled reassuringly back. The British soldiers on the beach watched closely the movements of everyone on the beach. They understood clearly their priority to protect the general's sister at all costs.

Cathair Mar turned back to face Augustine. "It is known to us that ye seek scrolls, lord emissary. The scrolls are gone from Mungair into the hands of the *Tuatha De* and the King of *Iarmummu* is blinded. The country is in uproar and I am commanded to escort yez to our High King in Temair in the north."

Augustine swung round to glance at Ros Failge on the vessel who shrugged his shoulders in response. Being one from Eriu, but living in the service of the British and the Romans for many years, he could understand all that was being said.

"These scrolls belong to the Bishop of Rome and these *Tuatha De* will be required to hand them over to me," said Augustine.

"The *Tuatha De* are beyond command, emissary. Only the High King can negotiate with the *Tuatha De*. It is the law."

Augustine considered these developments. The whereabouts of the scrolls was known. He had someone of standing to negotiate with. That was good. Mention of a High King encouraged him. As emissary he was long accustomed to dealing with kings. He found lowly abbots problematic and tiresome in their unworldliness. He had not been relishing travelling in a strange land pursuing his quarry through rain-soaked, muddied hovels. So God had intervened on his behalf once more: he would gladly deal with this High King from the comfort of a palace and not with some half-starved rural monk.

"Very well, Cathair Mar. I accept your invitation to meet with your King."

At that Ros Failge who had been following the conversation from the vessel leapt ashore and spoke quietly in Latin to Augustine.

"Emissary, my men must accompany you and Sister Dorothea fully armed to the High King. On that there is no compromise," he said.

Augustine nodded in agreement.

"Chief Cathair Mar my soldiers will accompany me to the High King. The Bishop of Rome would have it so," said Augustine flatly.

"Very well, but we will hold yer vessel and its crew as surety. We have a good harbour in the next bay" said Cathair Mar pointing proudly over the headland.

"We will expect the vessel and crew to be treated well. My captain insists upon it. We will return when our business is complete."

"The Uí Bairrche are known for treating travellers, especially sailors hospitably and honourably. Manannán mac Lir insists that sailors are cherished while ashore. Yer vessel will be safe. Ye have my word, emissary."

XXI: The Meadow of the Sons of Nos

It was dark by the time Cormac and his friends arrived at the monastery of the Meadow of the Sons of Nós on the eastern banks of the great river Sionann. It was from here they would be taken to their final destination and a meeting with Colum Cille when they would be relieved of their sacred burden.

The wolf guard had been mounted on the monastery for the night. Their eerie calls could be heard across the water as Feth Fio silently slipped his curragh alongside the jetty. It was a black night with no moon and a gentle breeze carried the lingering scent of the day's wood smoke from the monastery. After the scourge of famine and the yellow plague when the monasteries in Eriu became a sanctuary for many, the *Tuatha De* had secured the help of the wolf to guard the communities against attacks from brigands such as the *dibergga*. It was this that began the collaboration between the people of the land and the *Tuatha De*. The wolf would guard the community and in return they would be fed. Such an arrangement also kept the community's livestock safe from the predations of the wolf.

"Ye'll not get past the wolf this night, Father Cormac," whispered Feth Fio nervously. "Better to lie on the far bank until morning."

All looked anxiously to Cormac. Standing upright in the boat he cupped his hands to his mouth and made a long, low howl into the night. As the wolf calls went silent the lady Melania gasped and pointed towards the monastery, "They are coming. Look!"

Across the meadow in front of the monastery's large embankment the shadows of a wolf pack could be seen racing towards them.

"Stay still and do not show any fear and do not look into their eyes," said Cormac. "I have dealt with the wolf before."

As they approached the jetty the wolf pack of around one dozen stopped and blocked access to the land. A single grey wolf walked soundlessly towards them, eyeing all closely. It sat calmly by their boat.

"Who called the Sons of the Country?" the wolf demanded.

"I did" said Cormac as boldly as he could.

"What is your business with the Meadow at this hour?"

"My name is Cormac mac Fliande, travelling a great distance with my friends from Egypt to meet with Abbot Colum Cille. We are to meet with his agent here in the Monastery of the Meadow. Abbot Mac Nisse expects us."

The wolf fixed Cormac with a glare and sniffed the air. Cormac avoided the wolf's gaze, to return their eye contact would be seen as a direct challenge.

"This is a strange band indeed: two monks travelling with two women and a golden hare." The wolf fixed Zachariah with a glare. This time the stare was returned. The hare had no love for the wolf since his own family's demise in Lucania.

Feth Fio spoke to break the tension, "Sarnat, the Great She Wolf, it is I, Feth Fio, boatman of the river. I can vouch for these good people. I was engaged by the *Tuatha De* to bring them to this place."

"I am not blind, changeling," snapped Sarnat. "I would recognise you from six fields away in the fog of Balor. I'd smell you first. Who are these by name?" demanded Sarnat of Feth Fio looking from one to the other.

"Well," began Feth Fio nervously. "This is Father Cormac from the desert of Egypt, but a son of this land and an ordinate of the great Colum Cille. This is the lady Melania from Egypt, a priestess of the goddess Isis." Sarnat stared softly at the lady Melania and sniffed the air. "And this is Brother Simon a scholar from the city of Alexandria and this, Bretha, daughter of Failge Berraide, the great *File* of *Iarmummu*," continued Feth Fio. Sarnat ignored Bretha and Simon and was looking again at Zachariah. "This is Master Zachariah, a changeling like meself."

Sarnat and Zachariah both stared at each other. Then the she wolf lowered her great grey head and gave out a loud wolf cry. The wolves on the bank at once turned and ran off towards the monastery compound fanning out to encircle the monastery, leaving their leader, Sarnat alone on the jetty.

"The Sons of the Country, welcome you, strangers to the Meadow. I will bring you to the monastery entrance where the Hospitaller will see you are accommodated. The changelings must remain here. They will be brought food and shelter for the night. Abbot Mac Nisse is in Vespers and will meet with you in the morning at the third hour in the hall. Prince Colum Cille's emissary is here before you."

With that Sarnat turned and walked back down the jetty to sit on the bank while the visitors stepped out of the curragh and onto the jetty.

"She has no manners on her! I will tell her who I am. I will come ashore!" said Zachariah angrily.

Feth Fio grabbed Zachariah and held him in a tight hold at the stern of the boat.

"Let me go, otter!" shouted Zachariah, nervous at the proximity of the wolf.

"Be still, Master Zachariah" said the lady Melania quietly holding a hand on the struggling hare. "It is but a short time. Feth Fio will look after you." The lady Melania had a skill with Zachariah. He ceased to struggle and sat sullenly beside Feth Fio while the others departed with the she wolf for the monastery. No one knew the reason that the wolf detested changelings, but it was known that they always had.

At the gates of the monastery they parted company with Sarnat and Cormac thanked her for her assistance.

The monastery's Hospitaller, a small elderly woman and aunt of the abbot, greeted them and brought the group to their rooms in the hostel just inside the embankment. The hostel was well built from sturdy local oak, hazel wattle and thatch. Men and women were accommodated separately in comfortable rooms with straw mattresses. Hot baths were being made ready, fires sparkled even though it was a warm spring night. A nourishing stew had been prepared.

It being the eve of the festival of Beltaine, the rooms were bedecked with the brilliant yellow of gorse, primrose and marsh marigold. The old ways blended without offence to the Christ or his church.

The lady Melania displayed the eagerness and delight of a small child at the prospect of a hot bath having only washed in rivers and sea water for many weeks. Bretha had rarely washed in a bath, preferring the convenience of rivers and the sea. However it was the eve of the Festival of Beltaine when a bath was taken to prepare the body for the purification of the fire, so she gingerly entered the bath.

"It's fierce warm, lady!" exclaimed Bretha. "There's not a chance our flesh could cook?"

Melania laughed. The water was barely hot, but perhaps much warmer than Bretha had experienced. "No child. The heat will cleanse your skin. In Egypt the baths are much hotter than this. Come and we will wash each other. You will not be boiled."

As they washed they talked as women do. Bretha began washing the lady Melania with sweet smelling soap.

"What will ye do when our task is complete, lady?" asked Bretha.

"Father Cormac will ask Prince Colum Cille for his advice and help. He may join a monastery and I would seek out your druids" said Melania.

"The *filid* will help ye. We still honour the druid ways. I will speak to my father on our return."

Bretha continued washing the lady Melania: thinking of how the *filid* could help one such as her.

Eventually Bretha spoke again: "Tell me about the goddess Isis, lady" asked Bretha.

"She is the Queen of heaven and the ocean. Isis has been my comfort since I was a child and has protected me all my life. She protects all the downtrodden. She is the daughter of Geb and wife of Osiris who is her brother."

"It is said that, Aine, my goddess, married her father, the sea god, Manannán mac Lir. Such things are against the law in our land. Only the gods do such things," Bretha observed.

"Will you marry, Bretha?"

"When I am a *file* I will marry a *file* and together we will compose beautiful verse while making our *filid* children."

Melania laughed.

"Why did ye leave yer home lady and travel here?" asked Bretha.

"My home was lost to me. The Christian church opposed my religion and would kill me and my people."

"Kill ye?!" exclaimed Bretha. "That would never happen in Eriu. Here the ways of the Celt and the ways of the Christ exist peacefully. No one is ever killed because of what they believe," said Bretha.

"I know. It is a good way to live. But in my land it is an old practice to kill whoever does not believe as you." Melania looked wistfully at the fire. "Tell me Bretha, why is the new religion of the Christ accepted in Eriu without bloodshed?"

"You're asking one such as I?" said Bretha. "Father Cormac would answer much better than I."

"I would like to know what you think, Bretha."

"The Christ's religion came here a long time ago. They say those from Eriu serving in the army of Rome at the time of the Christ brought his word here and many bishops have followed since. They use the cross as we do."

"You use the cross?"

"Yes. Ye see the ancient crosses all over our land. Some assume they are the Christ's, but they are the druids'. The cross we use is formed by the lines of the sun at the summer and winter solstices." To illustrate the point Bretha stood in the bath and raised her arms pointing to the opposing directions of the sunsets in winter and summer like a dancer. "Also we believe in resurrection after death, in life beyond this place and in the trinity in all things. Look!" Bretha lifted the gold medallion that hung about her neck and Melania leaned in close to look. "It is the triquetra: the symbol of the three in all things. Maiden, mother and crone; life, death and resurrection; earth, water and air and so with the Christ: the Father, the Son and the Holy Spirit."

"These are on temples to Osiris in Egypt," said Melania. "It is like the petals of a flower."

"Many in Eriu, like my father, believe that this Yeshua the Christ was a wise and brave druid. So his followers are gladly accepted here."

"Would that were the case in my land" said Melania sadly.

"Mind, people in Eriu are killed for different reasons: in battle for land, for cattle and for power, for women too. Maybe someone will kill for ye, lady."

Melania laughed, but for once Bretha was not joking.

"I am too old to be fought over, child."

Bretha held Melania's face in her hands. "Ye are a beauty, lady. Have no doubt. Men could well fight over ye in this land. Have a care and stay close to Father Cormac. I am protected because I am the daughter of a great *file*. If I was a poor girl I could be taken: even though the law forbids it."

Melania held Bretha's gaze.

"Yes, Bretha. I will be careful" said Melania respecting Bretha's obvious concern.

They remained in silence while Bretha finished washing Melania.

"Ye never took a husband, lady?"

"No. I am pledged to the service of the goddess."

"Have ye known a man?"

"No. I am a virgin. What of you, child? Have you taken a lover yet?"

"No I'm still a virgin. But I'd like a man to have me: one that I love and who loves me. I've kissed boys and touched them and they have touched me. But I do not want to be with child and without a husband. Both my father and my goddess would chide me."

"You are wise. Good men are a precious thing."

"Ye are attached to Father Cormac, lady, are ye not?"

"I am spiritually attached, child. I love him as a brother that is true."

"Would ye lie with him?"

"Do not talk of such things, child! It is wrong," said Melania sternly dropping the wash cloth. "Father Cormac would be hurt if he knew and I do not wish ever to see my brother hurt. Your words can hurt, Bretha. As a *file* you must know the power of words and the thoughts behind them."

"I am sorry, lady," said Bretha looking into Melania's fiery eyes. "I get too curious for the ways of people at times. It is the *file* in me. I am truly sorry. I love yez both and I too would not wish to hurt either of yez. He calls me an imp, ye know." She laughed.

"He is right. You are." Melania's eyes softened and took on a faraway look. "Father Cormac showed me great kindness during my life in Alexandria. Through our gods he was helped to save my life. He is a kindly man. I am pledged to him as a sister and he to me as a brother. We are celibate. Our gods wish it so. Come now. I will wash the imp out of you with this brush as a penance for your thoughts."

Bretha squealed as Melania brandished a stiff brush and the two women wrestled playfully in the water.

As the fire died and fatigue pressed upon them, the lady Melania and Bretha retired to sleep on a comfortable mattress close to the warm embers of the fire. Melania held the young girl in her arms and fell asleep with the fragrant smell of Bretha's newly washed skin pressed close to her nose and the sound of the wolf guard in the meadow below.

Cormac and Simon could hear the laughter of the women as they too prepared to bath. There was little conversation between the two men and there was no sharing of the bath. Cormac washed first followed by Brother Simon. As he sat warming himself before the fire, Cormac watched the young man bath. His body was thin and weakened by their weeks of travel. He trembled like a leaf in the breeze. Brother Simon did not have the constitution to withstand hardship caused by long hours of travel and a meagre diet. The desert father was hardened to such things. Cormac still worried on account of the burden the young man carried. Simon's knowledge of the scrolls was a heavy weight for one so young: heavier because Simon took much inside himself, the tradition with the eastern monks. This was made worse by the secrecy required and Simon's breaking of his vow of silence.

The Church of the *Ceile De* had created the *anam cara*: a soul friend or confessor for each monk to help him or her with their burden as the mind, body and soul wrestled with salvation in this life. It was an *anam cara* that Simon so desperately needed. Yet this was so difficult to provide on the journey. Cormac worried that if the young monk carried the burden much longer he would suffer great spiritual damage.

As Simon stepped out of the bath Cormac asked: "Is your body cleansed, brother?"

"It is, Father," said Simon.

They remained in silence. Then Cormac spoke quietly and simply: "Your welfare is important to God, brother, and to me."

"I am well, Father. Thank you," said Simon as he struggled to dress.

"God will not punish you, brother. You must know that in the depths of your soul. You are His chosen one in this affair and He will support you. Give Him your burden."

"You are the chosen one, father. I am a poor, outcast scholar."

Cormac ignored the self-pitying tone. "You have been given the knowledge of these scrolls, brother, not I."

"I do not want the knowledge any longer!" hissed Simon. "I was trained a scholar, not a desert father. I cannot carry this. It is too much!" With that Simon suddenly fell to his knees, whimpering like a wounded animal, tears flooding his pale cheeks.

Cormac rushed to Simon and held him in his arms.

"Then share it with another, brother. I will help you" said Cormac smiling at the young monk. The cleansing water had released something in the young monk as Cormac had hoped. The dam had broken. Simon was seeking help like a stream seeks the lough.

"I am bound to an oath of secrecy that only Prince Colum Cille can share," wept Simon. "I cannot give it to you. You have burden enough, father."

"Then will you share it with another?"

"It would be wrong to burden another."

"There are those who can take such burdens, brother. We must choose wisely. Will you trust me to find such a one?"

Simon hesitated.

"We must pray for guidance. Come to the church with me," said Cormac seizing Simon's hand.

Cormac led Simon by the hand across the enclosure where a night wind came off the river to chill their newly washed skins. Swiftly they entered the darkened church. It was empty save for a single monk standing as guardian by the door and one burning candle.

They knelt by the light of candle before the altar and prayed. As they did several monks began to file quietly into the church to form

a semicircle behind Cormac and Simon. One monk stood in front
and faced them. As they became aware of the monks in the church
around them both Cormac and Simon opened their eyes and raised
their bowed heads. The monk before them was Abbot Mac Nisse.
He stood with his arms held open towards Simon. Cormac gently
helped Simon to his feet.

"This is Abbot Mac Nisse, brother. He will be your anam cara. Go
with him in faith, brother," said Cormac quietly, gazing into
Simon's frightened eyes.

Simon did not resist: his trust in Cormac ran deep. He moved
towards Abbot Mac Nisse who guided him out of the church
followed by the other monks leaving Cormac alone in the church
with God.

When the bell for matins sounded and dawn began to break over
the river, the old Hospitaller woke the lady Melania and Bretha.
Cormac and Simon were already arisen and at prayer with the
monks.

After matins the four met in the great dining hall to eat with the
many merchants who visited the Monastery of the Meadows. They
waited for Colum Cille's emissary to present himself. All were
refreshed from their night's rest and bath.

While they sat, Bretha stared curiously at Simon. There was
something different about the young monk's appearance that
intrigued her. He carried himself differently, his skinny back was
no longer hunched. In return for her attention Simon allowed a
smile to flicker across his face. He was not accustomed to smiling,
so the smile fell awkwardly upon him. This crooked smile amused
Bretha and reassured both Cormac and the lady Melania.

"I am Luigbe mac Min, emissary of Colum Cille." A monk
announced abruptly standing by their table with hands clasped
before him in a very rigid manner.

"We are pleased to meet with you, brother," said Cormac standing
to greet the monk. "I am Father Cormac. We are refreshed and
eager to meet with Colum Cille."

The emissary did not return Cormac's warmth and enthusiasm. He
appeared a rough and a sour fellow with a warrior's scar on his

face. While many monks lacked fine manners and charm, Cormac had thought that Colum Cille would pick a monk with more warmth than this one to be his emissary on such an important matter. Luigbe mac Min neither smiled nor showed an open hand and he did not use Colum Cille's title of abbot.

"Colum Cille asks that I bring you to meet him at the Festival of Beltaine on the Hill of Uisneach this night. It is but a day's walk from here. We must leave now," said Brother Luigbe.

Cormac smiled to himself. His old mentor Colum Cille or Crimthainn as Cormac knew him, was ever drawn to a grand setting. Crimthainn could have chosen the quiet of his nearby monastery of Durrow, where he had ordained Cormac many years ago, but he could not resist the bright lights of the fires of Beltaine on Uisneach to receive the sacred scrolls from his desert monk.

In Eriu all fires were extinguished on the day of Beltaine and were only rekindled when two great fires were lit that night on the Hill of Uisneach in the very centre of the island. Once Uisneach was ablaze other fires fanned out from hill to hill across the land signalling the arrival of summer. The people of the land with their livestock then walked through the heat of the fire to drive out the winter darkness and to welcome in the fertility of the summer growth.

Crimthainn will have a performance planned, surmised Cormac. He was, after all, the great magician and performer. But Cormac wondered what his mentor had planned following the excitement of Beltaine in regard to the demands of the Bishop of Rome and his forceful emissary. Crimthainn will need all his skills as a diplomat and as a man of God to deal with the challenge posed by the scrolls.

Simon was dispatched to fetch Zachariah from the curragh and to bid Feth Fio farewell.

As they left the great hall, many monks had gathered in the enclosure to give God's blessing to Cormac and his party on their journey. As a desert monk Cormac was much revered by the monks of the *Ceile De*. Word of his journey to meet Abbot Colum Cille with the sacred scrolls from the Holy Land had spread and was already passing into folklore even before the journey was complete. As torches burnt in the half light of the dawn, monks sang the Te Deum in Cormac's honour.

Abbot Mac Nisse stepped forward. He embraced each in turn, holding Simon especially close. He whispered something in Simon's ear which made the young monk smile again. Simon nodded and clasped his hands to his chest and bowed to the abbot. Standing before them, Abbot Mac Nisse gave Cormac a small block of finely shaped wood. On it were carved verses from the Gospel of John much favoured by the Ceile De. The abbot recited:

"Let not yer hearts be troubled. Believe in God; believe also in me. In my Father's house are many rooms. If it were not so, would I have told ye that I go to prepare a place for ye? And if I go and prepare a place for ye, I will come again and will take ye to myself, that where I am you may be also.' And ye know the way to where I am going."

The abbot kissed the tablet and presented it to Cormac who in turn kissed it, wrapping it in cloth and placing it in his leather bag next to the sacred scrolls.

Much affected by this display of love Cormac waved farewell to all who were gathered, tears wetting his cheeks for he would have gladly remained with them. Instead he turned his face towards the east, towards his duty and their onward journey to the Hill of Uisneach. It seemed that even the emotions of a desert monk could be stirred.

XXII: Road to Uisneach

Brother Luigbe set a fast pace towards Uisneach that allowed for no distractions such as Bretha's fondness for gathering plants or Zachariah's many observations. Brother Luigbe set the pace from the front and no one was minded to keep him company. As he strode the monk kept a close watch on the road behind, where they had left the river Sionann and the great monastery of the Meadow. Luigbe's concern about pursuit was clear and not misjudged. Knowledge of the scrolls and the Bishop of Rome's pursuit of them were now well-known throughout Eriu. Many would have an interest in securing the scrolls in order to bargain well with a powerful bishop. Rumours abounded concerning the riches on offer from this bishop: an emperor's ransom and more, they said.

Yet here they were on the Slighe Mhor – the kings' road that runs from the east coast of Eriu all the way to the west – without any protection save for God's good grace and a couple of stout monks' staffs which would be employed if the need arose. However the road was quiet in the early hours as the sun came up over the central plain of *Mide*. The land was gentle: meadow and woodland abounded, streams and lakes sparkled in the early sun. No smoke curled from the thatch of the farms as they walked because all fires were being laid in readiness for Beltaine and the signal from Uisneach.

Cormac was interested to discover how matters of faith sat with Brother Simon after his time with Abbot Mac Nisse. While he had no wish or right to interfere between a monk and his anam cara, he needed to know about the young monk's spiritual well-being. Certainly from his demeanour Simon appeared much better as he struck up many joyful melodies on his flute as he walked.

"You are well this morning, brother, I trust?" asked Cormac of Simon as they walked side by side.

Simon smiled the same awkward smile. "Yes I am well, father. The abbot was very helpful and I am grateful to you for making such a meeting possible. A heavy load has been lifted from my mind. Even my flute feels a new spirit!" he said playing some new notes.

"I am pleased, brother. It brings joy to my heart to see you with such bright airs. Abbot Mac Nisse is a valued friend to troubled souls."

Simon smiled and nodded in agreement. The two walked on. Simon returned to his flute playing. Cormac considered further enquiry unseemly and unnecessary.

Eventually Simon volunteered more information: "I told the abbot of my torment having read the scrolls."

"Brother, you have no need to share this with me. It is enough for me that you are returned to the grace of God," said Cormac, holding up his hand. He did not wish Simon to feel he was obliged to reveal more.

"Please, father, I would like to relate some of what took place with the abbot if you will hear me. I think it may help all of us," said Simon. Then casting his eyes heavenward he continued, "Forgive me, but I presume too much, father. It is not for me, a young monk, to judge what a desert father needs. I am sorry."

"Brother, do not be sorry. We never stop learning. I will hear your thoughts on your meeting with Abbot Mac Nisse if you wish to tell me," said Cormac.

"I told the abbot of the nature of my torment since reading the scrolls and that they challenged the teachings of the holy church and caused me to question my loyalty to the church. I believe this may be the case with many who read them – if they are permitted to be read. As you know I have said that I will not be silenced any longer about the scrolls, but that conviction has tormented me. I have been unsure about how to speak out and to whom. The words would not come. I now know I was too angry and God did not wish me to speak with a hot tongue. The abbot has cooled my tongue with his kind words and wisdom."

Simon stopped speaking and considered his thoughts and the words he would use.

"The abbot told me of a legend from this land. It's about a great warrior and chieftain – Conal Cearnach from the far north of Eriu. He served in the Roman legions as a centurion and was there at the crucifixion in Golgotha. He was mightily offended at the injustice and cruelty meted out to our lord Yeshua by the Romans and the Jews and swore he would be His champion from that moment onward. He returned to Eriu and brought the true Word with him. He told the people what the apostles had told him: that one day the true Word would come to Eriu in a physical form carried by messengers of the Christ.

"Abbot mac Nisse has said that he believes that we are these messengers sent by the Christ, the fulfilment of the centurion's legend. Isn't that wonderful news, father!? Once we deliver the scrolls to Prince Colum Cille I will bring the word to all of Eriu. I believe I have been guided to do so by Lord Yeshua himself!"

Simon sounded some playful notes on his flute. Cormac considered Simon's words and sought guidance on this response. "That is good, brother. It is a legend I have heard something of, but it is so long ago, I had forgotten it. There were several warriors from Eriu who served in the legions and brought much back to this land from far off places, including the word of the Christ," said Cormac. "It is thought that this is how the word first came to this land in the years following the Crucifixion."

They walked in silence for a while, considering what each had said. Cormac was anxious not to discourage the young monk's new found enthusiasm.

Cormac then spoke: "I am pleased that you have found your voice in the Christ, brother. We all must consider our sacred purpose when the scrolls are safely delivered to Prince Colum Cille. But can I ask you, brother, to stay your hand in this matter until Colum Cille has considered the scrolls and we have consulted with him? You will find that he is a wise and just abbot who understands *The Word* of the Christ better than many in Rome and Alexandria. He has helped lead the church in Eriu on a true and just path. I hope you will not be disappointed."

"Father, you must think me a young upstart," said Simon. "I did not presume to know better than Prince Colum Cille or you. Colum Cille is held in high regard and I am honoured to be meeting with him. I will listen closely to his counsel and be guided by it, but I am fired with the Holy Spirit, father."

"You have experienced a holy moment, brother, and the Holy Spirit cannot be denied," said Cormac. "You will be guided on what to do by the divine and you must follow that guidance, as must we all. It is enough for now that you feel the divine within you. You are blessed, brother. Rejoice!"

Simon chuckled with delight and looked around at the wise desert father and at all creation about him. He wanted to run and jump, instead Simon continued to play his flute.

Zachariah scowled at the world that morning. He had not enjoyed his night in the curragh with Feth Fio. It had been cold and wet, not a condition that the otter had found uncomfortable, but Zachariah had. When Brother Simon arrived in the early morning to tell him that they were continuing overland to meet with Colum Cille, Zachariah was relieved and not sorry to say farewell to Feth Fio.

Now out on the open road and in the sunshine Zachariah's spirits lifted somewhat, but his annoyance was replaced by something else. The emissary from Colum Cille made him uncomfortable. The fellow was impatient with people and had a surly manner. He spoke to Cormac disrespectfully. There appeared nothing of kindness about him that Zachariah had found in other monks in Eriu and he had no Latin which was odd for a monk. At first he ascribed such manners to the fellow's nervousness at the task his master had given him. The scrolls were attracting more attention by the day and on the open road they were vulnerable to everyone from brigands to kings eager to strike a bargain with the Bishop of Rome. Zachariah cursed the Bishop of Rome for setting this land ablaze with greed and speculation.

Brother Luigbe glanced constantly over his shoulder in the direction of the monastery, but did not appear anxious at what lay ahead or to either side in the woods and meadows. It was as if he was expecting any attack to come only from one direction, the monastery. But why?

Finally Zachariah could not tolerate his growing unease any longer. When they stopped to eat, he quietly disappeared into some nearby bushes and was gone. He was strongly guided to retrace their steps back to the monastery – the apparent source of Brother Luigbe's anxiety.

Brother Luigbe became greatly disturbed at Zachariah's disappearance and demanded to know where he had gone. The group of friends were unperturbed by the hare's absence and confidently expected Zachariah to return in due course. It was only when Cormac told Luigbe of Zachariah's history and his eccentric nature that the monk shrugged his shoulders in bewilderment and continued on the journey: this time looking over his shoulder even more.

In the late afternoon they had arrived within sight of the Hill of Uisneach. It rose gently out of the surrounding plain to command views across the kingdom of *Mide*. Many people were travelling along the road towards the hill for the Festival of Beltaine: some were flaithe (lords) on horseback accompanied by their vassal people on foot, also boaire (farmers) in carts who brought tribute of firewood and food. There were *filid* who brought song and verse and musicians too, many who were monks, bringing great horns, flutes, fiddles and drums.

One flaithe in a splendid red cloak stopped to ask the business of the strange band. Brother Luigbe spoke to him in whispered tones. The flaithe regarded Cormac and his leather bag closely and then rode off towards Uisneach leaving Cormac uneasy at such a whispered exchange. His unease grew apace as soldiers on horseback passed by on their way to Uisneach. Cormac considered it unusual for soldiers to attend the Festival of Beltaine unless customs had greatly changed. Yet Brother Luigbe did not find it so unusual. In fact he appeared much less anxious after seeing the flaithe and the soldiers. Cormac told the others to stay close to one another and he too looked back along the road beginning to wonder why Zachariah had disappeared.

As they drew near to Uisneach they could see the ramparts encircling the hill. Above them on the summit of the hill, two large wood piles were in place ready for the fire which would be set ablaze at nightfall.

Dusk was falling when they arrived at the foot of the hill and smoke was beginning to emerge from the wood piles at the top. Huge horns sounded, signalling that the fires had been lit. Along the rampart circling the first enclosure on the lower part of the hill was a line of drummers dressed in long yellow cloaks, the colour of Beltaine, matching the blaze of gorse that garlanded the hill. The drums now welcomed the people of the country to the hill. As the noise of the drums became ever louder, the horns fell silent creating an expectant air.

"Where is Abbot Colum Cille, brother?" asked Cormac of Luigbe over the sound, anxious to attend to their business in spite of the distractions.

"At the top of the hill: he will meet us after the third pass. Until then we wait," said Luigbe.

Animals were in pens at the bottom of the hill, many cattle, sheep, pigs and horses and even some goats, all baying and bleating to add to the noise. They would be herded between the two fires and thereby purified of their winter dross. This kept them free from disease for the rest of the year and increased their value. The ritual would go on as long as the fires burnt, but the first three passes were the most powerful representing the elements of earth, water and air.

Passing through the first enclosure, they climbed the gentle slope in a sunwise direction into the main enclosure where the players of the horns now stood silently in a circle in front of the fires waiting for the flames to reach a height where they could be seen from neighbouring hills. At this point a great blast of sound would go out from the horns signalling the relighting of fires all over Eriu starting from Uisneach and moving from hill to hill, north, south, east and west. Then summer was truly welcomed across the land.

Many people stood in a large group on the east side of the hill ready to walk between the fires following the direction of the sun towards the west. Rank was respected with the *Ard Ri* (High King) and the *Ard Ollamh* (High *File* of Eriu) proceeding first followed by the *Breithem* (judges), the *Ard Draoithe* (High Druid), the *Ri Cuicidh* (provincial kings), the *Ri Mor* (clan kings) and the *Damna Ri* (lords of the kindred), to the *boaire* (wealthy farmers) and so on down to the *feiders* (tenant farmers). The *bothaig* (slaves) could not join the walk through.

Of course many would attend fires in their own lands. The Hill of Uisneach was attended only by the most powerful and by those living close by in the land of *Mide*.

Cormac overheard talk in the crowd that the *Ard Ri*, Aed mac Ainmuirech of the *Ui Neill* was not present, but was delayed in Temair, meeting with the Bishop of Rome's emissary. Instead the Ri Cuicidh of the *Laigen*, Brandub mac Echach and Colman Bec of Uisneach were together, standing in pride of place strutting to and fro in long flowing purple robes much like courting cocks. This was seen by the people gathered as a snub to the *Ard Ri*. It was known that Brandub and Colman both hated the *Ui Neill* who had invaded their lands in the *Laigen* and in the *Mide* and that Brandub would soon challenge Aed for the high kingship in battle.

"Come, lady, I shall show ye something" said Bretha to the lady Melania.

In the half-light they slipped away from the group, Melania following Bretha over to the other side of the hill. There, a large round stone the size of a house, sat on the land as if dropped from the sky.

"This is the Stone of Divisions, lady," said Bretha proudly. "It marks the centre of Eriu: a powerful place, dividing the five kingdoms of Ulaidh, *Laigen*, *Mide*, *Iarmummu* and Connacht. It is the burial place of the mother goddess, Eriu. She was one of three sisters of the *Tuatha De*. It was here on this hill that the *Tuatha De* gave this island to the Gael on condition that it bore the name of the goddess Eriu. Since then this hill has been the seat of the underworld power for the *Tuatha De*. Their king has his palace under our feet."

Melania lovingly touched the great stone in wonder and said, "It is good. This is a thin place between worlds. I can feel it."

At that, a loud blast from the horns shattered their contemplation of the stone. The fires were blazing and the purification ceremony was beginning. Bretha and the lady Melania re-joined the others in the waiting crowd.

The two kings, Brandub and Colman Bec, led the first pass between the blazing fires. The intense heat meant that no one lingered and many were quickly passed through, with many running. As the animals were herded through on the second and third passes, their calls added to the noise of the fire, the horns and of the drums to create a cacophony so loud that no voice could be heard.

Bretha pulled the lady Melania forward and the two walked through the fires on the third pass behind the goats and some sheep. The wind was whipping the flames into a frenzy and the animals leapt in all directions in fear of being burnt alive. Both women screamed in fear and delight at the spectacle and at the thrill to their senses. They helped herd the frightened animals through the fires on either side. At the end of the tunnel of fire a large full moon had risen in the night sky beckoning them forward to safety and rest.

Once they were clear of the fires and the panic-stricken animals, the two women embraced in joy at the thrill of the experience.

"Do you feel purified, lady?" asked Bretha.

"Yes I do! It's wonderful, Bretha!" shouted Melania. "But where are the others?"

They looked around and realised in their excitement that they had lost contact with Brother Luigbe, Cormac and Simon.

The three monks had declined to go through the fires for one very good reason: the scrolls could be damaged. So they were led by Brother Luigbe around the great fires and all the noise to the other side where Luigbe said Colum Cille was waiting. They followed a path lower down the hill beside a small copse of beech and ash which shielded them from the bright light and heat of the fires. In the shadow of the copse it fell dark as the moon slipped behind a cloud and they struggled to see clearly as their eyes adjusted to the sudden, sultry gloom.

Ahead of them on the path Brother Luigbe seemed to fall to one side into a thicket. Suddenly there was the sound of great commotion beyond sight in the bushes, a muffled scream and the snarling of a beast.

Cormac shouted: "Brother what has happened? Where are you?"

Both Cormac and Simon looked at each other in alarm. Cormac turned to run into the bushes to investigate and help Brother Luigbe, but as he did so he was thrown to the ground with his bag of precious scrolls and found himself pinned down by someone very strong.

"Father!" shouted Simon in alarm frozen in fear.

XXIII: Slighe Chualann

The troop of horses and men surrounding Augustine and Sister Dorothea was a fearsome sight for any who chanced upon them as they cantered northwards along the Slighe Chualann through the fertile lands of the *Laigen*.

The twenty British horse soldiers of the Gododdin with their captain Ros Failge leading them, set a fast pace as they rode in tight formation. Each held a shield emblazoned with the Cross of the Christ. Ros Failge himself held the standard of the Gododdin, a red dragon entwined around the holy cross.

The British cavalry were in essence Roman cavalry, having been schooled by Rome for many generations. The Gododdin had believed their Roman birth right and fought loyally in the legions from the time of Hadrian until 407AD when the Emperor in the West, Constantine III, led the legions out of Britain to defend the empire against the barbarians in Gaul and along the Rhine. This left Britain at the mercy of many barbarian invaders and it was in this struggle for the survival of the British tribes that the Gododdin discovered their manifest destiny as the guardians of Britain, organising their renowned horse soldiers into a powerful fighting force of almost one thousand strong.

Under the leadership of Artur's ancestors, Uther Pendragon and Ambrosius Aurelianus, the Gododdin inflicted defeats on the Picts in the north, the Angles in the east, the Saxons in the south and in the west they forced the Scotii back to Eriu. By age twenty-four Artur, as Guledig or general had shown himself to be capable of continuing his family's legacy of military prowess.

In long campaigns far away from their northern lands, the horse soldiers of the Gododdin developed close bonds of comradeship which Artur nurtured and fashioned into a code of honour known as the Code of the Horsemen. This code required the horsemen to give their lives in the defence of their people and to bring justice to the weak and the vulnerable. Their oath of loyalty bound them to each other and to their Guledig, Artur.

It was therefore with a mixture of some pride and trepidation that Cathair Mar of the Uí Bairrche mounted his chariot to lead this troop of fearsome British horse soldiers escorting the emissary of the Bishop of Rome to meet with the *Ard Rí* at Temair. While the honour was great, so was the risk. He was accompanied in the chariot by his brother, Daire, who had brought with him two heavy axes, two broadswords and some knives for close work should they be needed.

At the rear of the caravan was a troop of Uí Bairrche horsemen who closely studied the Gododdin whose equipment was superior to that of the Uí Bairrche. The British horses were large, muscular beasts with metal shoes on their hooves and their riders sat on heavy leather saddles; whereas the horses of the Uí Bairrche were smaller and had none of these refinements. In Eriu horses were unshod and a simple blanket served as a saddle. It was no wonder that a host of these horse soldiers had forced the kindred out of west Britain. The Gododdin would be a formidable force to stop and turn back.

The wily Cathair Mar had sent a fast rider ahead as soon as Augustine had landed to forewarn the *Ard Rí* in Temair. He calculated that to deal with the challenge presented by this emissary, the *Ard Rí* needed to be prepared. He prayed to the gods that the *Ard Rí* and his advisers could conclude this business with the Bishop of Rome peacefully and that no more of these British horse soldiers would arrive in Eriu to enforce the bishop's demands. While the warriors of Eriu were skilled and fearless in battle, they were untested against a foreign force of any kind, least of all one mounted on these beasts and schooled in the military tactics of the once great Roman Empire.

It was midday when they saw men gathered on the horizon ahead, blocking the Slighe Chualann.

Ros Failge rode up beside Cathair Mar: "My men will not stop. If these men attempt to block our path we will cut through them like a scythe," Ros Failge said in warning to Cathair Mar.

"Do so and you will be embroiled in a war before you even get to the *Ard Rí*," responded Cathair Mar. "These are men from the Ri

Cuicidh of the *Laigen*, one named Brandub mac Echach. He is a powerful king and you would be very mistaken to treat his men with such contempt."

Ros Failge remained impassive. At this Cathair Mar spoke a command to his two horses pulling the chariot and instantly they broke into a gallop. While these horses were smaller than the British, they were fleeter of foot and quickly left the group of Gododdin behind. They sped towards the group of men gathered on the horizon. Ros Failge watched the ease with which Cathair Mar's chariot left them behind. In turn the horse soldiers acted as one. Without an obvious command they too broke into a gallop, reaching for their broad swords in preparation for the challenge that lay ahead.

Reaching the group of men first, Cathair Mar slowed his horses and in a swift movement swung his chariot across the road between the charging Gododdin and the men on the road. He and Daire quickly dismounted carrying their broad swords and stood facing the fast approaching Gododdin with Augustine and Sister Dorothea left some way behind in great concern. Ros Failge considered the scenario before them as he charged at the front of his troop. A battle now would leave his troop isolated in a hostile land, most likely without their guide to the *Ard Ri* and with Sister Dorothea and the emissary at risk. Cathair Mar was right. Ros Failge made a small, almost imperceptible signal with his left hand and within a few paces the Gododdin halted their charge and stopped to face Cathair Mar, his brother and the men of the *Laigen* beyond, their large horses snorting and sweating from the gallop.

The men of the *Laigen*, some thirty strong, on seeing the charge of the horse soldiers towards them had assumed a crouching position across the road holding sharp wooden stakes angled towards the galloping horses. Cathair Mar and Ros Failge eyed each other and waited for someone to declare their hand in this affair. They did not have to wait long. As Augustine's wagon caught up a voice came from the men of the *Laigen*.

"The men of the *Laigen* bid ye welcome to our land, emissary," said the voice. "May all the gods smile upon ye and yer mission in Eriu."

The welcome was lost on Augustine who was still collecting himself after the shock of seeing his guard gallop off to confront local forces blocking their path. His translator, Sister Dorothea, was still inside the wagon and had not heard the greeting above the snorting horses.

Augustine was angry at the behaviour of men he believed to be under his command and was determined to reassert his authority to control the situation that lay before them. As was his habit in all such situations, Augustine strode up towards the man who had emerged from the group blocking their path, ignoring both Ros Failge and Cathair Mar. Sister Dorothea followed him in order to translate. Immediately four Gododdin horse soldiers swiftly dismounted and accompanied her, swords drawn. Ros Failge followed them by horse.

Swinging his cross from over his shoulders and holding it upright in front of him, Augustine spoke and Sister Dorothea translated: "I am Augustine of Nubea, emissary of the Bishop of Rome, God's most favoured upon this earth. I am travelling to meet with your High King in Temair on a sacred matter of great importance. Who am I speaking to and what is the purpose of this blockade?"

"I am Eugan Laib, lord of the kindred, Uí Dúnlainge. We are sent here by our king, Brandub mac Echach, king of all the *Laigen*. The king wishes to meet with yez and discuss yer mission. His *rath* is close by in Aillinn where ye will be very welcome and well cared for, emissary."

"Lord Eugan, I am pleased to meet you. The King of the *Laigen* is kind and I would like to meet with him, but I must meet with the *Ard Ri* in Temair first. He has invited me and I would not wish to insult him as a visitor to his land."

"The land does not belong to the *Ard Ri*, emissary. It is the people's land," said Eugan Laib correcting Augustine's perception of kingship in Eriu. "Brandub mac Echach is a powerful king who can help yer bishop greatly in this land. We know of the scrolls and my king wishes to help ye secure them for the Bishop of Rome. This night at the Festival of Beltane on the Hill of Uisneach the scrolls will be secured by my king."

Augustine looked in surprise to Ros Failge and Cathair Mar. Both shook their heads imperceptibly.

"Lord Eugan, your king is indeed wise and resourceful, but I must consult with my advisers," said Augustine turning away to speak to Ros Failge and Cathair Mar.

The three huddled out of hearing from Eugan Laib. Cathair Mar was the first to speak.

"It's a trap, emissary. Brandub is a trickster. I doubt he has the scrolls. He has betrayed the Uí Bairrche in the past," said Cathair Mar. "This is the politics of kings. Brandub wishes to be *Ard Ri* and will use the scrolls for his own ends. Beware, emissary. Let me take ye to the *Ard Ri* first and then ye can make yer own assessment of affairs from there. Although he is a northern king, the *Ard Ri* is a just man and has a powerful army."

Augustine turned to Ros Failge: "Can your troop force a way through these vagabonds, captain?"

"It's not so easy now we are stopped, sir" said Ros Failge glaring at Cathair Mar. "But yes, we can butcher these farmers where they stand and ride on to the *Ard Ri*."

"That would be a bad business, emissary. Ye will start a war between Brandub and the *Ard Ri* with the Church of Rome in the middle and the scrolls lost for all time in the Spy Wood," said Cathair Mar.

"It sounds like there may be a war between these two anyway," said Augustine eyeing the force opposing them.

"That may be so, emissary, but I doubt if ye want the scrolls caught up in such a war" said Cathair Mar.

Augustine nodded and considered. He could see the sense of Cathair Mar's counsel.

"God will find us a peaceful way through. This is His work we are engaged upon," said Augustine smiling confidently. "Put your swords aside."

Clutching his cross before him Augustine marched up to Eugan Laib accompanied by Sister Dorothea.

"God has commanded me to meet with your *Ard Ri*. This is God's holy cross. I must go where it leads me. Any man who touches this cross or impedes its progress will be struck down. I will meet with your king when I have met with the *Ard Ri* and I will make him a generous offer for the scrolls , if they are truly in his hands – that will make his royal heart swell with delight."

With that Augustine marched forward holding the cross on high towards the line of men.

As Augustine approached, the men of the *Laigen* looked to their lord for guidance for they too were mightily intimidated by the black priest carrying the bright shining cross so fearlessly before him like a divine beacon. Eugan Laib was surprised by this emissary's boldness. Could he risk the anger of the Christian god? He had heard that this god could smite the most powerful and this black skinned man was clearly one of his close disciples. King Brandub mac Echach had not met the emissary to appreciate the power he wielded.

Reluctantly Eugan Laib signalled to the men to let the emissary pass.

Augustine continued to march boldly down the road holding the cross aloft to shine in the bright sun. Sister Dorothea and her guards followed closely with the *Ui Bairrche* and the *Goddodin* horse soldiers behind, while the men of the *Laigen* looked on with fascination.

It did appear indeed that God was smoothing the path for Augustine of Nubea in Eriu. Augustine was now greatly emboldened and even more convinced that this was the case. As he proceeded along the Slighe Chualann he could see in his mind's eye his glorious return to Rome with the sacred scrolls: crowds would line the Circus Maximus to applaud his progress towards the Lateran Palace and his place of honour would forever be assured beside his protector, the Holy Father.

Only when he was safely out of sight of the men of the *Laigen* did Augustine retire to his wagon to proceed in comfort to his meeting with the *Ard Ri*.

That evening as Augustine's caravan arrived beneath the sacred Hill of Temair the place was busy with preparations for the Festival of Beltaine. Crowds were on the Slighe Chualann travelling by foot, by horse and by chariot towards the hill where the great fires would be lit after those on Uisneach.

Ancient oak trees formed a dense canopy over all roads approaching Temair; their huge overarching branches hung like the beams of a great church nave or the arms of a powerful god scrutinising all who approached the hill. All who walked underneath the great trees were awestruck, preparing them for their entrance onto the sacred hill itself. The caravan slowed to a respectful walk as it passed underneath the dark canopy. Augustine once more dismounted from his wagon and holding his cross aloft began his procession towards the hill and his meeting with the *Ard Ri*. He was dutifully followed by Sister Dorothea and her guards. People stopped to watch this strange figure pass by. Many were disturbed by the sight of the black-skinned priest and called for protection from the evil eye.

Suddenly Augustine let out a cry of pain and lowering the cross, held his forehead in his hands.

"What ails you, Father?" asked Sister Dorothea looking round for an assailant. The Gododdin drew their swords.

"Something hit me on to forehead," said Augustine. "Are we being attacked?"

"I see no one," said Sister Dorothea perplexed.

Before Augustine could reply something again hit Augustine this time on the back of his bowed head. The missile fell to the ground in front of Dorothea. It was an acorn and it had come from overhead. Looking up Sister saw a red coloured animal glaring at them defiantly from one of the tree beams. It was a small squirrel.

As Sister Dorothea's bodyguard surrounded her she too was hit in the arm with an acorn.

"Why is that creature so hostile?" said Sister Dorothea. The defiant squirrel continued to confront the caravan from the safety of the high branches of the canopy. He showed no signs of the timidity normally displayed by such creatures.

"That's Bran Mut, King of the Squirrels," said Cathair Mar. "He does this to all coming to meet the *Ard Ri*. Some say he is jealous of the *Ard Ri* and wants the position for himself; others say he is one of the *Tuatha De* protecting the hill and the *Ard Ri*."

"But how would acorns thrown by such a small creature protect the *Ard Ri*, sir?" asked Sister Dorothea as another acorn hit Augustine.

"Well, many travel this path with pride and anger in their hearts to confront the High King on matters dear to their ambitions, but once they are harried by Bran Mut they find themselves less prideful. Bran Mut is not a great and ferocious bull, but a tree mouse who can subdue warrior kings and bishops alike. Believe me when I say that once such people reach the hill they are strangely subdued and much more willing to talk with humility and honesty in their hearts with the *Ard Ri*."

Sister Dorothea laughed and smiled up at the defiant creature. But Augustine did not smile as another acorn thrown with great accuracy and force hit him on the nose.

"Throw one more and I will have you torn from that tree and burnt on the fire!" screamed an angry Augustine at Bran Mut.

To someone of Augustine's dignity such disrespect was maddening no matter its source, but especially so from such a small creature who operated with apparent impunity from on high. Augustine's threat did nothing to deter Bran Mut. He simply threw another acorn at Augustine, this time even harder.

Turning in anger to a grinning Ros Failge he commanded: "Captain, have your men capture that creature or knock him down with sling shot."

"We have no sling shot, Father."

"Do I have to endure this creature's insults, captain?" demanded an enraged Augustine as yet another acorn hit him.

"If we move along quickly we will soon be away from these trees," said Ros Failge.

Reluctantly and with as much dignity as he could muster, Augustine continued to carry his cross as before, but this time rather less sedately. Bran Mut pursued him from the canopy above, forcing Ros Failge to hold his shield over Augustine's head. This only made Ros Failge the target of Bran Mut's attacks instead of Augustine. The amusement of the horse soldiers following behind was cut short when they too were attacked by other squirrels from elsewhere in the canopy. Acorns rained upon them all. The bombardment continued until the caravan was clear of the trees and grouped in confusion at the foot of the hill.

Like many before him, Augustine's ambition of making an impressive entrance to the Hill of Temair, one befitting his status as emissary with his sacred cross held majestically aloft, had been successfully undermined by Bran Mut, King of the Squirrels and his kin folk. For their part the Gododdin, for all their experience in battle, had never encountered such a determined foe whose tactics utterly defied them.

Men of the royal household troop approached them accompanied by the king's hounds.

"Welcome to the Royal Hill, strangers" said their captain.

As Augustine knocked acorns out of his cloak and sought to regain his composure, he replied through Sister Dorothea:

"I am Augustine of Nubea, emissary of the Bishop of Rome, God's most favoured upon this earth. I am come at the invitation of the High king on a most urgent and sacred matter."

"The *Ard Ri* has been expecting ye, emissary. I will show ye to him," said the captain. "But yer soldiers must wait in the hostel where there are stables for the horses. No soldiers are allowed on the Hill. The one named Cathair Mar of the Uí Bairrche may accompany ye, no other."

"I must bring my translator and assistant, Sister Dorothea," said Augustine.

"The *Ard Ri* has the Latin, sir: though a woman is allowed."

Ros Failge attempted to accompany Sister Dorothea, but his path was blocked by several men and hounds.

"Soldiers must remain here. The Hill is a holy sanctuary. No one is harmed here. Yez are safer here than anywhere else in the land," said the captain sensing their unease.

Cathair Mar raised a hand to reassure a nervous Ros Failge of Sister Dorothea's safety. Augustine asked Ros Failge to ensure his wagon was always guarded.

The captain led Augustine, still clutching his cross, Cathair Mar and Sister Dorothea along a broad avenue between large earthen ramparts towards the summit of the hill. Such was the design of the route to the seat of the *Ard Ri* at the summit that little could be seen beyond the ramparts.

"You would do well to cull the evil creatures in your woods, captain," said Augustine, still ill-tempered from Bran Mut's assault and feeling he must make some protest, but also noticeably subdued after his encounter with the squirrels.

The captain simply ignored him and spoke no further.

As they continued along the avenue towards the summit of the hill, more large wooden palisades on raised earthen ramparts became visible and within them could be glimpsed the roofs of substantial roundhouses. While these were much larger than any Augustine had seen on his journey, they were not what he was accustomed to in relation to kings he had dealt with elsewhere in Rome, Gaul and Hispania. It began to dawn on Augustine that no royal villa awaited him and that he would have to work in less impressive structures.

Since his arrival in Eriu and hearing of the High King, Augustine had anticipated being welcomed to a grand villa or castle on a hilltop where he could recover from his arduous journey in civilised comfort and deal reasonably with men like himself who understood how power and politics worked. Yet on his journey from the coast he had not seen even a modest villa, city or even a town. All the buildings he had seen were constructed of wood, wattle and thatch, grouped in small settlements with not a sign of strong military fortifications. He had seen no buildings made of stone. Yet he hoped the High King would have such a building with stout walls where Augustine could work in confidence without fear of being overheard by spies and gossips. Such a building would demonstrate the king's power and his intentions. For Augustine, wood had such a sense of impermanence and weakness. His experience taught him that no empire had been built on wood and he worried that strong agreements could not be made in buildings made out of sticks and mud; strong walls were needed to contain the secret words uttered within them and give to them the force needed for the world beyond.

They reached the top of the Hill of Temair as the sun was setting in the west towards the Hill of Uisneach from where the signal would come to light the fires of Beltaine. They were met by a crowd of people gathered in a large open area in readiness for the festival. They gasped and stood aside to watch in breathless wonder as the tall black-skinned priest moved through them with his bronze cross held high. The people whispered to each other about the legends now surrounding the emissary, the desert father and the sacred scrolls. Some said the black priest had divine powers; he could walk on water like the Christ and float on clouds like the ancient prophets. Others said the desert father was wise, protected by the *Tuatha De* and could weave ancient Celtic magic. It was said that when these two meet Yeshua the Christ will come back to earth on this sacred hill to save the world.

All this was lost on Augustine who did not understand their language, but Sister Dorothea did and was alarmed when she heard their whispered speculations. She clutched her own small crucifix to her bosom as it dawned on her that they were caught up in something that was growing beyond human control. They were all actors in a divine drama that would test them to their limits. She began to pray outwardly for the strength to play her part and to dutifully serve God's wishes in this affair. She prayed too for Father Augustine, the *Ard Ri*, the desert father and most of all for her brother, Artur. She did not wish Artur to become part of this drama through his ambitions to hold these scrolls in Britain.

XXIV: Royal Temair

The captain of the household troop led Augustine, Sister Dorothea and Cathair Mar through an entrance in the largest rampart. They walked through a series of circular earthen ramparts and then they emerged into a large central enclosure. To Sister Dorothea's immense relief the crowd had not followed them.

The last of the setting sun cast a shaft of light through the rampart entrance. It fell on a chalk-white burial mound causing it to gleam eerily in the half light. Beyond this were two further enclosures on raised mounds each containing a large roundhouse. They were led towards the first enclosure where music could be heard. It was a bright sound of whistle, pipes and drum that helped lift Sister Dorothea's sombre mood. When they entered the enclosure they were met by two men guarding the door of a large roundhouse. Above the door a beautifully carved wooden cross hung on some deer antlers and decorated with purple heather, gorse and marigolds.

The captain motioned them to enter as one of the men held the heavy door open. Stooping to enter the doorway Augustine saw people sitting in a semicircle. They were shown to chairs facing the semi-circle and, as soon as they had taken their seats, the musicians and cup bearers in the roundhouse were ordered to leave.

While waiting for the roundhouse to empty Augustine gathered his senses for the meeting and let his eyes grow accustomed to the gloom: all light from candles and fires was extinguished in readiness for the lighting of the Beltaine fires. Augustine set his cross on a bench beside him. Plates of salted beef, wheat bread and beer were offered and each accepted gratefully.

Augustine noticed the figures opposite watching him closely. He in turn scrutinised them. A ruling council, he wondered. He must reach an early assessment of them.

In the centre of the group, sitting on large chairs were a man and a woman clothed in purple: the universal colour of kings and emperors. Around their necks both wore magnificent golden torcs sparkling even in the darkened room. The man had a strong, lively face with dark eyes that flickered with intelligence and cunning. The woman was poised with long black hair which fell in tresses over the gold of her torc. She had sharp yet handsome features. Augustine judged the couple to be the *Ard Ri* and his queen. He had not expected women to be present and had been uneasy at the presence of Sister Dorothea.

On the other side of the queen sat a monk in a shabby gown and muddy boots. He was a tall figure sitting very still and upright on a simple stool. The queen was half turned away from the monk as if in disgust and embarrassment. The monk stared at Augustine in a manner that disturbed him. It was as if he was examining his very soul.

When the roundhouse was empty of all others Augustine set aside his food in readiness, but an elderly man sitting to the left of the *Ard Ri* held his hand up and smiling, said gently: "Eat first, guest"

They sat in quiet for several moments regarding one another as the visitors ate. The excited crowd could barely be heard as the huge ramparts dulled sound from the main enclosure. This reassured Augustine somewhat, but sitting in the company of a king in silence and with strangers watching him eat made him uneasy. When they had eaten and the plates cleared away, the silence was broken by a gravelly voice. It was the *Ard Ri* speaking.

"I am Aed mac Ainmuirech, *Ri Cuicidh* of the *Cenel Conaill* and *Ard Ri* of this place." He paused weighing his words and looking directly at Augustine. "This is my queen, Ronnat and these, my advisors. Ye are welcome to our land, though yer mission has brought great disturbance as ye will have seen. I have asked that ye attend this place so that we can hear from ye what yer business is with us."

At that he stopped speaking and sat passively waiting for Augustine to reply. This caught Augustine unawares. He had been expecting a longer, more dramatic speech of royal welcome.

The *Ard Ri* had spoken in his native tongue, not Latin. Therefore Sister Dorothea with great nervousness had to explain her role as translator to those before them. The *Ard Ri* nodded, but made no offer to speak Latin.

Augustine rose to his full height to deliver his response and Sister Dorothea stood beside him to translate.

"I am Augustine of Nubea, emissary of the Bishop of Rome, God's most favoured upon this earth. My bishop has long taken an interest in the development of the Christian church in this great land. He marvels at the success of your Church and the graceful manner in which the pagan ways are being set aside to make way for Yeshua the Christ. My bishop believes it is an example to the world that must be elevated and learnt from. So now the Holy Father wishes to form an alliance with Eriu: an alliance that will raise up the Celtic church to take its rightful place in the eyes of God. Rome can provide what is needed both to the bishops and to the temporal authorities to facilitate the building of a great and powerful church as befits Eriu and its people."

Reaching into his cloak Augustine withdrew a small leather pouch: "As a token of his friendship towards you, *Ard Ri*, the Holy Father asked me to give you these gold coins handed personally to an earlier Holy Father by Constantine the Great. It was he whom God rewarded in battle and chose to convert the empire to the one true faith. These coins are given by the Holy Father only to kings of Christian lands such as Gaul, Hispania and Italia as a token of our holy brotherhood."

Augustine handed the pouch to Sister Dorothea to pass to the *Ard Ri*. Aed mac examined them and turning to his queen pointed to the inscription on one of the coins. He obviously understood the Latin.

"Your majesty will see the inscription 'By this sign you shall conquer'. It was the sign from God received in battle by the emperor. These sacred coins are given only to kings who have conquered and can be enabled to conquer further through the power of the Christ and the Church of Rome."

"But we are an island. What would we conquer, emissary? We have no wish to conquer other lands," said Aed Mac.

This was the first king Augustine had encountered who had no ambitions to conquer so he had to think quickly. "Men's souls, sire" answered Augustine weakly. He added: "and the ability to rule your enemies within."

"Your bishop would send me warriors and weapons?"

"The Holy Father can help good Christians defend themselves, sire."

"Will he send me monks to fight? Have ye seen monks fight, emissary? They fight like girls. They strike a blow, apologise and then spend an age in penance for their sin. This would be a strange army to behold."

This produced great hilarity among those gathered around the *Ard Ri* and discomfort for Augustine. But the monk seated next to the queen did not laugh.

This king was unusual. He did not take the same bait as the Franks, the Lombards or the Goths. What did this one need? Augustine had learnt over the years not to make offers lightly. In time the adversary always made their needs clear. So he would withhold any precise offer of riches and likewise any threat of invasion until the way was clear. Instead he would make vague references that may initiate thinking.

"This proud island has never been conquered, sire," said Augustine. "But elsewhere conquering armies are on the move in Italia, in Gaul and in Britain. In Britain the Saxons and the Angles move ever westwards, forcing the British off their fertile lands and into the hills and marshes. It is possible that they will one day arrive on your shores; the British looking for a home or the Saxons and Angles seeking more land. An alliance with Rome will give you protection, sire."

"Rome itself has been conquered by the Lombards, emissary. Has it not? The Emperor has fled to the east. So if yez cannot protect yer own lands how can ye offer protection to us?"

A worthy adversary, thought Augustine. The *Ard Ri* knew of affairs beyond his shores.

"The Holy Father never fled, sire. He has defended the sacred city of Rome against all the barbarian invaders. No one governs the holy city but the Church, through and by God's grace. That is a sign of how God supports his own true church in the face of the invaders. Now we help the Christian Franks and the Lombards build strong empires against the barbarians. Now the British seek our patronage," said Augustine.

"The British, ye say!? Who? They have had no king since the great Foirtchern" snapped Aed Mac this time looking directly at Sister Dorothea. She twitched nervously. From her tongue he already knew she was British.

"The British are keen to join the communion of the Church of Rome, sire" said Augustine. "They wisely understand that this union will help them withstand the pagan assaults on their lands."

"Hmmmm." Aed Mac scratched his chin and he whispered to the elderly adviser sat to his left.

"What of these sacred scrolls we hear so much about, emissary?" said Aed Mac bluntly, changing tack.

"What of them, sire?" replied Augustine. He would play this king at his own game, thought Augustine.

"We hear that sacred scrolls have arrived in Eriu carried by a desert monk and that yer bishop wants to get his hands on them and that's really why ye have come to this place. Is this true?"

"My mission is twofold, sire," said Augustine. "to help you build a strong church in Eriu as a bulwark against the barbarians and to return these scrolls to Rome for safe keeping."

"Can ye prove yer ownership, emissary? Our judges have very firm views on such matters. So we must be very careful. Our laws may not allow us to simply give ye or even sell ye these scrolls. Theft of sacred documents has caused war in this place before now."

The monk turned to stare at the *Ard Ri*.

"There is canon law, sire" said Augustine. "We believe there is strong canon law on this matter to establish Rome's claim."

"But surely our good clergy can be trusted with these scrolls?"

"That may be, sire, but until the church has an ecclesiastical structure and formal leadership in Eriu how could these scrolls be kept secure? The church would help with building such a structure with strong church buildings and much more, sire. Until such time the scrolls must return to Rome."

The monk shifted on his stool.

"There are many who would argue with yer view, emissary: my cousin for one. Is that not so, Crimthainn, or what do they call ye these days? Colum Cille isn't it?" The *Ard Ri* turned to the monk smiling.

A quiet descended on the meeting.

Colum Cille replied in fluent Latin: "They call me many things, cousin: druid, abbot, trickster, politician and simpleminded monk. I am all these and more. But above all I am a servant of my god and his people. All of you in this room, forby our guests, know that we have built a church in this place from the destitution of the famine and the plague." His voice rose. "It is unkind for the emissary to suggest that we could not be trusted with these sacred scrolls. We have held the true word of the Christ safely in this land since the dawn of Christendom, while Rome still worshipped a divine emperor. Perhaps Father Augustine does not know us and our history. I would be glad to escort him to our monasteries where we have thousands of brothers and sisters in study and devotion."

"That is a generous offer, cousin," said Aed Mac who now also spoke in Latin. "This is my cousin, Abbot Colum Cille of Aio and all points north, east, south and west. Would you like to learn more about our church, Father, so that you are better placed to help us?"

This was a clumsy attempt to delay matters and distract Augustine. He had no intention of accepting.

"Of course I would be glad to accept the abbot's invitation, sire. I am sure there is much we can learn from each other."

Augustine's calculating mind was racing. He knew now that the *Ard Ri* and his cousin had no intention of releasing the scrolls to Rome and that the whole issue could become a legal wrangle with judges. It seemed ridiculous to him that such a primitive place would have judges. This so-called king appeared to be subject to these judges. Augustine had never come across such a king in all his years as an emissary. However it was Augustine's experience that judges always buckled under threat of arms and that clarity in these matters was always useful. He would have to find a more persuasive tactic, if indeed they had the scrolls in their possession. He still had several throws of the dice.

"Good! "said Aed Mac. "Father Colum Cille, I will provide the horses and men to take you and the emissary on your tour. When will you leave?"

"Tomorrow. We will leave after matins," said Colum Cille.

With that Colum Cille bowed to Aed Mac, ignoring Augustine and left the roundhouse accompanied by some other clergy.

"Now light the fires of summer!" said Aed Mac. "Father, you and your friends will accompany me to the Festival of Beltaine and stay the night with us? It may help you understand our ways."

That night Augustine tossed in his bed in the guest hostel. His mind was calculating his next steps to counter the *Ard Ri*'s clumsy tactics. Eventually he resigned himself to a sleepless night. He rose, dressed and went outside to a moonless sky. The smell of wood smoke from the Beltaine fires lay heavily on the night air. He walked around the smoking embers of the fires pondering his strategies.

As he did so, he became conscious of a figure watching him. He turned and squinted through the dark to see someone standing by a small roundhouse on the far side of the enclosure. It began to walk towards him. As the figure drew close he saw it was Queen Ronnat. She spoke to him in Latin:

"Father, I am glad we have been able to meet," she said. "I feel you were roughly treated in the council meeting. Please accept my apologies."

"Thank you, my lady" said Augustine. "It is the work of an emissary, nothing more."

"We can be rough folk in Eriu. We have not the polished ways of you Romans. The abbot is beyond endurance, is he not?"

"He is a rural monk, my lady. It is their way."

"The *Ard Ri* indulges him because they are close kindred and Colum Cille is a powerful figure in Eriu. The abbot does as he wishes and seems beyond authority. I find it tiresome."

"He does seem to exceed his powers as an abbot."

"I pity you travelling with him. He farts like an ox and pisses where he pleases. He has no grace."

Augustine smiled at her observations, but said nothing.

"Would you care for some wine in my house, father?" asked Queen Ronnat. "It may help you sleep in readiness for your journey with the ox."

Augustine could see the hand of God moving in his direction and smiled to himself.

"I would be honoured, my lady."

Normally Augustine was awkward around women, especially those of high birth, except when they were important to his strategies. This one appeared to want something without any encouragement from him. So his manner became quite relaxed and courteous, even charming. He liked to feel needed.

As they sat by the fire in the queen's roundhouse Augustine watched the light from the fire flicker over her face as she talked. She did not possess the classic beauty he was accustomed to in women of high birth. Her eyes were dark with heavy eyebrows and shallow cheeks, but she possessed a dignity and a physicality that attracted him. He was fascinated by the whiteness of her skin. It was like ivory. He longed to touch, to discover its nature and how it covered her body. He also calculated that he fascinated her. However, the mutual interest went much deeper than skin colour. It was clear to Augustine that the queen wanted something from him and she in turn could be enormously useful to him.

"We can talk freely here, father, the king is with another wife tonight," said Ronnat.

"There is more than one queen, lady?" said Augustine wondering if he was wasting his time with this one.

"No. I am the queen. I am the first wife. The king may take others, but they have few rights and cannot replace me. Only I can take an interest in the king's affairs. I advise him. Sometimes he listens and other times not."

"And this time, lady?"

"Colum Cille has Aed mac's ear on matters of faith," said Ronnat. She eyed Augustine closely as if weighing up how much she could trust him. "Let's talk plainly, father. I may be able to help you and you may be able to help me. Can we explore our needs?"

"I would be glad to, lady."

"Very well. It is clear that you are here because of the scrolls. What will you give for them?"

"I admire your directness, lady, and I will be equally direct. The Bishop of Rome will in the first instance give one thousand gold solidi for the scrolls. That is enough to buy a fleet of ships, to build a palace or buy an army. Whatever you heart desires."

"And, in the second instance, father?"

"More support would be forthcoming, lady. It is not just the scrolls, I assure you. The Church of Rome wishes to build alliances throughout the known world. It is written:

> '*And I also say to you that you are Peter, and upon this rock I will build My church; and the gates of Hades shall not overpower it.*'

"So you see, lady, it is our sacred mission given to St. Peter by the Christ. We can do no other. The church now holds sway over large areas of the old empire. Even the barbarians convert to Christianity under our influence."

"I understand, Father. But we do not use coins in Eriu. So such support is of limited use to us. It is your alliances we seek; alliances with Gaul and even with the British. Can you offer these?"

"I can, my lady. We have close alliances with the Franks in Gaul and with some of the most powerful in Britain. How would you use such alliances, lady?"

"We need support in this land. Abbot Colum Cille and his many allies dislike your Church. They believe it is an extension of the old empire and wish to remain independent. But this leaves us weak and isolated. We see what has happened in Britain since the empire withdrew with the Angles, Saxons and others stealing land. We are not a rich powerful people, father, able to withstand foreign forces. Your church could help us secure support, but we will need military force too."

"May I ask who 'we' are, lady?"

"My cousin is Brandub mac Echach, King of the *Laigen*. He is the most powerful king in Eriu, more powerful than the High King. Brandub and the King of *Mide*, Colman Bec, wish to see the Church of Rome installed in this island and will trade the scrolls for the practical support of the Church of Rome. You were right in the council meeting to point out that we have never been conquered. But that may not always be the case unless we have powerful friends. Eriu cannot continue to be so isolated."

"You are very wise and brave, my lady. Your cousin has already declared his interest. His men attempted to stop me on the road here. I now regret not accepting his invitation to meet."

"If you had you would have the scrolls this night."

"Your cousin has the scrolls?"

"The scrolls were taken from the desert father earlier this night at Uisneach," said Ronnat smiling slyly at Augustine.

"That is good news, lady. The Holy Father will be most grateful, I can assure you," said a delighted Augustine. "I must meet with your cousin immediately."

"You must make some excuse to the abbot in the morning and accept my cousin's invitation to meet at his *rath* in Aillinn. It is half a day's journey south from here."

"I have no need of an excuse. My business is concluded here for the moment. But what of you and the *Ard Ri*, lady?"

"Aed Mac will be replaced as *Ard Ri* when the people see he does not possess the scrolls and how he has rejected the friendship of the Bishop of Rome. I ask you to keep our relationship a secret until all is in place."

"You have my word as a priest, lady."

"Very well. Our business is concluded, father. It is as I hoped and prayed. Our needs coincide beautifully," said Ronnat clapping her hands in delight. "But now I pray you will keep me company for a while longer."

"Er, yes, yes. I would be glad to keep your company, lady."

Ronnat giggled quietly at his uncertainty and licked her lips. She became playful. "Our minds may be as one, but don't you find the difference in our skins intriguing, Father? I know you do because I have seen your glances," she chided him.

"You are an attractive woman, lady. Your skin has the appearance of expensive ivory. I apologise if I have caused offence." Augustine could feel his heart quicken. This woman was seducing him and he felt an unstoppable urge growing in him.

"There is no offence, Father. You fascinate me with your Roman ways and your black skin. It is like ebony. Just like this beautiful piece. She opened her gown to reveal a large piece of magnificent ebony jewellery suspended from a gold necklace and lying between her now naked white breasts. She held it up for Augustine to examine. "I wish to know you. You may touch my skin to satisfy your curiosity."

Augustine leaned over and gently touched Ronnat's marble white breasts with the back of his hand. She held his hand, kissed it tenderly and then placed it on her sex further beneath her gown.

"Is this not what you really want, Father? To worship at my temple."

He gasped. It had been some time since he had been with a woman and that had been a simple sister of Christ in Rome, not a queen with power and the skills of a courtesan. He thanked God for the gift of this one and asked forgiveness for his carnal lust.

Augustine mounted the queen with energy, his lust was in full flow as he felt the warm ivory skin beneath him. Yet as he entered her he saw himself falling into a dark tunnel to emerge onto a hillside, holding the scrolls and being pursued by a great black raven. The raven pursued him, attacked him and stole the scrolls. Augustine shook his head to be free of the image and continued to copulate enthusiastically, but he would not look in her eyes in spite of her need for him to do so. He was afraid she would see what he saw. As he moved above so the lady writhed and bucked beneath like a young excited mare. And while they moved in harmony he understood clearly that their agreement had to be sealed by this union of their bodies, without it this woman would not trust him. It bound them to each other like no other covenant. Besides the queen held him in her tightly so that their destinies were securely joined.

Suddenly she stopped him and forced him to look in her eyes: "Do you like to worship in my ivory temple, black Augustine?" she demanded.

He looked at her for a moment. Then smiling he said, "Yes. You are the ivory goddess, Queen Ronnat."

She laughed with delight and began to move against his loins once more. "Then worship in my temple, high priest of Ronnat!"

As they both achieved fulfilment and Augustine fell upon Ronnat's ivory altar exhausted with his eyes closed in ecstasy, Augustine saw a second vision. The black raven was now pursuing a white dove. It grabbed the dove and with its long, sharp black beak pierced is heart, its red blood staining the white feathers, yet the dove did not die and both flew away together.

As dawn broke Augustine lay alone sleeping in his room. He was awoken by a gentle knocking on the door and a letter being pushed under it into the room. Augustine found no one outside. Examining the package he discovered a hastily written note from Queen Ronnat asking him to deliver a letter with all haste and the utmost discretion to her cousin the King of the *Laigen* at the royal fort of Aillinn. The package contained something small, firm and round. It was a small white brooch of the purest ivory. It was the shape of a white dove.

XXV: Running north

"Iucharba!?" cried Cormac as he lay on the ground looking up at the face of his assailant.

"It is, Father. Your life and the scrolls are in danger. That was not Colum Cille's emissary leading you to him. He was an impostor sent by those who seek the scrolls."

"I don't understand what's happening" said Cormac in a daze reaching for the precious bag of scrolls lying in the dirt.

"That man was not Luigbe mac Min. He was a spy from the King of *Mide*, bringing you here to steal the scrolls and kill you all. Colum Cille is not here. He is in Royal Temair with the High King."

Sitting upright Cormac stared blankly at the ground, "God help me. What a fool I have been!"

Iucharba and Simon helped Cormac to his feet.

"You must hurry back to the monastery of the Meadows and to the river. It is too dangerous for you to travel by land here," said Iucharba . He turned to a monk standing silently on the path behind them. "This man is the true Luigbe mac Min, Colum Cille's emissary." The monk bowed to Cormac and moved to stand close beside him.

The true Luigbe mac Min whispered to Cormac, "Abbot Colum Cille told me that Moninna says the weeds are growing tall on the lower field in Killabuonia."

Cormac nodded in recognition. It was the proof he should have sought back at the monastery of the Meadows. Only Colum Cille could know this detail from his past. What a trusting fool he had been, thought Cormac, shaking his head.

"We must get to Colum Cille soon. We are all growing tired, brother," whispered Cormac in a weary sigh.

"There are horses waiting for us at the entrance to the hill, Father," said Luigbe mac Min, "that will take us back to the Meadow. I will take you on northwards to Colum Cille where you will be safe. I will tell you the place of our meeting when we are away from here."

Cormac turned to Iucharba. "Thank you, kind friend, once more." Then pointing into the bushes where he had heard the noise of the beast, Cormac asked, "Is that man dead in there?"

"Yes, Father, he is. He was to kill you and all your companions."

"But if I had not been so reckless I would never have come here and that poor man would still be alive with a chance of salvation. Now he is condemned to hell for his sin without the opportunity of redemption. It is my fault. God forgive me."

Cormac began to weep, shaking his head repeatedly in sorrow.

"I must go to him to pray for his poor soul."

Luigbe mac Min exchanged a worried look with Simon. They needed Cormac to be strong and not to delay. Iucharba reached out and touched Cormac's breastbone with the palm of his hand. Cormac's eyes closed and he remained completely motionless. Then holding Cormac's head in his other hand for a few brief moments Iucharba said: "When Father Cormac awakes he will not recall the death of this man or his own distress. As you see it upsets him greatly. Please do not refer to these events in Father Cormac's presence."

Simon and Luigbe nodded silently, unsure about what to make of the *Tuatha De*'s magic. Iucharba released Cormac and the monk's eyes blinked open.

"We have to find the lady Melania and young Bretha. They became separated from us," said Cormac with no sign of his previous distress and no reference to the dead spy in the bushes..

"They are with the horses. Come, you must leave this place immediately," said Iucharba glancing over his shoulder towards the fires.

At the entrance to the hill Zachariah, Melania and Bretha were waiting for them with five good horses.

"Brother, are you well? We were worried," asked Melania.

"I am, sister. I tripped and fell in the dark. Iucharba says we must go back to the Meadows. We are to travel north on the river." Cormac with brother Luigbe turned to look for Iucharba, but he had disappeared.

"Can everyone ride a horse?" asked Cormac of the group as he recovered his senses.

"No, Brother Simon and I have never ridden a horse," said a worried looking Melania, "besides these large beasts alarm us both."

The horses were indeed large physical beasts that pawed the ground restlessly and snorted loudly into the night air. Then one of the horses came forward and with a great snort and shake of his mane he spoke.

"I am Gaeth, which means 'like the wind'", he said in a clear voice. "I am sure of foot and as fast as an eagle. Fear not, lady, you will be safe on my back."

"Very well, Master Gaeth," said Cormac in delight and moving close to Gaeth, stroked his flanks with tenderness. "I had a horse like you who spoke to me as a boy. I thought your kind were no more."

"We speak, monk. But only some will hear. It is a great frustration."

Cormac laughed. "I know a hare that doesn't let that bother him. He makes you listen."

"There's another skill I have, monk," said Zachariah suddenly reappearing. "I can run fast. So I will be back at the Meadows before any of these great lumbering beasts."

The horses snorted their outrage at the hare's remarks. But men's angry voices could be heard on the other side of the rampart on the hill.

Gaeth spoke again: "Enough! This hare is boastful fellow, father. We will prove him wrong. But I sense danger approaching. We must be gone before it finds us."

At that Zachariah took off down the road towards the west. The horses also became impatient to be gone from the hill. Cormac quickly helped Simon and Melania to mount. Then he and Luigbe mounted two other horses. It was true that they were safe on Gaeth's back, for while the animal galloped fast towards the Meadows and in the dark of the night, he somehow kept Simon and Melania secure on his back throughout.

Dawn was trickling over the western sky as they arrived at the Meadows to see Zachariah grooming himself on the jetty beside Feth Fio. Gaeth was downcast at not winning the race. So much so that Zachariah felt guilty at having goaded the horses and felt he had to offer some reassurance to them.

"You were carrying two novice riders, Lord Gaeth. I had none. It is no shame. I am sorry for my thoughtless remarks. Zachariah likes to play even in these hard times," said Zachariah.

"You have done us a great service, Gaeth," said Cormac stroking the big horse once more. "You and your kind have got us here safely and quickly. You have your place among God's anointed. God bless you. God bless all you magnificent creatures."

"We will race in better times then, hare, when the hills do not hold such danger," called Gaeth.

"I look forward to the day, Lord Gaeth," shouted Zachariah as Gaeth and the other horses turned and galloped off towards the rising sun.

They stood by the river honouring the horses' departure, watching as they disappeared over the first hill on the Slighe Mhor towards the rising sun.

Feth Fio was already in his boat and setting the oars.

"To the farthest reaches of the river, boatman, and hurry," said Luigbe and glancing behind them, "There may be others following us and we do not wish to be caught."

"Feth Fio loves a race," said Feth Fio as he bent to his task. "None can catch this boatman."

As before, Cormac helped Feth Fio on the oars for a time, but as the river was quiet in herself with a kind morning wind out of the south, they raised the sail allowing Cormac to rest and speak with Brother Luigbe.

Without saying a word, Brother Luigbe handed a sealed letter to Cormac from Colum Cille. It read:

> 'To my blessed brother monk, Cormac mac Fliande,
> 'My soul sang when I learnt of your return to our land in the service of the Creator and the Lord Yeshua. Many years have passed since your peregrinatio and in that time our church has prospered here.

'I believe your years with the desert fathers have brought you to a deeper knowing and a strength that enables you to carry out this divine mission. You would not have been chosen otherwise.

'We in this land are also divinely honoured to be chosen as the guardians of the Word.

'God's work has taken me to an island in the north, in the land of Dal Riata where we have built a community to His glory and where we await the end times.

'Since learning of your arrival with the scrolls, I have returned to speak with the people, their kings and judges.

'You must know, my dear one, that there are those in this land who would wish to trade the sacred Word for Rome's overlordship. It has always been our prayer to be a true vessel for the Word in this land and I believe that is why the Word in its earthly form has been sent by God to us in this time. That said, the judges and the kings must have their say on the legal ownership of the scrolls. But God and his servant Yeshua will be the final arbiters, I pray.

Be careful in your dealings, dear brother. Eriu is still a land where intrigue and greed sit alongside kindness and love. Some would do you harm to possess the scrolls.

It has been God's will to place a kindred of mine on the high throne as Ard Ri who, I pray, will stand fast with us. However there is bad blood between he and some others such as the King of the Laigen and the King of Mide. These two are ambitious for power and may well trade with the Roman emissary to get it.

I have seen this Roman emissary in a vision coming to this land as a ravenous black eagle offering gold and threatening war. He will stop at nothing to obtain the scrolls for his master in Rome. He will land in the south and meet with the Kings of Laigen and Mide at an early stage.

We will soon be calling an assembly to decide this matter. So fly north, my brother, where we can protect the scrolls, as well as you and your companions.

273

*Brother Luigbe is my loyal emissary who you can trust with
your life and your soul. He will tell you where we will meet. I
cannot commit such information to pen.*

*I look forward to the hour when we two will embrace once
more.*

God protect your kind soul,
Your loving abbot,
Colum Cille.'

Cormac kissed the letter and put it with the scrolls in his bag. He
was mightily relieved to hear from his old mentor and immediately
gave thanks to God for Colum Cille, asking Him to protect the
abbot in the task before him. It was clear that challenges were all
around them both.

When Cormac had finished his prayer for Colum Cille, Brother
Luigbe spoke: "As you now know, Father, Abbot Colum Cille is at
Royal Temair to meet with the *Ard Ri* and his counsel. We are
blessed that the *Ard Ri* and the abbot are both of the *Cenel Conaill*
and that the *Ard Ri* seeks Colum Cille's counsel on many spiritual
matters. The abbot is minded to ask him to call an assembly of all
the judges to address the matter. He will meet us at the monastery
of Saint Molaise on Ox Island on the great lake of *Érainn*, four
days journey north from here. We will be safe there until the abbot
can meet us on the island one week from today. If there is to be an
assembly, he will take us to it."

Cormac had no knowledge of such assemblies and what purpose
they would have in regard to the scrolls.

"It is a meeting of all the kings along with the *Breithem*, the *Ri
Cuicidh*, the *filid*, the senior abbots and the bishops," said Luigbe.
"The law will not allow us to decide on the matter of these scrolls
on our own, Father. Abbot Colum Cille believes that an assembly
must be allowed to decide: although with God's grace he will guide
its decision."

Cormac smiled to himself. Colum Cille was ever the wily
politician as well as a churchman. He would be proposing such a
gathering only if he felt he could win the day, whatever men's law
said. He surmised that his old mentor was still attached to getting
his own way in temporal matters, which ownership of the scrolls

would be in the eyes of the judges. Yet it was a wonder that no one was more obedient to God's will than Colum Cille. His magic lay in aligning the temporal with the sacred.

In the days that followed they moved quickly up the river, stopping for only a few hours to rest each night, forever keeping a watchful eye for pursuers on the river behind them and the banks to either side.

They made good progress for Feth Fio had enormous stamina and strength as an oarsman. Cormac, Simon and Luigbe were hard pressed to keep up with his pace on the oars.

By the third day Feth Fio had brought the group of exhausted pilgrims north as far as the river would take them. There on the banks of a lake they rested overnight in readiness for their walk over hill and bog to the lake of *Érainn*. They gave thanks to the spirit of the river and to God for holding them safely. Bretha, the lady Melania and Feth Fio swam in the cool waters as the evening closed in around them. As before, Feth Fio nipped Bretha's behind and she in turn pulled his tail as they played together in the lake. The lady Melania looked on with amusement, but did not take part in their game.

Being part otter Feth Fio was a skilled fisherman and brought back several fine fish for their evening meal. As they ate, he regaled them with stories of the great river and the things he had seen.

"Will you return to your river work now, Master Feth Fio?" asked Zachariah.

Feth Fio looked all around and sniffed the air. He seemed unclear on his answer.

"In truth, Master Zachariah, I would like to travel on with yerselves, if ye will have me. There may be more boat work up ahead on the great lake of Erainn."

As he said this, Feth Fio looked at Bretha who was still busy eating the delicious fish. She heard none of what he said. It had become obvious to all, except for Bretha, that Feth Fio was in love with the young poet and now struggled to part with her.

"We would be glad to have your company, Master Feth Fio, would we not, Cormac?" said Zachariah with a knowing smile.

"You would be most welcome, Master Feth Fio" said Cormac while looking at Bretha who continued to ignore their conversation and at Brother Luigbe who seemed doubtful. "But we have many miles on foot from here and we must not delay. Can you manage such a task away from your beloved boat?"

Feth Fio was not an able walker having short legs and soft feet. All his life had been spent on or in the water. Walking any distance was not a skill he possessed.

"The goddess of the river will mind me boat and me legs are improving, sir. While ye were away at the Hill of Uisneach I walked up and down that jetty for many an hour. See, when this Brother Luigbe turned up looking for yez and ye were gone, I was fierce worried until Master Zachariah returned. And I have got these new boots too." He thrust out his feet to display his new leather boots. "I could keep yez in fish and…and entertain Mistress Bretha," he smiled nervously at his little joke and again looked imploringly at Bretha hoping to get a response, but Bretha remained oblivious to their conversation and to Feth Fio's attention.

Brother Simon snorted in his attempt to suppress his amusement at Feth Fio's attachment to Bretha. Cormac gave him a stern glance. Simon mumbled an apology and buried his head in his cloak.

They all looked on in bewilderment at the attachment Feth Fio had formed with Bretha and her complete ignorance of the nature of his attention. But to Feth Fio the water games he and Bretha regularly engaged in was a courting ritual to an otter and unknowingly Bretha had encouraged his attention.

Feth Fio was known throughout the great river as the most handsome of otters, accustomed to attracting females. But sadly Feth Fio was unaware that this handsomeness did not translate into human form. Daily he expected to be united with Bretha.

It would have been heartless to turn such a stout fellow and ally as Feth Fio away. So it was agreed that he would accompany them on foot. Cormac, concerned at these developments, quietly asked the lady Melania to explain matters to Bretha so that she may make her own decisions.

They set off for Ox Island at first light. The path wound through low lying marsh near the lake and then climbed steeply into hills. As expected, Feth Fio soon struggled to keep up with their pace. His soft feet and short legs began to cause him a pain that he would not admit to. Eventually Brother Luigbe took the protesting boatman to one side to examine his condition, after all he must be exhausted after getting them up the river so quickly.

"It's bees that have stung my feet, brother. See how they are swollen."

True enough Feth Fio's feet were badly swollen, but there were no bees to be seen so early in the summer.

"We have often had arguments, the bee and I. But I could keep out of their way on the river. Now they have seen their opportunity, turned on me in cruel vengeance and I am made a burden to you all in your time of greatest need," said a sorrowful Feth Fio.

They would not leave their friend by the side of the path in spite of his demands. Instead the men took turns to carry the boatman and, as they did, Bretha rubbed his back to give him comfort and when they rested she applied herbal ointment to his swollen feet. Such attention went a long way to healing both the boatman's feet and his damaged pride. So that by the time they reached the crest of a ridge of hills Feth Fio was able to stand to admire the view of the land beyond and the great lake of *Érainn*.

"It is the ancient land of Emania," said Brother Luigbe pointing to the land that stretched out below them as far as the eye could see. "Once ruled by the Ulaidh, but now many kindreds fight over it."

"There is no king of Emania?" asked the lady Melania.

"No, lady, there is not. There is one who claims to be and we may meet him, Aed dub mac Suibni, Black Aed as he is known. But his kindred have been forced ever eastwards by the *Ui Neill*, Abbot Colum Cille's kindred and the lands of the Ulaidh are much reduced."

"Then do the abbot's family connections make our task more difficult in this land, brother?" continued Melania who sought to understand this new land and their situation.

"No, on the contrary, lady, the abbot's cousin is the *Ard Ri* and more importantly, Colum Cille is respected well beyond his kindred as a monk interested only in the kingdom of God. The abbot is both diplomat and missionary. He moves between the worlds of kings and monks and farmers with ease. He has the gift of prophesy. Some say he is a druid smith," said Luigbe smiling, "but I only see a great leader of men to the glory of God. Many would give their lives for his holy mission, as would I."

"You know the abbot, brother?" asked the lady Melania turning to Cormac.

"I do, sister. He ordained me as a young monk before I left on my peregrinatio. He is all that Brother Luigbe says. He and other great monks saved this land from destitution after the famine and the plague. We owe him and his like a great deal," said Cormac. "We can rely on Colum Cille in this affair. He will be guided by God, as ever. In that regard the Patriarch of Alexandria chose most wisely."

"You will meet him soon, lady, at the monastery on Ox Island," said Brother Luigbe. "Come, let us arrive there before morning."

They set off once more. This time Feth Fio was able to walk.

As they came to lower ground they passed through farms where the people greeted them with curiosity and hospitality. Without asking they were given food and drink to help them on their way. Word of the scrolls appeared not to have travelled this far north.

By the time that dusk was closing in they had arrived on the shores of the lake of *Érainn*. At the sight of water and the prospect of boats Feth Fio regained his confidence.

"Is there a boat waiting to take us to this monastery on the island?" asked Feth Fio of Brother Luigbe.

"There is a ferry further along this shore."

That was disappointing news to Feth Fio. It was not possible for Feth Fio to be carried on a ferry. The indignity of being carried over land was one thing, but becoming a passenger on a ferry would bring him great shame. He would swim to the island instead. Indeed he wondered to himself if Bretha would accompany him and at that prospect his spirits rallied greatly.

In a nearby settlement they were directed to the jetty where a boat was awaiting them with a young boy guarding it.

"Is this the ferry to the monastery, boy?" asked Brother Luigbe.

"It is, sir, but I am to tell you that the ferryman, my father, is taken ill with fever. He is sorry he cannot take you to the monastery tonight," said the boy. "There is a good boatman in the next settlement. I will fetch him."

"No need, no need," said Feth Fio leaping into the boat and seizing the oars with glee forgetting all about the prospect of a swim with Bretha.

"How will you get the boat back to my father?" asked the worried boy.

"Boy of the lake, I am Feth Fio, boatman of the great River Sionann, the greatest river in the land," said Feth Fio. "I will return this fine boat to you as soon as my friends are safely on the island."

"Then how will you get back to your friends, sir?" asked the boy.

"Why I will swim, boy of the lake," said Feth Fio.

"It is very far, sir. No one swims that distance."

"I do," said Feth Fio.

"Feth Fio will do as he says, boy. You have no need to worry. Your boat is in good hands as God is my witness," said Brother Luigbe placing a reassuring hand on the boy's shoulder.

"What about the goddess of the lake? She may not welcome strangers at this hour." asked the boy.

"I will vouch for the goddess. I am a priestess of the goddess, Isis," said the lady Melania knowing that Brother Luigbe could not give any assurance about a goddess. "I will make a sacrifice of these flowers to her." She threw some marigolds and bluebells she had picked earlier onto the water and Bretha placed a small triquetra she had made from twigs onto the placid water. Then Melania and Bretha bowed solemnly to the lake.

The boy appeared satisfied with this and handed over the rope holding the boat.

As they set off Feth Fio shouted back to the boy, "Boy of the lake, I will have the ferry back by sunrise, as the goddess is my witness."

The boy waved and once more Feth Fio strained at the oars with pleasure, his pride as a boatman restored for all to see.

XXVI: The Two Kings

In the late afternoon Augustine sat quietly in a room in the great *rath* of the King of the *Laigen* reflecting on his first tumultuous day in Eriu. Much had happened in such a short time and he needed the quiet to steady his mind, before meeting Brandub mac Echach.

After learning that the attempt to seize the scrolls at Uisneach had failed, Augustine had travelled at speed that morning from Royal Temair to Dun Aillinn, the royal residence of the Kings of the *Laigen*. While he reasoned that he had not secured the scrolls during his first day on Eriu, an unlikely outcome even for one such as him, he had learnt much of value. He reflected that with God's help he had made good progress. The game was in play and God was with him. That much was plain.

In Augustine's world reliable information was everything and now he had such information in abundance.

He knew the scrolls were close-by and still in the hands of the desert father. He had met with the High King and learnt that he was in thrall to his judges and to his coarse abbot, and not presently of a mind to trade the scrolls. However the High King had an ambitious and treacherous wife who was in alliance with those who would take whatever steps were needed to trade the scrolls and in so doing seize the land for themselves. Augustine smiled in deep contentment as he recalled his own alliance with Queen Ronnat.

Augustine's priority now was to quickly come to an understanding with the queen's cousin, this King of the *Laigen*. He still had his British ally, Artur, the Guledig of the feared Gododdin, to hold as a negotiating ploy. After all, he had twenty of his horse soldiers as living proof of his alliance with the general. The presence of the Gododdin was already causing the necessary fear and consternation. However he could not reveal that Artur had a similar desire to possess the scrolls. That was a complication he would leave for another day.

Beyond this he had one more weapon, Artur's beloved sister, the demure Sister of Christ, Dorothea. He had not made up his mind how he would use that tender morsel. God would show the way at a given point, after all. He had placed her in his hands to use as Augustine saw fit for the greater good.

The King of the *Laigen* obviously had high ambitions supported by at least one other provincial king and by the High King's own wife. That was more than enough to work with, Augustine reasoned. What did the High King have, save for an eccentric abbot, a traitorous wife and some pedantic judges who would disappear into their rooms at the first threat of violence? It was for Augustine now to secure the support of the rebels and force the issue to a successful conclusion as quickly as possible and return to Rome in triumph.

The letter from Queen Ronnat to her cousin, the King of the *Laigen* that he been given in Royal Temair was not sealed and was written in Latin, so it was obvious to Augustine that he was meant to read it.

> *'Dear Cousin*
>
> *Your news that the scrolls were not secured at Uisneach is not the setback it may seem for I have secured the support of the Roman emissary, Father Augustine who I met with in private last night and he comes to you with this letter.*
>
> *He offers all that we need to secure this land in return for the scrolls.*
>
> *Cousin, speak frankly and courteously with him as I have done and reach an early understanding.*
>
> *It seems likely that my husband will call an assembly hoping to settle the matter. If the judges and Colum Cille have their way the scrolls will be lost to us and with them the chance to secure Eriu. Therefore I believe we must conclude matters with the emissary before the assembly, so that we can pose a strong argument to destroy the forces of weakness and secure the scrolls. I pray you and your allies will be of the same mind.*
>
> *I will continue here with my husband and will send you news until matters dictate otherwise.*

Then there were words in a strange text that Augustine could not understand the meaning of which said:

> *Boann coupled with Goibhniu to make a great sword to defeat the brown bull of Cúailnge.*
> *Your loving cousin,*
> *Ronnat.'*

Augustine was reassured by the letter, except the final line in a strange tongue. He puzzled at it, convinced it was a coded message. The queen may copulate like a sweet angel, but his years of experience had taught Augustine that powerful, attractive women used their bodies as a spider uses its web and he was no fly, not Augustine of Nubea.

Augustine chuckled at the memory of his delicious coupling with the High King's wife. Normally he would be racked with guilt after such weakness, but bedding a queen in pursuit of his holy mission was no sign of mortal weakness and only filled him with delight. A little carnal knowledge in a holy cause would not disturb his sacred contract, he calculated.

As Augustine was recalling his moments of passionate embrace with the queen, Sister Dorothea came to his door. He watched her move timidly into his room. Thankfully, since having her breasts bound, the sister had been unable to tempt him on their long journey and he could deal with her on a formal basis without the distraction of wayward lust. He already had power over her through her obedience to the church and he would use it when he saw the need. That was satisfaction enough.

"Excuse me, Father Augustine, the two kings invite you to meet with them in the counsel hall," said Dorothea demurely.

"Both are there? That is very good. Stay close by, sister, and translate well. Keep your wits about you and expect God's intervention."

"I will, Father."

With his bronze cross strapped to his back Augustine followed Dorothea towards the counsel hall. As they emerged into the evening sunlight the four Gododdin horse soldiers fell in behind them. Augustine resented their presence, but he knew they would not let Sister Dorothea out of their sight.

They were shown into the counsel hall where many men stood around while two sat alone in the centre of the hall by a large fire They were clothed in purple and surrounded by large hunting hounds lying at their feet. A hush fell on the room as Augustine walked in which emboldened the emissary. He liked to make a dramatic entrance. It gave him a certain advantage at the beginning of an encounter.

It was a very different grouping to that which Augustine had experienced in Royal Temair. There appeared to be no judges or monks present. A man introducing himself as the king's house steward motioned Augustine and Sister Dorothea to be seated opposite the two men. A cup bearer brought them wine and bread. The horse soldiers remained standing behind them.

The house steward spoke first and loudly in his native tongue: "This is King Brandub mac Echach, King of the *Laigen*, son of Echu mac Muiredaig of the *Uí Cheinnselaig* and this is Colmán Bec, King Of *Mide* and son of Diarmait mac Cerbaill, *Ard Ri*."

Both men watched Augustine closely and remained silent.

Sister Dorothea stood up, bowed to the two kings, apologised for presuming to speak and once again explained her role as translator.

Augustine reasoned he would meet these two as equals. He would remain seated and would stand for no provincial king who needed his support.

"I am Augustine of Nubea, emissary of the Bishop of Rome, God's most favoured upon this earth. I am come to this land to help build a strong church here and to return some important sacred scrolls to Rome" Augustine began. He had no time now for weasel words and these two looked as if neither had they. "I have met with the *Ard Ri*. His queen gave me this letter for King Brandub."

Augustine handed the letter to Sister Dorothea who began to approach the king with it. Immediately the hounds stirred and began to growl menacingly. The king held up his hand for her to stop. The steward took the letter and approached the king through the hounds who accepted his presence.

As Brandub read the letter the steward explained to Augustine: "These are royal slaughter hounds, father. They guard the kings and will permit no strangers near their masters. If any come close they will rip their throats out. It happened only last week to a foolish merchant from Gaul. He left all his fine wine behind." He laughed.

Dorothea gasped at the risk she had just taken and clutched her small crucifix to her throat. Augustine was unimpressed with such displays. The King of the Visigoths kept a pride of leopards around him. They were nothing more than a distraction.

Brandub looked up from reading the letter, he passed it to Colman Bec and ordered everyone to leave the counsel hall except the steward and the Minder of Hounds. The slaughter hounds remained eying Augustine and Sister Dorothea suspiciously.

"So, Father, ye now know my cousin, the queen" said Brandub grinning.

Augustine ignored the implication. He surmised that the foreign text in the letter must have informed the king of their liaison. It mattered little to Augustine who knew of their coupling. The queen had asked him to be discrete yet she had not reciprocated. It told him to be careful with this queen regardless of his strong physical attraction.

"I met the queen at Royal Temair. We had a meeting where we discussed the issues before us," said Augustine flatly.

"What are those issues as ye see them?" asked Colman Bec bluntly, irked at not receiving any deference from this black monk.

"You want powerful allies which the church can provide and the church wants certain scrolls held in this land returned to it. It's quite simple." Augustine was not going to play games with these two. If they wanted powerful overseas allies to further their cause in Eriu, then they would have to obtain the scrolls for the Church. "Tell me if you see it differently."

"So who are these powerful allies ye have in yer pocket, emissary?" asked Brandub in return.

"King Brandub, it is not I, but the Holy Father who has allies. The Holy Father has built alliances with the Franks in Gaul, the Lombards in Italia, the Visigoths in Hispania and the Gododdin in Britain."

"The Gododdin?" asked Brandub. "The Gododdin plundered our settlements in west Britain and drove our kindred to the sea."

"Then you will know what a powerful ally they would make. I travel with a troop of their horse soldiers. This is a clear sign of their support for the Church."

"Why would the Gododdin help us?"

"If you are an ally of the Church, they will help you. They desire to have the holy communion of the one true church and, like you, wish to have the church's powerful support against their enemies. I can persuade them that such support will only be offered if they join an alliance with you to secure the sacred scrolls for us."

"So what form would yer support take, emissary"?

"First we need to know what your ambitions are, King Brandub and King Colman" said Augustine, "to see how they coincide with the church's."

Brandub nodded and conferred with Colman Bec.

"Eriu is not a large and powerful country, emissary. Some say we were fortunate to escape invasion by Rome, others say that we would have benefitted from their rule. But for meself, I hear of what is happening in Britain since the legions left and I doubt that we would have benefitted in the long run. We hear reports of Angles, Saxons and Jutes stealing land in Britain.

"The old people of the sanctuaries tell us of visions of warriors in the far north who will come upon us in Eriu if we are not powerful enough to resist them. We must prepare for that day. We do not want them here. We do not want any foreign masters. If you seek dominion over us, emissary, then we will be united against you," said Brandub.

He turned to Colman Bec who continued:

"We see the presence of yer Church in a different light, helping us to build the alliance ye speak of with the British and the Franks in Gaul. In that way we both benefit. Ye get yer faithful church in this land supported by the kings and we get our security to continue to rule this land without threat of foreigner overlords," said Colman Bec.

"And the scrolls?" asked Augustine.

"We will secure the scrolls for the church," said Colman Bec.

"I am curious to know how you will do that," said Augustine.

"Aed mac Ainmuirech, the *Ard Ri* and *Ri Cuicidh* of the northern *Ui Neill* is not a powerful *Ard Ri*, emissary. We two together," said

Colman Bec indicating Brandub and himself, "are more powerful. Many foreigners suppose that our *Ard Ri* wields great power over others, but he does not. It is an honorary role. He is a guardian of the laws and the roads, but little else. He is not like your Frankish kings or a Roman emperor. War will be his last resort. He will hope to win this by cunning or by force of legal argument."

"Aed is stupid and thinks not of the future, only of today. A High King must plan for his people's future, this High King does not," said Brandub. "Colum Cille is a different matter. He was born a prince and should be *Ard Ri*, but he chose the church instead. He's a clever one. A devout and humble monk of that there is no doubt, but when the need arises he is a great diplomat and a cunning strategist. He will no doubt see this as a holy crusade to secure *the Word* in this land.

"He was fostered to a high druid and knows the old ways and uses them when it suits him. He has the gift of second sight. Colum Cille is your adversary, emissary. He is the power behind Aed mac Ainmuirech."

Brandub called for more wine and went on, "We two together, with the support of the Church of Rome, have the power to isolate Aed and the puppet-master, Colum Cille. Most of the other kings will see this and will support us for the common good. There is no desire in Eriu to hold onto these scrolls. They mean little to us. If the *Ard Ri* holds onto them and by doing so alienates important allies in Rome, in Gaul and in Britain and gambles with the safety of this land, the people will turn on him. He will have broken his sacred covenant to govern according to the three principles of wisdom," Brandub held up his hand with three fingers raised, "obedience to the laws of man and God, concern for the common good and courage in the face of adversity."

Colman Bec nodded and spoke: "It seems that Aed, persuaded by his cousin the abbot intends to keep the scrolls for some religious reasons best known to themselves. They will hold an assembly, probably in the north where he and his priestly cousin feel strongest. But that will be their mistake.

"Eriu may not have had the benefit of the empire, emissary, but we have a strong system of our own laws especially around ownership set down by the *Breithem*, a powerful class of judges. They will hold that it is a simple matter of agreeing legal title to these scrolls. They will argue that because the scrolls have been sent here for safe keeping that they have proper title. Ye on the other hand will have to establish yer title. Can ye do so?"

"Of course," replied Augustine confidently. "We have the highest claim, above the law of mere men, God's law, which you say your High King must obey. It is written that our lord Yeshua passed his divine mission on earth to St Peter. It was St Peter who established the one true church in Rome. Therefore any sacred scrolls pertaining to Lord Yeshua belong in Rome under the care of St Peter's church and not in this land. This land has no claim, as this Abbot Colum Cille, if he is a true believer, will have to admit. He wants these scrolls purely for his own selfish purposes, I'll wager. It will not stand in the eyes of God and in the eyes of men. God will curse any who withhold the scrolls from his church."

"Ye make a strong case, emissary, which many will find persuasive," said Colman Bec.

"But we must not underestimate our opponents and their strong determination to hold onto these scrolls," cautioned Brandub. "Already an agent of ours was set upon by wolves and torn limb from limb before he could secure the scrolls. This was the work of the *Tuatha De* who live in the underworld and have long been close to Colum Cille. It was they who blinded Tigernaig, King of *Iarmummu*. They have powers beyond our understanding. However they have little power in the north. So if the assembly is in the north it will be to our advantage."

"This is good. So we must pray that the assembly is held there," said Augustine.

"Indeed we must," said Brandub.

"Very well, let us pray," said Augustine. Taking his cross from off his back, Augustine held it in front of him while he kneeled in prayer. The two kings looked at each other uncomfortably and followed suit. So did a surprised Sister Dorothea for she had never seen Father Augustine pray before.

Augustine began: "Dear Father, we, your humble servants, do pledge our lives and efforts in your service in this sacred mission to recover the scrolls and in all other matters as you may decide. It is our sacred duty to see these scrolls returned to the safe keeping of your church in Rome. We humbly ask that any meeting be held beyond the power of the *Tuatha De* in the north of this land and pray for your divine guidance in this matter today and every day. Allow these righteous kings and your humble emissary to be your loyal servants in this matter as in all others. Give us the strength to vanquish your enemies and build in this land a strong church to your everlasting glory. In the name of the Father, Son and Holy Ghost."

The two kings and Sister Dorothea waited patiently for Augustine to say "Amen". Even the Gododdin guards were on their knees. For several moments they remained in quiet contemplation in the counsel hall while the slaughter hounds became uneasy seeing their royal masters in such a pose. Still Augustine remained in the praying posture.

Eventually the "Amen" came and they rose to their feet and sat back on their chairs, except Sister Dorothea who remained standing.

Augustine smiled across at the kings.

"It is good we are now joined with God in this sacred mission. The church is pleased to have your loyal support, King Brandub and King Colman. As soon as the scrolls are in my possession work can begin building both a strong church in this land and strong alliances for you both beyond your shores, you have my word."

The two kings looked uneasy at this. Colman Bec was the first to speak: "We hoped we could see an initial gesture of good faith, Father: something to give us reassurance of yer support."

At that point a messenger entered the room carrying letters bearing the seal of the *Ard Ri* addressed to the two kings and to Augustine. They opened them immediately.

"Our prayer has indeed been swiftly answered, father," said Brandub smiling. "The meeting will be on the north coast two weeks from today. It will be an *airecht*. An *airecht* is a legal assembly, a court. This shows that they wish to use legal arguments. We are invited to bring our advisers. The *Ard Ri* will bring the *Breithem* and Colum Cille will bring the abbots and bishops. They hope to outnumber us."

Augustine smiled in quiet satisfaction. Their prayer had indeed been swiftly answered. There was no doubt God wished to give these two a clear indication of his power in this matter. Augustine watched the kings quietly for a few moments. He considered that having worked closely with God in so many trying circumstances he knew Him better than most. Perhaps these two took their God for granted. A dangerous belief for God was a jealous god who punished those who believed He was merely their play thing. The path was not always as smooth as it appeared and God tested your faith at key moments. Being prepared for all possible outcomes was always wise and this strategy earned divine respect. So Augustine asked the two kings: "If you should lose this *airecht*, what then?"

"We take the scrolls by force," said both kings without hesitation.

Their answer pleased Augustine enormously.

"Then this will be my reassurance to you of the church's earnest endeavour in this affair. If we lose this convention and war is the outcome, and we pray it will not be so, I shall pledge to bring you many Gododdin horse soldiers from Britain to affect a swift and speedy triumph."

BOOK THREE

XXVII: Ox Island

The monks in the monastery of Ox Island were devout followers of St Antony's strict ascetic lifestyle with no concessions to physical comfort. The island was not large and sat in a narrow stretch of water before the lake of *Érainn* widened westwards into its great expanse of fresh water.

There was a demanding daily routine of prayer and meditation, beginning with the first office just before dawn and continuing every three hours until midnight: between the offices of prayer there was manual work in the monastery farm. All this activity was supported by a meagre diet so that a lack of sleep and hunger quite often reduced the monks to delirium. But in spite of the harshness of their lives, they were kindly folk who saw to it that any guests and visiting pilgrims were as well accommodated as their resources would allow. The beds in the hostel were liberally covered in straw, fires were lit and hot baths were offered.

On arrival in the early hours Cormac, Simon and Luigbe felt the need for prayer and joined the monks in *Iarmeirge*, the first office after rising, before dawn broke in the east. It was obvious to them that their presence and the expected arrival of the renowned Abbot Colum Cille had the monks in an excited condition. After *Iarmeirge* the monks were drawn to Cormac in great curiosity. His status as a desert father recently returned from Egypt with sacred scrolls for Abbot Colum Cille elevated Cormac to living sainthood in their eyes. While none spoke, as idle chatter was forbidden, many kissed the hem of Cormac's mantle and kneeled before him for a blessing in the hope that his saintliness would be conferred on them.

Cormac obliged the gentle, half-starved monks, but was none the less embarrassed by their attention. Presently Brother Luigbe rescued him and asked the abbot to remove the curious monks as Father Cormac and his companions were exhausted after their flight from the Hill of Uisneach. Cormac, Simon and Luigbe then took to their beds and slept until they were woken for the next office.

As pagans, the lady Melania and Bretha were not required to take part in the life of the monastery, which was much to their relief for they too were exhausted and much in need of a bath after their journey.

A forlorn Feth Fio had immediately set out to return the ferry to its owner: forlorn because Betha rejected his invitation to return with him and then swim back to the monastery. She thought the boatman was half mad to suggest such activity after the journey they had just completed and bluntly told him so.

The bath was the first destination for the lady Melania and Bretha; it gave Melania an opportunity to advise Bretha of the true nature of Feth Fio's attention.

As they lay half asleep in the bath Bretha made her views of Feth Fio clear as soon as Melania mentioned his name.

"I know, I know he's a divil" she said sleepily. "But until this night I didn't realise that he was a mad divil. Do you know lady he asked me to take the ferry back and to swim back here with him!? What possesses him?"

"Bretha you must know that Feth Fio is in rapture. He loves you and wishes you for a... for a mate." said Melania.

Bretha sat upright in the bath with a start.

"For a mate!? What? To be... to be my husband?"

"Yes. We think your play in the water was a courting ritual to him."

"What? That nipping and tugging wasn't just a game?"

"No, it meant a lot more to him than that."

Bretha thought for a moment.

"I forgot he is a changeling. So the divil wanted to mount me in the water?"

"It was coming close to that I think," said Melania.

"That's why he wanted me to swim back with him just now. So he could have me among the reeds and the fish!"

"I think it's more than simple lust, Bretha. Feth Fio is a kind and loyal soul. He loves you and wants you for a mate. He respects you too much to have forced himself on you."

"You never can tell with changelings, lady. I don't want to give birth to baby otters. I am a *file*!"

"I'm told that changelings do marry humans."

"It's true. That's how you get creatures like Tocca the Hen. I don't want to give birth to something like that!"

They both laughed and lay quietly in the warm bath considering the situation.

Bretha giggled some more.

"I'll have to let the divil know. Changelings lead such complicated lives, poor confused creatures that they are, neither one thing nor another. It's a shame as I enjoyed his friendship and his games."

"You can still be friends. As long as he knows it's just friendship."

"Like ye and Father Cormac?"

"Father Cormac is not an amorous changeling!" giggled Melania.

"Feth may go back to the River Sionann now. It must have been me that brought him on this far," said Bretha wistfully. "I suppose there was no harm in the poor divil."

"No there is no harm in dear Feth Fio. He has been a good friend to all of us on this journey. We would not wish to hurt him."

Feth Fio did not return when he said he would.

They were idyllic days as they waited for Colum Cille to arrive, even though they all knew in their hearts that Ox Island was but a temporary sanctuary in the eye of a surrounding and gathering storm. The island was the perfect haven. The calm waters of the lake of *Érainn* sparkled in the warm summer sunshine and gave the island a peaceful solitude. Few visitors appeared save for a delivery of cloth and fishermen exchanging some of their catch for bread and cabbages. The sweet scent of the yellow gorse was mixed with the bitter of wild garlic; the purple of orchids and garlands of white thorn crowning the crest of the island near the church.

The land was fertile and the monastery farm grew cabbage, carrot, parsnip, herbs, some oats and barley. The monastery's beehives were coming to life in the warm summer air to provide wax for candles and honey for medicine and mead.

Cormac welcomed the familiar discipline of the monastery: it restored a much needed rhythm to his life after the fraught journey since landing on Inish Cathaig. The gentle poetry of the psalms and the physical labour of the farm brought body, mind and soul together in the worship of creation in the same way as the simple smell of the warm, freshly dug earth and the cut grasses took Cormac back to his youth in Killabuonia. All was bound up in sacred life and simple memories. Yet with the familiar leather bag secured on his back he was ever reminded of his greater obligation beyond the pull of this tranquil and simple place.

On the far side of the island there was a plain shrine to the founder of the monastery, Saint Molaise, who had ascended to heaven a few years earlier. Cormac began to visit the shrine to pray for the saint's guidance in the quiet of the evening before vespers. While in prayer on the third day he felt a presence beside him and when his prayer was complete he saw the lady Melania seated on the ground beside him.

"Forgive me brother, but I like to watch you in prayer," she said in her native Greek. "I hope I am not an intrusion."

"You are never an intrusion, my dear sister."

"It is some time since we talked; brother and I miss your discourse. May I talk with you now?"

"Please sister, do so. I too have missed the sweet caress of your voice. Our circumstances have not allowed it and I have wondered about your wellbeing in this strange land. This must have been a testing time for you and I am sorry I could not be closer to you."

"I have known that you are hard pressed, brother. Your welfare has been upper most in my mind. How are you?" asked Melania looking deeply into Cormac's bright blue eyes.

He held her gaze and said, "God sustains me, sister. It is quite remarkable. I ask for his guidance and it is always forthcoming."

"Your burden is great," she said pointing to the ever-present bag containing the scrolls.

"Lord Yeshua's burden was greater."

Melania smiled and picked a buttercup and held it in her hand.

"What will happen when the abbot arrives, brother?" she asked.

"This affair may test even Crimthainn's powers," said Cormac deep in thought. "He is not a quiet person, except when he is at prayer or in the scriptorium."

"I mean where will we go and what will happen?"

"That I cannot say, sister," said Cormac. "I expect Crimthainn, or Colum Cille as he is known now, will want to read these scrolls and God will then guide us on what is to be done with them."

"Do you think Crimthainn will be minded to keep the scrolls and deny the Bishop of Rome?"

Cormac thought for a while.

"Crimthainn loves scrolls. He loves reading and writing. He creates libraries in his monasteries, I'm told. He has written a beautiful book, I hear. The abbot of this place tells me that some years ago he even caused a great battle to be fought not far from here over the ownership of a book he had copied. Many died and because of that Crimthainn went into exile for years as a penance. So God may guide him to take a different view now and tell him to hand them over to the Roman emissary. But Crimthainn has little time for Rome. He sees their church as an extension of their military empire."

"What do you think should happen, brother?" asked Melania.

"It is not my place to say. It is a sin to presume to know the mind of God. Please do not ask such questions, sister. Ask them of God."

"I am sorry. I forget the mind of a desert monk. It is not like the Greek mind."

They smiled at each other seeing the Agora in each other's eyes and recalling their days together in debate.

"We must continue to place ourselves in the hands of the divine, sister; you with the goddess and me with Yeshua and his father."

"That, I will do willingly."

They sat quietly in the soft evening light while mayflies flew about their heads. Cormac watched the lady play with the buttercup in her tender hands. Her eyes focused on its beauty. Cormac was reminded of his wife's love of buttercups and then dismissed the memory as quickly as it had come to him.

Presently he said: "What does the goddess call you to do, lady, with your life now in this strange place? I would help you if I can."

"You are, as ever, kind, dear brother," she said looking up from her contemplation of the flower. "I have grown close to Bretha. She has offered to take me to a kindred called the 'old people of the sanctuaries'."

"Yes, the people of the sanctuaries. They are guardians of the old ways, the old places in this land. They worship the sun and the gods of the earth, the wind and the sky. You may find harmony there with your own gods. They would welcome you, but I do not know them now. They live separately from the kindreds. Bretha and her father will help you, I am sure."

"I am guided towards these people." Melania looked at Cormac with eyes full of sadness. "We will part, brother, and that vexes me."

"There may be no other way, sister. It is our separate calling that pulls us apart: as it has done before. So it will do again."

"What of you, brother?"

"Listen," said Cormac with his hand raised. "Can you hear that sound?"

Melania listened. She wondered what sound Cormac meant. She heard only the wind in the trees and the cattle lowing on the far shore.

"It is the sound of God laughing when I presume to know what I will do with my life in this place of shadows."

Melania laughed. "You blaspheme and you tease me, brother."

"I will hold you in my prayers daily, dear sister. I will visit you in my dream time."

"I see you often in my dreamtime, brother."

"I know," said Cormac. "Until the end of days we will meet there." They sat in quiet again listening to the divine.

"Come, it is time for vespers," said Cormac. "The abbot will be concerned if I spend more time alone with a pagan priestess."

The next day saw the arrival of Abbot Colum Cille. As Cormac turned to leave the church after the midday office he realised that a large framed monk covered in dust standing at the rear of the church was his old mentor, Colum Cille. He had quietly slipped in at the back and was standing silently with his head bowed just as any other monk would do, except Colum Cille was not just any other monk, much though he claimed to be. His given name meant 'Dove of the Church' and so he strived to be. He had built monasteries throughout the land and now had begun to build monasteries in Alba where they say he had converted the king of the Pictish people to be a Christian. To many Colum Cille appeared as if lit by an internal flame that never went out. This attracted many to him, much like moths to a flame.

He had a manner about him that was mighty, hot tempered and impatient and at other times secretive and then meek and mild. He could be as rough as a great bull, as gentle and quiet as a spring lamb and as cunning as the fox, his birth animal. In his presence kings were cowed and slaves lifted up. He was of royal birth, but as a boy he had renounced his lineage to walk a spiritual path first with the people of the sanctuary and then as a follower of Yeshua to build His church in Eriu and beyond.

The first thing that struck you about Colum Cille was his eyebrows. They were bushy and of vivid red hair set on a wide and high forehead. They moved as he spoke and gave him a fierce appearance.

Neither Colum Cille nor Cormac acknowledged each other while in the church. That would not have been seemly. When they walked outside to the wide enclosure surrounding the church and overlooking the lake they turned to each other, standing silently in recognition of the immense duty that had been placed upon them by their God.

Colum Cille was the first to break the silence.

"The desert has toughened ye, boy. That I can see. Ye no longer have the softness of a farmer about ye."

Cormac smiled and simply said: "The desert strips us bare, Crimthainn, and you taught me well."

"The naked soul can accomplish much in the world," said Colum Cille.

Colum Cille could no longer withhold his pleasure at seeing his young novice from many years ago stand before him as a well-honed desert father. His craggy face broke into a smile and he strode over to Cormac, held him powerfully by his shoulders and looked closely into his eyes.

"It is good to see ye returned to be amongst us after all these years, Cormac mac Fliande of Killabuonia. Ye are welcome among the free people of the Celtic Church. I have expected yer return for many a day. I can see in yer eyes that ye have prospered under God."

"I have striven to be God's instrument, Crimthainn, in the years since you tutored me in Durrow."

"Well I see ye are much loved by God for He has chosen ye for this most holy of missions."

"I hope I am worthy, Crimthainn," said Cormac quietly.

Colum Cille nodded. Looking round at the monks who were intently watching the two eminent churchmen talk, he said, "Come, dear brother, ye have carried this cross for many miles. We have much to discuss. Let us find a private place where we can unburden ye."

As they walked across the monastery enclosure Colum Cille called Brother Luigbe to him and asked that Simon join them also. Somehow he seemed to know of Simon's important role in translating the scrolls.

Ever since he was handed the scrolls by Acacius, on that day in the Patriarch's consistory, Cormac had allowed his mind to speculate about his meeting with Colum Cille. Now the true moment had arrived and as always the truth of the present moment was different. He was in an island monastery he had never known, further north than he had ever been and pursued by men he did not know. The only constant was his old mentor, Crimthainn. He prayed that God would give Crimthainn the wisdom to know what was to done about the scrolls he had carried for so long.

Colum Cille led them to a small roundhouse under the north wall of the church where he said they could speak in private.

Inside, candles burned and a table was set with bread and milk. To the side was a pitcher of water and soap for hand washing. It was a ritual before eating, but also before handling the written word.

Colum Cille sat down and tore off some bread, dipped it in the bowl of milk and ate hungrily while he waited for others to arrange themselves on the chairs provided.

"Well, boy, let's see what ye have ye in that bag," he asked Cormac. It was his way to call most people 'boy' young and old.

Cormac placed the leather bag on the table, opened it and slowly and carefully removed its contents. First he gave the letter from the

Patriarch to Colum Cille, then he set out the bag of gold coins on the table and unwrapped the cloth protecting the scrolls.

At the sight of the scrolls Simon instinctively shuddered. He remembered the huge uncertainty he had felt in the Great Library when he first understood the implications of what he read. He recalled the fear that came over him when he learned that he was to be exiled and a vow of silence imposed by the Patriarch upon him and on his teacher, the good Father Clement. Simon had prayed each day for Father Clement since their parting.

Yet he also recalled with relief how his old fears and uncertainties had been washed away by Abbot Mac Nisse in the Monastery of the Meadows and how he had found faith and courage in *The Word*.

Cormac noticed Simon's reaction to seeing the scrolls once again and placed a reassuring hand on the young monk's arm.

Colum Cille saw Simon's reaction. "What bothers the boy?" he asked Cormac.

Simon smiled nervously at the abbot and answered for himself haltingly in the language of Eriu: "These scrolls have powerful associations for me, father," Simon began. "Discovering *The Word* was a shock to me and to my teacher, Father Clement. It was not what we had been taught. The Church in Africa had concealed *The Word*. The Patriarch was angry at how it contradicted the Church's teachings and exiled both of us for fear we would reveal the contents. Father Clement was sent to the desert and I to Eriu, both with a vow of silence. All this was done so that *The Word* might remain hidden."

Colum Cille raised his great eyebrows. "Ye are very clear in yer opinions for a young monk, brother. Ye have also broken yer vow of silence in defiance of yer church," said Colum Cille accusingly.

"My vow of silence, father, was putting my good friends at great risk for they did not know what they carried. *The Word* that I have read guided me to break this vow. My conscience would not allow otherwise," Simon said looking at Cormac. "My silence was also designed to hide the truth and protect those in positions of power. Therefore it had no divine authority, father."

"Ye sound like a freethinking theologian, boy. Obedience to the rules is an important aspect of our life as monks. Do ye defy rules?" asked Colum Cille looking from Simon to Cormac and back.

"I have learnt from my experience and from reading *The Word*, father," said Simon calmly pointing to one of the scrolls lying on the table before them, "that a rule must only be followed if it is just and follows His teachings. This rule did neither, father."

Colum Cille fixed Simon with a long, silent stare. His fearsome eyebrows knitted above piercing grey eyes. Simon returned Colum Cille's glare.

"Good!" said Colum Cille eventually his eyebrows lifting. "Ye have learnt something valuable from yer experience, boy. We have no patriarchs in Eriu. We are a free people, but we must have rules in our communities. It is how we have survived. But they are fair rules according God's holy order and the demands of His creation and no other. Is that not so, Father Cormac?"

"It is, Crimthainn," said Cormac.

"Do ye wish to stay in the land of yer exile, brother, and serve our community of God?" Colum Cille asked Simon and before he could answer Colum Cille raised a large finger, shook it at Simon and stabbed the table for emphasis, "Be mindful of yer answer because this is yer holy contract with God and with me now in this place, boy. The only politics we play here is to serve the true word of God and His creation, not something made up by clever theologians and preening bishops. So do not suppose the ways of yer Alexandrian or Roman church apply in this place."

"I have learnt much since coming here, father. Father Cormac and Father Mac Nisse in the Meadows have taught me much. I have learnt that *The Word* has come to its natural home. I am guided that it should stay here and so should I."

Cormac interjected: "Brother Simon has been on a spiritual journey since reading the scrolls, father. Only he among us knew the content of the scrolls. That was a heavy burden for one so young. I believe he has grown closer to God as a result."

"That is good," said Colum Cille, "for I have work for ye to do, Brother Simon. Will ye serve God and His people loyally in this land?"

"As God is my witness, I will, father," responded Simon with a broad smile.

"Pray with me, brothers," said Colum Cille as he sat with his head bowed and hands clasped before him. "We welcome Brother Simon to our Celtic Church in Eriu and pray that he continues on his path to know and love the true word of God and His creation. Amen."

They sat in silence for several moments.

"Now to work, brothers," said Colum Cille. "We have much to do in very little time. It is my understanding that ye, Brother Simon, can translate *The Word* for us from the tongue of Lord Yeshua to the Latin. Is that so?"

"It is, father."

"Very well. Now Brother Simon, for that is yer birth name is it not?" Simon nodded. "Ye are well acquainted with these scrolls. Please explain what each of these is."

Simon identified each scroll in turn: *The Word*, St Mark's letter and Ciaiphas' letter to the High Priest of the Sanhedrin..

Colum Cille then broke the seal on the Patriarch's letter and his great red eyebrows knitted as he read the Latin text out loud.

> *'Esteemed Prince Colum Cille, Bishop of Eriu*
>
> *'The Holy Church of St Mark the Evangelist in Alexandria and all Africa has instructed Father Cormac of Scetis to deliver the sacred scroll known as The Word and the letters of St Mark and the High Priest Caiaphas, into the safekeeping of your church in Eriu for now and for all time and beseeches you to keep St Mark's sacred covenant.*
>
> *'You hold in your hands the very words of the Christ written down by Joseph of Arimithaea from words spoken by our lord as He lay on the third day before he ascended. This is The Word that St Mark carried out of the holy city and into Alexandria and upon which our church in Africa was built.*
>
> *'Witness to this was the Magdalene woman, St. James, Joseph of Arimithaea and Nicodemus. There is a letter from St Mark himself and another document penned by the creature Caiaphas of the Sanhedrin who crucified our lord.*
>
> *'To our shame these have lain in the Great Library of Alexandria since the time of St Cyril and were discovered by the Church in the present time. These sacred scrolls are no longer safe in our land pressed as we are by the heathen,*

Sassanid empire that will soon invade and threaten our holy church.

'Take heed that the Bishop of Rome desires The Word and will use and distort it to build a new empire to the glory of man on this earth and not to the glory of God as He intended. Be aware that Rome's emissary will pursue these scrolls to the ends of the earth.

'We humbly beseech the prince to keep these scrolls safe according to His glory and to His desire and to keep the holy covenant that is set out within. To our eternal shame we in Alexandria failed to keep our saint's holy covenant and over many years failed to honour the Word. So we pray that by entrusting The Word to the church in Eriu our failure will in some measure be forgiven, that we will be spared and allowed to continue our mission in Africa according the wishes of our blessed saint.

'The desert father who carries The Word to you has in his company a young monk by the name of Bartholomew who has translated The Word and will do so for you. We ask that he remains in your service and does not return to this land where his mortal life will be in danger. While in your service the one called Bartholomew is no longer bound to his vow of silence. We bless and pray for you and all who are in the service of your church, Prince Colum Cille. May Lord Yeshua give you the strength and the wisdom to be a worthy guardian of His Word and through this to become the Light of the World.

'This letter is written under my hand and with my God-given authority, Damianos I, Patriarch of the Church in Africa in the Year of the Word 575.'

The letter was signed by Damianos and his *Oikonomos*, Acacius.

Colum Cille lit a single candle and carefully broke the seals on the three scrolls that Cormac had removed from the leather bag.

"I humbly ask for the presence of the Father, the Son and the Holy Ghost to attend upon us now," said Colum Cille solemnly.

The air in the roundhouse had been perfectly still, yet the candle beside the scrolls fluttered in an unseen draught. Colum Cille let a contented smile drift across his face as he watched the small flickering flame.

When the three scrolls were opened on the table before them Colum Cille looked up at each monk in turn and said softly: "Not many lives are given to holy moments such as this one. So we must thank God for this great privilege in our humble lives on this earth, brothers.

"Brother Simon, Please read the contents of each to us starting with our Lord's sacred Word."

XXVIII: The Plot

King Baetan mac Cairill had just settled himself on a large comfortable chair provided for him in the Great Hall of Trimontium in Alba after his long journey from Dunethglas in Eriu. Artur pressed him for news of his sister, Dorothea.

"My spies tell me she is in Royal Temair with the emissary and the *Ard Ri* and is well. They also tell me that she will be travelling south to Aillinn to meet with the Kings of the *Laigen* and the *Mide*. All did not go well for the emissary with the *Ard Ri*. Colum Cille saw to that. Although the emissary did manage to bed the queen or maybe it was the queen who bedded him."

"He's a dog of the dung heap, that one," said Artur. "If he lays a hand on my sister I will take his black skin off, emissary or no."

"Your sister is safe, Artur. She does not appeal to his taste in women, I'm told."

"People say the black skinned people are closer to God on account of being closer to the sun, but I did not see any godliness in this emissary," said Artur.

"His master is his foster father, the Bishop of Rome and not God," said Baetan taking a large mouthful of wine and drawing a letter from his cape. "Now to business, Guledig; I have come with this letter from the *Ard Ri* received just two days ago. He is calling a meeting of the judges, an *airecht*, to decide on the ownership of the scrolls."

"Judges!?" said Artur dismissively.

"You must know that in Eriu the law is an important aspect of all things and the judges are powerful folk, Artur. Our laws did not disappear with the legions as they did in Britain," said King Baetan teasing Artur for the lawless state of Britain since the legions left in 410AD. He turned to the Ard Ri's letter in his hand, "It is Aed mac Ainmuirech's habit to do the bidding of the priest king. This is Colum Cille's doing. He means to hold these scrolls in Eriu to secure his church. One thing we can be sure of is that Colum Cille will not surrender the scrolls to Rome without a fight."

Both men drank deeply of the wine.

"But all this plays into our hands as soldiers do not attend these legal meetings," continued Baetan mac Cairill. "So there will be no armies in attendance to stop us. The *airecht* will be held close to the north coast in a place known as Druim Ceit in two weeks. It is on Cenél nEóġain land so the *Ui Neill* will be all around us. Can your horse soldiers be assembled in time?"

"I have been preparing since returning from Armorica. We are ready and the boats await us," said Artur and laughed. "The emissary believes he has me in his pocket and will be expecting my men to seize the scrolls on his behalf."

Baetan mac Cairill was King of the kindred of the *dal Fiatach* on the east coast of Eriu and rivalled Black Acd for the leadership of the Ulaidh and the kingship of Emania. It was Baetan who had helped Artur of the Gododdin rescue his sister from bondage on his lands and who now was plotting with Artur to secure the scrolls for Britain in return for Artur helping Baetan remove the hated *Ui Neill* from the lands of the Ulaidh and the high kingship to place Baetan of the Ulaidh and the dal Fiatach on the high throne of Eriu.

Their plan was for Artur to land with the Gosgordd, a crack troop of three hundred Gododdin horse soldiers, one day's march from the *airecht*, surround the gathering and seize the scrolls, slaughtering all *Ui Neill* present. At the same time Baetan's soldiers would march south from his stronghold in Dunethglas and seize Royal Temair while the *Ard Ri* was absent. It was an ambitious plan, never before attempted in Eriu, but Baetan and Artur were nothing if not ambitious.

Baetan had travelled in great secrecy to Artur's stronghold in the old Roman fortress of Trimontium in Alba to finalise their plans as soon as he had received the letter from the *Ard Ri*.

"What of the priest king, Colum Cille?" asked Artur.

"What of him? If he resists, slay him and all his followers."

"No I cannot harm a man of God, Baetan. God would punish me. Colum Cille has no weapons and is no threat. At worst we will hold him hostage until he accepts your authority in Eriu."

"Be warned, Colum Cille has powers beyond the physical, Artur. He has chosen this place Druim Ceit because it is a sanctuary of the old people with whom he is in alliance. He is also in alliance with the *Tuatha De*. They have no power in this place, but they do in Royal Temair. He is seeking to work some spells in Druim Ceit, I'll wager."

Artur stared in the fire in the great hall of the Roman fortress for a few moments.

"Last night I saw a vision in my sleep, Baetan. A great raven landed on our sanctuary, the high Hill of Eildon. I spoke with it. It said it was the spirit of these islands. I questioned it. It told me that Colum Cille and I could hold the heathens at bay in all these islands, but this would only happen if we worked in harmony. We could not accomplish this separately. It said that we could hold the scrolls in common ownership and that if we did this you would indeed rule as a wise and just *Ard Ri*, but only if we shared the sacred Word as one church with Colum Cille as its bishop."

Baetan made a dismissive noise to show his disbelief in Artur's vision.

"Remember," Artur said, "that it was my vision that led me to you, Baetan, and to my sister, and a vision told me of the emissary coming to meet with me in Armorica. These are not a boy's wet dreams, my friend. Colum Cille is not the only one with the power to see beyond this world."

"So what would ye have us do in Druim Ceit?" asked Baetan.

"Do all that we have agreed: seize the scrolls; slaughter any *Ui Neill* who opposes us, except for any clergy, and you seize the high kingship. But then I will negotiate peaceably with Colum Cille on holy matters for the sake of our Christian faith in these islands."

"Artur, it is true Colum Cille is a holy man, but he is also a *Ui Neill* and a trickster," said Baetan. "Ten years ago under the cover of a devilish mist at the Battle of Cúl Dreimhne he caused thousands to be slaughtered in a dispute over the ownership of a holy book. Do you think he will make a treaty with ye in regard to these scrolls?"

"He will if I hold him hostage in the Kingdom of *Rheged* and I have the scrolls," smiled Artur.

307

Baetan smiled, "So ye will take the priest king back with ye to this place?"

"If he will not agree terms with us at Druim Ceit," said Artur.

"Very well. Do with him as ye will. These matters of faith are not my concern. My purpose is clear: to seize Royal Temair from the *Ui Neill*, to rule for all the tuatha of Eriu and to see Emania reclaimed for the Uladh."

"After these events my sister will no longer be safe with Rome," said Artur. "So she will come back to the church here. My men in Eriu will see the emissary to a boat that will take him back to Gaul. I have no wish to further upset the Romans. I believe that with *The Word* in our possession they will treat us with respect and not seek to subdue us once more; besides their army is in Constantinople."

They drank more wine while the flames of the fire leapt high and the shadows of the day lengthened.

"Time is important," said Baetan. "If ye land too soon they will have time to oppose ye and defend the scrolls. Too late and the scrolls may be spirited away to one of Colum Cille's many monasteries or be in the hands of the emissary on their way to Rome.

"Black Aed, King of the *Cruithin* will allow you to land on his kindred's shores in the east," said Baetan. "Like I, he hates the *Ui Neill* because of their conquest of the lands of the *Ulaidh* in the west. Black Aed is a fearsome warrior and killed an *Ard Ri* many years ago with his bare hands. But he is an older man now with few ambitions, save to see the lands of the Ulaidh restored to our people."

"It is resolved then. We land in Eriu the night before the *airecht* and seize the scrolls while you march south," said Artur. He raised his glass to Baetan and both men spat into the fire to seal their contract.

XXIX: The Word

They had sat in silence listening intently to Simon reading from the sacred scrolls. After hearing him read *The Word*, Colum Cille nodded quietly his great head resting on his chest and then asked for it to be read a second time and more slowly. Cormac and Luigbe sat in silence.

Colum Cille was the first to speak at the end of the second reading: "Brothers, I must pray alone. When I have listened to God I will return to this house and discuss with ye what is to be done. Please meet me here after the offices of Sext."

He gently folded the scrolls and placed them back in the leather bag which he then secured on his back as Cormac had done for so long. He handed the bag of gold coins to Brother Luigbe as if it were nothing more than a bag of beans and left the roundhouse without further word.

Colum Cille had visited the kindred of the *Cruithin* as part of his preparation for the *airecht*. It was only when he had reminded Black Aed of his ancestor, Conal Cearnach's presence at the crucifixion and his role in bringing the teachings of Yeshua back to his kindred that the old king's loud demeanour suddenly became subdued.

By the time Colum Cille was leaving his roundhouse Black Aed's mood had deepened. Then and there the old king confessed to Colum Cille his pact with Baetan and Artur and wept for his betrayal of his ancestor. He offered to raise an army of the Ulaidh to stop the Gododdin as they landed on his kindred's shores. However, determined to prevent a repeat of his part in the slaughter of Cúl Dreimhne, Colum Cille dissuaded Black Aed from his plans. Such plans might well have stopped the Gododdin stealing *the Word*, but would have drenched them in blood and plunged Colum

Cille into eternal damnation in the eyes of God. So he persuaded the king that they must place their faith in God and not in the sword in this matter. Black Aed knew of the magic at Colum Cille's command and was content to leave the matter in the abbot's hands. Even though Colum Cille was by birth a *Ui Neill*, he was widely trusted as a holy man by the Uladh.

Now as he prayed for divine intervention alone under a tree on Ox Island a golden hare appeared to Colum Cille in a vision. The hare led him back to the shore where he had departed into exile many years before with a heavy heart and blood on his hands. It guided him to a waiting boat with his most loyal monks at the oars once more. When they were at sea the monks turned to him for direction as they had done before.

"Where do we go Colum Cille?" they asked.

"Let God decide," said Colum Cille looking over the waves. "Hoist the sail and God's wind will take us to our destination. If we are brothers in Yeshua we must believe that our boat will be guided."

So they drifted for many days and eventually arrived safely on the Island of Aio many miles to the north where they built a monastery to the glory of God. It was indeed a true telling of how Colum Cille and his loyal monks had arrived on the island of Aio some years before.

Now in his vision those same monks reminded Colum Cille to let God look after the scrolls to prevent repeated bloodshed. When he asked what he should do, it was the hare that replied, smiled and simply said:

> 'Redeem yourself by doing what you did before and all will be well.'

With that the vision melted away leaving Colum Cille mightily annoyed. His purpose was to avoid repeating his previous behaviour. He cursed the teasing hare's senseless riddle. But as he wrestled with his anger, the answer to the riddle came to him.

Colum Cille exclaimed to the sky: "God bless all hares! Amen." He arose from his prayers, amused at the simple nature of the answer to such complexity and set off to plan the implementation.

Cormac's first reaction at no longer carrying the scrolls was immense physical and spiritual relief. He felt lighter and freer in many ways, yet when he began walking across the monastery enclosure many questions started to flood his mind now that the contents of his hitherto secret burden were known.

All at once his mind began to spin, he sought the simplicity of physical labour as he had done in the desert. Cormac and Brother Luigbe joined other monks in the sowing of peas, cabbage and carrots in the main field on the southern slope of the island. Brother Simon retired to the sanctuary to pray and be still. The morning was a cool one, but the work quickly warmed the monks as they hoed the soil and prepared the ground for the seeds. Sinking his hands into the cool earth soothed Cormac and the rhythm of planting in some measure helped settle his mind to understand *The Word*.

Then something curious happened. Two small robins landed close to where he dug the earth in apparent search of some tender morsels of food. This was curious because robins were solitary creatures and defended their aloneness with vigour. Yet these two appeared like siblings. Instead of foraging they stood together on a stone, preened their feathers and sang to Cormac. For some moments Cormac was transfixed by the small creatures' song. Nothing was more beautiful and fitting to that moment. When they were finished the robins began to search for food in the freshly dug soil without fear and further reference to the nearby monk. Cormac remained motionless to allow the birds to feed. It was the least he could do after their gift to him. The robins' song had done more than any theological discussion to bring calm to his fevered mind. When the robins had finished feeding they looked directly at Cormac, held his gaze with their heads cocked to one side for a moment and then flew off to a nearby bush where they were joined by a third robin.

Cormac shouted over to them: "God bless you, birds of the air and land, for your gift to me. I will honour you all my days."

As he worked with renewed vigour, Cormac let the words he had just heard Brother Simon read float across his mind.

Before his ascension Lord Yeshua had left *the Word*: an exhortation to the world and a final reiteration of his central teachings. He spoke of angels appearing to Him in the tomb. He urged people not to allow His teachings to be usurped and twisted into a doctrine that debased and enslaved the people by those who wished to build a new empire using His name. According to *the Word*, God was within each living being and it was to His divine power that all must answer. Yeshua declared his human form and said that through God and his own sacrifice on the cross all are capable of greatness.

Where did that leave the resurrection and the belief that Yeshua was the Son of God, the Messiah, if not the very Godhead? The church had become bitterly divided over these issues since the time of Emperor Constantine. Great men had been anathematised, ostracised and even killed for questioning the church's teachings: theologians and good men like Origen, Nestorius, Arius, Pelagius and Clement. The church was now set against itself with Alexandria, Rome, Antioch and Constantinople each taking strongly opposing views on Yeshua's divinity and the resurrection.

Beyond these questions it was a simple phrase from the gospels that was repeated in *The Word* and used by Yeshua that echoed again and again inside Cormac's head as he worked:

> *"Therefore, whatever you wish that others would do to you, do also to them, for this is the Law."*

This was the *"Golden Rule"* according to Yeshua in *The Word*. Moreover it was how Yeshua explained this *"Golden Rule"* that gave it such meaning:

> *"On this rock must nations be built" he said.*

As he hoed and dug Cormac wondered where this left the church with its serried ranks of priests and bishops supported by kings and princes. No wonder the Patriarch wanted *The Word* sent faraway and the Bishop of Rome sought possession of it. How can men claim dominion over others if the *Golden Rule* is to be followed?

"You are hoeing the earth like a man preoccupied, monk. Is your mind tormented?"

Cormac turned to see Zachariah with a quizzical look standing behind him.

"We know the contents of the scrolls, hare, and my mind is seeking to make sense of them," said Cormac in explanation while continuing to hoe.

"I know. I have seen them," said Zachariah nodding.

Cormac looked at him curiously.

"The veil has been lifted. I can see the scrolls quite plainly at long last," said Zachariah.

"Then you will understand my confusion, hare."

"Look at it in this fashion: God is in his heaven just as before. The plants grow, the robin sings. It's as I said in Babylon," said Zachariah referring to his time as a prophet. "These other issues are of men's creation, not God's. Now that has been made clear in the *The Word*. It is good and I rejoice. It is a new dawn."

"Then be grateful you are not a monk, hare, taught to believe in many other things," said Cormac.

"I am. I don't doubt your confusion, but these are times of great change and monks given this revelation are chosen and must make clear the path."

"The path to where?" asked Cormac. "I am presently unsure of the route and the destination, hare."

"It has been set out clearly for you in *The Word*," said Zachariah. "Follow only the divine within you. Allow no other authority to have power over you."

"What of bishops, kings and the church?"

"Impostors in many cases," said Zachariah, "agents of another calling, not Yeshua's. He rejected them all. Now they have given their own name to a religion claiming Yeshua as its fountainhead. Have you ever wondered why your religion carries a Greek root, 'Christos' and does not bare Yeshua's Judaean name?"

"But who was Yeshua?" whispered Cormac so no other would hear.

"A great soul."

"The Son of God or God himself?" asked Cormac.

"No more than you are. He was a man and so are you. He was divine and so are you."

"No one is following me and building a church in my name," said Cormac.

"Your soul has not chosen that path. Yeshua's soul made a different choice and made great sacrifices for all creation," said Zachariah.

"It's that simple?"

"Yes. It's that simple," said Zachariah. "Honour this man for the great sacrifice he made, the message he has given you. Understand that as you are of the same stuff as him you are capable of great divinity also. You have shown this by how you have lived your present life, Cormac mac Fliande. You have brought *The Word* out of the darkness and into the light. I am proud to be your friend and to have helped you on this path."

Cormac stopped hoeing and leaning on his hoe smiled at the hare sitting before him.

"It has been my honour too, hare," said Cormac. "I sense we have a way to go yet."

"We have, brother."

Cormac continued to stand. He looked out over the land and the lake that stretched out below the monastery and above to a wide sky.

As if Zachariah could read Cormac's thoughts, the hare said: "Who are the 'others' mentioned in the *Golden Rule*? *The Word* says, "Therefore, whatever you wish that *others* would do to you, do also to them, for this is the Law."

"Go on, hare," said Cormac wishing to hear Zachariah's discourse on *the Word*.

"The Gospels, and now *The Word*, say: 'Go into all the world and preach the gospel to all creation.' So we are all partners in His creation, monk: hare, robin, the earth, the sky and you. We are the 'others'. Why else would I choose the hare if not to learn about creation? It is men's arrogance that makes them believe that God cares only for them. Men must relinquish their lust for power over the 'others', over women and over all creatures. Yeshua did not teach men to seek control over 'others'. Whom do you follow?

Yeshua or some other prophet? Look to *The Word*, is what I am saying, monk."

"You make a strong argument, hare. I have tried to live my life by his teachings and not those of men or more ancient prophets. I hope you will forgive me," said Cormac mindful of Zachariah's own past as an ancient prophet.

"I forgive you. But was it not I who prophesised his coming? Now *the Word* is the plain truth for our times and will help others follow his teachings," said Zachariah.

"There is much to be done, hare," said Cormac. "The Bishop of Rome wants to possess *The Word*. We may not be allowed to show it to the world. What then? Will it be hidden again? Will we continue to live in ignorance enslaved to a false doctrine created by men contrary to Yeshua's teachings?"

"Whether *the Word* is hidden or no, *The Word* says very little that has not already been said in the gospels. What *The Word* does is brings clarity to men's minds, that is all; that and the knowledge that *The Word* is Yeshua's most direct and final teaching. It leaves little to interpretation. There are no parables. His mission is complete. So he has nothing to hide from the authorities. They have done their worst."

"You are wise, hare. It baffles me why you play the fool at times," said Cormac. "His teachings are hidden in full view in the gospels. In *the Word* Yeshua refers much to his Sermon on the Mount as the cornerstone of his mission. His vision in the tomb that much of his teachings would be ignored or distorted after his ascension has been shown to be true. The Church is busy building a new empire to control all creation with clergy as it's legionnaires, just like the emperors did before them."

Cormac returned to hoeing the soil in silence. Then spoke again: "Colum Cille has *The Word* away with him. I pray he gets clarity on the way forward in this matter. We will meet again this evening. Without doubt he will have a plan, unless I don't know this man."

"*The Word* has come to the right place, monk," said Zachariah. "Of all the Christian churches the church in Eriu is closest to Yeshua's teachings. Now it can become closer and become a light to the world. Colum Cille has always refused to become a bishop. He understands the *Golden Rule* and how power can be misused.

Indeed he has in the past been guilty of such misuse himself and suffered for it. The Patriarch for all his shortcomings was well guided to choose this place and this man."

Zachariah watched Cormac work the soil and plant the seeds and considered how he could best help in the task that lay before these guardians of *The Word*. They had many challenges ahead if *The Word* was to remain in the light of day for all to see and understand. Finally he spoke: "You will not see me for a few days, monk. But let that not concern you. You will be preoccupied with your task. I shall be with you when you need me."

"And I with you, hare," said Cormac smiling at his friend. "God be with you on your journey."

"And with you, monk."

With that Zachariah skipped down the field, disappeared into some bushes near the shore and was gone.

As Cormac and Luigbe approached the small roundhouse after the office of Sext for their meeting with Colum Cille, they heard the familiar notes of Brother Simon's flute coming from inside. On entering they saw both Colum Cille and Simon sat together on a bench. Colum Cille was obviously enjoying the young monk's music and gestured for them to sit. They sat in silence as they listened to Simon play. Colum Cille made no effort to stop Simon. Cormac concluded that he too needed to hear a different sound from his own thoughts. Presently Simon stopped and Colum Cille thanked him.

The bag of scrolls was on the table and Colum Cille gestured towards it and began speaking quietly, but firmly.

"We each of us heard Brother Simon's reading of the sacred scrolls earlier, especially our Lord Yeshua's final testament in *The Word*. I am sure each of ye have had yer struggles with this as poor Brother Simon had on his own until Father mac Nisse heard him and released his torment.

"We four must journey on with these scrolls," continued Colum Cille looking closely at each monk who sat before him. "So we are bound together in this very sacred task. We have been chosen and I am sure none of us will shrink from our duty to God and to Yeshua.

There is an *airecht* that has been called by the *Ard Ri* further north from here in a week's time where the ownership of the scrolls will be decided. There the Bishop of Rome will make a strong claim on these scrolls, I believe."

They all shifted uncomfortably at this prospect.

"My experience with the ownership of books and scrolls has been a painful one. Brother Luigbe knows of what I speak, but Father Cormac and Brother Simon may not. Brother Luigbe is free to enlighten ye in his own time, but for now I need ye to know that these are very delicate matters where the future of Christendom is at stake, as well as human lives in this time. So we must tread carefully."

As he spoke Cormac watched his old mentor speak. His red hair was flecked with grey and his face was lined, but he had lost none of his energy and his old intensity. There was magnetism to Colum Cille that held your attention and even mesmerised you causing people to follow him loyally, even though he could be headstrong and hot tempered in pursuit of his calling. Cormac could understand if Colum Cille's fiery nature had led him into behaviour that was not seemly for a man of God. The tension between the impulses of high birth and his sacred calling was a work of never ending reconciliation for Colum Cille.

However Cormac noted a mellowing in his old mentor perhaps due to the experiences he alluded to. His manner was gentler and quieter, yet it still held great force within his being, perhaps more so as it was more disciplined and had the benefit of age and the wisdom it can bring.

"For my own part my soul would not withstand further loss of innocent life in any matter especially to do with scrolls. So I must be as wise and as cunning as a serpent and as cautious as a lamb. I have been guided by God that we have a strong claim to these documents that the Patriarch has placed in my care and through me the church in this land. However the divil is ever resourceful and if our mission fails to safeguard *The Word* here in this place, then the divil will have them for himself and Yeshua's sacrifice will have been in vain. So we must use every just means and righteous power at our disposal to ensure that *The Word* remains in this land as God intends."

Colum Cille paused and looked again at the three monks. No one spoke.

"I am to go to *Bheitheach Mhór*, brothers," said Colum Cille, "and I ask that ye come with me to assist in a very great task to protect *the Word*."

They nodded in response without speaking. Luigbe mac Min and Cormac looked at each other. They knew of this place. *Bheitheach Mhór* was an ancient sanctuary of the old people, known as a place of great magic, a place through which spirits of other worlds entered this realm for good or ill. Colum Cille had druid ancestry and had learnt their ways well when a boy in fosterage, before he joined the church. He had the power of prophesy and still visited the old places to call upon the hidden powers in times of great challenge. The church in Eriu was still close to the old ways and had not forsaken them as Rome and Alexandria had done. To many in Eriu these were all the powers of the Creator, the Holy Trinity of Earth, Wind and Water.

"Ye have two women in yer group, I'm told, Cormac," said Colum Cille.

"That is true, Colum Cille," answered Cormac. "The lady Melania, who comes from Egypt and Bretha, a young woman, who is training to be a *file* and comes from *Iarmummu*. Both follow the old ways."

"That is very good. Their feminine energy is needed," said Colum Cille. "Will they come with us to *Bheitheach Mhór*?"

"I will ask them. But can I know what you need them for, Colum Cille?"

"Their presence is all that is required. They will not be put in harm's way, Cormac. If they are familiar with the old ways they will not be alarmed," said Colum Cille smiling at Cormac's concern.

Cormac nodded in satisfaction.

"Praise God!" said Colum Cille. "We will leave in the morning after Iarmeirge. Horses are waiting for us on the north shore. *Bheitheach Mhór* is two days travel from here. After *Bheitheach Mhór* we will travel to the *airecht* which is another two days journey."

Colum Cille smiled at the monks gathered around him in the small roundhouse. He did not explain what would happen after the *airecht*: though all knew the enormity of the task before them and the uncertainty, but none gave voice to it. They were in God's hands and Colum Cille's. That was sufficient. Faith alone must guide them and provide the strength that would be needed. They prayed together for some time in the small roundhouse while *the Word* lay before them on the table.

XXX: Bheitheach Mhor

Colum Cille spoke little on the journey to *Bheitheach Mhór*. Cormac and Luigbe understood his silence, but it unsettled the others especially the lady Melania and Bretha for they wished to know what was expected of them. Cormac reassured them both as best he could, but had no idea what Colum Cille had in mind at the place of magic. At the end of the second day with a full moon high in the night sky they found themselves close to *Bheitheach Mhór* in gently rolling uplands. Colum Cille dismounted at the entrance to an avenue of alder trees. As he did so a figure approached.

"Ye have travelled far, Crimthainn and are welcome."

"Ruadhan, it's good to see ye, boy," said Colum Cille as he embraced the figure. The man carried a heavy oak staff with a large carving of a wolf's head at its top. "Are the people of the sanctuary gathered?"

"They are, Crimthainn, gathered and eager to bring in the energy this night. The fires are lit. Have ye the women with ye?"

"I have two," said Colum Cille pointing to Bretha and the lady Melania. It was the first time he had acknowledged them.

"Good. We can get down to it," said Ruadhan.

Colum Cille signalled to the others to dismount and follow him.

"Will that man acknowledge us, brother?" asked Melania hotly.

"Quietly, lady, Colum Cille has much on his mind," whispered Cormac.

"He requires our presence yet has not spoken to us for two days! What manners are these?"

Bretha looked worriedly from Cormac to Melania. She had not seen the lady so inflamed. Whereas Cormac had and feared a storm was brewing within her.

"I will have no more. I will not be used. He will explain himself." Then turning to Colum Cille, "Abbot Colum Cille, I need to know why you have brought us here and what is to be done," shouted

Melania in Latin at Colum Cille's back as he walked up the avenue of alders.

Colum Cille and the man called Ruadhan turned to look at the source of the voice. Cormac shock his head in despair. People did not question Colum Cille, especially not before a ritual. His fury would come at you like a storm.

"What is to be done? What is to be done?" thundered Colum Cille his eyes flashing with anger.

"I wish to know why you have brought us here. We are not cattle or slaves. I will be spoken to," said Melania who met Colum Cille's rage with her own angry defiance.

"Who is this woman? She behaves like an ill bred mare," he asked Cormac.

Cormac was about to answer when Melania held her hand up.

"Be quiet, brother. I will speak for myself to this ill-smelling hound," said Melania trading insult for insult. No one had spoken to Colum Cille like that for many a long year. Cormac in desperation mumbled under his breath to Melania, but she heard nothing as she focused on Colum Cille, who stood glaring back at her.

"You," said Melania pointing accusingly at Colum Cille, "have dragged my friends and I to this hillside across valleys and bogs for two days to perform a ritual without so much as a kind word or explanation. Yet I hear you are a great follower of the prophet Yeshua. But he never treated women so, never mind his other followers. Why do you?"

At that angry thunder roared overhead and lightning flashed behind Colum Cille briefly revealing a series of stone circles on the hill behind them beyond the alders with people standing close by. Cormac could be heard praying quietly. The others stood transfixed to the ground. A wolf howled in the distance adding to the tension as Melania and Colum Cille faced each other.

"I have travelled over many great oceans and rivers with Father Cormac and brother Simon to bring these scrolls to your land and into your hands. I will not be treated like some slave. I am Melania, daughter of Ausonius and priestess of the Goddess Isis. Your reputation does not make me tremble like many others in this land, Abbot Colum Cille."

Lightning flashed again and caught the glint in Colum Cille's eyes. This time even Melania looked apprehensively at the dark sky. Cormac moved to stand close beside her. Bretha and Simon followed his example.

Ruadhan moved behind Colum Cille and spoke to him: "Now steady, Crimthainn. You need your energy for the work and we need these women." He glanced over his shoulder to the stone circles. "The people of the sanctuary grow restless."

Colum Cille nodded and noticed the group gathered around Melania. He sighed, partly in exasperation and partly in regret and all at once his anger seemed to disappear.

"For yer education, lady," said Colum Cille regaining his composure and hesitating as he considered his response, "Lord Yeshua had no Greeks about him, thanks be to God, and that's the issue here: Greek women with sharp tongues and big feet."

"Big feet?" shouted Melania looking down at her feet. "My feet are not big!"

"Ha!" exclaimed Colum Cille in contempt, pointing to Melania's feet and looking to others for confirmation.

Brother Luigbe shuffled up to Melania and whispered, "Admit yer feet are big and he'll apologise, lady."

"It's true," whispered Cormac. "He knows he's in the wrong. It's his way, sister. Your feet are fine. Play along and he'll be like a lamb now. Trust me."

Melania's anger began to subside into confusion at this strange turn of events. She was being asked to admit to having big feet so that this man could apologise to her.

"In my country women need big feet for kicking men with large, thick heads," Melania said defiantly lifting a foot off the ground slightly. "I have kicked a good many, abbot."

"Have ye kicked an abbot though, lady?"

"Not yet, they run too fast."

Colum Cille let out a great belly laugh that echoed across the hillside and everyone visibly relaxed.

"Ye're a woman of spirit, lady," he said smiling at Melania. "No wonder that boy is so skinny. It's from all the running." Colum Cille pointed at Cormac and they all laughed except Bretha who did not have the Latin, yet understood with relief that the angry confrontation was over.

"I have not behaved well, lady Melania. That I admit and I humbly apologise to ye and yer good friends," said Colum Cille still grinning. "Your feet are as beautiful as any I have seen since Eastertime. Come let us sit by a fire and I will explain."

Melania smiled in acknowledgement. Her anger disarmed by Colum Cille's fulsome apology.

As they turned towards one of the fires at the end of the avenue, Colum Cille placed a hand very lightly on Melania's back to guide her over the rough ground. As he did there was a tremendous sensation of heat passing through her body from Colum Cille's hand that left her feeling cleansed of all anger and fatigue. He did the same with Bretha who squealed in surprise at the sudden sensation.

When they sat on logs by the fire Bretha whispered excitedly to Cormac, "He has the power alright, that Colum Cille. He touched me and my ears near popped off my head! I feel like I could chop down trees with my bare hands!"

Cormac simply smiled.

"I am preoccupied with this vital business of the scrolls and will appear distant and uncharitable," said Colum Cille to the group gathered around him sitting on the logs. "That was not my intention. The lady was right to question me. I cannot expect yer support without yer understanding. Forgive me."

People were adding wood to the fires as Colum Cille spoke. There were several fires dotted around and each was placed close to a stone circle. From where they sat they could see that one larger stone circle had a tall straight tree trunk embedded into the centre with the carving of a square cross at its head.

"I am a follower of Lord Yeshua, that is true, but I am also a druid smith. These powers were given to me as a boy from my ancestors and I cannot deny my heritage," said Colum Cille shaking his great head. "This is not a denial of my belief in Lord Yeshua for he had these powers and more, the power to heal with a touch and the gift of prophesy for example. These are powers given by God, not the devil. This place has been a sanctuary of sacred energy for thousands of years," continued Colum Cille. "It is a thin place between this world and the others. It has been used by the peoples of this land to channel the energy needed for crops to grow, healthy children to be born and enemies to be vanquished. The people of the sanctuary are here this night to help us channel such energy. This time the energy will be used to anchor the blessed scrolls in our land, making it much more difficult for them to be removed and taken elsewhere.

"What we do here tonight must remain a secret known only to us. The people of the sanctuary allow us to use this place on that understanding. Are we agreed, dear ones?"

Everyone nodded.

"The moon is full which is good," he said looking up at the fullness of the golden orb. "In a short while I will stand in the centre of this circle with the channelling pole. This channels energy into the earth from the heavens and is used in many of our monasteries. I will have the scrolls with me. Four of you will stand just inside the stone circle looking towards the centre, one each in the north, south, east and west. The four will be the lady Melania, Bretha, Brother Simon and Brother Luigbe. The women will stand at the east and west points. You will feel charges of energy moving through your bodies. That is normal. Do not be afraid. No harm will come to ye. But ye must not move from the spot until the ceremony is complete. After the ceremony I shall journey to the *airecht* in Druim Ceit with Brother Simon. Father Ruadhan will bring Father Cormac, the lady Melania and Bretha to Druim Ceit where the ownership of the scrolls will be decided."

Colum Cille looked at Simon who nodded.

"We are all in God's hands, dear ones," said Colum Cille holding his own hands open. "After the *airecht* we will each go where God directs. I thank each of ye for yer courage and yer care of *the Word*. The church here will be forever grateful to each of ye and ye will be honoured among us for evermore."

Melania and Bretha smiled warmly. Their faces shone like lanterns in the night and their eyes were full.

"The people of the sanctuary will form a large circle behind us," continued Colum Cille. "They will perform the *cresa imdegla*, the ceremony of the protective girdles to protect us from any evil while performing the ritual. The ritual removes the membranes between this world and the others. So in theory anything can come in. That is why we need the protection. If ye do see or hear anything amiss do not be afraid and do not move yer feet. The divine will be close, closer to ye than perhaps ever before in yer life. Close yer eyes if ye wish.

"Father Ruadhan will tell ye when the ceremony is over. Then and only then can ye move. Is there anything else yez wish to know?"

Brother Simon's mind was full of questions, but the words would not come to his tongue.

"I can answer yer questions as we travel, Brother Simon. I have a need of yer skills in the scriptorium," said Colum Cille acknowledging Simon's unspoken urge. "We can't do this with empty bellies, dear ones. So now we will eat."

The people of the sanctuary distributed fresh bread, butter, salted meats and a thin barley gruel.

Melania was taken aback by how very different looking these people were from those she had met in Eriu. The most noticeable aspect was their hair. It was blue. It was difficult to tell in the half-light if it was dyed or was natural. Their skin was very clear and unblemished. They moved gracefully dressed in long black robes woven from a material that Melania did not recognise. An unusual scent followed them that Melania knew, but could not remember.

"What's that scent, brother?" she asked Cormac.

"Frankincense and myrrh," he said.

She looked at him quizzically seeking further explanation for why such exotic scents would be used by these people. He simply smiled in response.

"Who are these people?" she asked.

Cormac was silent for a moment, and then he spoke quietly: "The people of the sanctuary. These are the people that Bretha's father will introduce you to. Legend says their ancestors built the great circles and mounds in Eriu, later most moved to Egypt in search of better sun alignments. There they built the pyramids while some remained here as guardians of the sacred sites."

Melania watched with fascination as the people moved silently around her.

When the food was finished Colum Cille put on a purple robe and a gold chain holding a square cross. He asked that everyone except

Cormac join him in the stone circle. As they moved into the stone circle Simon let out a gasp. Colum Cille had touched him and Luigbe in the same manner as he had Melania and Bretha producing the same rush of heat to their bodies.

Melania and Bretha were positioned opposite each other and likewise Simon and Luigbe, all were facing the centre where the tall tree trunk stood. Behind them cut out on the ground were five concentric circles surrounding the circle. Ruadhan gave each inside the stone circle a small bunch of the herbs that Bretha had collected and a small bag of pebbles along with some spring water to drink. With ash from the fire he made a mark on their foreheads. Quietly the people of the sanctuary moved behind them to form a large encirclement outside the stone circle but inside the five concentric circles. When all this was in place Colum Cille called for absolute silence and stillness.

Placing the bag containing the scrolls at the base of the tree trunk and a wooden staff at his feet, Colum Cille raised his arms skywards. Simultaneously the sound of a single horn was heard piercing the night air. It played a long low note and then all was silent again as a cool wind whipped round the gathering.

Colum Cille stood motionless; with his face turned to the night sky he said a lorica in a booming voice:

> *"Today we gird ourselves*
> *With the strength of heaven,*
> *Light of the sun,*
> *Brightness of the moon,*
> *Brilliance of fire,*
> *Speed of lightning,*
> *Swiftness of wind,*
> *Depth of sea,*
> *Firmness of earth,*
> *Stability of rock"* [4]

[4] *Druids, deer and 'words of power': coming to terms with evil in medieval Ireland. J. Borsje)*

With that the wind whistled through the trees to tug at their robes and fan the flames of the fires.

The people of sanctuary then began to chant the lorica in a low, melodic fashion.

> *"We call on the God of the Earth, Wind and Water*
> *See us in this place of admission*
> *Your dutiful man and maid servants*
> *Bring your elements to bear on us tonight*
> *Channel your power to the centre of all things"*

Colum Cille continued his incantations, except now they were softer and inaudible above the roar of the fires, the wind and the chanting.

Those standing inside the stone circle could feel the sensation of something unseen pushing gently down on their bodies from above and the very stones appeared to be vibrating with sound. This pressure continued for several moments until Melania felt a quickness of breath and her heart began to race. Just as she felt she could endure no more, all went silent and motionless as if quietened by a single mighty hand. Colum Cille seized the wooden staff at his feet in both hands and pointing it to the bag of scrolls at the base of the channelling pole, held it there.

Overhead there was a single clap of thunder. A stag appeared from the woods and moved with ease through the circle of the people of the sanctuary right into the stone circle. He stopped in the centre before Colum Cille where the two silently regarded each other. The stag sniffed at the bag of scrolls and walked calmly around the circle looking at Bretha, Melania, Simon and Luigbe in turn; then strode unhurriedly out of the circles on to a nearby hill. There he stood looking down on them.

The chanting from the people of the sanctuary began again. Colum Cille removed the staff from the bag of scrolls, sank to his knees and prayed for several moments clutching the cross hung about his neck. Standing erect he lifted the bag of scrolls onto his back and taking up the staff held his hand out to Simon. Both walked off in the same direction as the deer without looking back.

As Colum Cille and Simon departed the people of the sanctuary began to sing joyously in a strange tongue.
Ruadhan walked into the circle.
"It is complete, my friends. Ye may rest. God bless ye."

XXXI: Camus

After the ritual at the stones of *Bheitheach Mhór* the people of sanctuary disappeared into a dense mist that lingered into the next day, making for a slow journey northwards to the *airecht* for Cormac, Melania and Bretha accompanied by Father Ruadhan of Lorrha.

Ruadhan and Colum Cille were old friends who had studied under Finnian of Clonard as young men. Both monks had crossed swords with a previous *Ard Ri*, King Diarmait mac Cerbaill, thirteen summers ago in a bitter dispute which led to sad slaughter and the self-imposed exile of Colum Cille to the isle of Aio.

The *Ard Ri* had greatly offended Colum Cille and Ruadhan by killing a prince who had sought holy sanctuary with Colum Cille The *Ard Ri* had also passed judgement against Colum Cille on the ownership of a sacred book. These were offences of great magnitude to any abbot, but especially to one such as Colum Cille for whom the sanctuary of the monastery and written word were so important. Outraged by the *Ard Ri*'s behaviour, Colum Cille had encouraged his kindred, the *Ui Neill* to fight a great battle in the west against the forces of the *Ard Ri* in which many were slaughtered and the *Ard Ri* defeated.

"Crimthainn was overcome with guilt at what his hot temper had caused to happen," said Ruadhan shaking his head. "Some said it was rightly so that Crimthainn should feel ashamed and wanted him excommunicated from the church for causing such death. But to my mind that would have been wrong considering what good works he had done. Besides, the *Ui Neill* had wanted a war with Diarmait. They were looking for an opportunity. It wasn't all Crimthainn's doing, that's well known."

The four were on horseback passing alongside a slow river on the second day of their journey. Gentle rain fell as they moved along a broad track. The lady Melania had mastered the basic elements of horseback riding after her experience with Gaeth on the flight from the Hill of Uisneach and so she sat comfortably on a small Gaulish mare named, Uasal.

"Instead," continued Ruadhan, "Crimthainn went into exile of his own choice well beyond the shores of Eriu to the isle of Aio and remained there until the arrival of *The Word* forced him back to his homeland. Since his exile he has pledged to dedicate his life to saving as many souls for God as were slaughtered in that battle and has remained steadfast to this pledge ever since. People flock to his monastery in Aio from all over these islands and he has converted the King of the Picts to Yeshua's teachings. In truth I should have gone into exile with Crimthainn, but I was called to Lorrha to build a community of God there."

"How many died in the battle?" asked Melania.

"They say three thousand souls were taken," said Ruadhan sadly. "Crimthainn and I believe that *The Word* has been sent to us by God so that we can build with it a true church of Yeshua in Eriu and beyond. If *The Word* remains in Eriu Crimthainn believes thousands of souls will be saved for God."

"If *The Word* goes to Rome, what then?" asked Cormac.

"The truth will die," said Ruadhan simply. "*The Word* will be hidden again, as it was in Alexandria. A religion will grow in the west more akin to an empire and based on men's lies."

"And you and Crimthainn?" continued Cormac.

"Why we will both die sinners, I fear. I pray that God will allow me to do whatever I can to prevent that happening to a good man like Crimthainn."

They journeyed on in silence for a while, meditating on Ruadhan's words.

Melania broke the silence: "Why will you both die as sinners? What wrong have you done, Ruadhan?"

"I should tell ye, friends, that I too had a part in those ill doings. I cursed Diarmait for his sins and also the royal hill of Temair. Within a short time Diarmait was killed in battle by his own foster son, Black Aed of the *Cruithin*, and his kindred lost Royal Temair to the *Ui Neill*. It was a wicked act on my part. Diarmait was a bad king, but it was not my place to take vengeance that belongs to the divine. I sinned against God. But now I pray that I too am being called to redeem my soul."

"It is good that you have this opportunity to atone, Father," observed Cormac.

"Aye it is, boy. It is the answer to our prayers these thirteen years," said Ruadhan. After the business with Diarmait I concentrated on my work as a monk in the monastery of Lorrha: until now that is, when Crimthainn called for my help. It is right that all our past deeds rebound on us in this time. God is forgiving and the opportunity to atone is offered. Yeshua taught us that. Yeshua wants our life to have abundance and to flow like the river, for that to happen we must remove the dams we have built and to face life with love and courage and honesty." He paused and reflected further. "We face great challenges. Ye see I hear Diarmait's son is Colman Bec, King of the *Mide* is in league with the Roman emissary to obtain *the Word* for the Bishop of Rome. Colman will give Crimthainn and I no quarter. It will please him to thwart us."

"This emissary is known for his ruthlessness, Father" said Cormac. "He will stop at nothing to obtain these scrolls. I warn you. There is no limit to his ambition. It is indeed an unholy alliance."

"They are welcome to each other along with that trickster Brandub, King of the *Laigen*: a parcel of thieves and no mistake. We will see that at the *airecht*," said Ruadhan shook his head sadly. "Aye, but we will keep the scrolls in our land where they belong because that is God's will. Why else would they have been sent to us? That said we must prove we are worthy and there is nobody more worthy than Crimthainn. Our hearts are settled on building a church in this land that will truly honour Yeshua's life on this earth and be the light of the world."

As he finished speaking Bretha offered Ruadhan some strawberries she had collected on the way to lift the abbot's sombre mood.

"Bless you, child. Ye are kind," said Ruadhan.

They spoke little more on the journey, each reflecting on what Ruadhan had told them and what the *airecht* held for all.

At dusk on the second day they arrived at the small monastery of Camus beside the waters of the Ban Dea in the land of the *Cenel nEógain*, a kindred of the *Ui Neill*. Colum Cille and Simon were already there and busy in the Scriptorium, where they were not to be disturbed. The monastery was full to its rafters with abbots and bishops on their way to Druim Ceit and Cormac and his companions had to bed down in a barn. Much to the dismay of the lady Melania there were no baths available and a wash in the river was all that could be managed.

Cormac went immediately to the church to pray and stayed for some time. He asked God to guide all those with influence to seek a peaceful resolution to the issue of *the Word* while allowing Yeshua's true teachings to be heard.

At the office of Midnocht he was joined by Colum Cille, Ruadhan and Simon and noticed that the hands of both Colum Cille's and Simon's were stained with ink from the Scriptorium. It was like Colum Cille to seek the scriptorium at times of great stress. He found writing brought him closer to the divine and often times he would write the sacred books in his cell for several days managing without sleep and with a meagre diet.

On leaving prayers Colum Cille embraced Cormac and told him they would be leaving after the early office of Prime the next day to travel west to the *airecht* at Druim Ceit which was a short journey by horse. As their eyes met, Colum Cille smiled sadly, he looked tense and tired. Cormac sensed that his mentor had been very busy since leaving *Bheitheach Mhór*. Cormac simply smiled in reassurance and held his mentor in a loving embrace without speaking. At times like these words were often unnecessary.

XXXII: Druim Ceit

The birds were on their singing posts bringing a lightness of being to that auspicious morning. But this was not reflected in men's hearts as Colum Cille and his large party of abbots, bishops and monks arrived at Druim Ceit.

Druim Ceit was a small settlement on the wooded banks of the River Ró near the north coast of Eriu that had the advantage of a large hall used by the *Ui Neill* for their assemblies. It was a long, low structure with a circular area for meetings positioned on a hill at the edge of the settlement giving it a prominent aspect befitting its status.

Below the meeting hall was a large *airlise* or green, used for fairs. Many temporary structures had been erected there to accommodate all the delegates ranging from kings to abbots and their retinues. The kings were arriving each with their judges, advisors, stewards, guards and attendants. No armies were allowed at such gatherings lest they influence the outcome, but no king travelled without his personal guard of around twenty trusted and battle-hardened warriors.

Market traders had gathered on the airlise to sell their wares to the growing crowds. Stalls were being erected to sell clothing, furniture, linen, bedding, swords, musical instruments, jewellery and all manner of foods. The smell of new leather, spices and wood smoke lay on the still morning air as the tradesmen worked busily to prepare their stalls for trade that might last several days if the *airecht* struggled to find agreement.

Brother Luigbe greeted Cormac and Ruadhan and showed them to the meeting hall where Colum Cille, Luigbe and Simon were already waiting for the *airecht* to begin. A large group was gathered around Colum Cille which Ruadhan thought was a good sign. He pointed out some of the kings to Cormac.

"That tall, skinny one is Aed mac Echach, King of Connacht. His son was the prince killed by Colman Bec's father, Diarmait, the old *Ard Ri*, which vexed Colum Cille and I. So the King of Connacht will be for us. To his right is Fidelmid mac Coirpri, King of *Iarmummu*. He replaced Tigernaig whom yer friends, the swans, blinded in Mungair. He has already crossed swords with Colman Bec in battle and defeated him. So he is for us as well. To his right is Black Aed. Ye can see why he is given that name."

An enormous man occupied a bench that normally accommodated three men. He was wrapped in a purple cloak as befitted a king. He had a large head of the blackest hair tied back in a long tail and a beard to match that reached to his chest. He sat with his arms folded and stared straight ahead.

"He's otherwise known as Aed Dub mac Suibni, King of the *Cruithin*. It was he who killed his foster father, the *Ard Ri* Diarmait mac Cerbaill in battle. But he hates the *Ui Neill* because they took land from his kindred, the *Ulaidh*. Colum Cille is not sure of him and Black Aed says little at the best of times. However he is sat near Colum Cille which may be a good sign. It's hard to tell with that one."

As they spoke Colum Cille walked over to Black Aed. He bowed to the king and spoke closely with him for a moment. Black Aed listened intently and nodded as Colum Cille spoke.

"To Colum Cille's left is Aedan mac Gabrain, King of the Dál Riata," said Ruadhan as he pointed to a young man not much older than Simon, but more powerfully built. "Much of their land is now over the water in Alba as the *Ui Neill* have pushed the kindred of *Ulaidh* ever eastwards. He is close with Colum Cille who ordained him as king last year.

"Then in the centre there is the *Ard Ri*, Aed mac Ainmuirech, King of the *Cenel Conaill* in the west. He is a powerful *Ui Neill* king within these parts and is cousin to Colum Cille, but as an *Ard Ri* at Royal Temair he is weak and as a *Ui Neill* he is hated by the *Ulaidh* as well as the *Laigen* and the *Mide*. His wife beside him is Ronnat. She is a cousin to Brandub, the King of the *Laigen*, who I do not see here yet. She gives the *Ard Ri* his power in the south. The *Ard Ri* will control the discussions which gives Colum Cille an advantage, we pray."

"I have never been to one of these gatherings, father. It is truly a confusing spectacle to behold," said Cormac looking around bemused.

Ruadhan nodded and smiled. "Is it any wonder Colum Cille chose the church? But he still has to deal with these folk and is a master at the politics, when he puts his mind to it. If anyone is to get agreement from these it is Colum Cille."

Standing behind them looking on were the lady Melania and Bretha, their mouths agape at all they were witnessing.

"The lady Melania and Bretha will not be permitted to remain in the main hall, Father, because they are not kindred to any of the parties," said Ruadhan. "I will get one of my monks to look after them. There is much to be seen in the fair."

Melania looked at Cormac with concern: "May the gods protect you and the scrolls, brother, in this gathering and provide the outcome you seek for your religion," she said. Unseen she touched his arm gently.

At that Ruadhan called over an elderly monk who shepherded the two women out of the hall and into the fair on the *airlise*.

As Melania and Bretha left the hall a loud horn blast announced the *Breithem*, the judges, who made their solemn entrance. There were nine of them in all, dressed in white robes and led by the Ard Ollamh, Dallan Forgaill, who was also the Chief *File* of Eriu.

As the judges took their seats on a high bench opposite the *Ard Ri*, the kings of the *Laigen* and *Mide* arrived. They did not acknowledge the *Ard Ri* but took their seats on the opposite side of the hall to Colum Cille. A whisper went round the hall as heads were turned to see the Bishop of Rome's emissary, the tall black skinned Augustine of Nubea, who took his seat beside the two kings, Brandub mac Echach and Colman Bec. It was the sort of entrance that Augustine enjoyed. He looked straight ahead except for a fleeting glance at Queen Ronnat who returned his look.

"They say he is close to God on account of his skin colour," said Ruadhan. "But you doubt this, father."

"His reputation in Egypt is not that of a holy man," said Cormac. "He was fostered by the Bishop of Rome and has been his emissary for many years. Some doubt he serves God at all. But I would not be so harsh."

"Well we will know soon enough, I expect," said Ruadhan.

Brother Luigbe approached the two monks.

"Father Cormac and Father Ruadhan, Abbot Colum Cille asks that ye join him. Father Cormac, ye will be asked to speak at some point about yer instructions from the Patriarch. This may have a bearing on the issue of ownership."

"I see," said Cormac with some trepidation as they walked across the hall towards Colum Cille.

"Do ye understand the law in Eriu, father?" asked Luigbe.

"I could not claim any understanding, father. It was never an interest of mine and I have spent so many years in foreign lands."

"Well it is not the law that ye may have known in other lands. It is not Roman law, nor is it Christian. It is the Brehon law that the people of Eriu have devised over many hundreds of years. We have strict laws on the ownership of all things," said Luigbe as they took their seats. "One thing ye should know is that visitors from overseas, such as the Roman emissary over there, are allowed to pick the judges to hear their case. This has allowed the emissary, guided by his allies Brandub and Colman to select judges who may be more favourable to his case for ownership of the scrolls."

Cormac looked worried. It was a very strange environment for one such as he and he worried he would let down Colum Cille.

Luigbe continued to advise Cormac: "However, as ye are now classed as a visitor from overseas and are the current guardian of the scrolls, ye too can pick judges."

"I don't know any judges, father."

"Abbot Colum Cille has helped in that matter: so half of the judges have been selected by us and the other half by the emissary and his friends. The Chief Judge remains his own man," said Luigbe smiling. "On one matter ye must be clear: until this issue is decided ye are the legal owner of the scrolls. It is ye that was given them by the Patriarch and brought them to this land."

"But the Patriarch told me to give them to Colum Cille. They are not mine, I assure you, father," said Cormac nervously.

"In Brehon law they are, father, until the judges decide otherwise. Colum Cille must prove his title. If he does not the emissary may well take them to Rome."

"That must not happen. I have a duty to the Patriarch and to God in this matter," said Cormac anxiously.

"I know, father. So speak of this and of yer conversation with the Patriarch, of his instructions to ye when he gave the scrolls into yer hand," said Luigbe. "Colum Cille has the letter from the Patriarch gifting the scrolls to him. That is important. Ye will be asked to bear witness to that."

"I can do that," said Cormac swallowing hard.

"Ye'll be grand, boy," said Colum Cille reaching over and slapping Cormac's knee. Their eyes met. Colum Cille had his familiar glint back and his tiredness seemed to have lifted. "Just tell the truth and shame the divil. God will guide us. Ye'll see."

Cormac nodded. Colum Cille's confidence was always reassuring, even in this strange place.

Another horn blast was heard.

"Is the *airecht* assembled?" a voice boomed across the hall. It was the *Ard Ri*'s Marshall.

"Baetan mac Cairill is not present," said another.

"I speak for Baetan," said Black Aed.

None sought to challenge Black Aed. The *Ard Ri* nodded. "Very well we are complete. The *airecht* is in session. Let no man interfere with the law or the penalty is death."

XXXIII: Airecht

The great doors of the hall closed and the assembly fell silent as all awaited the opening remarks of the Chief Judge, Dallan Forgaill. The distant sound of the market could be heard from the airlise below.

"We are called to decide the ownership of scrolls that have arrived in this land in the hands of a desert monk. Will this monk make himself known to the *airecht*?" said Dallan.

Cormac stood up. "I am the desert monk, Cormac mac Fliande."

"Thank ye, Father," said Dallan. "How did ye come by these scrolls?"

"They were given into my safe keeping by my bishop, the Patriarch of Alexandria in the land of Egypt and I was instructed to bring them to Eriu."

"Why Eriu?"

"I understand from the Patriarch that he believed that the scrolls would be kept safe here and well away from the Church of Rome. He did not wish Rome to possess the scrolls," said Cormac.

"Why not Rome?"

Cormac cleared his throat. "He, the Patriarch, believed Rome would misuse the scrolls or destroy them."

"What were ye instructed to do with these scrolls once ye arrived in Eriu?"

"To give them into the hand of Abbot Colum Cille for safe, keeping," said Cormac.

"Will Abbot Colum Cille please make himself known to the *airecht*?"

Colum Cille stood up.

"Have ye the scrolls with ye, Abbot Colum Cille?" asked Dallan.

"I have."

"Then please place them on this table in front of the judges for all to see."

Colum Cille removed the bag from his back and gave it to Brother Simon who took it over to the table.

"Please empty the bag."

Simon gently emptied the bag and set the three scrolls out on the table.

"Can ye tell us what these are?"

Answering for Simon Colum Cille pointed to the three scrolls and explained their provenance. Everyone was straining to look at the sacred scrolls lying on the table. Augustine was on his feet to get a better look.

"Now, Abbot Colum Cille, do ye contend that ye are the rightful owner of these scrolls?"

"I do."

"Who disputes this claim of ownership?"

Sister Dorothea rose to her feet shaking with trepidation.

"I speak for Father Augustine, emissary to the Bishop of Rome. The emissary does not have the language of this place, sir."

"Who are ye, lady"?

"I am Sister Dorothea, sir, of the Church of Rome in the service of Father Augustine."

"Very well, sister. Please ask Father Augustine to identify himself."

Sister Dorothea asked Augustine to stand.

"I am Augustine of Nubea, emissary of the Bishop of Rome, God's most favoured upon this earth," said Augustine.

"What brings ye to this land, Father Augustine?" asked Dallan.

"I am instructed by the Holy Father, himself. Here is my letter of instruction," said Augustine holding up the letter. "My mission is twofold, sir, to help you build a strong church in Eriu as a bulwark against the barbarians and to return these scrolls to Rome where they rightfully belong."

"I see," said Dallan and then turning to the other judges: "Fellow judges ye may begin yer examination."

The first in the line of judges began.

"Abbot Colum Cille, can ye show me yer deed of ownership of these scrolls?"

Brother Simon brought the letter to the judge who examined it and then read it out loud translating from the Latin for all to hear.

"The letter is signed by the Patriarch I see and by someone by the name of Acacius," concluded the judge.

A buzz went around the *airecht* that was silenced by a horn blast.

The next judge was handed the letter and examined it.

"Abbot Colum Cille, are ye a prince or an abbot?" he asked.

"I was born a prince and became an abbot," answered Colum Cille.

"Are ye the Bishop of Eriu referred to in this letter from the Patriarch?"

"No, I am not."

"Then who is? This letter is addressed to the Bishop of Eriu."

"There is no such person," said Colum Cille. "The church in this land does not have a ruling bishop or patriarch unlike Rome or Alexandria."

"But this letter gifting the scrolls is addressed to such a person. If such a person does not exist then how can the sale proceed?"

"It is addressed to me," insisted Colum Cille.

"But ye are not the Bishop of Eriu. Ye are an abbot," said the second judge flatly and passed the letter to the next judge.

"What do ye have to say about this letter, Father Augustine?" he asked.

Augustine and Colum Cille eyed each other across the hall: both looking to get some measure of the other.

"Abbot Colum Cille has no claim on these scrolls. As you have rightly identified, sir, he is not the Bishop of Eriu," said Augustine. "In fact my observations tell me that there is no church in Eriu, but a series of monasteries, each under the control of an abbot who is answerable to no one. So there is no suitable home for these scrolls in this land at present."

"Is this so, Abbot Colum Cille?" asked the judge.

"No, it is not so. The church in Eriu is a body of devout Christians united under our God and Lord Yeshua. We do not need an earthly master when we have a divine one," said Colum Cille. "This is not Rome and we do not have Roman ways."

"So the church here is unified in spirit, but not materially, Abbot Colum Cille?" asked the judge.

"That is so."

"Does any churchman here disagree with Abbot Colum Cille?" asked the judge of the *airecht*.

340

It was true there were rivalries between abbots as each were bound to a kindred who had granted land to each monastery, but would any now speak out against Colum Cille and declare that the church in Eriu was not united?

Colum Cille glared around him and the hall remained silent.

In turn the next judge, a woman, examined the Patriarch's letter.

"Why are these scrolls so important to the church, Abbot Colum Cille?" she asked.

Colum Cille paused before he replied and then walking out from the seated crowd to stand in front of the judges and the *Ard Ri*, he began to address the whole *airecht*.

"My lady, *The Word* is the last testament of Lord Yeshua the Christ. He sets out what he most wishes us to remember of his teachings. We know from this that while in the tomb an angel appeared to him and warned of false prophets misusing and twisting his teachings to found a false church, a new empire in effect, for the aggrandisement of rich men and the oppression of the poor and the needy.

"*The Word* was written down by Joseph of Arimithaea as Yeshua spoke just before he ascended – and this is that very document," said Colum Cille pointing to *The Word* laid out on the table for all to see and then kneeling before it to say a brief prayer. "The document is witnessed by Mary Magdalene, Joseph, St James (Yeshua's brother) and Nicodemus and it is testified to by St Mark himself in his scroll and by the High Priest, Caiaphas as evidenced in his letter to the Great Sanhedrin.

"*The Word* is what Yeshua most wishes us to remember about his teachings while on this earth.

"It is written in *The Word* from words that Yeshua spoke:

> *'The Emperor in turn will fall and in the end days men will come to this new faith seeking to maintain Rome's power. Their love for the divine and His creation will be corrupted by a love of power, riches and self. There will be a closing of minds and an intolerance of others. So the Word must leave this land of David and go to a place far beyond the temporal powers where it will be the light of the world, nurturing saplings to grow to mighty oaks.'*

Colum Cille hesitated and looked around at the stunned assembly to let the words sink in to men's hearts.
"Yeshua quotes from the Beatitudes in *the Word*:

> *'Blessed are the poor, for theirs is the kingdom of heaven.*
> *Blessed are those who mourn, for they will be comforted.*
> *Blessed are the meek, for they will inherit the earth.*
> *Blessed are those who hunger and thirst for righteousness, for they will be filled.*
> *Blessed are the merciful, for they will be shown mercy.*
> *Blessed are the pure in heart, for they will see God.*
> *Blessed are the peacemakers, for they will be called children of God.*
> *Blessed are those who are persecuted because of righteousness, for theirs is the kingdom of heaven.'*

"These are the teachings that the church in Eriu was founded upon. We do not seek an empire. We do not seek mastery over others or other nations and their beliefs: only mastery over ourselves in communion with Him."
In the great hall, even kings and bishops and abbots sat in silence, watching and listening as Colum Cille delivered his homily with all the power of his passion.
"It was Yeshua's teachings that so attracted the people of this land, not some later interpretations by men who had never known him.
"In *the Word* Yeshua reminds us of the divil tempting him:

> *'Then the devil, taking Him up on a high mountain, showed Him all the kingdoms of the world in a moment of time. And the devil said to Him, "All this authority I will give You, and their glory; for this has been delivered to me, and I give it to whomever I wish. Therefore, if You will worship before me, all will be Yours." And Jesus answered and said to him, "Get behind Me, Satan! For it is written, 'You shall worship the Lord your God, and Him only you shall serve.'*

"So we serve no earthly authority of bishops or so-called divine emperors in their palaces in Rome or in Alexandria." He pointed to the kings sat in their purple cloaks. "Our kings are elected by their people and are bound by the laws, as we all are. They must keep the *King's Truth* or be driven out. In Alexandria where *the Word* was delivered by St Mark it was hidden in a library. Hidden! Why? Because it became an embarrassment to a church as it grew greedy and sinful in its lust for power over others. People were driven out or killed in the streets because they disagreed with the church's teachings, women skinned alive I am told while the priests hid *the Word* in a darkened room. The Church of Alexandria and Rome have made men worship them and not God, they have mistreated women and taught children that they are born in sin. This is not what Yeshua taught. It is this perversion of faith that he warns of in *the Word*.

"Let me remind all ye learned men and women that no one in this land has died because of their belief in God or in gods: no one! Why is that? Because we followed his true teachings and not the dogma of some preening, latter-day prophet or theologian who would turn men against each other. And where did these teachings come from? Why were the people of Eriu so marked out?" asked Colum Cille.

He let the question sit on the air while he looked around his audience. He knew he had their attention so he took his time. He could see his adversary, Augustine, smirking in response. Those with a mind to judge these matters found such demeanour in a man of God offensive.

Colum Cille pointed directly at Black Aed sitting rock like on his bench. "Why, from an ancestor of this man, Conal Cearnach of the *Cruithin*, a Roman centurion who witnessed our Lord's crucifixion and then met with the apostles and was the first to bring back Yeshua's teachings to this place hundreds of years ago. This is why his teachings took root here without bloodshed. This is why *the Word* belongs here and why God has guided it here in this time."

Black Aed looked straight at Colum Cille for a moment. He thumped a great staff on the ground and stood up: "Colum Cille speaks the truth. My ancestor witnessed the crucifixion and in his sorrow and anger he brought the true teachings to this land. *the*

Word should have come here then." He shook his great head. "God forgive me, a poor sinner, who has strayed far from the wisdom Conal brought to his people. I have sinned a great many times. I have disrespected my heritage." Black Aed held up his great hands. "These hands have killed many men, both good and bad. Your father and my foster father, King Diarmait," he said pointing to Colman Bec who shifted uneasily. He then turned to Colum Cille and shouted in some anguish, "God forgive me for what I have done, Colum Cille!"

"He will, sire. I promise: for you truly repent this day."

Black Aed sat down heavily on his bench, his head bowed.

Now Augustine's party were looking distinctly uncomfortable at the case Colum Cille was presenting. Colum Cille was stealing the *airecht* from them. Brandub and Colman Bec looked to the emissary to intervene and challenge Colum Cille on his doctrine. Even Sister Dorothea looked to her master expecting his intervention. However Augustine remained strangely quiet and even looked as if he was enjoying the performance.

Then Sister Dorothea recalled Augustine's whispered warning to her as they approached the *airecht* that morning.

"Sister, expect a few surprises this day and when they happen stay close to me and do as I say, if you wish not to be carried off into slavery once more."

Now it was becoming clear to Sister Dorothea that Augustine had a strategy in mind that did not involve winning a doctrinal or legal argument with the abbot or the judges. She knew what deceit her master was capable of in his service to the Holy Father and what disregard he had for any that stood in his way. Her unease grew by the moment. Dorothea could see that this poor abbot was quoting the sacred word to a man who had little respect for holy teachings, except when they could serve his ambitions.

Colum Cille looked directly at Augustine: "I understand the emissary has a cart full of gold to give us should we foolishly give *the Word* into his hands, but again let me quote from *the Word*:

> *'For what shall it profit a man, if he shall gain the whole world, and lose his own soul?'*

and

'It is easier for a camel to go through the eye of a needle than for a rich man to enter the kingdom of God.'

"*The Word* will nourish us and our children and our children's children. Gold and fine temples will not. Have you forgotten that it was our obedience to God that saved this land and its people from the destitution of the famine and the misery of the plague: a plague that came out of Constantinople as a judgement on its corrupt emperor, Justinian!" Colum Cille pointed accusingly at Augustine.

Then turning to the whole *airecht* he said: "*The Word* has come home. It is God's will. With this divine power we will build a church in this land and beyond in the true image of God and Lord Yeshua and not some resurrection of the Roman Empire that never ruled this land and, while God permits me to breathe, never will. Send *the Word* away for a cartful of gold and ye will risk God's wrath for flouting his clear design."

Many nodded and stamped their feet in approval. Colum Cille bowed to the judges and the *Ard Ri* and kneeling before scrolls prayed once more. While he knelt no one knew if he had finished his address, so they waited in a respectful silence. Eventually Colum Cille rose to his feet and resumed his seat.

As he did so a low vibration in the ground could be felt. Many looked to Colum Cille for it was known he could conjure the elements when the passion was on him, but he simply turned to Brother Luigbe who nodded. The only person in the hall who did not look perplexed at this vibration was Augustine, whose face had broken into a wide smile from its previous smirk.

Ros Failge of the Gododdin horse soldiers burst into hall short sword drawn, he walked straight up to Augustine and spoke quietly with him for some moments. Then Augustine whispered to Sister Dorothea at his side, "You are about to be reunited with your brother, sister. Stay close to me and Ros Failge and we will be on our way to Britain with the scrolls shortly."

Sister Dorothea stood in shock. "No, no there will be slaughter, Father! You must not do this," she turned to Ros Failge. "Please stop them, Ros Failge. We cannot spill blood on these sacred scrolls."

"There will be no blood spilt if the scrolls are handed to us, sister," said Ros Failge. "Now I must take you and the emissary to a place of safety."

"I will not be party to this theft of sacred scrolls from a God-loving people!" shouted Sister Dorothea and broke away from Ros Failge.

Someone ran into the hall breathlessly shouting: "Horse soldiers are coming, many hundreds. Save yourselves!"

There was great confusion in the hall. The kings were huddled in conference. Men were shouting, monks were praying. Colum Cille could be seen with Brother Simon hastily placing the scrolls back in the leather bag.

Dorothea was already out of the hall and running in the direction of the thunder. She ran across the airlise where the market traders were standing around wondering what was afoot and towards the wide road at the entrance to the settlement of Druim Ceit. She ran past Melania and Bretha who were holding hands in terror.

Artur was at the head of the Gosgordd as they left their vessels on the eastern shore of Eriu in the lands of the *Dal nAraide* according to the agreement with Black Aed, their king. The horse soldiers had arrived in the dark and were ashore before they were seen so that no one could raise the alarm. The Gododdin travelled too fast for any messenger to get ahead of them to warn others. This was the element of surprise the Gododdin used.

It was known that no armies attended the *airecht* so there would be only a small number of warriors in Druim Ceit protecting the kings. They would be no match for the Gosgordd assisted by Ros Failge and his men and would be slaughtered if they resisted handing over the scrolls.

However as three hundred large British horse thundered westwards, the Gosgordd became unsettled by a black raven that was closely following their progress. They had noticed it perched high on a cliff as they landed at early dawn and again it was seen on a barn by a river ford later in the morning. It was quite clearly following their progress from on high, swooping occasionally to take a closer look. To the British a raven was not a good omen

346

especially before a battle. Legend told of the god of slaughter, Aeron, sending his ravens ahead to spy on the enemy.

Though privately disturbed by the raven's persistence, Artur told the men that they were a gaggle of suspicious old women. But their concerns were not allayed. It was only after they crossed the Ban Dea when the raven disappeared that the Gosgordd forgot their concerns, concentrating on their race towards their quarry at Druim Ceit.

Artur had sent word to Ros Failge through Baetan mac Cairill's spy network that he was launching an expedition to capture the scrolls as Druim Ceit with Baetan's support and that he wanted to both ensure the emissary's compliance and his sister's safety. For his part Augustine was very happy to comply with this change to his plans. Having the scrolls removed to Britain and into the hands of a single, powerful leader who openly desired the presence of the Church of Rome was preferable to the infinitely complex nature of the political and religious alliances he had discovered in Eriu. If the raid failed he could deny all knowledge and still pursue his former strategy in Eriu. In effect God had now given him two horses to ride. One was bound to win.

XXXIV: The trade

As the Gosgordd entered the road that their scout had told them led to Druim Ceit and the meeting hall on the hill, they went into battle formation with their short lances drawn. Such a charge was able to punch through the shield wall of an army ten thousand strong, sending warriors into panic and confusion. Once through the shield wall the horse soldiers would draw their short broad swords and axes to make short work of men's heads as they slashed through the ranks.

Their battle readiness was disturbed when the black raven reappeared flying directly at the advancing charge along the road in front of them. To avoid the raven the Gosgordd split in two with horses charging off into the woods on either side. It took many minutes to recover the charge as men fought through the dense woodland to return to the road where they reformed for the final approach towards the settlement. On reaching a point where the road opened out from the woods into Druim Ceit, Artur saw the small figure of a woman running towards them. As he strained to understand what this figure was doing, the raven once again flew at them. This time it flew across the ranks of the leading horses so close that its wings touched their muzzles, startling the beasts, who reared, reducing the charge once more to chaos.

"Artur, my brother!" Dorothea called in as loud a voice as she could muster above the sound of the horses whinnying and men shouting.

Artur wheeled round from checking his men to see his sister standing in direct line of the charge and immediately gave the command to stop.

"You could have been killed!" shouted Artur at Dorothea. "Get away from here, sister. Where is Ros Failge and the emissary?"

Dorothea did not move.

Behind her loomed the bulk of Black Aed and his *Cruithin* bodyguard with swords drawn, standing between the Gosgordd and the *airecht*. In truth they could not hope to stop three hundred horse soldiers, but Black Aed was guilt-ridden and would now lay down his life in a blood sacrifice to atone for his betrayal of his ancestor, Conal Cearnach.

"You will not pass me, brother," said Dorothea calmer now that she had made her decision. "I will throw myself under your horses before I will allow you to attack these people and steal *the Word* for yourself."

"It is not for myself!" said Artur hotly. "It is for the Britons. It is so we can build a strong faith in our land to withstand the Angles and the Saxons."

"This is not the way. God intends *the Word* for this land in this time, brother, not Britain. I am sure of it."

"Why are you so sure?"

"Because I have seen their faith in their monasteries as I have travelled their land and I have seen faith in Rome. Yeshua's teachings are not to be found in Rome: in cities and in grand buildings. They are to be found here in simple buildings and rural folk. I have heard Colum Cille speak. His passion and faith moves me. I never heard such passion and truth in Rome. Rome will bring you no succour from the Angles and Saxons, brother."

"We cannot discuss this now, sister," said Artur impatient as always to lead his men to success in battle. The horses were nervous at the sight of the raven and needed as much reassurance as their riders.

"Then I will stand with these men," said Dorothea moving back to stand beside Black Aed. Even though he understood none of their language, it was plain to Black Aed what was afoot with this little sister and he pushed her back amongst his men and stood forward to face the onslaught of the Gododdin. Artur knew that if he wanted the scrolls he would have to sacrifice his sister. His heart turned cold as he told his men to prepare to charge.

Just then the doors of the meeting hall opened and Augustine emerged into the sunlight with Ros Failge and some of his men. As they walked past the group of *Cruithin* warriors Dorothea noticed Augustine carrying the leather bag that she had seen in the hall.

"No, no!" she wailed, realising Augustine had the scrolls. Dorothea ran from the *Cruithin* towards Augustine. She was stopped by Ros Failge and held.

"I always suspected your woman's faith was weak," said Augustine sneering at Dorothea in his triumph. "That's why it is men who build the church of St Peter and not weak and treacherous women," he spat on the ground at her feet.

At that the *Cruithin* drew swords and prepared to charge the Augustine to rescue the scrolls.

"There is to be no blood, Aed of the *Cruithin*!" shouted Colum Cille striding across the airlise towards them. "We agreed to be guided by God in this. No blood!"

Black Aed hesitated as Colum Cille accompanied by the *Ard Ri* and Cormac walked up to face Artur and Augustine.

"If it is God's will that these scrolls should be in Britain then you shall have them. We will not spill blood in the name of God," said Colum Cille.

Holding the scroll bag Augustine sneered at Colum Cille. "Then your church will wither and die, abbot. The Church of St Peter will flourish and grow. Yeshua said:

'Do not suppose that I have come to bring peace to the earth. I did not come to bring peace, but a sword.'

"I wish we could have debated the true nature of God for you misunderstand him, abbot. As you can see," Augustine indicated the Gododdin horse soldiers, "God has answered my prayers, not yours."

With that Augustine mounted a horse next to Artur.

Cormac was close by with tears rolling down his cheeks. He could not comprehend what was happening. He had failed his God and his Patriarch. His legs could barely hold him upright. The thought of losing *the Word* to these men was an indescribable loss akin to that of losing his wife and sons. He could not carry a second loss. As he stood in utter devastation he looked over to the woods at three figures standing looking at him. He looked again. It was Moninna, Ternoc and Etgal, his wife and sons. They looked so happy and healthy. They were waving at him and laughing. He could not understand their obvious joy. He looked away in confusion and back at the tragic scene unfolding before him.

On Artur's order all the Gododdin mounted their horses and without another word turned around and set off down the road with Augustine and the scrolls at their head. Unknown to them the black raven followed once more.

Cormac sank to his knees with an unearthly cry of anguish.

The lady Melania and Bretha had been watching the tragedy unfold from the *airlise* now rushed in despair to their fallen friend and leader. Without thought and with Colum Cille looking on, both embraced the sobbing monk with their own tears joining his.

"Our love is with you brother for now and all time. Do not let your heart break. Go to your God, go to God. He will heal your pain," pleaded Melania as she held her brother.

"We love ye, Father Cormac. I love ye," whispered Bretha repeatedly as she choked back her tears.

Colum Cille stood watching them comfort the distraught monk for several moments. Such contact with women was forbidden for a monk, but these were unusual circumstances.

He walked over to the women and signalled for them to allow him close to Cormac. Melania and Bretha stood aside as Colum Cille knelt beside Cormac.

Placing a hand on Cormac's shoulder he whispered: "Ye have carried a heavy burden well, dear Cormac. One that God had prepared ye for. We have each learned much from these events. Let the sorrow wash through ye. Ye know from your time in the desert that such despair is but a holy moment that brings the soul closer to the divine."

Cormac looked up as he heard Colum Cille's words of comfort and again he saw Moninna, Ternoc and Etgal standing at the edge of the wood smiling and waving at him. They did not share his sorrow.

Colum Cille looked in the direction of Cormac's stare.

"I see them too, brother. Why do they smile so?" said Colum Cille as he gently lifted Cormac to his feet. "Come let me tell ye. I could not tell ye before, brother and so in yer ignorance ye suffered. But yer suffering is the only casualty of this affair. When I tell ye will know why the souls of yer kin are happy, their happiness is for ye, their dear one."

Colum Cille led Cormac back towards the meeting hall.

As they walked past those gathered Colum Cille spoke to them cheerfully, "Come let us go back to the hall and have some food and give thanks for the gift of this day."

Then he whispered to Cormac.

"Do ye know why I got into trouble before over scrolls, brother?"

"Yes, Father Ruadhan told us. You copied some scrolls and....." said Cormac as Colum Cille held up a hand not wishing to go into the detail of it.

"I did so again. I copied the scrolls," said Colum Cille fixing Cormac with his glinting eyes. "I had prayed for guidance and in a vision a golden hare advised me to repeat the exercise. Imagine, brother, repeating such a misdemeanour, but this time to save life, not lose it? It was such a simple solution, staring me in the face. I did it with much help from yer young scholar, Brother Simon. He was sent by God and no mistake, that boy. Who else in all the land can write Aramaic? He has a talent for myth making and riddles too."

Cormac stopped in his tracks before the door of the hall and stared at Colum Cille as the realisation began to dawn on him.

Colum Cille nodded: "The British thieves have a bag full of gibberish. Riddles and rhymes, myths and legends, nothing more. The originals are safe elsewhere."

Cormac did not know whether to laugh or to cry. He closed his eyes and thanked God and the wily fox, Colum Cille. Then a thought occurred to him.

"But they'll come back when they find out, Crimthainn."

"They have to find someone who can translate Aramaic first. There's not many of those boys around as we know," said Colum Cille smiling. "I don't believe they will return to us. The Angles and the Saxons will keep them busy, God help them. So come, let's give thanks and break some bread on this good day when God's will was honoured without bloodshed."

Cormac felt as if he had died and been resurrected. His relief was overwhelming. He would pray that Colum Cille was right that the Gododdin would not return seeking vengeance. It was a great risk, but one that he considered Colum Cille had been right to take. The alternative was the loss of the scrolls to Britain or to Rome with all the consequences that would flow from that for the people of this land.

Sister Dorothea was standing alone while all attention had been focused on the desert monk. As they returned to the hall she remained alone, a small figure looking down the road after Artur. She had been deserted by the brother she had loved since a small child: a brother who today might well have killed her to obtain the scrolls for his kindred. Yet her pain was bearable as she felt sure she had acted according to God's wishes. She had been given the strength to speak the truth in spite of her enormous fears for her safety and her duty to the Church of Rome. So she began to feel a great sense of liberty, she felt cleansed from oppression. It had become clear to her on this day and in this land that she could be a faithful follower of the Christ and still honour herself as a woman. Looking around she noticed the king who had offered to protect her, standing in desolation with his men. He was in great sadness at losing *The Word* to the Britons.

Sister Dorothea felt moved to speak to this broken, yet fearsome man. She walked over to Black Aed and said: "Great king, I feel your sorrow and have shame for my brother. You would have protected me from the horse soldiers and I thank you for your great courage. I am now alone in this land and wish to serve the church here. I am a Sister of Christ and I humbly ask to be given sanctuary."

Black Aed blinked through his sorrow and stared down at this small woman standing before him seeking his help. A smile slowly crossed his sad, weathered face.

"I promise I will help ye all I can, brave little sister. Ye tried to save the scrolls for this land. There are some fine monasteries that would be glad of yer devotion and yer courage, as would I," said Black Aed who was moved to use more words than he normally cared for. He was even minded to say more to the little sister, but his nostrils smelt the roast pig. "Come our bellies need food, even one as small as yers."

With that Black Aed and Sister Dorothea followed by his guards walked together towards the meeting hall.

As they reached the doorway they heard the sound of horse galloping towards them. They turned to see Artur and Ros Failge rushing towards them. Black Aed and his men immediately drew their swords and stood between Dorothea and her brother believing he was returning to steal her away or worse, kill her.

Instead Artur came to a halt a few steps away and threw the bag of scrolls at Black Aed who caught them against his huge chest.

"They are yours, Black Aed. I cannot defy God." Turning to Dorothea Artur said, "Your courage makes me proud and ashamed of my actions, sister. I ask for your forgiveness."

"You are already forgiven, Arthnou," said Dorothea emerging smiling from behind Black Aed.

"You will stay in this land?"

"Yes I will, brother. I will be safe now. This good king will be my guardian."

Looking at Black Aed Artur said: "I had to rescue my sister from bondage in this land before. If I have to do so again I will hold you responsible, Black Aed."

"The *Cruithin* look after their women. The little sister will be safe. She is already praised in this land, while her brother is not."

Looking back to Dorothea Artur smiled, "Pray for me, Dorothea, and all the Gododdin."

"I will, Arthnou. Every day you will hear me." She removed a cross from around her neck and threw it to Artur. "Stay close to God, my brother."

Artur caught the cross and kissed it. He smiled at Dorothea one last time and with that he turned his horse and in an instant was charging down the leafy road away from Druim Ceit followed by Ros Failge.

Black Aed was like a butcher's dog on a feast day. He held the bag of scrolls to his chest with much pride. He burst open the doors of the meeting hall and strode over to the table where Colum Cille was breaking bread with Cormac, Simon, Luigbe and many others. He threw the bag of scrolls on the table before them.

"The Gododdin thought the better of it. Praise be to God. We are saved this day by the grace of God and by this little sister," said Black Aed placing a large hand on Dorothea's slender shoulder and thrusting her forward with pride for all to admire. He then walked off to celebrate with Sister Dorothea walking self-consciously by her guardian's side.

Colum Cille stared at the bag speechless in wonder. He checked the contents and turned to Cormac and Brother Simon: together they burst into laughter that brought tears of joy to their eyes. Many in the hall gathered around to see the miracle that Colum Cille had performed. They all believed Colum Cille's laughter was of sheer joy at God's mercy in returning *the Word* that all believed they had lost to the Gododdin. In truth it was indeed a joy, but also delicious relief at the wondrous twist in divine providence that meant no one, except Colum Cille, Simon and now Cormac, would ever know of the deceit that had been practiced to save the true scrolls for Eriu.

As the peals of laughter rang out a group of harpists, who were sat in shadows of the hall, caught the mood and began a sound of celebration that touched the hearts of all present. It drifted on the air out to those on the airlise and some say that on hearing the sound the *Goddodin* stopped their furious homeward charge to listen.

XXXV: The way home

People who witnessed the events on the airlise that day told their story long into the night as they recalled each moment of the legend played out before their eyes. Bards were already composing song and verse. But few knew the real story that the British general had unknowingly returned a bagful of gibberish. Nothing is ever as it seems in Eriu. That night Colum Cille returned to the monastery of Camus with his companions to pray and give thanks to God and all hares for the glorious delivery of *The Word*.

The *airecht* was to continue in session the next day on less weighty matters connected to a dispute between the kings and the *filid*, so Colum Cille would remain in the area a while longer.

Sister Dorothea had asked leave of her new guardian, Black Aed, to travel with Colum Cille to the monastery. Dorothea's courage in facing her brother had impressed many, so the 'little sister', as they called her, could have had anything her heart desired in Eriu. Yet her heart desired only one thing, beyond belonging to a loving community that served God, and that was to unbind her breasts. This she did without seeking permission that very night.

While the sun set on the Ban Dea that night by the monastery of Camus, four companions sat by the river in silence reflecting on the tumultuous events that had brought them together and to this place. As they did so, they were disturbed by a rustling in the bushes behind them and out came Zachariah the Hare looking very travel worn.

"Master Hare you are back among us!" exclaimed Cormac. "I hear you have been busy with Colum Cille."

Zachariah merely smiled.

"It is so good to see you, Master Zachariah," said the lady Melania. "You appear tired. Come rest with us."

"I tell you friends I have had some long and arduous times," said Zachariah. "This hare is growing too old for this work."

"What work is that Master Hare?" asked Brother Simon.

"God's work," said Zachariah simply.

The others knew not to press Zachariah on where he had been since he left them on Ox Island and what he had been doing. They knew some things of magic should not be given to words. So Simon smiled and sensed that he should press the hare no further.

"Still all is well, I hear," continued Zachariah.

"Indeed it is," said Cormac. "*The Word* is safe with Colum Cille and the emissary is on his way to Britain as far as we know."

"Huh! Thanks be to God," said Zachariah. "So do we go back to Egypt now, monk?"

"No. My days in the desert are over, hare," said Cormac. "My place is in Eriu, in the place where I was born. I will journey to Killabuonia where my kindred have a monastery. I hope you will travel with me."

"I might," said Zachariah.

The hare lay in the grass with the others as they ate fruits picked by Bretha. Presently Zachariah spoke again.

"And you Brother Simon where does God call you?"

"Abbot Colum Cille has asked me help bring *the Word* to the people of Eriu, to keep it in the light," said Simon. "As you know I have the Latin, the Greek and the Aramaic. I am mastering the language of Eriu now too."

"You have become well versed in our tongue since you arrived, Brother Simon, in spite of your vow of silence," Cormac smiled. "Is that what you are guided to do?"

"It is, Father. That would make my heart sing."

Zachariah turned and stared at the lady Melania, smiling. She returned his smile ten-fold.

"Well, Master Hare, do you wish to hear from me?"

"Indeed I do, lady. I wish to know that you will be well accommodated in Eriu now that all this business of scrolls is seen to," said Zachariah.

"Bretha and her father will introduce me to the people of the sanctuary where I hope to find a calling," said Melania.

Zachariah looked at Cormac quizzically, but Cormac ignored his look.

"And I will compose an epic poem, a saga of this adventure. It will pass into legend through my work and ye'll all be famous through the ages," said Bretha not waiting to be asked. "I knew I was right to leave Mungair with yez that day. What an adventure it's been!"

They mumbled assent with no one wishing to define the detail any further. It was all too fresh an experience to be able to put words to it. They were content to leave that to Bretha.

"Will you write it down, Bretha?" asked Melania.

Ha!" laughed Bretha. "I have learnt much from this adventure, lady. One lesson above all is that writings can cause great difficulties. If all these clever *Chresten* men had never written down their words we would not have had so much trouble. No, my ancestors are much wiser. It is better to remain with the spoken word. In that way there are no books to be fought over or lost."

"You grow wiser by the day, child," said Cormac.

"Where is that magical hare of yers, Cormac, so I may thank him?" said Colum Cille across the monastery enclosure after prayers the next day.

"Zachariah dislikes drawing attention to such matters, Crimthainn," said Cormac. "It is enough for him to know he has helped. He is anxious that we are on our way."

"We will say prayers for him daily in Aio," said Colum Cille. "Is it God's will that you leave us again, dear one?"

"It is, Crimthainn. God willing I will end my days as they started with my kindred in Killabuonia."

The two men embraced for some moments. Then Cormac reached round his neck and removed the holy relic he had been given by Aba James in the monastery of St John the Short.

"You are to have this sacred relic, Crimthainn. It protects who ever has guardianship of the scrolls. Now it will protect you," said Cormac placing it over Colum Cille's head.

"What is it, boy?" asked Colum Cille examining the heavy silver phial.

"It was St Mark's. He brought it out of Jerusalem. It contains the blood of Lord Yeshua and the tears of Mary Magdalene," said Cormac. "St Anthony wore it and it was passed down through the

Fathers of Scetis to Aba James today who gave it to me. It is meant for you now."

"God bless ye, Cormac of Killabuonia for yer strength and courage and steadfastness. Ye have served God well, my brother. The glories of heaven await ye. There will always be an honoured place for ye in our community on Aio," Colum Cille kissed Cormac's forehead and then kissed the phial.

"And God's eternal blessings on you, Crimthainn," replied Cormac.

"I pray the work I have done in this matter has absolved me of my past wrongs and strengthened the church. My past sin has been a heavy burden on my work," said Colum Cille. "But now the real work begins. *The Word* must be seen in all corners of Eriu for it to take root and we must be worthy of Yeshua's true teachings. God forbid that we should end our time in shame with *The Word* hidden in some dark hole as in Alexandria."

"I will pray daily that Eriu will be worthy of *The Word*."

"Our prayers will go out from all our monasteries each day for ye and all yer companions from this day and for evermore for what ye have brought to this land, brother," said Colum Cille.

"I am thrice blessed, Crimthainn."

So it was that Cormac left Colum Cille to build a true church in Eriu founded on *the Word*. Monks would go out to the known world from Eriu guided by Yeshua's true teachings. In this time the Celtic church became known as the Light of the World for its learning and its guiding example.

Leaving the monastery of Camus that day on horseback with Cormac were the lady Melania and Bretha with Zachariah following. Retracing their steps south, they made good progress towards the head of the River Sionann where they hoped to find a boat to take them downriver. Bretha worried that Feth Fio might again be their boat man and would press his affections upon her.

"I don't wish to hurt the divil, but I will not marry a changeling," she said.

As luck would have it when they arrived at the same waters where Feth Fio had left his boat to journey overland with them, there was his boat waiting for them and Feth Fio sitting in it, oars at the ready.

"My friends it is good to see yez," he shouted. "They said you would pass this way. Feth Fio and the river are at your service once more."

"It is good to see you, Feth Fio," said Cormac. "We are honoured once more."

Feth Fio chuckled in delight as he eyed Bretha who returned his look in a less friendly manner.

"Alright, boy," Bretha declared. "Ye come with me. Ye and I must talk before this journey begins."

Feth Fio look delighted and sprang onto the shore to follow Bretha. They went off together to seek some privacy and returned some time later eager to be under way: matters between the two having been settled, it seemed. So without further ado they set off down the river as a soft, warm rain began to fall.

"What did you say to Feth Fio, Bretha?" asked Melania in a whisper, anxious to know how matters stood.

"I told the divil he was a fine fellow and my friend, but that I was pledged to my art and no other. So I could not be his wife nor would I play with him in the water."

"How did he respond?"

Bretha began to cry, "He said that he knew his love was not returned and he had come to accept this. But that he would always love me. He said I was the most beautiful water spirit he had ever seen and he had seen many in his years as a boatman. He asked to kiss me before we parted."

"Yes."

"I let him," said Bretha in some distress. "I felt I owed him a parting little kiss. It was the best kiss I have ever had! While he kissed me he became this gentle, handsome young man and now look, he's a changeling again. Half man, half otter. Oh what will I do, lady? This divil has me tormented!"

Melania could only laugh at Bretha's predicament. Such complexities were beyond even her.

Their journey down the great river was wondrously uneventful after their recent experiences: meadows and farms along the river bank slipped quietly by them as Feth Fio guided the boat with ease.

The land seemed more at peace with itself now. No one pursued them or challenged them as before. It was as if some hidden hand had removed all discord.

They slept in farms known to Feth Fio as they wished to avoid the attention of monasteries on their return journey with all the excitement that their presence might attract. So there were no warm baths, only the cool river waters to wash in. This time Bretha and Melania played in the water without Feth Fio's attentions and Cormac kept his usual discrete distance where he bathed alone listening to the women's laughter.

He recalled the tenderness they had shown him in his distress at Druim Ceit and yet he had not found the words to thank them, but knew he must. So awaiting their return from the river one day he composed his words of gratitude. Then seeing Bretha walk off from the river to a nearby farm in Zachariah's company, he resolved to wait on the lady Melania.

When the lady did not appear Cormac became concerned and set off to look for her. He found Melania swimming alone and naked in a quiet pool, but this time he did not look away. Instead, unseen he watched, mesmerised as she moved like a nymph through the water; movements that were so becoming of her nature: gentle, quiet and all in a rhythm.

Cormac could never recall deciding to join Melania in the water. It had been unthinkable to him. But that day he awoke as if from a dream and found that he was swimming naked towards her and that she had turned to welcome him. Then part of him wanted to turn back from his foolishness before the lady was offended, but another part could only see this goddess in the river before him, calling him towards her divine embrace. He ached for her sweet embrace. Now he could no longer resist the urge to hold her and to be held.

On seeing Cormac enter the water as naked as she, Melania's heart beat quickened. She had never seen a man naked and the sight of her friend, Father Cormac, naked before her was confusing, even disturbing. Then her fear vanished when all she could see was her friend swimming strongly through the water towards her. She ached to hold him tightly to her as she had done in Druim Ceit. She raised her arms to him and called him onwards. He seemed to gain in confidence and soon he was beside her, his arms encircling her and holding her to him in the water. No words were spoken.

While they swam closely together Melania turned her head to Cormac and he kissed her. She lay in the water beside him as he caressed her body like a fisherman would gently tickle the belly of a trout. He raised her up until she lay half out of the water and kissed her belly softly while she looked up into the wide blue of the sky. As small white clouds drifted past and the world fell silent, Melania offered herself up to him, her arms moving to touch Cormac lightly as she explored the nature of him. In return he directed her body towards him in the river. She felt his strength and power come into her as she surrendered to his blessed fullness and soothing warmth.

They remained entwined in the water for some time, watched by the birds and the creatures of the river bank until they released each other and swam to the bank to dress; still not a word was said between them.

Few words were spoken in the coming days as they journeyed further south towards the river end as it widened out in to the sea. What had happened between Melania and Cormac was accepted without discussion or inquiry. Each understood that time was needed for all of them to adjust to changed circumstances.

When Melania told Bretha that she would travel on with Cormac and Zachariah to Killabuonia and would not seek out the people of the sanctuary, she accepted this with joy for her close friend mixed with not a little sorrow that she would lose Melania's warm embrace.

The parting when it came was deeply felt all round.

"I will miss our baths," whispered Bretha to Melania.

"And I will miss holding you in bed," said Melania.

"You have Father Cormac now to hold."

"I think the 'father' is a title he will no longer use. We will farm on his kindred's land instead."

Bretha chuckled. "You have never farmed, lady!"

"Cormac believes I can learn. He is hopeful that he has cousins who will help us."

"It's a wondrous world, lady."

"It is Bretha. Alexandria is a faraway place," Melania said wistfully. "But I have found my temple in this land and, like a good pagan, I worship my god daily."

"And does Cormac worship his goddess in her temple, lady?" said Bretha with a grin.

"Of course he does. He worships at my altar daily and I at his. We are still priest and priestess after all."

They looked at each other and laughed.

XXXVI: Postscript: Derry 2015

"This was no casual theft! Are you telling me that someone has replaced the scrolls with professional fakes without being noticed by anyone," demanded Sir Francis in the seconds following the discovery of the missing scrolls. "How could this have happened? These scrolls are a threat to national security. These scrolls must be found."

Later Bryony wondered at Sir Francis' choice of words regarding the loss of the scrolls. It seemed an exaggeration of the importance of the scrolls to her. But back in that charged atmosphere her mind in a panic raced through the events of the morning. She remembered the busker arriving in the corridor and asking to use the toilet. She assumed security must have let him into the building and he had such a pleasant and familiar manner that she forgot the rules and let him in.

Now Bryony was running down the corridor before she could be stopped and throwing open the front doors of the building on to the street. It was a bright autumn day and the street was busy with shoppers. Frantically she looked around for the busker. The corner that he had been playing in was now occupied by a harpist.

"Where's the busker with the flute who was here earlier?" she asked at the harpist interrupting his flow.

"Who? Cormac?" asked the musician. "He just left."

"Where'd he go?"

"Just up the street," he pointed. "Ye'll catch him if ye hurry."

He calmly watched her go while he resumed a traditional air on his harp.

Bryony ran up a steeply sloping street and there ahead of her she saw the man, as bold as brass carrying the distinctive leather bag over his back. Bizarrely sticking out of the bag there was a hare's head, curiously looking all around him. As the busker walked he played his flute. She called out to him using the name the harpist had used.

"Cormac, wait!"

He turned at the sound of his name. He appeared to be in no hurry, not like a man who had just stolen something. He smiled at her and waved and in that momentary exchange something passed between them that made Bryony hesitate. She was disturbed by an unknown but strong familiarity between them. It felt like a close family bond. She felt she knew this man, knew him well, yet she couldn't place him. She knew no buskers, flute players or tramps. The familiarity of this total stranger was so strong it made her cautious about approaching him until she understood the reason for how she felt.

He too stopped to watch her for a moment smiling openly as a friend would and then with another wave he disappeared round a corner. When she reached the spot where he had stood he was nowhere to be seen.

As the existence of the scrolls had never been revealed to the media it was not difficult to keep their existence a continuing secret. Instead they gave the media the Dunseverick Chalice and no mention was ever made of the scrolls.

Bryony never revealed her strange encounter with the busker in the street and admitted only to having let him use the toilet. Security denied letting anyone into the building. Yet internal CCTV showed the busker going into the toilet. The camera in the meeting room covering the scrolls was faulty and revealed nothing. Everyone at the meeting was detained, investigated and questioned by the security services. The busker with his pet hare, the scrolls and even the harpist disappeared without trace.

Suspicion continued to linger around Bryony. Disillusioned with professional archaeology and disturbed by the suspicions of the authorities, she found she could no longer live within the straight jacket of government service and objective science. She left her job to become a professional storyteller and poet. To her everlasting frustration there was one story she could never tell.

Appendices

Place names

Aillinn
Also known as Dun Aillinn, near Kilcullen, Co. Kildare, ancient seat of the Kings of Leinster in Ireland. (See map)

Aio
Ancient name of the island of Iona off the western coast of Scotland where Colum Cille founded his monastic community in 563 A.D. Also known as Ioua. (See map)

Al Asqueet
A wadi in Egypt between Scetis and Alexandria

Alba
Roman name for Scotland

Armorica
Ancient name for Brittany, France. (See map)

Ban Dea
River Bann, Northern Ireland

Bheitheach Mhor
Beaghmore Stone circles near Cookstown, Co. Tyrone, Northern Ireland

Camus
Monastery near Coleraine, Northern Ireland. Founded in 6th century by St Comgall of Bangor and used by Colum Cille before the Convention of Druim Ceit. (See map)

Canopian Way
One of the main and most attractive thoroughfares in the ancient city of Alexandria. It was known for its elegant houses and displays of flowers

Church of Dionysius
Former temple of Dionysius in Alexandria and named after St Dionysius, 3rd century Patriarch of Alexandria. Used to accommodate the residence of the Coptic Patriarch.

Cill Dalua
Monastery of Killaloe in Co. Clare. (See map)
Dal Riata
Celtic kingdom spanning north eastern Ireland and western Scotland founded around 6th century. Through this the Scotii (Roman name for the Irish) came to Alba eventually conquering the country and giving it the modern name of Scotland. (See map)
Derry
Modern city on the north coast of Northern Ireland, also known as Londonderry. Ancient name is Doire (Oak Grove). A monastery was founded there by Colum Cille in 546 A.D. (See map)
Druim Ceit
Also known as Drumcett. Site of the Convention of Drumcett in 575 A.D. thought to be in the Roe valley near Limavady, Northern Ireland. (See map)
Dunseverick
Also known as Dun Sobhairce. A small settlement and harbour on the north coast of Northern Ireland. The site of the discovery of the scrolls in 2015. A large fort existed here in the 6th century and the great road travelling the entire length of Ireland, the Slighe Midluachra ended there. (See map)
Durrow
Monastery in Co. Offaly, Ireland founded by Colum Cille in 553 A.D. who ordained Cormac there in the same year.
Eildon Hill
A large ceremonial site in the Scottish Borders used for ritual and celebration in Celtic times.
Emania
Ancient province of Ulster in Ireland. (See map)
Érainn
Lake of Érainn, modern Lough Erne in Northern Ireland. (See map)
Eriu
Ancient name for Ireland, named after the goddess Eriu of the Tuatha De.
Great Library
In Alexandria: was held to be the biggest store of written knowledge in the known world, founded in 3rd century B.C. by the Ptolemies. The date of its destruction is confused. It may have lasted in some form until sacked by the Sassanids in 642 A.D.

Forest of Brocéliande
Legendary forest in Brittany, France associated with Arthurian legend. (See map)
Hill of Uisneach
Held to be the centre of Ireland and the burial place of the goddess Eriu. Also known as the Hill of Balor, the god of fire and was used for the Festival of Beltaine in May 1. Near Loughnavalley in Co. Westmeath. (See map)
Iarmummu
Ancient name for the Kingdom of Munster, one of the five provinces of Ireland. (See map)
Inish Cathaig
Scattery Island, Co. Clare in the Shannon Estuary. The site where Cormac landed in Ireland. A large monastery was founded by St Senan in 6th century. It was also a great centre of trade. (See map)
Killabuonia
Birth place of Cormac mac Fliande in Co. Kerry, Ireland. Monastery founded there in 5th century. (See map)
Laigin
Ancient name for the Kingdom/ province of Leinster in Ireland. The most powerful and richest province. (See map)
Lucania
Ancient province in southern Italy
Lugdunum
Modern city of Lyons, France
Maigh Choscain
Macosquin, Co. Derry, Northern Ireland.
Massilia
Modern city of Marseilles, France (see map)
Meadows Monastery of the Meadows of the Sons of Nos
Clonmacnoise monastery in Co. Offaly, Ireland. Founded by St Ciaran in 543 A.D. It became a great centre of worship and trade. (See map)
Mide
Ancient kingdom/ province of Meath in the centre of Ireland (see map)

Molua
Monastery of Molua at Killaloe, Co Limerick founded by St Molua in the 6th century.

Mungair
Modern village of Mungret, Co. Limerick, Ireland, Seat of the kindred, the Maic Brocc. (See map)

Neustria
An ancient kingdom in northern France during the time of the Franks from the 5th to the 7th century A.D.

Ox Island
Devenish Island, Lough Erne, Northern Ireland

Paestum
A city in Greek and Roman times located in southern Italy. It became home to a Christian community in the 6th century when Cormac stayed there and met Zachariah. (See map)

River Sele
Near Paestum in southern Italy.

River Sionnan
River Shannon, largest river in Ireland (See map)

Rheged
Ancient north British kingdom possibly stretching from Dumfries and Galloway down to north Wales. Strongly associated with the Gododdin.

Rodonos
River Rhone in France. (See map)

Skellig
Skellig Michael Island off the south west coast of Ireland. Home to a Coptic ascetic community of monks from the 6th to the 8th century.

Slighe Chuallann
Ancient road in Ireland running from Waterford to Dublin.

Slighe Mhor
Ancient road in Ireland running from Dublin westwards to the coast near the modern day Galway city.

Spy Wood
Ancient, mythical woods in Connacht.

Temair
Royal Temair or the Hill of Tara, near Navan, Co. Meath. The legendary ancient seat of the high kings of Ireland from around 2000 B.C until it went into decline after St Ruadhan cursed it in 563 A.D. (See map)
Trimontium
Former Roman cavalry fort in the Scottish Borders used by the Gododdin horse soldiers. (See map)

Uisneach
Sacred hill held to be the centre of Ireland. Near Mullingar, Co. Westmeath. Used for the annual Beltaine festival to this day. (See map)

Main Characters

(In order of appearance)

Cormac mac Fliande
Irish monk from Killabuonia, Co. Kerry, Ireland. After losing his family to famine and disease in Ireland in 545AD he became a monk and spent over ten years living as a desert father in the western desert of Egypt. B. 520 A.D.

Zachariah the Hare
A golden hare and long term muse of Cormac. The golden hare is a sacred animal in pagan culture. Zachariah claims to have been the biblical prophet, Zachariah from Babylonia. He is a changeling with special powers, able to move in and out of different worlds.

Simon of Bezatha
Also known as Bartholomew. A young monk and academic from the outskirts of Jerusalem, speaks and writes several languages – Greek, Latin, Hebrew, Aramaic and latterly Old Irish. He is also a skilled scribe and worked in the Great Library of Alexandria.

Melania
A philosopher and priestess of the goddess Isis in Alexandria, of Greek descent, born in Alexandria and close friend of Cormac.

Augustine of Nubea
Priest and Emissary to the Bishop of Rome, his foster father. Born Ouggamaet in Nubea.

Bretha
A young Celtic poet or file and herbalist from Mungair (Mungret) in Co. Limerick, Ireland. Daughter of an eminent file (poet), Failge Berraide.

Dorothea
Young British nun serving in the Lateran Palace in Rome in 575 A.D. and assigned to Augustine as a translator during his mission to Ireland. She spoke the different Celtic languages of Britain and Ireland, as well as Latin and Greek.

Artur*

Guledig or general of the Gododdin (a tribe in northern Britain, who were well known for fielding a large force of horse soldiers). They learnt their military tactics under the Romans. Artur at this time was around twenty-four years of age and brother of Sister Dorothea. Artur of the Gododdin is held to be the historical figure that the legend of King Arthur was created around. The real Artur was never a king, but was a highly successful general who led his army against the Angles and Saxons in Britain.

Colum Cille*

Eminent abbot of Iona (Aio), an island monastery on the west coast of Scotland. Born in Co. Donegal, Ireland of royal blood within the Ui Neill dynasty. He is a cousin of the High King (Ard Ri) of Ireland, Aec mac Ainmuirech*. Colum Cille founded several monasteries throughout Ireland and brought Christianity to Scotland. He initiated the tradition of monastic book writing in Ireland which led to the creation of Book of Kells. He was instrumental in keeping 'the Word' alive in Europe during the 'Dark Ages'. He was known by several names:

Given name: Crimthainn (the fox), then he became known as Colum Cille (Dove of the church), this was later Latinised to Columba. He is referred to as a saint, but was never canonised by Rome. One of the 'Twelve Apostles of Ireland'.

B. 521. D. 597.

*Denotes historical figure.

Secondary Characters

Acacius
Oikonomos or chief lay advisor to the Patriarch of Alexandria.
Aed dub mac Suibni
Ri Cuicidh (King) of the Dal nAraide (the Cruithin) in Co. Antrim. Also known as Black Aed.
Aed mac Ainmuirech*
Ard Ri (High King of Ireland) and Ri Cuicidh of the Cenel Conaill in Co. Donegal, Ireland.
Ausonius
Greek philosopher living in Alexandria, father of Melania.
Baetan mac Cairill*
Ri Cuicidh (King) of the Dal Fiatach in Co. Down.
Berossus
Chief Editor of the Great Library of Alexandria and cousin of the Patriarch.
Brandub mac Echach*
Ri Cuicidh of the Laigen, King of Leinster. The most powerful regional king in Ireland.
Bran Mut
King of the Squirrels in Ireland and protector of Royal Temair.
Bryony MacDirmaid
Irish Archaeologist who found the scrolls in 2015.
Catelinus*
Roman churchman who became Bishop of Rome (John the Third) in 561 A.D. he became Augustine's foster father around 530 A.D.
Cathair Mar
Chief of the kindred, the Uí Bairrche in south east Ireland.
Ciaiphas*
High Priest of the Great Sanhedrin in Jerusalem 18 A.D. to 36 A.D.
Colman Bec* Ri Cuicidh of the Mide, King of Meath, Ireland.

Connor of the Dreams
Ten year old boy with psychic ability, living in Mungair. He lost a hand in a savage attack by a wolf. This event triggered his gift of second sight.

Damianos I*
Patriarch of Alexandria, Bishop of all Africa, Coptic Church: 574 A.D. to 605 A.D.

Dr Jacob Shamir
British Museum's expert on ancient Semitic languages, 2015.

Failge Berraide
Eminent poet (file) in Iarmummu (Munster) and father of Bretha.

Feth Fio
Boat man on the River Sionnan (Shannon) and changeling.

Gaeth
A horse in Ireland

Gregory of Tours*
Bishop of Tours in France, eminent clergyman. B. 538. D. 594 A.D.

Igider
Also known as the "Eagle" because he could talk to birds and appeared to sail his boat as if it were flying. He was from Cyrenia in North Africa; eminent captain in Patriarch's fleet in the Mediterranean.

Iucharba
A lord in the Tuatha De, the underworld tribe of ancient Irish. A pagan with mystical powers.

James the Just*
Brother of Yeshua and leader of Yeshua's followers in Jerusalem after the crucifixion.

Jonathan of Ananus
Nephew of Caiaphas and his successor.

Joseph of Arimithaea*
Member of Sanhedrin Council in Jerusalem, merchant and apostle of Yeshua.

Luigbe mac Min*
Irish monk and trusted emissary of Colum Cille.

Luigbe mac Min#2
Agent of Colman Bec who pretended to be Colum Cille's emissary in order to secure the scrolls.

Mac Nisse*
Abbot of the Monastery of the Meadows of the Sons of Nos
Mary of Magdala*
Mary Magdalene, wife of Yeshua.
Nicodemus*
Merchant in Jerusalem and apostle of Yeshua.
Ronnat
Queen of Ireland, wife of the High King (Ard Ri), Aec mac Ainmuirech* and cousin of the King of the Laigen (Leinster),
Brandub mac Echach*
Ri Cuicidh (King) of the Dal Fiatach in Co. Down.
Ruadhán of Lorrha
Saint and founder of the monastery of Lorrha near Terryglass, Co. Tipperary in Ireland. Close friend of Colum Cille and one of the 'Twelve Apostles of Ireland'.
Tocca mac Aedo
Also known as Tocca the Hen because of his hen-like mannerisms. An Irish merchant belonging to the kindred of the Maic Brocc in Mungair.
Rabanus
Jewish Chief Librarian of the Great Library of Alexandria
Ros Failge
Captain of the Gododdin troop of horse soldiers in Ireland and of Irish origin.
Sarnat
She wolf guarding the Monastery of the Meadows
Senan*
Abbot of Inish Cathaig (Scattery Island), Co. Clare. Saint and one of the 'Twelve Apostles of Ireland'.
Sheila Donald
Chief Executive of Heritage Ulster in Northern Ireland in 2015
Sir Francis Hedding
Senior civil servant in British government in 2015
Vitalios
A Greek monk running a mission to prostitutes in Alexandria and a friend of Cormac's.
Yeshua ben Pandira*
Jesus Christ aka Yeshua ho Xristos   *Denotes historical figure.

Terms

Aba
Aramaic term for an abbot
Agora
Main square in ancient Alexandria used for meetings and markets
Aine
Irish goddess of summer, wealth and sovereignty
Airecht
Legal assembly under Irish Brehon Law
Alba
Roman name for Scotland until it took the name derived from the Roman name for the Irish, Scotii.
Anam Cara
Soul friend or confessor. Concept introduced to Christianity by the Celtic Church.
Anexodos
Alexandrian beggars
Aramaic
The language of Jesus. Jewish Aramaic was spoken by Jesus and his followers, not Hebrew.
Ard Ri
High King of Ireland. Only a ceremonial position in 575AD.
Ard Ollamh
Chief Poet and Judge
Arians
Followers of Arius, 4th century ascetic monk. Arius believed Jesus was effectively human and not divine. His beliefs caused the first schism in the church.
Beltaine
Celtic Festival of Fire to welcome in the summer, held in early May.
Berber
North Africa tribe
Bouleutai
Alexandrian merchants

Brehon law
Pre-Christian legal system developed by the Irish people over many hundreds of years. It was not written down until the fifth century, but was passed around orally by the filid (poet class).

Brithemain
Class of lawyers in ancient Ireland: also known as Brehon lawyers.

Cenél Conaill
Tribe or tuath in Co. Donegal within the Ui Neill dynasty. Their king in 575 A.D. was Aed mac Ainmuirech also Ard Ri (High King). Colum Cille was a prince within these kindred.

Cenel nEógain
Tribe or tuath in Co. Derry within the Ui Neill dynasty.

Changeling
Mystical being that can change shape between human and animal.

Chresten
Early Celtic word for Christian.

Consistory
Meeting place for the Presbytery of the Coptic Church in Alexandria

Cruithin
Early Irish tribe or kindred holding land in the north east of Ireland in the 6th century. Rivals of the northern Ui Neill dynasty who forced the Cruithin ever eastwards until they migrated to Scotland.

Dal Fiatach
Celtic Kingdom centred around Co. Down in Northern Ireland. Ruling dynasty within the Ulaidh. King in 575 A.D. was Baetan mac Cairill.

Dal nAraide
The territory of the Cruithin in County Antrim, Northern Ireland. King in 575 A.D. was Aed dub mac Suibni or Black Aed.

Dal Riata
Celtic kingdom spanning north east Ireland and western Scotland (Argyll and Kintyre) in the 6th and 7th centuries. One of the kingdoms within the Ulaidh people. The Dal Riatan king in 575 A.D. was Aedan mac Gabrain.

Dibergga
Wild young warrior/hunters in Ireland. Usually drawn from the upper class.

Druim Ceit
Drumcett, Roe Valley, Limavady, Co. Derry. Held to be the site of the Convention of Drumcett called by Colum Cille in 575AD.

Druid smith
A class of philosophers, teachers, counsellors and magicians In Celtic Ireland.

Espartu
A time of daily prayer in the Celtic church

File
Poet, storyteller, lawyer. It took up to twenty years of study to become a file.

Filid
The powerful poet class, storytellers and lawgivers. Before writing arrived in Ireland in the 5th century the filid (file: singular) were the holders of all oral records for the kindred; also known as seanchaí.

Gododdin
A Celtic tribe in northern Britain

Gosgordd
Elite force of three hundred horse soldiers within the Gododdin cavalry

Guledig
General of the Gosgordd. See Artur.

Hegumenos of Scetis
Leader of the ascetic monastery community of Scetis in Egypt

Honestiores
Alexandrian aristocratic class

Iarmeirge
One of the offices of prayer. Iarmeirge was said on rising. Also known as Prime

Immram
A class of old Irish tales concerning a hero's sea or river journey

Inish Cathaig
Scattery Island, Shannon Estuary, Ireland.

Isis
Ancient Egyptian goddess of nature and magic. She was a patron of slaves, sinners, sailors, artisans and the downtrodden. Adopted by the Greco-Roman world.

Kindred
Tribe or clan: also known as tuath, plural tuatha.

King's Truth

An Irish king must be just and virtuous and his reign peaceful. If this was not so he could be forced from his throne. A decision taken by the king to enforce the King's Truth overruled all other laws

Lorica

A Celtic prayer

Maic Brocc

A sept of the Eoghanacht (the dominant kindred of Iarmummu) living the area around the Shannon estuary in the sixth century.

Manannán mac Lir

Irish god of the sea

Manaig

Married Irish monks who farmed the monastery lands. Ascetic monks were not married.

Martyrdom

A monk could not become a saint unless he was martyred. This was a strong tradition in Christianity since the days of persecution by the Romans prior to the recognition of Christianity in 313 A.D. by Constantine. In Ireland Christians were not martyred in the conventional sense and this was one of the reasons monks left Ireland. They created other forms of martyrdom e.g. Green martyrs left behind the comforts and pleasures of ordinary human society to live hermits' lives. White martyrs sailed into the sea without a known destination.

Matins

Office of prayers around 9 a.m. Also known as Terce.

Mazices

North African tribe known for looting monasteries.

Maghreb

North and West African tribe who later became known as Moors.

Mide

Ancient province of Meath in central Ireland. (See Maps)

Midnocht

One of the offices of prayer. Midnocht was said at midnight. Also known as Nocturne.

Myaphysites
Also known as monophysites. A strand of Christian theology
believing that Jesus had one nature, both human and divine. This
was the belief of the Alexandrian or Coptic Church

Nazorean
A term used to describe Jesus. It has nothing to do with Nazareth.
The Nazoreans were a Judaic sect possibly linked to the Essenes.

Nestorians
Followers of Nestorius, 5th century Patriarch of Constantinople.
Strand of Christian belief which asserted that Jesus had two separate
natures, human and divine. They were branded heretics and moved
eastwards to found the Assyrian Church.

None
Office of monastic prayers around 3 p.m.

Ollamh
Master Poet and lawgiver or file. It took up to twenty years of study
to become an Ollamh.

Parabalini
Alexandrian church militia. Militant, fundamental Christians.

Pelagius
Celtic moralist (he was not a monk). He was closely identified with
the Celtic Church. He believed in free will and opposed the concept
of Original Sin advanced by St Augustine of Hippo.

Peregrinatio
A monk's travels seeking martyrdom. (See Martyrdom.)

Pharisees
Middle class Jewish political, social and religious movement at the
time of Jesus. They often clashed with the aristocratic Sadducees.

Plague
The Justinian or Yellow plague ravaged the Middle East and Europe
from 540 - 545A.D. In Ireland it killed up to a third of the known
population. It was similar to the later Black Death or Bubonic
Plague in the 14th century. Name after the Roman Emperor
Justinian who reigned at the time.

Prime
One of the offices of monastic prayer. Prime was said on rising.
Also known as Iarmeirge

Rath
Irish name for a circular earthen fort topped with wooden ramparts occupied by a lord or a king. The size of the rath was an indication of social status with the larger ones having several circular mounds each within the other. Inside the rath was a compound containing homes, barns and shelter for animals.

Ri Cuicidh
Provincial king in Ireland

Ri Mor
Local king ruling over a single tuath or kindred.

Sanhedrin
Jewish rabbinical court in Jerusalem

Sadducees
Ruling class among Jews in Jerusalem. The High Priest Caiaphas was a leading member. They ceased to function as a power after the destruction of the second temple in Jerusalem in 70 A.D.

Samhain
Celtic festival marking the end of the growing season and the start of winter. It was replaced by Hallowe'en in Christian times.

Sassanids
The last Persian Empire before the rise of Islam. They conquered Alexandria in 613 A.D. destroying what remained of the Great Library.

Satirising
A powerful form of verbal attack used in verse form by the filid in Ireland to condemn their enemies. It was believed that their words could inflict actual physical injury much like a curse.

Scotii
Roman name for the Irish which later was used to name Scotland when the Irish/Cruithin tribes conquered the native Picts.

Scriptorium
Room where books were written and copied in monasteries.

Serapeum
Temple of Serapis, the divine protector of Alexandria, mostly destroyed by Christians in 4th century.

Sext
Office of monastic prayers around midday.

Sidhe
Underground home of Tuatha De. Usually a hill.

Terce
Office of monastic prayers around 9 a.m. Also known as Matins.
Tonsure
Form of hairstyle used by monks. The Celtic tonsure was similar to the Jewish Hassidic hairstyle, shaved at the front and long at the sides. The Roman tonsure saw the hair shaved at the top of the head
Tuath
Tribe, clan or kindred. Plural tuatha.
Tuatha De
Ancient mythical pre-Christian tribe that lived underground in Tir na n'Og ("Land of Youth"). They were also known as the Tuatha De Danaan. They were forced underground after the invasion of Ireland by the Gaels around the 1st century AD according to legend.
Ui Bairrcche
Irish tribe or tuath in south east Ireland around late 6th century
Uí Cheinnselaig
Irish tribe or tuath in south east Ireland around late 6th century
Ui Dúnlainge
Irish tribe or tuath in south east Ireland around late 6th century
Ui Neill
Aka O'Neill. A powerful regional dynasty of Irish kindred centred on Donegal, but expanded into most of western Ulster and Mide by the 6th century. They dominated the high throne of Ireland for centuries.
Ulaidh
Name for the people of the ancient Irish province of Ulster (See Emania) comprising all of the north of Ireland. By the 6th century they had been forced eastwards and into Scotland by the expanding Ui Neill dynasty and occupied only counties Antrim and Down in 575AD. (See kingdoms of Dal Fiatach, Dal nAraide and Dal Riata on Maps). See Cruithin.

Selected Bibliography

Aalen, F. H. A., *Atlas of the Irish rural landscape*, Cork, Cork University Press, 2010.

Adamson, Ian, *The identity of Ulster*, Belfast, Adamson, 1982.

Adomnan, ed. Sharpe, R, *Life of St Columba*, London, Penguin, 1995.

Aslan, Reza. *Zealot*, London, Westbourne Press, 2013

Bellesheim, Alphons, *St. Columba and Iona*, British Columbia, Eremetical Press, 1887.

Bhreathnach, Edel, *Ireland in the medieval world*, AD 400-1000, Dublin, Four Courts Press, 2014.

Bhreathnach, Edel, *The kingship and landscape of Tara*, Dublin, Four Courts Press, 2005.

Black, Jonathan, *The Sacred History*, London, Quercus, 2013.

Bradley, Ian, *Columba: pilgrim and penitent*, Glasgow, Wild Goose Publications, 1996.

Cahill, Thomas. *How the Irish saved civilisation*, London, Hodder & Stoughton, 1995

Clarkson, Tim, *The Picts*, Edinburgh, Birlinn, 2010.

Crossan, John, *The power of parable*, New York, HarperCollins, 2012.

Ehrman, Bart, *Did Jesus exist?* New York, HarperCollins, 2012.

Fleming, Robin, *Britain after Rome: the fall and rise, 400-1070*, London, Penguin, 2011.

Freeman, Charles, *A new history of early Christianity*, Yale, Yale University Press, 2009.

Freeman, Philip, *St. Patrick of Ireland*, New York, Simon & Schuster, 2005.

Gardiner, Laurence, *Bloodline of the Holy Grail*, Shaftesbury, Element, 1996.

Geissel, Hermann, *A Road on the Long Ridge: in Search of the Ancient Highway on the Esker Riada*, Naas, CRS Publications, 2006

Ginnell, Laurence, *The Brehon Laws*, London, Forgotten Books, 2012.

Green, Miranda, *Celtic Myths,* London, British Museum Press, 1993.

Haas, Christopher, *Alexandria in late antiquity*, Baltimore, The John Hopkins University Press, 2006.

Hamlin, A., & Hughes, K., *The modern traveller to the early Irish Church*, Dublin, Four Courts Press, 1997.

Heather, P. J., *The restoration of Rome: Barbarian Popes & imperial pretenders*, London, Macmillan, 2013.

Hutton, Ronald, *The pagan religions of the ancient British Isles*, London, John Wiley & Sons. 1993.

Kelly, Frank, *Early Irish farming*, Dublin, Dublin Institute for Advanced Studies, 1997.

Losack, Marcus, *St. Patrick and the bloodline of the Grail*, Annamoe, Ceile De, 2011.

MacFarlane, Robert, *The Old Ways: A journey on foot*, London, Penguin, 2013.

Markale, Jean, *Women of the Celts*, Rochester, Inner Traditions International, 1972.

McClintock, Chris, *Columba: the last Irish druid*, Coleraine, Aesun Publishing, 2012.

McCulloch, Diarmaid, *A history of Christianity*, London, Allen Lane, 2009.

Minahane, John, *The Christian Druids*, Dublin, Sansas Press, 1993.

Mitchell, F & Ryan, M. *Reading the Irish landscape*, Dublin, Town House & Country House, 1993.

Moffat, Alistair, *Arthur and the lost kingdoms*, London, Weidenfeld & Nicholson, 1999.

Molloy, Dara, *The globalisation of God*, Inis Mor, Aisling Publications, 2009

Montifiore, Simon, *Jerusalem: the biography*, London, Weidenfeld & Nicholson, 2011.

Moorhouse, Geoffrey, *Sun dancing*, Orlando, Harcourt Brace, 1997.

Newell, Philip, *Christ of the Celts*, Glasgow, Wild Goose, 2008.

Norwich, John Julius, *The Popes: A history*, London, Vintage, 2012.

O'Croinin, Daibhi, *A new history of Ireland*, Oxford, Oxford University Press, 2005.

O'Croinin, Daibhi, *Early medieval Ireland 400-1200*, Harlow, Pearson, 1995.

Oliver, Neil, *A History of Scotland*, London, Weidenfeld & Nicholson, 2009.

O'Rourke, Benignus, *Confessions of St. Augustine*, London, Darton, Longman and Todd Ltd., 2013.

Pagels, Elaine H, *Beyond belief: the secret gospel of Thomas*, London, Vintage, 2004.

Robb, Graham, *The ancient paths*, London, Picador, 2013.

Simmans. Graham, *Jesus after the Crucifixion*, Rochester, Bear & Company, 2007.

Slavin, Michael, *The Book of Tara,* Dublin, Wolfhound Press, 1996.

Thom, Catherine, *Early Christian monasticism*, London, T&T Clark, 2006.

Ward, Benedicta, *The desert fathers*, London, Penguin, 2003.

Webb, J.F., *The age of Bede*, London, Penguin, 1965.

Wesselow, Thomas, *The sign*, London, Viking, 2012.

Wright, Tom, *Simply Jesus*, London, Society for Promoting Christian Knowledge, 2011.

Young, Simon. *A.D. 500*, London, Phoenix, 2005

Maps

JOURNEY TO ERIU 575 AD

Cormac's route ---
Augustine's route ---

ERIU 575 AD

Cenél Conaill Kindred
Cenél n Eogain Kindred
Dal Riada Kindred
Dal nAraide Kindred

NORTHERN UI NEILL
ULAIDH
Dal Fiatach Kindred

KINGDOM OF CONNACHT
KINGDOM OF MIDE
KINGDOM OF LAIGEN

Uí Dunlainge Kindred
Uí Cennselaig Kindred

Maic Brocc Kindred
Uí Bairrche Kindred

KINGDOM OF IARMUMHU

N
W · E
S

Author's note

The book is based in the sixth century, a pivotal time in Christianity. The Roman Empire had collapsed in the early fifth century and the Christian Church had split into the four patriarchies of Alexandria, Antioch, Constantinople and Rome. The church in the east was threatened by the Sassanid Empire which later overran Alexandria, Antioch and Constantinople in the seventh century. Rome was still in a chaotic state following the fall of the empire with successive invasions by Goths and Lombards. At this time the Church of Rome had not yet gained its hegemony over Europe and the British Isles.

On the western fringes of the known world, largely untouched by Rome, a different strand of Christianity was flowering on the island of Ireland with its close connections to the old pagan beliefs.

It was against this back drop that the story suggests an ancient scroll, '*the Word*' was removed from Alexandria by the Coptic Church, which feared invasion from the Sassanids (Persians), and sent it to Ireland for safekeeping, well away from the clutches of Rome or so it was hoped.

Ireland was one of the few Christian countries that had a degree of stability at this time. Uniquely in Europe, Ireland had its own ancient legal system and a uniform language, yet it had no central government or church authority.

Ireland's relative isolation meant that the island had never been conquered by Rome and had developed its own brand of Christianity, the Celtic Church. Indeed there is some suggestion that Christianity was brought to Ireland shortly after the crucifixion, long before St Patrick and even before it arrived in Rome; so that by the late sixth century it could boast large monasteries of up to three thousand monks peacefully coexisting with Celtic paganism.

The island had been devastated in the mid sixth century by both a famine caused by successive wet summers and the Justinian plague. This cataclysm may have been a motivating factor in the rapid growth of the monastic system in the latter half of the sixth century. It was monasteries that provided a means of sustaining many destitute communities and this necessity lead to the rapid expansion of the monastic movement throughout Ireland led by men like Colum Cille and Ruadhan.

Many of the early monasteries were much more than simple religious communities. They became self-sufficient communities supported by married monks who farmed the surrounding land. Each monastery was headed by an abbot or abbess who ruled with the consent of his or her monks. These abbots were independent of any central authority, but owed their allegiance to the local clan or regional dynasty. Monks studied astronomy, geography, mathematics as well as the gospels and took their learning into Europe at a time of great uncertainty and darkness.

This was a time well before rational and scientific thought when belief and imagination were indistinguishable from our more modern perceptions of 'reality'. Religious and spiritual belief was at the heart of daily life. The Hare's Vision reflects this close connection with the world of the imagination.

Ireland's transition from Celtic paganism to Christianity was accomplished without violence and with considerable tolerance of differing beliefs and ancient traditions. Pagan worship and Christianity continued to function side by side for many centuries and in many cases up to modern times the practices were interwoven.

While the Celtic Church in Ireland was independent of Rome at this time, it had strong connections with the Alexandrian Church and the monastic movement of the desert fathers in Egypt. However from the ninth century onwards the Celtic Church suffered at the hands of marauding Vikings while Rome continued to seek dominance. Eventually Rome succeeded when the Normans invaded Ireland in the twelfth century and brought with them the European monastic sects such as the Cistercians and Benedictines. Soon after this the independently minded Celtic monasteries ceased to exist.

The book suggests that the presence of '*The Word*' in Ireland which with its mystical properties led to the great flowering of Celtic Christianity during what is known as the 'Golden Age' from the sixth to ninth century A.D. It was during this period that Irish monasteries became seats of great learning, creating eminent works of art such as the Book of Kells, attracting students from all over Europe and sending Irish monks out across Europe to found monasteries.

The Hare's Vision is a work of fiction, but uses many historical figures set in an accurate historical context to weave its story. There is much to be learnt from this period about the development of the Christian Church, of religious and political tolerance, connections with the world around us and of the role of imagination in everyday life.

Acknowledgements

This book could not have been written without the continuous support of my wife, Jenny. Not only did she provide never ending encouragement, Jenny used her skills, developed over a lifetime of reading widely, academic study and teaching, to provide critical feedback as well as a vital editing service. In addition Jenny provided all the internal illustrations.

My research over a wide range of authors - both popular historians and serious academics - revealed a great deal of valuable information and material on this little known period of history and also gave inspiration for many of the concepts and plot lines.

In particular I am grateful to the work of Edel Bhreathnach, Bart Ehrman, Christopher Haas, Charles Freeman, Laurence Gardiner, Laurence Ginnell, Katherine Hughes, Peter Heather, Frank Kelly, Chris McClintock, Diarmaid McCulloch, John Minahane, Alistair Moffat, Dara Molloy, Daibhi O'Croinin, Graham Robb, Graham Simmans and Catherine Thom.

My friend and fellow author, James (Jaap) Hiddinga helped me secure my first publishing offer mid-way through writing the book. This greatly helped my confidence as a writer; as did the encouragement of Emy ten Seldam, whose professional input was critical to the book's completion and to my own belief in my writing.

My next book will be based on mysteries surrounding the creation and fate of the Book of Kells during the 9th to 11th centuries.

Watch this web site and blog for news of its release
www.temairpublishing.com
https://williammethven.wordpress.com/

Made in the USA
Charleston, SC
01 October 2015